ENGRAVED IN STONE

Madhulika Liddle lives in Delhi and has worked in hospitality, advertising and instructional design before giving it all up to focus on writing. Her short stories have won several awards, including the top prize at the Commonwealth Broadcasting Association's Short Story Competition, 2003. *Engraved in Stone* is her third book about the Mughal detective, Muzaffar Jang. Besides fiction, Madhulika also writes on travel and classic cinema.

Engraved in Stone

A Muzaffar Jang Mystery

Madhulika Liddle

First published in 2012 by Hachette India
(Registered name: Hachette Book Publishing India Pvt. Ltd)
An Hachette UK company
www.hachetteindia.com

1

ISBN 978-93-5009-448-8

Hachette Book Publishing India Pvt. Ltd
4th/5th Floors, Corporate Centre,
Sector 44, Gurgaon 122003, India

Typeset in Gentium 10/13
by InoSoft Systems Noida

Printed and bound in India
by Gopsons Papers Ltd., Noida

To Pallavi, one of my favourite people. Thank you for being part of my world.

1

'LOOK AT HER, huzoor. *Touch her.*' The voice was enticing. 'She is beautiful, is she not? Beautiful *and* strong. Ride her all day and all night, and she will not protest.'

The double entendre was doubtless deliberate, the speech often rehearsed and just as often used. Muzaffar Jang, whose attention had been wandering, glanced sharply at the speaker. A good head shorter than Muzaffar's own imposing height, the man made up for it with a magnificent turban, a pristine white silk of no less than ten yards. It blossomed out like the canopy of a stunted and spindly tree above the narrow shoulders and almost skeletal figure of the man. Below that remarkable turban was a face of unusual beauty. Yes, beauty, thought Muzaffar; not a rugged handsomeness, as one might expect in a man. It was a slim face, with a well-trimmed grey beard and moustache. The lips were thin, the eyes hooded but occasionally sparkling with sudden brightness. A serene, tranquil face. The face of a saint and the words of a pimp.

'You will not see another like her, huzoor,' the horse trader purred. 'Why, the atbegi himself – the Master of the Imperial Horses – has bought palfreys from me, and Turcoman horses like this one. If huzoor seeks a horse, there is none more reliable than Shakeel Alam. You may ask anyone.'

Muzaffar looked away, letting his gaze wander across the vast covered stretch of the Imarat-e-Nakhkhas, the building in which Agra's nakhkhas, the cattle market, was held every morning. He had expected crowds and chaos; the sights and smells of horses, oxen, and camels; the bustle and din of men and animals mingling; but he had not expected it on this scale. The nakhkhas was huge, stretching along the bank of the Yamuna north of the fort. The courtyard, its flagstones already littered with straw, grain and steaming dung – where stable boys had not yet been quick enough to clean up – was a large rectangle, its peripheral walls holding in a constantly shifting mob that haggled and wheedled, laughed and fumed, and occasionally resorted to fisticuffs.

The wall facing the fort was pierced by a massive gate. It was red sandstone like the encircling walls, and devoid of any decoration but for an inconspicuous repetitive pattern of carved lotus buds. Nearest the gate were the sellers of equipment and accessories: the men who had been granted stalls, little rooms built along the inside of the wall. A couple of steps up, and buyers could examine for themselves the feed bags, the saddles, bridles, and the mane coverings known as yalpusts. Some stalls were occupied by the wealthy merchants who dealt in the more luxurious goods, the items reserved for the stables of the Emperor or those of his highest ranking noblemen.

One merchant, a rotund but energetic man in his late forties, was prattling on while his servant exhibited their wares to a trio of noblemen. A caparison embroidered in gold; another of fine brown leather – soft as cotton, said the merchant's plump fingers as they flitted, curling and uncurling in rapid succession. There were saddlecloths of chintz, quilted and finely embroidered; flocked yalpusts to decorate horses for festivals – or for the supreme honour of carrying an amir to his wedding – and metal rings in the shape of bells, to be attached to fetlocks.

'Huzoor appears to be more interested in the equipment than in the horses,' said the horse trader peevishly.

Muzaffar looked at the mare Shakeel Alam was exhibiting with such pride. She *was* a beauty, muscular yet slender and utterly feminine from the tips of her fine ears down to her tiny hooves. A superb palomino, her golden coat glistening with a coppery sheen that contrasted with the creamy silken mane and tail. Muzaffar reached out a hand and stroked gently down between the large eyes to the tapering muzzle.

'Can you imagine her in the field, huzoor? Swift, turning with the speed of lightning. An archer could shoot from that back, now here, now there – without missing a shot. And she would be equally fine as the mount of a noble gentleman such as huzoor. I can well imagine *her* being the mount of a bridegroom, her legs red with henna and her equipment embroidered with gold. Ah, that would be a sight to please any eye.' The man paused, watching Muzaffar for signs of weakening.

The young amir ran his fingertips down the horse's sloping shoulders and along her gleaming flanks before asking, 'How much?'

The merchant smacked his lips. 'Ah, the love and care I have lavished on this one, huzoor. She has been fed from the day of her birth on nothing but barley, mutton fat, raisins and dates. With my own hands have I covered her with thick felt to sweat out every last pinch of fat –'

'Muzaffar!' The name rang out across the interior of the Imarat-e-Nakhkhas, distorted by the many competing sounds: the lowing of cattle, the neighing, the occasional whicker and grunt, the dozens of simultaneous conversations in progress. Muzaffar frowned, puzzled, then turned back to the horse trader. It may well have been another word, not even his name. And even if it had been what he had thought he heard, Muzaffar was not an uncommon name. There were probably a dozen Muzaffars in the marketplace at the very moment. One of the servants patiently displaying caparison after caparison for an indecisive buyer, perhaps. Maybe even one of the stable boys mucking out the Arabian grey's stall in the next bay. It was a sobering thought.

The horse trader was blabbering on, but Muzaffar whirled around, a smile lighting up his face as the voice – now recognizable and just a few feet away – bellowed his name again. A gorgeously attired figure pushed through the rabble of the nakhkhas, weaving an intricate path between the dung and the straw. The fine woollen choga of the newcomer was a bluish grey, embroidered along the hems in crimson and silver. The boots shone, the turban was a dream in scarlet; and three necklaces of perfectly matched pearls hung down the front of the choga. Even the large muslin handkerchief being hurriedly pulled out of the choga pocket was prettily embroidered.

Akram, thought Muzaffar with a sudden surge of affection, was well capable of asking Iz'rail, the angel of death, to wait while he tried out yet another jewel or straightened his turban.

The man came to a halt amidst an awed silence. He glared briefly at the stable boy who had stopped in the middle of currying the grey Arabian and was staring fixedly. Then, with the handkerchief whipped up suddenly to his nose, the man let out an explosive sneeze. When he had wiped his nose and pitched his handkerchief into the heap of rubbish in the corner of the stall, he looked at Muzaffar with watery red eyes. 'I've been yelling for you for the past five minutes,' he said hoarsely. 'What in the name of Allah are you doing in Agra?'

It took Muzaffar less than a minute to have the horse trader's assurance that he would be there the next day – and the day after. Muzaffar said that he would be back in a day or two, then moved off, threading his way through the crowds with his friend Akram at his heels.

Beyond the horses were the camels, long-lashed, supercilious animals from the Thatta region of Sind and darker double-humped ones from up north. One of the traders had fitted out his best specimen in a style befitting its value. The camel had been rubbed down with pumice and sesame oil, then given a final scrub with buttermilk; the faint, slightly tart aroma of the buttermilk still hung in the air. The camel's saddle was of intricately embroidered leather, its edges fringed with heavy tassels. A young amir, goaded on by the shouts of his friends around, was climbing into the camel's saddle as Muzaffar and Akram squeezed their way past.

'I hate camels,' Akram muttered as the camel lurched to its feet, the bells festooned from its girths and breast bands tinkling merrily. 'They jerk about so dreadfully. I always think I'm going to be sick.'

They passed the cattle pens, each with its own lowing, shifting herd. One trader even had a small herd of prized silver-grey buffaloes, but the farmers milling around merely glanced covetously at the buffaloes and then moved on to the more affordable milch cows, examining the udders, peering into the cows' eyes, and standing back to look at the animal from a distance. A high-yielding cow, it was widely believed, would be one with a body shaped like a wedge.

Muzaffar and Akram stepped out through the gate and onto the riverbank. Three hours past sunrise, the mist had still not lifted completely. It curled moist tendrils through the trees, obscuring the boundary between river and land, throwing a shifting blanket of white across the blurred outlines of the havelis dotting the shore.

'Uff,' Akram said, with a sudden shiver. 'I'd forgotten it was so cold outside.' He pulled his choga closer about him and huddled deeper into it. 'Where's your horse, Muzaffar?' His breath floated on the chill morning air in a wisp of white.

From beside the gate, a beggar scuttled forward, one arm withered and the other clutching a chipped earthen bowl. Muzaffar reached into his choga and handed the beggar a daam as he replied to Akram's question. 'At a haveli down the river, recovering from a bout of thrush. That's why I came to the nakhkhas; I need another mount. I had to hire a boat to bring me here.'

The beggar, mumbling blessings on Muzaffar, retreated to his post near the gate, just close enough to the path to draw the attention of passers-by, just far enough to not get trampled underfoot.

'Thrush?'

'Yes, a bad case. Hooves gone very black in places, and smelling like death. I couldn't possibly ride him.'

Akram tut-tutted. 'Not lame, is he?'

'No.' Muzaffar looked at his friend sympathetically as Akram sneezed again. Akram fumbled around in his choga pocket for a fresh handkerchief and muttered, 'I should be like the Europeans, eh, Muzaffar? Blow one's nose in a handkerchief, then shove it back into a pocket as a keepsake. I thought I had some spare bits of muslin in here... ah, yes.' He wiped his nose and threw away the handkerchief.

'Standing out here in the cold and damp isn't going to do anything for this cold of yours,' Muzaffar said. 'I'd liked to have gone to a qahwa khana for a cup of coffee, but not having a horse is a problem –'

'I have a spare. I'd brought a groom along to the nakhkhas, just in case I decided to buy a horse. He has a horse you can borrow. It doesn't look much, but it's sturdy enough, I daresay.' Akram paused. 'But on one condition. We will not go to a qahwa khana. We will not venture anywhere *near* a qahwa khana. I will not be bullied into having any more of that horrid beverage.'

'I'd gone to Ajmer,' Muzaffar said, swirling the steaming coffee around the earthenware cup. Chowk Akbarabad, Agra's main market, had its share of eateries and kabab-sellers, but the stench of reused oil wafting from the first such establishment they had entered had sent Akram scurrying out, looking faintly bilious. After that, it had required little persuasion on Muzaffar's part to steer his friend to a qahwa khana.

Despite the low hum of conversation from the groups of patrons scattered across the hall, Muzaffar guessed the coffee house was not thriving. The plaster was peeling in places; one corner had a large patch of damp, and the mattresses were thin and cold underneath the greying sheets. Muzaffar dug absently with the tip of his dagger at a grimy encrustation of long-ago food along the inside edge of the salver on which the tall, narrow-necked coffee pot stood.

'My sister, Zeenat Begum, wanted me to accompany her to Ajmer so she could offer prayers at the dargah,' he said. 'On the way, she made friends with a young woman from Agra, who was also headed for Ajmer. By then, Zeenat Aapa was longing for some female company. Before I knew it, she'd befriended Shireen and her entourage and made them part of *our* entourage.'

He grimaced as he examined the greasy black tip of the damascened blade. 'Anyway, when our pilgrimage to Ajmer was over, Zeenat Aapa insisted that we accompany them back to Agra. She wouldn't hear of Shireen travelling without a female chaperone.'

Akram raised a curious eyebrow. 'Shireen, is it?' he grinned, somewhat lopsidedly. 'I see.'

'I'm sure you do,' Muzaffar's voice dripped acid. 'You see things where there is nothing to be seen. But what are *you* doing in Agra? I thought you had no plans of moving out of Dilli for a while at least.'

The tepid sunlight streaming in through the doorway of the qahwa khana was blocked out momentarily as a small group of men, European mercenaries by the looks of them – and one man in a long robe, his hair cut strangely in a fringe around a perfectly round, bald patch at the crown – stepped in. Akram watched them move to one of the tables at the far end of the room, next to one of the windows that looked out on the bustle of Chowk Akbarabad.

He sighed. 'I'm here giving Abba company.'

Muzaffar waited.

'*He* was ordered by the Diwan-i-kul to accompany him to Agra.'

'Ah. With a substantial army, I suppose? I noticed much activity off towards Sikandra when I was riding into Agra yesterday. Elephants, horses, much dust and noise. I didn't stop to find out what it was all about.' Muzaffar sipped his coffee. 'The Diwan-i-kul, eh? His arrival in Agra has nothing to do with the mess down in Bijapur, has it?'

Akram nodded sombrely. 'It does. He's headed for Aurangabad, to join up with the armies of the Shahzada Aurangzeb.'

Muzaffar frowned, suddenly filled with a sense of foreboding. It had been less than six months since the arrival in the court at Dilli of the cunning Mir Jumla, the former wazir of the peninsular kingdom of Golconda, fabled land of diamonds and wealth untold.

The tales whispered about Mir Jumla were legion: that he had cast a spell on the Shahzada Aurangzeb, who danced like a willing puppet to Mir Jumla's every command; that he had presented cartloads of diamonds, rubies and pearls to each of the Baadshah's most influential noblemen and Allah alone knew how much to the Emperor himself; and that he had actually succeeded in seducing the mother of the king of Golconda.

All bazaar gossip, of course, but there was perhaps a grain of truth hidden deep in it. Zeenat Begum's husband and Muzaffar's brother-in-law, Farid Khan, the kotwal of Dilli and a man not inclined to exaggerate or gossip – had shared with Muzaffar some of what he had learned through his connections at court.

Mir Jumla was originally from the city of Isfahan in Persia. Born Mohammad Sayyid, he was from a Sayyid family, respected only for its supposed descent from the Prophet; the head of the house, Mir Jumla's father, had been an oil merchant of little consequence. Mir Jumla, however, was a different kettle of fish, ruthlessly ambitious and ready to use intrigue and bribery to earn him both wealth and power.

Mir Jumla's ambitions had resulted in his gaining employment as the clerk of a diamond merchant, and eventually arriving in India at the entrepôt of the diamond trade: Golconda. Gifts left, right and centre, accompanied by much flattery – and perhaps even some of that seduction which people hinted at – had made Mir Jumla the wazir, the chief minister of Abdullah Qutb Shah, the king of Golconda. Mir Jumla hadn't stopped at that; his ambitions were higher and his nest far from adequately feathered. He spent his time at Golconda farming out diamond mines, gathering in gems by the sackful – and finally attracting the attention of his boss Abdullah Qutb Shah, who had realized all too late that he was being hoodwinked. Secret plans were hatched to get rid of the corrupt wazir; but Mir Jumla, a step ahead of his sovereign, had wriggled free and opened negotiations both with the Sultan of the neighbouring state of Bijapur, and with the prince Aurangzeb, Mughal governor of the Deccan.

In Shahzada Aurangzeb, Mir Jumla appeared to have found the

ultimate champion, though Farid Khan, in his recounting of Mir Jumla's past to Muzaffar, had a cynical comment to make: 'No doubt the shahzada has his own axe to grind. The Baadshah lacks the will or the power to hang on to the throne much longer. And Dara Shukoh, no matter if he is the proclaimed heir, does not have the military experience to be able to withstand an attack if Aurangzeb decides he wants the throne for himself – which I am convinced he does. The more powerful friends Aurangzeb makes, the more he strengthens his own hand.'

And so, supported by a commendatory letter from Aurangzeb, Mir Jumla had been appointed a Mughal mansabdar or 'holder of rank' – and awarded an army of five thousand horsemen of his own. With Aurangzeb, he had gone off to plunder Golconda, and had withdrawn only after the Emperor Shahjahan, bribed by the Qutb Shah, had ordered the two Mughal commanders to accept the indemnity offered by Golconda.

Six months later, in July of what was, to the Europeans, 1656 AD, Mir Jumla had presented himself in the court at Dilli. It had been a typical Dilli summer: blisteringly hot, the sun blazing down mercilessly, reducing the Yamuna to a trickle and leaving man and beast yearning for the monsoon. But Mir Jumla, bowing and scraping and mouthing insincere words of endless fidelity to the Baadshah, had brought relief at least to the Emperor, if to no one else. He had presented his liege lord with a diamond of almost unbelievable beauty and size, along with a mouth-watering array of lesser diamonds, rubies and topazes. The Baadshah had summarily bestowed the title of Muazzam Khan on Mir Jumla and had appointed him the Prime Minister, the Diwan-i-kul. And Mir Jumla had reciprocated by suggesting to the Emperor that instead of distant Kandahar – which the Baadshah had been considering invading – Bijapur, closer home and by far the wealthier, would be a more lucrative target for a military expedition.

The king of Bijapur, ailing for months now, had died in November, and word had soon spread that the new Sultan, the late king's eighteen-year-old son, had no right to the throne. A bastard, an illegitimate upstart whom no self-respecting kingdom should accept as ruler, said many. Among those who had refused to acknowledge the new Sultan was Aurangzeb. A letter had arrived in Dilli from Aurangzeb to the Baadshah shortly after, and the Emperor's response had been to give carte blanche to his son and his Diwan-i-kul: *Deal as you feel fit with the situation.*

And this was how they were dealing with it. Muzaffar sighed.

'So they're off to plunder Bijapur now? And how do they know it won't be a repeat of Golconda? What if Bijapur also bribes Dara Shukoh and sends the Baadshah piles of diamonds, begging for mercy? To be pulled off from yet another invasion will do no good to the prestige of either the Shahzada or the Diwan-i-kul.' His voice rose in agitation.

Akram held up a hand, gesturing to quieten Muzaffar. Two men sitting on a mattress nearby were staring, curious.

Muzaffar shrugged. 'Ah, well. Perhaps some good will come of it. Who knows?' He lifted the edge of the mattress, wiped the dirty blade of his knife surreptitiously on the underside, and replaced the knife in his boot. 'Don't tell me the Diwan-i-kul has ordered Abdul Munim Khan Sahib to accompany him to Aurangabad.'

Akram shook his head at the mention of his father, a venerable old amir. 'No, of course not. Abba has never been any good as a soldier; he'd be a liability on the field, and he knows it. So does the Diwan-i-kul. No, he's just got Abba to come up to Agra with him, because he wants to meet Mumtaz Hassan Khan.' Akram noticed the blank look on his friend's face and grinned. 'You have no idea whom I'm talking about, do you?' He paused, waiting for Muzaffar to say something, then carried on.

'Mumtaz Hassan Khan is an amir who came to Agra from Bijapur years ago. His fortune was made in precious stones; primarily diamonds, but just about everything else too. He's well-respected, extremely wealthy, and – as luck would have it – married to Abba's half-sister. My uncle, so to say.'

Akram sniffled and peered into his cup. 'In the few months the Diwan-i-kul has spent in Dilli, he hasn't lost his touch,' Akram said in a voice so low that Muzaffar had to lean forward to listen. 'He appears to regard bribery as the most dependable means of conquest. They say he's had it already put about in the armies of Bijapur that any officer who defects, along with a hundred men, will be given two thousand rupees. Underhand, but that's the way he works. And he thinks Mumtaz Hassan Khan will be able to help him.'

'Why?'

'Because Hassan Sahib is still well liked and respected in Bijapur. He has contacts, and people will listen to him. Many of the wealthiest and most influential men of Bijapur – the diamond traders, the ministers, the big landowners – will pay heed if my uncle suggests that it would be a good idea to throw in their lot with the armies of the Shahzada and the Diwan-i-kul. Not all of them will agree, but the Diwan-i-kul seems to think most will. Enough, at any rate, to tilt the balance.'

'So what is he planning to do? Take your uncle along with him to Aurangabad and then to Bijapur?'

Akram shrugged expressively. 'I suppose so; Abba hasn't thought it fit to take me *that* far into his confidence. I'd think the Diwan-i-kul might need to exert himself a bit to first bring my uncle around to his way of thinking. They've known each other a long time – I'd even say they were more friends than mere acquaintances. And Mumtaz Hassan is loyal enough to the Baadshah. But I'm not sure he'd be willing to stoop to bribery of the sort Mir Jumla wants to incite him to.' He tipped back the cup, then put it down and regarded the dregs glumly before looking up at Muzaffar pleadingly. 'Do visit us at the haveli, Muzaffar. I'm bored to death. The Diwan-i-kul, Abba and Mumtaz Hassan are closeted in the dalaan all day long, and the only other people in the haveli are the servants or the women in the zenana.'

Muzaffar allowed a half-smile of sympathy to flicker across his face. 'So how do you spend your time?'

'Going to the nakhkhas and trying out different mounts. Wandering around Kinari Bazaar. Touring the sites and gawping appreciatively at everything I see, just so I don't look out of place.'

This time, Muzaffar grinned broadly. 'And what, may I ask, have you been gawping at, that wasn't worthy of your admiration?'

Akram's eyes twinkled. 'Nothing, I suppose. I went to Sikandra, to Bihishtabad. And through the gardens on the east bank of the river. I even went to the tomb of Itimad-ud-Daulah. Abba had known the man years ago, when he wielded a lot of power.'

Muzaffar nodded absently. Itimad-ud-Daulah, 'Pillar of the State' – for that was what the title meant – had not been merely a powerful nobleman, but had also eventually been successful in building a connection, by marriage, with the Emperor himself. Itimad-ud-Daulah's accomplished and beautiful daughter Mehrunissa had married Shahjahan's late father, the Emperor Jahangir; and had, in one fell swoop, not just made herself the most influential woman in the empire, but had also cleared the path for her family. Jahangir had bestowed on her the title Nur Mahal – Light of the Palace – and had later elevated her even further, by naming her Nur Jahan, Light of the World. Nur Jahan's niece, Itimad-ud-Daulah's granddaughter by his son, had been born Arjumand Bano Begum, but had, after her marriage to Shahjahan, become known as Mumtaz Mahal. The lady for whom a grieving husband, an unwarrantedly extravagant emperor and an unabashed aesthete, had built the most magnificent tomb in Agra – perhaps in all the world.

'Have you been to the Taj Mahal?' Muzaffar asked.

'*Of course* I have. I'm nothing if not fashionable, Muzaffar, you know that. And going to the Taj Mahal is extremely fashionable. Have you been?'

'Not since it was in the process of being built.' Muzaffar's mouth curled in a half-humorous, half-regretful smile. 'It's strange, you know; I have so much in common with Gauhar Ara Begum. We were both born in the same year, and we both lost our mothers soon after. Ammi's grave is of course a paltry one compared to the Empress's...' His voice petered out. Akram looked on silently. After a moment,

Muzaffar continued. 'Zeenat Aapa and Khan Sahib brought me up, but Khan Sahib was constantly on the move: this year Lahore, the next Gwalior; then in the Deccan, and then off to Kashmir. When I look back at my childhood, it seems a whirlwind of long caravan trails, and of tented camps and Khan Sahib imparting lessons to me on horseback.'

'And you acquiring a menagerie of small pets,' added Akram with amusement as he recalled a long-ago confession of his friend's.

'That too.' Muzaffar gulped down the last of his now tepid coffee. 'And we seemed to be in Agra only now and then – on our way from one outpost to another. I saw the Taj Mahal rise, but in occasional glimpses. One year we passed through Agra, and they were excavating the land for the foundations and carrying away cartloads of earth. There was a yawning maw alongside the river, where they were digging deep shafts and sinking boxes of wood. Zeenat Aapa forbade me to go anywhere near the site; she was terrified I'd fall in.'

'I saw the rauza – the cenotaph itself, not the mosque or the other subsidiary buildings that surround it – when it was all brick. They didn't put in the white marble cladding till later, and frankly, I couldn't imagine then what it would look like. Somehow, that vast building all in brick didn't inspire any admiration in me.' He smiled ruefully. 'Then one year they were building the mosque. There was that Persian calligrapher, Amanat Khan, creating his paper prototypes for the verses that were going to be inscribed all across.' His eyes brightened perceptibly as a thought struck him. 'What I liked best was when Khan Sahib took me to see the stone cutters at work. I'd seen tulips and daffodils in Kashmir, but never in Agra – and these men were creating them, slicing the gemstones and carving the marble, inlaying flowers. I'd never seen anything like it before. I still haven't.'

'You must see the finished work for yourself,' Akram said fervently. 'It's spectacular. *And* you must meet my uncle, Mumtaz Hassan. He was one of the purveyors for the gemstones used at the Taj Mahal. I'm sure he'll have some interesting stories to tell.'

2

ABBAS QURESHI, THE uncle of the young lady whom Muzaffar had found himself escorting to Ajmer, was a minor amir with a haveli tucked away on the western bank of the Yamuna. All the powerful noblemen, the mansabdars with their huge endowments, their vast households and dozens of servants, had their havelis – each competing with the next for grandeur – along the western bank, between the fort and the luminous Taj Mahal. The Taj Mahal, also known as the Taj Bibi, had itself been built on land acquired from a nobleman, the Raja of Amber. The raja had been amply compensated for his bequest; he had received not one, but four separate stretches of land in return.

The chances of anybody ever requesting Abbas Qureshi for any of *his* land were slim. His haveli was a modest one, the white marble cladding of the dalaan its only attempt at ostentation. The rest of the mansion was affordable brick, plastered over and polished. It was a neat house, clean and airy, and with a small khanah bagh – a private garden – where the women and children could come out for a breath of fresh air. In the dead of winter, with a chill breeze blowing in from across the river, the inhabitants of the zenana remained indoors, huddled under their light quilts and wrapped in their fine shawls. Zeenat Begum, Muzaffar's elder sister and adoptive mother, had taken advantage of the emptiness of the khanah bagh. A tersely worded note had been presented to Muzaffar by one of the eunuchs from the zenana. Muzaffar was to present himself at the khanah bagh an hour after lunch.

Zeenat was already seated on the single stone bench when Muzaffar entered the garden. Her eyes lit up when she saw him, and she rose to her feet, gathering her shawls about her. Her thin face, with wisps of grey hair escaping from below the dupatta covering her head, was still attractive. The smile as she came towards Muzaffar and reached out to take his hand made it more so. 'Thank you for coming,' she said, moving back to the bench, with Muzaffar following in her wake. 'I'd wondered if you'd come.'

'You didn't give me much choice, Aapa,' Muzaffar said, with an affectionate grin. 'That note told me to come; you didn't say I was allowed to refuse.' He lowered himself beside her onto the bench, careful not to step on the silken skirt of her flowing ankle-length jagulfi, its fitted sleeves and fine bodice hidden beneath a flowing qaba, a long gown of pashmina.

'Have you bought yourself a new horse, as you said you would?' she asked as she stroked the qaba down with long, slender fingers, luxuriating in the feel of the soft wool.

Muzaffar told her of the unexpected meeting with Akram. 'I thought I'd return to the nakhkhas tomorrow, perhaps,' he explained. 'But at lunch today, Qureshi Sahib was strangely magnanimous. He insisted that while I am in Agra, and until my horse is well enough, I *must* use one of his own horses.'

Zeenat Begum raised a shapely eyebrow. 'I shudder to think what the stables of this haveli are like,' she murmured. 'Or the horses in them. I suppose you were given a choice between a newly foaled mare and one with colic or rain scald or some such affliction?'

Muzaffar chuckled. 'On the contrary. Qureshi Sahib himself presented the horse he had chosen for me. It's a gelding, a lovely black creature, better than my own stallion.'

'And you accepted?'

'It would have been churlish to refuse; he was very insistent. But it will only be for a few days, I think. I had a look at my own horse after Qureshi Sahib had gone. It's improved vastly. The keeper said he had the hoof and the frog cleaned out; he showed it to me – the blackness has diminished and that appalling stench is gone. There's clean hay, the floor of the stall is good, packed earth, and they're even feeding the animal cooked legumes. I was a little taken aback,' he admitted. 'In a household that is so obviously derelict, to have such care lavished on a near stranger's horse?'

Zeenat Begum bent, a slim hand reaching to pick up a long-dead peepal leaf, the green decayed and disintegrated sometime in the wetter months of the year. All that was left now was the silvery, filigree-like tracery of the leaf's veins, as perfectly symmetrical as the dome of the Taj Mahal itself. Zeenat gently stroked a fingertip along the stem of the leaf, up past its swelling waist and to the tapering tip. 'It appears to me that Qureshi Sahib is trying his hardest to ingratiate himself with you.'

'*With me?* What on earth can he hope to gain by that?'

'The mahal sara is a tedious place,' Zeenat murmured, and Muzaffar blinked, mystified. 'Qureshi Sahib's three wives are empty-headed, shallow, selfish women, with no desire to further any interests but their own. Their daughters are as vacuous and dull as them, incapable of thinking of anything except clothes and jewellery and how they may marry a wealthy man someday. There are eight of them, did you know? The youngest is a toddler, but the five eldest are all in their teens.' Zeenat twirled the peepal leaf, watching absently as it spun, delicate as a spider's web. 'Shireen does not fit here. She is miserable, and they tolerate her presence simply because she happens to be Qureshi Sahib's niece.'

Muzaffar frowned. 'What does that have to do with Qureshi Sahib's unwonted benevolence towards *me*?'

'Do you *really* not see? Qureshi Sahib has eight daughters to marry off. He has little wealth of his own, and no position to speak of. If his daughters are to make good marriages, he will have to be not just vigilant but also perhaps a little wily. Now if he can ensure a handsome and reasonably wealthy young amir – and that too from Dilli – is obliged to him, it just might be possible to get one of the girls hitched to that young man.' She smiled deliberately at Muzaffar. 'You're a good catch, little brother,' she whispered.

Muzaffar gaped at her, stricken. 'I have no desire whatsoever to be married to any of Qureshi Sahib's witless daughters,' he replied.

'I thought as much.' She gave the dried leaf one last twirl, then dropped it into his lap. 'But what about Shireen?'

Muzaffar, dressing with exceptional care for dinner that evening, mulled over Zeenat's question. He had not expected it, and had not known – *did not know*, even a few hours later – what to say. He had been spared the necessity of replying to Zeenat by the fortuitous arrival of a deferential eunuch, stepping into the khanah bagh with a discreet cough to address Muzaffar. A messenger, it transpired, had come from the haveli of Mumtaz Hassan Khan Sahib with a note for huzoor. Khan Sahib had requested a reply, to be sent back with the man.

Muzaffar had taken hurried leave of his sister, with a vague hint at resuming their conversation later. Zeenat Begum had given him an enigmatic smile and had nodded wordlessly.

The note from Mumtaz Hassan Khan was courteous but to the point. Mumtaz Hassan's nephew, Akram Khan, who was (as Jang Sahib already knew) residing temporarily in Mumtaz Hassan's haveli, had informed the writer of Jang Sahib's presence in Agra. Abdul Munim Khan, Akram Khan, and the writer himself were eager to meet Jang Sahib. It would be a privilege for them if Jang Sahib were to partake of the evening meal that night with them. If Jang Sahib would consent, an escort would be sent to guide him to Mumtaz Hassan's haveli.

A comparatively informal postscript had been added at the end in a handwriting that Muzaffar recognized as his friend's.

Has Qureshi had the decency to lend you a nag? If you're still without a mount, let me know. My uncle has offered to let you have a horse. Whoever comes to fetch you this evening will bring it along.

Muzaffar, with a muttered instruction to Mumtaz Hassan's servant to wait for the reply, had made his way to his chamber.

A reply, suitably grateful but not obsequious, had been quickly penned, along with an assurance that Muzaffar had indeed been lent a horse. The messenger had gone off and Muzaffar had retired to his chamber to think over the question Zeenat had so nonchalantly tossed at him.

Now, as he tucked the end of his turban in and pinned a turra – an enamelled aigrette, set with emeralds – on the side of the turban, his mouth was set in a grim line. No, he thought; he could not imagine being married to Shireen.

True, in the few days he had spent travelling alongside her, he had noticed things about her that had intrigued him. She remained veiled, like a well brought-up young lady of the upper classes; but she was not averse to pulling that veil across and peeking out now and then. Both literally and metaphorically speaking. He had seen her ride a horse with skill; effortlessly break up a fight between maids at a sarai; and attend to his sister when the older woman was weary from a long day of sitting in a jolting, swaying palanquin. He had seen Shireen's face, oval and striking, framed in the dupatta she had allowed the wind to whip back. He had been impressed by the quiet confidence in her expression, the intelligence in those beautiful brown eyes.

But he could guess what lay beneath. Shireen may be different, but how different could she be, after all? On closer acquaintance, she would be like any other woman. Fickle.

Mumtaz Hassan Khan's haveli stood along the riverside, ringed by a wall, an orchard abutting it on one side, a garden – now barren and dead in the winter – on the other. There were an inordinate number of soldiers milling around, men in heavy leather tunics, the officers in more durable mail, armed with lances and swords. A dozen or so soldiers were ranged on either side of the drum house, weapons at the ready. A small group of archers had taken over the drum house, having evicted the musicians who would normally have been seated in the balcony. The musicians now sat, along with their pipes and kettle drums, in a cold and unhappy huddle at the base of the building. One of them was trying to kindle a fire on a heap of twigs.

Muzaffar dismounted as a servant came forward to lead his horse away. His escort was exchanging a few words in a low voice with a grizzled officer who had emerged from the drum house. The officer, his mail shining, glanced towards Muzaffar, gazing at the nobleman in the yellow light of the torches fitted into sconces in the façade of the drum house. The officer's eyes sized up the newcomer and found him adequate. He nodded, gesturing to the two men through the drum house.

It was a standard drum house, a four-sided, double-storeyed building. The ground floor consisted of a large gate, with a steep narrow staircase built into one of its thick walls. A plain dado of red sandstone covered the bottom half of the walls; above it, on the polished white lime plaster, were paintings of trees laden with fruit, tiny wisps of cloud curling about the canopies of the trees. Two soldiers, wrapped in blankets, were sleeping, snoring in different keys, on the low platforms along the inner wall of the gate.

Muzaffar and his escort stepped through the gateway and out of the drum house. Muzaffar shivered. The short stretch of paved path till the main entrance of the haveli was flanked on either side by a grove of mango trees, now enshrouded in a clammy grey mist. Torches had been inserted into stone rings set on either side of the path, but the mist had swallowed them up too, reducing them to formless spots of light that did little to pierce the gathering gloom.

A dark figure emerged from the bulk of the house and paused briefly in the arched doorway, silhouetted against the warm glow of torches inside the house. An arm held aside the heavy padded curtain that hung from iron rings along the bottom of the overhang. The figure stood still for a moment before the man stepped out, letting the curtain fall back into place behind him.

'Haider Miyan,' called the man walking beside Muzaffar. 'Jang Sahib is here. Will you bring a torch, please? The mist is getting worse.' The man in front of the doorway reached up to pull out a torch from one of the sconces beside the door.

It was a middle-aged man, saw Muzaffar, lean and with a prematurely greying beard. Reaching them, he held up the torch and scrutinized Muzaffar keenly. 'I am Haider, huzoor,' he said. 'The steward of this haveli. I beg your pardon for the inconvenience –'. He wagged his chin in the approximate direction of the drum house beyond. 'The soldiers are a necessary evil,' he added with distaste.

'They are here for the protection of the Diwan-i-kul, I suppose.'

'Yes, huzoor,' Haider replied as he led the way up to the entrance of the haveli. The other man fell back, slowing down to allow Muzaffar and the steward to proceed. 'But the Diwan-i-kul has been gracious enough to give orders that none of the soldiers be allowed into the haveli itself.'

Muzaffar glanced about him, at the orchard of mango trees, their canopies shutting out the moonlight, the swirling mist obscuring the trunks. Somewhere, not too far away, he could hear the baleful hooting of an owl, and from the drum house behind him, the muted sounds of conversation. 'None even within the grounds?'

'None, huzoor. They patrol the outer walls. The Diwan-i-kul said he did not want his privacy shattered.'

They had reached the doorway, a broad cusped arch, flanked on both sides by a row of identical arches, marching away into the mist. The steward climbed the six steps to the doorway and held the curtain aside for Muzaffar to pass inside.

Muzaffar's eyes widened as he looked about him. Akram had told him of Mumtaz Hassan Khan's wealth, but even Muzaffar had not expected splendour on a scale such as this. There were prosperous omrah in Dilli who had sumptuous havelis, their dalaans gorgeously decorated with carved and painted panels, some – like Muzaffar himself – even going to the expense of getting a strip of inlay added. There was one man, an erstwhile Persian adventurer and now a trader in musk and silver, who had got the ceiling of his dalaan covered in intricate mirrorwork and silver. It was an unabashed imitation of the Sheesh Mahal at the Qila Mubarak in Dilli, and had resulted in a marked increase in the number of guests who attended the orgies the man was so fond of hosting. Looking up and seeing themselves reflected a thousand times seemed to gratify an astonishing number of people, thought Muzaffar.

But Mumtaz Hassan outdid them all. The floor of the room was of a warm golden stone from Jaisalmer. The dadoes of the walls were white marble, inlaid with a geometric pattern in black slate and more of the Jaisalmer stone. Above that, the plastered wall curved up into a vaulted ceiling, painted in curlicues and flowers in red, gold and a dull green.

And this was just the entrance to the house. Muzaffar drew in a deep breath and followed Haider into the heart of the haveli.

Each successive room was equally magnificent, even oppressively so. The dalaan into which Muzaffar was finally shown was painted and inlaid in shades of muted red and blue, with a rich Persian carpet in the centre and urns of blue-painted Chinese porcelain on either side of the arched doorway. Haider fussed over Muzaffar, seating him on the thick mattress along the right wall and pulling the brocaded bolsters closer. He carefully moved a large vase of full-blown white chrysanthemums off to one side as a servant entered, bearing a salver with cups of Chinese porcelain, a small bowl of sugar, and an ornate silver pitcher. On the servant's heels, bustling in importantly, came Akram. 'Ah, you're here. Had a good ride? Is Qureshi's horse sound?'

The servant placed the salver where the vase had been standing, and then left the room, followed by the steward.

Akram seated himself next to Muzaffar, arranging the skirts of his heavy brown choga about him. 'I told them you liked coffee,' he continued when he had settled down. He leaned forward and lifted the pitcher from the salver, carefully pouring a cup of coffee for Muzaffar before handing it over and sitting back against a bolster.

His lips curved into a teasing grin. 'So? All well? How is the lady, Shireen – I assume you will allow me to call her that? Only as a brother of sorts, I hasten to add; as the friend of the man who –'

'Shut up, Akram.' The words were clipped, Muzaffar's voice low and brimming with anger.

Akram regarded Muzaffar watchfully for a few moments, waiting for an explanation for his friend's unwarranted bluntness. When Muzaffar continued to sip absently at his coffee without another word, Akram said cautiously, 'Abba is waiting to meet you. And my cousin Basheer is with him. Mumtaz Hassan Khan's son. Perhaps once you've had your coffee, I can let them know you're here.'

Muzaffar nodded, and with a forced smile, launched into a discussion of Mumtaz Hassan's haveli. It was a safe, innocuous topic, but ended up petering out into a long, uncomfortable silence. After Muzaffar had finally tilted the cup and drunk down the last swallow of still-hot coffee, he put the cup back on the salver and looked up at Akram to find his own tension mirrored in the other man's face.

'More coffee?'

'No, I think not. It keeps me awake late into the night if I drink more than a cup.'

'Shall I fetch Abba and Basheer, then?'

'Please. I shall be honoured.'

Akram departed from the dalaan with unseemly haste and a sigh, almost of relief. Muzaffar gazed at the silver pitcher of coffee, mentally chastising himself for his rudeness. Akram's remark had been undoubtedly light-hearted and harmless: a mere jest. Coming just a few hours after Zeenat Begum's startling question, however, it had touched on a raw nerve. Still, it had not been fair to have snubbed his friend so brutally. Muzaffar sat back, leaning his head against the quilted curtain behind him. Later in the evening, he would make it a point to draw Akram aside and apologize for his conduct.

'Take care! I'm depending on you! If you mess this up – you know!'

The words came out of the blue, the muffling mist doing little to disguise the viciousness in the voice. Muzaffar, snapping out of his reverie, straightened immediately, his eyes instinctively searching the room. It was pointless, of course; the dalaan was too small and too well illuminated for anybody to be hiding in it. He glanced towards the doorway. Another whisper, in that same impatient voice, made him turn and look suspiciously at the quilted curtain behind him.

Where a curtain hung, there would be a window – a panel of stone filigree. He had felt the carving, a solid net of worked stone, probably marble, behind his head when he had leaned back. The voice had come from somewhere beyond that window. Muzaffar bent closer to the padded chintz of the curtain and listened, but all he could hear now was an indistinct mumble.

Muzaffar looked swiftly back over his shoulder, his gaze sweeping across the room. The niches in the walls held lamps; an ornate faanoos, a candlestand shimmering with the light of dozens of candles, stood on one side. There was too much light in the room. If he lifted even a corner of the curtain, the light would shine out. Muzaffar twisted to one side, pulling the skirt of his choga up over his head as he bent towards the lower left corner of the window. He draped the thick wool of his choga over the edge of the curtain, then lifted both over his head.

The mist was too thick and clammy to allow him to see anything; it obliterated everything beyond the lattice of the window. But he could hear the low murmur of conversation, just a little bit better now.

'The third window from the burj overlooking the river. Don't forget.'

'You can depend on me, huzoor.' The other voice was a deeper, heavier one, somewhat nasal. It sounded as if the speaker had a cold, and a bad one at that.

From beyond the doorway of the dalaan, Muzaffar heard the sounds of people approaching. Boot heels clicked and thumped on stone floors; there was the swish of chogas and the sound of laughter as someone made a joke. He whipped his head out from under the curtain and his own choga, just in time to hear one last sentence: 'And don't leave the note behind, whatever you do!'

Muzaffar had his choga in place and was sitting upright and formal, the very picture of decorum, when three men trooped into the dalaan. Akram's father, Abdul Munim Khan, was as deceptively frail as ever, the thick veins standing out on his hands, his beard nearly white. Akram, looking a little subdued in the presence of his father, preceded him. Behind the two of them was a portly young man dressed in a startlingly bright green choga. His eyes were close set and bulged slightly in an aquiline face, strangely incongruous with the girth of the body below.

Abdul Munim Khan was genteel and gracious. 'We met the last time – and the first, if I remember correctly – last year, when the Emperor was travelling. It has been a while since then. So much has changed.' He shook his head in a gesture that Muzaffar found hard to interpret – resignation? Sorrow? Cynicism? Or pure weariness? Whatever it was, it didn't indicate joy. Akram's father placed a paternal hand on Muzaffar's broad shoulder. 'My brother-in-law would like to meet you. He is on his own at the moment; the Diwan-i-kul has retired to his chambers... would you?' His voice trailed off as his eyes, still keen, looked up into Muzaffar's. Muzaffar nodded.

The plump young man, who had stood beside the doorway through the course of the short conversation, turned and stepped out into the corridor. Muzaffar gestured, head bowing briefly in respect, to let Abdul Munim Khan precede him. Akram, falling into step with Muzaffar, directed a shrewd glance at his friend. 'What were you up to? Listening at the window, if I'm not mistaken? Something suspicious?'

His voice was a mere murmur, and Muzaffar replied in an equally low tone. 'Nothing that concerns me, I think.'

From the momentous day when he had first made the acquaintance of Akram, Muzaffar had known the young amir to be fastidiously fashionable. Akram's attire was always impeccable, always rich and never either too opulent nor, at the same time, too understated to be inconspicuous. His friend had, if nothing else, the knack of treading the line between fashion and ostentation with an enviable panache.

Watching Akram's half-uncle from beneath hooded eyelids, Muzaffar decided that Mumtaz Hassan Khan, at least, did not share that knack. As Akram had already given Muzaffar to understand, Mumtaz Hassan was a very wealthy man. Muzaffar, cringing inwardly, realized that the man had also no compunctions about showing off that wealth. The dalaan in which he received Muzaffar outdid all the other rooms Muzaffar had seen in the haveli. A ceiling of silver and mirrors shimmered above a floor and walls of white marble inlaid with lapis, turquoise and jasper. The mattress on which Muzaffar had been invited to sit was the thickest he had ever seen, and the fat bolster against which he leaned self-consciously was of crimson velvet embroidered in gold thread. There was too much glitter here, thought Muzaffar; and in his experience, a profusion of glitter meant there was dross beneath, not gold.

A servant quietly put down a goblet of sherbet beside Muzaffar, while another placed a silver salver of samosas, fried pastries filled with spiced meat, between the men. Other servants followed, laying out an array of snacks: bowls of pistachios, almonds and walnuts; a tray of apples; imartis so syrupy they disguised the earthy flavour of the ground lentils of which they had been prepared. Muzaffar preferred his lentils savoury. He helped himself to a scant spoonful of dalmoth, the spiced roasted lentils for which Agra was famous.

'Jang Sahib,' said Mumtaz Hassan as he leaned forward, holding out a platter of balushahis toward Muzaffar. 'Surely you shall have a balushahi?' He winked and inclined his head slightly towards the sweets. 'Gold leaf, as you can see,' he murmured as, with a dramatic flourish, he moved the platter closer to one of the lamps. The heap of deep-fried sweets, rich and flaky with ghee and sugar, caught the light and gleamed golden. Muzaffar, watching his host, looked up to see the gold reflected in Mumtaz Hassan's eyes. They were close-set, a rich beautiful amber brown in colour. His eyebrows curved sharply above his eyes, sweeping down at an angle that gave Mumtaz Hassan a look of almost permanent surprise.

'No, thank you,' Muzaffar said. 'Later, perhaps.'

Mumtaz Hassan grinned in response and placed the platter on the thick Persian carpet. 'Do not pass them by, Jang Sahib,' he said. 'Not everybody is privileged enough to be offered such sweets. Basheer here –' he indicated the plump young man in green, whom Muzaffar had since been informed was Mumtaz Hassan's eldest son, Basheeruddin – 'is inordinately fond of them. Should you not have at least one, you may not find *any* at the end of the evening.' Mumtaz Hassan's full lips, set in a weathered but still handsome face, twisted in a contemptuous sneer. In the awkward silence that followed, Muzaffar glanced towards Basheer and their eyes met. There was embarrassment in Basheer's, as one would expect, along with suppressed fury.

'Akram told me that you were one of the purveyors when the Taj Mahal was being built,' Muzaffar said, turning back to Mumtaz Hassan. 'You must certainly have some interesting tales to recount of those times. I myself was too young to remember very much. And in any case, we spent little time in Agra. But I would give much to hear your recollections of its building.'

'Would you indeed?' Mumtaz Hassan swirled the reddish-gold contents of his goblet, looking intently at the sherbet before taking a long sip of it. 'I thought your generation was hardly interested in what has gone before. Eating, drinking, spending money on transitory pleasures –.' His gaze had once again moved deliberately towards his son, and he broke off as he realized, perhaps, that Muzaffar might be offended. 'But I can see you are not one of those, Jang Sahib.

'Those were interesting times, as you so rightly say. Hectic, too. I wasn't here all through, you know; being a purveyor of gems for the Taj Mahal meant a lot of travelling, many negotiations and much work. I spent very little time in Agra: a month here, a fortnight there. Less than six months, I think, all told. But yes, we had some adventures.' He raised his goblet so that it caught the light, and carefully holding the stem between his index finger and his thumb, turned it around, silently admiring the finely carved relief of lilies along the rim.

Around him, the room gradually fell silent. The steward, with a last whispered instruction to the servants, withdrew; the perfunctory conversation between Akram and Basheer petered out; even Basheer's chomping of the much-loved balushahis died out.

A stray moth fluttered drunkenly across the room and into one of the lamps, expiring with a barely audible hiss. One of the servants moved soundlessly forward to remove the lamp, and Akram broke the silence by sneezing. Mumtaz Hassan blinked, regarded his nephew with disgust, and turned back to Muzaffar with a bright smile.

'You see this goblet, Jang Sahib? This is from then. Of course, there is no rock crystal at the Taj Mahal – or none that I supplied' – Muzaffar caught a whiff of pomposity in the words and felt a welling of anger at the man's egotism – 'but this piece I obtained around that time. I had gone to the Kokcha River Valley in Badakhshan to purchase lapis lazuli... the best lapis is mined there, you know: a deep inky blue, so intense it draws you in. And it's flecked with gold. Like golden stars in a midnight sky.' His eyes flickered bright and dreamy, and in that moment Muzaffar glimpsed another side of the conceited and wealthy amir: an enthusiast whose love for the merchandise he dealt in was profound enough to border on reverence.

'Have you been to Badakhshan?'

Muzaffar shook his head. 'No. I have never been north of Kabul.'

'A mere three months from Dilli,' Mumtaz Hassan said, as if Kabul's relative proximity to Dilli was its downfall. 'And nothing to write

home about, either. I hate Kabul. The place to see is Badakhshan.'
He reached out to pick up an apple from the tray. He polished it
briskly on his thigh. 'It's a beautiful country. Rugged and bitterly
cold most of the year, and with almost no vegetation to speak of –
but beautiful. There is exquisiteness in the myriad shades of blue all
around: the river, the sky, and the lapis, of course. Not that you'll
see *that* beside the river. For the stone, you'll have to first climb up
a mountain and then descend into the mines, through stretches of
black and white limestone. It's eerie inside, claustrophobic and dim;
all you can see are the dark tunnels and the occasional fire which the
miners light to soften the stone enough to be able to gouge it out.'
His eyes glazed over and his voice dropped to a near-whisper. 'It is
hard to describe the thrill of holding a piece of still-warm lapis in
the hollow of your hand. Warm and rich, worth a king's ransom.

'I met a man at the Sang-e-Sar mines, where the lapis is quarried.
He was a miner who had a penchant for lighting fires just in order
to keep warm. He'd been many things: horse trader, thief, pimp,
soldier – *and* jeweller. A very odd mix of professions, I thought. But
we struck up an acquaintance while I was patrolling the Kokcha
Valley, searching out the finest lapis for the Baadshah. That man was
one of the shrewdest I've ever met; he could scent an opportunity
a kos away. Came down to Agra with me, finally. A very interesting
man.'

Muzaffar, watching Mumtaz Hassan, was reminded of the
Venetian merchant he had been taken to visit a few months earlier.
They were similar, he realized: both fond of ostentation, and both
given to long, rambling monologues that led nowhere.

'*He* gave me this goblet. Said it had been sold by a penurious
amir forty years ago, a man so desperately deep in debt he had
been reduced to selling off all his possessions. That may have been
true, but I've always had a sneaking suspicion my friend acquired
the goblet by less legitimate means. That's history, of course; now
he's a well-respected trader. Nobody would think of pointing fingers

at him. But ah, what adventures we had.' Mumtaz Hassan's eyes
twinkled. 'With a past like his, he was well suited to provide just
anything a man could ask for. A good mount, a pretty trinket, a girl
who knew how to please a man. There were times when it seemed
to me he knew Agra better than I did, even though I had been here
a week for every hour *he* had.'

He paused, and in that moment his son yawned – a loud, expansive
yawn that welled up from his well-padded stomach and hung in the
stricken silence of the room.

3

'*HUZOOR!*' THE VOICE was just above a whisper, troubled and urgent. 'Huzoor, please wake up!'

Muzaffar jerked up, bleary and disoriented, sucking in his breath at the chill of the air outside the warm cocoon of quilts. It took him a moment to blink, to accustom his eyes to the dimness of a room in which only a dull greyness filtering through the edges of the padded curtains indicated that the night had passed. He hauled one of the quilts up around his shoulders, shivering as he peered at the shadowy figure hovering nervously by his bed.

'Who the hell are you?' Muzaffar croaked. He had not imbibed; Mumtaz Hassan, for all his confessed love of decadence, did not believe in serving wine to his guests – but the night had been long, too long for a man who had come home in the small hours of the morning only to toss and turn, his mind flitting between Mumtaz Hassan's eccentricities, the embarrassingly obvious lack of love for his son, and inevitably for Muzaffar, his own feelings towards Shireen. He had finally fallen asleep, exhausted and with a headache, and had dreamt of her. A slim figure, resplendent in bridal silks and heavy jewellery, her henna-reddened palms stretching out towards him as she wept. Not with joy, but in sorrow – a deep, gut-wrenching sorrow that a befuddled Muzaffar did not understand, not even in his dreams.

He was jolted out of it by this insistent voice, almost on the brink of panic, which begged him to wake up.

'Qureshi Sahib's steward, huzoor. A rider has arrived from the
haveli of Mumtaz Hassan Khan Sahib with a message for you, huzoor.
He apologizes for the hour, but says that he has been instructed to
tell you that it is extremely urgent.' A hand held out a rectangle of
paper, barely visible as a fuzzy grey shape.

'Get a lamp. How am I to see in this darkness?'

The missive was in Akram's scrawl, made even more untidy by
the agitation of the writer.

Mumtaz Hassan had been killed during the night. Could Muzaffar
come as soon as possible?

Akram, looking haggard and uncharacteristically ill-dressed – his
turban had been hurriedly tied on and he wore no jewellery except
for his favourite emerald ring – emerged from the haveli as Muzaffar
strode up the path from the drum house. An amorphous and fragile
mist, its grip as tenuous and weak as a ghost's, had cloaked the river
as Muzaffar had ridden out of Qureshi Sahib's still-dozing household.
The mist had played hide-and-seek with the breast-shaped dome of
the Taj Mahal: one moment the mist would envelop the dome, as
if shielding it from the prying eyes of the world; the next moment,
a breeze would whip away the veil of mist, laying bare its rounded
beauty. By the time Muzaffar dismounted at the drum house of
Mumtaz Hassan's haveli, the breeze had carried away the last of
the mist, and the brass finial atop the dome of the late Empress's
tomb was twinkling fitfully in the weak sunshine. It was going to
be a cold day, thought Muzaffar, as he hurried up the path to meet
his friend.

'Allah be thanked you are here, Muzaffar! I am so sorry to have
hauled you out of your bed at such an unearthly hour –'

Muzaffar waved a hand in dismissal of the apology. 'What
happened? All you said was Mumtaz Hassan was slain during the
night. Are you sure of that?'

Akram, striding up the steps to the entrance, halted and turned to Muzaffar with a look of injury. 'An entire household cannot be mistaken in thinking its master dead. The hakim's had a look too, if you need reinforcement of the fact; Mumtaz Hassan is definitely quite dead.'

'I wasn't questioning his being dead. You wrote specifically that he had been *killed*. Are you sure of that? It cannot have been an accident, or death by a natural cause? Is there evidence that someone murdered him?'

'Oh.' Akram continued, into the flashy chamber Muzaffar remembered from the previous night, and down a broad corridor off to the right. 'This way – and yes, the hakim says it is murder. You can talk to him after we're through with the Diwan-i-kul. He wants to meet you.'

Muzaffar was of too little consequence to have ever been accorded the privilege of meeting Mir Jumla in person. He had seen the Diwan-i-kul in court, of course, an imperious figure standing at the front of the silver railings that separated the Emperor from the more important omrah, hailing the Baadshah's every utterance with flattering remarks. 'Mir Jumla,' a disgusted Farid Khan had whispered to his brother-in-law, 'is a firm believer in the dictum "Agar Shah roza goyad shab ast in, bebayed guft inak mah u parwin."' *If the King says that it is night at noon, be sure to cry, 'I see the moon'.*

A Mir Jumla seen at close quarters and in the restricted confines of a chamber a tenth the size of the Diwan-i-Khaas, was a less ludicrous figure, and more ominous. He was sixty-five years old, a year older than the Emperor, but with the vigour of a much younger man. Where the Emperor's years – and those too recent ones of stress, despair and disease – were written in the wrinkles of his face and the whiteness of his beard, Mir Jumla looked still young. True, the beard was flecked with grey and the jaw was fleshy, the hands spotted and with the dry, parchment-like skin of an old man; but the eyes were vividly alive, noting every detail, missing nothing. Muzaffar did not doubt that the mind behind those eyes was equally sharp.

'Abdul Munim Khan has spoken to me of you,' the Diwan-i-kul said without preamble as he gestured to Muzaffar to sit. 'You sit too, Khan Sahib – and you,' he added, looking briefly at Akram, who was standing timidly at the doorway. 'The rest of you, get out.' He waited for the little contingent of attendants to disperse, the last one staying a moment longer than the others to place the Diwan-i-kul's hookah close at hand; and then, when the room was empty of servitors, he turned back to Muzaffar.

'Khan Sahib here tells me you are an investigator of sorts.' It was a statement, but the suspicion in Mir Jumla's voice made it clear that he questioned the veracity of Abdul Munim Khan's assertion. It had, however, not been structured as a question, and Muzaffar held his tongue. 'He says you have successfully solved a number of cases, including one that involved an embezzlement of funds from the Imperial Exchequer.'

Muzaffar inclined his head. 'Khan Sahib is too kind.'

Mir Jumla's head snapped up. 'I don't care if he's kind or not!' he snarled. 'All I'm interested in is whether or not you're capable. Were you *right*? Were you *lucky*? Did you succeed simply because you are a nobleman and could bully people into confessions?' His hand had clenched around the pipe from the hookah; he now put the end of the pipe to his mouth and gurgled deeply. 'Tell me that, and spare me the niceties.'

'I may have been fortunate once or twice,' Muzaffar admitted, 'But I can safely assert that I am capable of successfully carrying out an investigation without the help of luck or the support of my status. In any case, luck I find to be too fickle and my status is hardly worth speaking of –'

Mir Jumla cut in, his lip curling. 'Do you coerce your suspects by talking ceaselessly at them, then?'

Muzaffar bit back a sharp retort. The Diwan-i-kul gurgled meditatively on his hookah before heaving a deep sigh and sitting up straight. He pulled the end of the pipe out of his mouth and coiled the pipe next to the hookah before looking up at Muzaffar. 'But we have no choice. The kotwal of Agra is a stupid fellow; he was presented to me yesterday and I have little faith in his abilities. I trust Abdul Munim Khan, though, and since *he* has spoken on your behalf, I feel the correct decision would be to hand over the investigation of this death to you.'

His voice had soothed into a magnanimous murmur, as if he were doing Muzaffar a favour by appointing him an official investigator. Involuntarily, Muzaffar's gaze moved to Akram's father, sitting at right angles to the Diwan-i-kul and watching the scene with worried eyes. He shook his head almost imperceptibly when his gaze met Muzaffar's. *Do not dare refuse.*

Mir Jumla noticed the silent interaction, but except for a sardonic smile, did not react. 'Very good,' he said, rubbing his hands on the front of his choga, down his thighs. 'You will get started immediately on your investigation. I will leave Agra as soon as my armies are ready to march – perhaps by noon, maybe later; certainly today. I do not know when I shall be back in town, but when I am – or when I return to Dilli – I shall expect a full report from you on what you have discovered. I sincerely hope that you will have found the culprit by then. I would not like to have the murderer of a dear and cherished friend of mine go scot-free.' He paused for effect, and added in a quieter voice, 'And I would also not like to have the brother-in-law of the kotwal of Dilli subjected to the ignominy of being branded an incompetent.'

He waited long enough for the words to sink in, then turned away to look at Abdul Munim Khan. 'Khan Sahib, there are some things the two of us must discuss. Be so good as to have someone go and fetch a scribe from that crowd camped at the gateway.'

He looked towards Muzaffar and raised an eyebrow. 'And *you* had better get started. I would not like to be in your boots should you fail.'

He's a martinet, isn't he?' Akram said when they were safely out of earshot. 'I wouldn't like to be in your place, Muzaffar.'

Muzaffar nodded grimly. 'I am aware of that. I wish Khan Sahib –'. He broke off, suddenly remembering that he was talking to Khan Sahib's son. 'Never mind. Where is your cousin?'

'Which one?'

Muzaffar huffed, annoyed. 'The only one you've introduced me to. Basheer. Are there others, too?'

'Of course there are others. I told you; Basheer's the eldest of the sons. There are some daughters as well, though I think all of them are already married.'

'I didn't get to meet any of Basheer's younger brothers,' Muzaffar murmured. 'Are they not in town?'

'They are, but they're too young for Mumtaz Hassan Sahib to have deemed them fit company for guests. One is thirteen years old, one eight, and the youngest three.'

Muzaffar's eyes widened. 'A large family.' But it was not unusual; in a time when disease and war and famine carried off thousands of children before they even reached puberty, exceptionally large families were common. Even among men like Mumtaz Hassan, who could well afford hakims and nutritious food to keep starvation and illness at bay. 'I meant Basheer,' Muzaffar added. 'Where is he?'

'In the room where my uncle's body was found. The hakim's with him.'

But Basheer and the hakim were not in the room; they were standing outside, in a corridor which overlooked a small garden. The hakim, hunched against the cold wind blowing in from the garden, was a frail little man with protuberant eyes, a red nose and a beard that hung in straggly wisps from a weak chin. Muzaffar was put strongly in mind of a catch of shrimp he had seen a fisherman drawing in near the coast at Karavali.

He put the picture firmly out of his mind and addressed a few words by way of condolence to Basheer, who was looking more aggrieved than grieving. The dead man's son acknowledged Muzaffar's words with a curt nod and an indistinct murmur, then asked, 'You'd like to see it, wouldn't you? Akram insisted everything should be left as it is, but Ammi and the other ladies of the house are making noises about how a corpse should not be left lying about like this. They say it's inauspicious, disrespectful to Abba, things like that.'

He waited just long enough to see Muzaffar nod in agreement before he pulled the curtain back from the doorway. 'Come on in.'

MUZAFFAR HAD BEGUN to get used to the vulgar opulence of Mumtaz Hassan's haveli. The room in which the man had died was like the rest of his house, glittering and overdecorated. A heavy curtain had been pulled aside from a jharokha, an oriel window at the far end of the room. Sunlight was beginning to stream in through it, but it would be a while before the sunshine was strong enough to illuminate the room. Instead, lamps had been brought in and set, two near the door and another beside the bed. A cold breath of air blew in through the open jharokha, stirring the flames of the lamps and making them dance. The hundreds of mirrors inlaid in the ceiling danced in unison. The effect was startlingly beautiful, thought Muzaffar as he stepped into the room behind Basheer.

But the corpse stretched out on the bed was ugly. Mumtaz Hassan, in life, had been a handsome man; in death, his throat ringed by a harsh reddish-brown bruise and his tongue protruding, he looked a distasteful caricature of himself. Muzaffar looked down at his host of the previous evening, before turning to the hakim, who had followed them in. 'Well? What do you say?'

'Throttled,' the hakim replied. 'Sometime during the night.'

'And,' Muzaffar spoke slowly, picking his words with care as he thought through what he needed to know, 'can you deduce anything about who might have killed him? Man? Woman? Was it done with bare hands? A garrotte?'

'A garrotte. Definitely. Look here' – the hakim indicated the bruising on the dead man's throat – 'fingers would have left splotches, not a continuous unbroken ring like this.' He grimaced, mouth working as he mulled over the condition of the body. 'I'd say the murderer was as tall as Hassan Sahib, or even taller. He would have sprung on Hassan Sahib from the back, you see, slinging the garrotte – maybe a length of rope, or a strip of twisted cloth – over Hassan Sahib's head and around his neck. Had the man been shorter than Hassan Sahib, the bruise would have been angled down at the back of Hassan Sahib's neck.' He turned the corpse on its side, indicating the bruise as he did so. Muzaffar leaned forward to look more closely at the dead man's neck, the mottled skin stretching across the Adam's apple in front, and curving up towards the nape.

Muzaffar straightened and glanced around the room, taking in the bedclothes, all richly embroidered velvet and heavy wool, the quilts and blankets tossed about, a sheet tugged right off the bed and half trailing on the floor. A ewer next to the bed had been knocked over, the water in it spilling in a still damp splotch across the carpet. One bolster, ripped to reveal its stuffing of cotton, lay on the floor a few feet from the bed.

'He certainly put up a fight,' he said.

The hakim contented himself with a shrug, reaching into the pocket of his choga to draw forth a large muslin handkerchief with which he wiped his hands. He replaced the handkerchief a moment later and rubbed his hands together briskly in a gesture eerily reminiscent of glee. No, cold; Muzaffar corrected himself mentally. It *was* cold in the room. He moved towards the jharokha, a window without bars or stone screens to shut out the wind.

Halfway across the room, Muzaffar paused and bent to retrieve something from the floor. 'Look at this, Akram,' he said to his friend, who was a step behind him. 'A pebble.' A stone, half the size of a walnut, smoothened and polished by centuries of flowing water, lay in his palm. 'A river pebble. What on earth is it doing here?'

'There's another one,' Akram said, pointing at the base of the jharokha. Under the window lay another pebble, smaller than the first one, but also definitely from the river. Muzaffar picked it up and stood at the window, gazing thoughtfully down at the two stones that nestled in his hand.

A quilted curtain, patterned in green and red, hung from rings above the jharokha; it had been pulled to one side and the end shoved behind a chest that stood next to the jharokha. Muzaffar reached out to tug the end of the curtain free, and pulled up short, staring fixedly at the corner of the jharokha.

A rope, about the thickness of a man's finger, snaked into the room from the corner of the jharokha. It was half-hidden by a hanging fold of the curtain, and in the half-gloom of the room, it had been nearly invisible. Now, Muzaffar could see it clearly – and could see, even as he stared at it, that it was straining towards the jharokha, as if someone was trying to pull it free of an anchor within the room. Muzaffar pulled the curtain aside and looked down, to where one end of the rope had been knotted securely around a handle of the chest. He spared it a single glance before moving forward, soundless as a shadow, to peer down from the jharokha to the ground below. It was no use; the mist may have begun dissolving in the sunlight, but it still hung thickly over the river.

Muzaffar whirled and raced for the door, grabbing Basheer by the arm and dragging him along as he did so. 'Where is the nearest exit towards the river?' he hissed, his voice low and urgent. 'Quick! Show me!' He propelled Basheer swiftly through the door. Akram had run out into the corridor too, following in his friend's wake. Basheer gestured towards the right, and Muzaffar tugged at him, trying to run with the weight of his unwilling guide pulling him back. Behind Basheer, Akram pushed and shoved, egging the other man on. A maid, twig broom in hand, emerged from a nearby room and shrieked as she stepped back hurriedly to avoid the three men careening down the corridor. A burly servant, apparently believing that Basheer was in danger of his life, lunged for Muzaffar.

Basheer squeaked in alarm. 'No, no! It's all right – here, Jang Sahib!' he panted. '– Maybe Gulrez will be better able –' but Muzaffar, switching his grasp to the arm of the fitter Gulrez, had gone racing down the corridor, Akram on his heels. Basheer followed at a more sedate pace.

The river-facing side of the haveli was derelict, a place of damp and neglect. There were no carefully tended gardens here, no orchards, no parterres bursting with flowers. A strip of land about twelve feet across, perhaps a little more in places, stretched between the outer wall of the haveli and the river. The ground was soggy and a morass of mud, broken reeds and grass. Basheer cursed under his breath as he picked his way through, pushing aside the bulrushes and the reeds, following in the wake of Muzaffar and Akram. Gulrez, having led them to the door looking out onto the riverbank, had returned to the haveli, passing Basheer on the way and giving his master a vaguely reproachful look, as if disapproving of the company Basheer had begun to keep.

Basheer arrived under the jharokha to find Akram standing at the wall, looking up at the jharokha from which the rope hung, its end about four feet above the ground. There was no sign of Muzaffar.

'Where's Jang Sahib?' Basheer asked, his voice ringing eerily in the whiteness of the mist that surrounded them. Somewhere close, a bird began squawking and flapping its wings. The sound built up in a matter of seconds, the birdcalls rising into a frenzied crescendo, the wingbeats growing louder – and suddenly, piercing the mist and rising up into the air, was a flock of ducks. For a moment, they were visible against the white blanket, and then they were gone, their cries echoing.

Akram glowered at Basheer. '*Thank you*. If there *was* anybody hiding out there, he'd have had ample opportunity to make his escape by now.' He looked away pointedly, staring out toward the invisible river, from where another sound, far less audible than the quacking of the ducks, had begun to make itself heard. Someone was wading, the gentle rippling of the water combining with the soft crunch of half-dry reeds crushed underfoot. Muzaffar emerged a few moments later, his bare feet muddy till the ankles.

'You no doubt heard our friend here,' Akram complained. 'Scaring away everything and everybody in sight – and all down the river, I'm sure. Did you find anything?'

Muzaffar had rolled up his pajamas to his calves, and now drawing out a large handkerchief from the pocket of his choga, cleaned up and pulled down his pajamas. He shivered, cursing under his breath, which curled up in a white cloud about his face. 'No,' he said, after a few moments. 'And don't blame your cousin,' – he looked up fleetingly, to bestow a smile of utter sweetness on Basheer – 'I am sure it was unintentional. In any case, I think we made enough noise running through the haveli and out here for us to have been able to catch anyone unawares. Whoever was here ran off long before we arrived.' He took out his shoes – tucked hurriedly into another pocket when he had been obliged to set off into the marshes – and put them on.

'He seems to have had a boat waiting for him. The footprints lead straight into the river. Of course, it may well be that he's a strong swimmer, but anybody who would voluntarily get into water as cold as ice on such a morning must be a lunatic.' He shoved his hands into his choga, pushing them deep into his armpits as he gazed out unseeingly over the river. Then, suddenly, he turned to Basheer. 'Do you have a boat here? Or can one be hired nearby?'

'A couple of boatmen moor their boats half a kos from here,' Basheer said, gesturing towards the south. 'But they won't be out this early in the morning.'

'Never mind,' Muzaffar muttered, already striding away in the direction Basheer had indicated. 'I'll row the boat myself if I must. Akram?'

'The mist seems to be dispersing,' Akram said, peering ahead from his position at the prow. 'But I can't see anything other than the river and the bank beyond. No boats on the river, at any rate.' Behind him, Muzaffar, pulling strongly on the oars, leaned back and then forward, finally having settled into the rhythm of rowing. Akram glanced over his shoulder at his friend. 'I'll take over, shall I?'

Muzaffar shook his head. 'We aren't far now.'

The shapeless masses that had formed the riverbank were now beginning to emerge from the mist that blanketed them, solidifying into recognizable shapes. A grove of mango trees. A spreading banyan with its heavy tresses anchoring it to the ground. A small pavilion. A group of men sitting on their haunches around a tiny fire that blazed a cheerful orange as someone moved away for a moment.

'Ah,' Muzaffar said with a satisfied grin. 'There are boats here. Maybe this is where our quarry alighted.'

Six men, all of them wrapped in drab grey blankets, were huddled around the fire. A seventh, his blanket folded lengthwise and slung across his shoulders, crouched in one of the small rowboats tethered to poles along the river bank. The men beside the fire craned their necks, watching the approaching boat with curious eyes; it was the lone man in the boat who straightened and came forward, the murky water of the shallows swirling about his ankles, to help draw the boat in to the shore. 'Where is your boatman, huzoor, that you should be pulling the oars by yourself?' he said, addressing Muzaffar with a grin. Polite but not servile, probably because he guessed that a nobleman who could condescend to row a boat would not balk at being chatted to by a mere boatman.

Muzaffar waited until the man had helped Akram out of the boat, then sprang out onto the dry sand. The group around the fire had finally given up its need for warmth in preference for a little excitement. The men came clustering around, murmuring among themselves, wondering who the aristocratic newcomers were and why they were on their own, unattended by servants or boatmen.

'Give them some space,' growled the man who had helped pull their boat in. 'What's the matter? Do you want to shove them back in the river?'

'I should hope not,' Muzaffar said. 'I've had a hard time getting us here in the first place.' He glanced across at the group in front. 'Has anybody else come here across the river this morning?'

But the men had already begun to lose interest. Someone mentioned something about the fish being nearly done, and almost simultaneously, all the men turned back to the fire they had temporarily abandoned. Within less than a minute of Muzaffar asking his question, the group had gone back to the fire and the spitted fish roasting above the flames. The occasional glance came their way, but other than that, Muzaffar and Akram appeared to have been forgotten for the time being.

'I'm sorry about that,' said the man who had helped them. 'We'll be beginning work soon, huzoor – the men want their breakfasts.' He smiled apologetically. 'You wanted to know if anybody else crossed over here this morning, huzoor? One did; but he didn't merely cross over. I ferried him both ways.'

Muzaffar raised an eyebrow. 'You mean from this side of the river and back again?'

The man nodded.

Muzaffar exchanged a glance with Akram before turning back to the boatman. 'When was this?'

'Not long back, huzoor. We set off before the sun had risen. When we reached the other shore, he made me wait while he got off. I must have waited a few minutes, I suppose – and then he was back, running as if a tiger was after him, telling me to pull as hard as I could.' He wagged his head, mouth curving into a mocking grin, as if marvelling at the foibles of his ex-passenger. 'What a creature. So much bluster and so much belligerence, but really just a bundle of nerves at the end of it all.'

'And when did you get back to this shore?'

'Just a little while before you arrived, huzoor. I was cleaning up my boat when you came in.'

Muzaffar directed a glance up and down the shore. The mist, rarely completely gone during these bleak days of deepest winter, was especially tenacious along the river. Visibility had improved since Muzaffar had first run out onto the riverbank, but the mist was still sufficient to provide only a limited view of the surrounding land.

'He's gone, of course. Did you see where he went?'

The man shook his head. 'I was preoccupied with getting my boat in, huzoor. He was in a tearing hurry, you see: he didn't even wait for me to bring the boat in. He leaped out and scurried off well before that.' He paused, then raising his voice, called out, 'Asif! Come over here for a moment!'

From the knot of men sitting around the fire, busy with their meagre breakfast, a youth detached himself and hurried over. Asif smiled nervously at Muzaffar, bobbing his head in a gesture of deference.

'Asif,' said his colleague, 'did you see where my passenger went?' The boatman had seated himself on the rim of the boat, one of the oars balanced, erect, between his knees as he slowly ran his fingertips along the handle, carefully feeling the worn wooden surface. There was a splinter there, perhaps, thought Muzaffar as he watched the man draw a knife from the cloth wound around his waist, and use that to begin trimming the handle.

Asif's smooth forehead creased. 'South, I'd say,' he said finally in a voice that, though it had broken, had not yet been completely brought under control by its owner. 'The last I saw of his horse, it was headed south.'

'His horse?'

The young man nodded, looking at Muzaffar. 'He had ridden out here, huzoor. There was a boy with him, who looked after the horse while the man was on the river.' He chuckled. 'An inept groom, if I ever saw one. He couldn't control the horse. Not one bit; it kept prancing about and dragging him through the sand. The boy tried giving it a lump of cane sugar, but no: the horse wouldn't even do him the honour of accepting *that*!'

'Hmm. And when the passenger got back, he mounted and rode away, is that right?'

Asif nodded. 'With the boy seated behind. They were in a big hurry.'

'And they went south, you say. What lies south of here?' he glanced from Asif to the other man.

It was the man who answered, after a moment's thought. 'Mainly gardens, huzoor. A couple of havelis. And there are those who tend the gardens, or who work in the havelis, or fish in the river: their huts are scattered about the place.'

'What do you think, Akram?' Muzaffar said. 'Will you come on what may be a wild goose chase?' He waited long enough to see Akram's nod of assent, then turned back to the two boatmen. 'One last question: what did he look like?'

'Piebald,' Asif replied promptly. 'White, but with large patches of black on his neck and belly. Very handsome, I'd say. I wondered how a man as down-at-heel as him could afford a stallion like that.'

Muzaffar grinned, amused. 'I meant the man. You like horses, do you?'

The young man looked embarrassed. 'I beg your pardon, huzoor,' he said in a stifled voice. 'I did not realize – but the horse *was* beautiful, and that boy who'd been left in charge was so *very* clumsy. Said they'd only just bought the horse, it hadn't been broken in properly yet, it needed time to get used to the saddle and the bridle, and so on. What rot!' He snorted derisively. 'I may be a boatman, not a groom, but I'm sure I'd have made a better handler of horses than he was.'

'I'm sure, given the opportunity. But tell me: what did the man look like?' He looked at the other man as he spoke, directing the question to him. The man had put away the knife he had been using on the oar handle. Now he bent, lifted a handful of sand from near his feet, and began rubbing it down the length of newly shaven wood, its colour a harsh cream against the dirty weathered brown of the handle.

His eyes narrowed and he chewed his lip as he worked, but whether that was because he was concentrating on the job or merely thinking over Muzaffar's question, Muzaffar could not say. Perhaps a bit of both. 'A middle-aged man,' he said, after a few moments. 'Perhaps forty years old. Tall and broad. Red-cheeked and grizzle-haired.' He looked absently down at his fingers, dusted over with sand; then, bending over to gather up another handful of sand, he added, 'Not a poor man, huzoor. But not rich, either, despite that grand horse of his. I could wager that horse wasn't his.'

5

MUZAFFAR GLANCED AT Akram. 'So? What do you think?'

Akram looked thoughtfully down at the hoofmarks in the loose sandy soil of the riverbank. 'I'm not the tracker, Muzaffar,' he said, with a shrug. 'You have more experience with things like this than I do. What do you say?'

'That the horse pranced around a good deal here. But *that* we already knew. The boatman said the boy who brought the horse had difficulty controlling it.' He indicated the confused welter of hoofprints and footprints. 'A skittish creature, I think. It certainly kept the boy on his toes. But where did they go once they picked up their passenger?' His eyes narrowed and his voice trailed off as he examined the area around them, trying to pick out possible trails that could lead off from the muddle of marks on the ground. 'Ah! Do you think –?' his eyes alight, Muzaffar moved off towards the north, following a line of hoofprints, before realizing that it looped back a few yards on. He returned to where Akram still stood, watchful and patient.

'That horse led the boy on a merry dance before he could bring it back,' Muzaffar grunted, sheepish. He moved on, now half bent, eyes scanning the ground and face taut with concentration. Suddenly, he straightened and stared ahead at a wavering line of hoofmarks that headed south. A moment's perusal, as if in confirmation, and then he called out over his shoulder. 'Come along, Akram! I think we have it!'

'Must we race along in this unseemly fashion?' Akram huffed a few minutes later, his cold exacerbated by the chill in the air, his voice hoarse and his nose red and running.

The trail, clear as the Milky Way across a dark and cloudless night, led roughly south-east of where they had disembarked. The sand in the soil had given way to the rich and fertile alluvium that the Yamuna had been depositing along its shores for centuries. Moist, dark soil that faithfully held the marks of a recent and hurried passage. A horse, laden down with the weight of two people, had left deep prints, unmistakable and clear enough for Muzaffar to not need to focus much attention on following the trail.

'The faster we move, the greater chance we have of catching up with our quarry,' Muzaffar replied. Akram's low-voiced protest, that two men on foot could not hope to catch up with two men on horseback, went unheeded as Muzaffar hurried on.

Ten minutes of brisk walking, interspersed with sporadic bursts of running, brought them to the end of the trail.

Directly across the Yamuna rose the Taj Mahal. Its dome sparkled in the sunlight, topped by the gleaming gilded brass finial – a pillar-like structure, one globe atop another, a lotus blossoming above the traditional kalash, an auspicious waterpot filled with mango leaves. All of metal, all shining like gold in the sunshine.

'They say the Baadshah plans to build an identical tomb for himself,' Akram remarked with a sniff. 'But on this bank of the river, to be connected to the Empress's tomb by a bridge. That will be a sight, eh, Muzaffar? White on one side, pure and unsullied: black on the other, brooding and mysterious. Black and white, man and woman, life and death –'

'We've lost the trail,' Muzaffar said bluntly.

Whether or not Shahjahan intended to build a mausoleum for himself on the east bank of the Yamuna was a moot point. Some said that the Emperor had chosen a spot for his own mausoleum –

opposite the Taj Mahal, and a reflection of the Empress's – when the Taj Mahal itself was being built. Others, more sceptical, scoffed at the idea. If the Baadshah had truly meant to build a structure on the same lines as the Taj Mahal, work on it would have begun long ago. The Baadshah would not have gathered up the court and shifted to Dilli, to devote his energies to creating a capital there.

Whatever the gossip about the east bank of the river, one thing could not be disputed: it commanded a fine view of the Taj Mahal. Perhaps because of that, it appeared to have acquired a certain degree of popularity among the local inhabitants. Where the riverbank sloped down to the river, a few boatmen had anchored their vessels. One boat was already out on the river, bobbing about in midstream. On the bank, milling about the tethered boats, was a motley crowd: fishermen with nets trailing behind them, one of them with a basketful of undersized silvery-black catfish on his head; a trio of women carrying bundles of laundry; two boys lugging a large, flattish, circular basket laden with the fibrous tubes of lotus stems. There were others too, people less obviously here on work. The idlers, the talkers, the sightseers and those who merely wanted to spend the first hour of the day basking in the warmth of the winter sun: they were all there, a couple of them looking curiously up at the two noblemen standing on the path at the top of the embankment.

'I suppose this is a thoroughfare?' Akram said gloomily. 'All that traffic coming up from the riverbank, up here and then' – he waved a hand vaguely about, as if scattering seed to the four winds – 'all over.'

Muzaffar gazed down at the mud churned up around their feet. The hoofprints of the piebald horse – so sharp and clear till now – had reached this point and been swallowed up, smothered into oblivion by a crowd of footprints, hoofprints, pawprints, drag marks and other signs of traffic. There was a strange, round and deep indentation, which Muzaffar realized was the print of a crutch; and the broad, all-obliterating sweep of a damaged boat that had been dragged almost halfway to the top of the embankment. There were the occasional footprints of leather- and wood-soled sandals, even a worn boot; but those were the exception. Muzaffar wriggled his toes, cold even inside the shoes he wore, and tried to suppress an odd pang of guilt. All around, pressed into the wet earth, were the rounded marks of bare toes. Bare in the deepest of winter. Bare, as the rest of the body would mostly be, perhaps clad only in a single shawl and dhoti.

All in the glorious reflection of the exquisite Taj Mahal. There was something distasteful about it.

It was heinous, this contrast between the wealth of the Emperor and his court on the one hand, and the grinding poverty of the general populace on the other. The aristocracy lived in comfortable cocoons where starvation, cold, and fatigue were strange and unknown to the point of being a novelty when experienced – if ever. He had once met, Muzaffar remembered, a group of amirs who had returned from a hunt, and had deemed it high adventure to have lived only on rotis and lentils for two whole days, and to have actually bathed in unscented river water. They had had to live *terribly* roughly, one had insisted; they could not take too many horses, so he had been obliged to leave behind his favourite hookah, his ivory chessboard, and a particularly fine slave girl.

Salim, the scraggy old boatman who was one of Muzaffar's more outspoken friends in Dilli, had doubled up in laughter on hearing the anecdote from Muzaffar. 'If I could eat lentils and rotis every single day, I would consider myself very well off, indeed!' he had said. 'Tell me, these men who bathe in scented water – do they piss perfume, as well? Perhaps I should keep an eye out, eh? If I see an amir relieving himself, maybe I should collect his piss, and make a fortune out of selling it. At least I'll be able to afford one square meal a day!' He had laughed again, but there had been not a trace of mirth in the sound, just anger and bitterness at the injustice of it all.

'There's a man there who looks as if he's been here a while,' Akram said, jolting Muzaffar out of his reverie. 'Shall we ask him if he saw anything?'

The man was bending over the boat that had been dragged up

onto the bank. Sleeves rolled up past sinewy forearms, he was using a crude chisel, with a heavy stone in place of a hammer, to chip away at something on the inside of the boat.

Though he admitted to having been in the vicinity since sunrise – 'even before, if you count the time I spent in my – um – ablutions', he explained, with a meaningful smirk – he had seen no signs of a piebald horse with two riders. 'Not that I would,' he said. '*Look.*' He waved the chisel, indicating the embankment. 'From here, you can only see someone up there if they stand right on the edge of the embankment. If they're further back, on the path, they'd be invisible from here.'

He looked inquiringly at Muzaffar, as if awaiting assurance that Muzaffar agreed, or at least understood. When Muzaffar nodded, the man exhaled deeply and bent to his work again. 'There are gardens up ahead,' he added, as he wielded the chisel, cleaning away the smashed and torn edges where a jagged rock appeared to have ripped into the hull of the boat. 'They're just off the path. If anybody saw that horse you're chasing, it would be the workers at one of the gardens.'

Akram nodded sagely when Muzaffar conveyed the advice and they moved off. 'Yes. That might be an idea. I've been to a couple of these gardens. With Abba, years ago, when I was a child. Abba knew some of the big mansabdars, and they had impressive gardens too. Herds of oxen and battalions of gardeners and sweepers and whatnot.' He fell into step beside Muzaffar. 'But you would know, Muzaffar. Your Abba left you very extensive lands too, didn't he? You must be the lord of many gardens.'

'Like the seven hundred and seventy-seven fabled gardens of Kashmir?' Muzaffar grinned. The more gullible believed that the Emperor Jahangir – so deeply interested in plants and animals and all things living that he was almost more a scientist than an emperor – had laid out that exaggerated number of gardens in the Vale of Kashmir. 'Hardly.'

Akram grinned back, and shrugged a little sheepishly as if in preparation for the question he was about to ask. 'You don't believe that tale, do you? About the seven hundred and seventy-seven gardens? I've been to Kashmir, and it's all very pretty, and the gardens are very beautiful, to be sure. But I only remember maybe about half a dozen. Not even a hundred, let alone seven hundred.'

'If the imperial family owned those many gardens, the need to wage wars in the Deccan would be substantially reduced,' Muzaffar replied drily. 'And I suppose the Baadshah would have built his black marble mausoleum. And had it inlaid with emeralds and rubies. I can well imagine the many maunds of roses that are harvested from the imperial gardens every month. Enough to keep every begum in the harem well supplied with rooh gulab, and with plenty left over to sell.' His lip curled. 'An empire founded on roses. Or funded by roses. How ironic! But I suppose with the blood they've spilled all across the land, a poet could say many millions of roses have blossomed – each a deeper red than the other.'

Akram grabbed Muzaffar by the sleeve, yanking him back just as they reached the top of the embankment. 'Muzaffar, for the love of Allah!' he hissed. 'What's come over you?! What if someone heard you?'

Muzaffar glanced at his friend, then frowned. A few moments passed in silence before he blinked and shook his head, as if trying to shake off the cynicism that had gripped him. 'I'm sorry; I hadn't meant to go so far. It's just that this isn't at all how I wanted to be spending my time in Agra, Akram. All I'd meant to do was help Zeenat Aapa bring Shireen safely home, and then go on back to Dilli. I hadn't bargained with being suddenly hauled up by the Diwan-i-kul and told to solve a crime about which I know nothing.'

'That's usually the way with crime,' Akram muttered half to himself. Muzaffar did not give any sign of having heard Akram; he continued as if uninterrupted. 'And now I find myself running about after an elusive horse. With no horse of my own, mind you. I had thought I'd be back home within a week. Now I'm stuck here in Agra till who knows when. And if I can't find Mumtaz Hassan's killer, the Diwan-i-kul will probably have *my* head instead.'

Akram pulled a face. 'Don't be morbid, Muzaffar. Come on.' He tugged at Muzaffar's sleeve, and Muzaffar, with a final dispirited nod, squinted down the dirt track. On their right, the embankment sloped down to the riverbank, a stretch of grass bordered by sand and pebbles, with the slow flowing Yamuna beyond. On their left, tussocks of coarse grass, beaded with silvery dew, fringed the dirt road. Beyond stretched more grassland, a few scattered trees, and – further away – what looked like a small village, its outlines blurred by distance and the last remnants of the morning mist.

'I suppose the gardens he meant lie further down that way,' Muzaffar said finally, gesturing towards a walled enclosure perhaps a quarter of a kos along the road. 'What do you think? Does that look like a garden?'

'At this distance? I don't have the eyes of an eagle.'

'Let's go find out, then, shall we?'

The eastern bank of the Yamuna had been given over to several gardens, among them the ones which the imperial family itself had created. To the north, beyond the tomb of Itimad-ud-Daulah, lay the Bagh-e-Nurafshan – the 'light-scattering garden'. Pining for the cool environs of Ferghana and Kabul and cursing the heat of Agra, the first of the Mughal emperors, Babur, had fashioned this garden, with its pathways and pavilions, its runnels and pools of shimmering water, its beds of roses and narcissi. The late emperor, Jahangir, had redone the garden and bestowed on it its high-sounding name. But to many, it still remained what Babur had called it: the Aaraam Bagh, or the 'garden of rest'. A retreat for lazy days.

Off to the south, the Mehtab Bagh – 'the garden of moonlight' – fragrant with night-flowering jasmine, lay opposite the Taj Mahal. Rumour had it that this was the garden in which the Baadshah had planned to build his own mausoleum, that legendary tomb of black marble. That had not yet happened – and seemed unlikely – but the vast octagonal pool in the Mehtab Bagh was positioned perfectly to reflect the Taj from across the river on a moonlit night. One Taj above the water; another below. Muzaffar had not visited the Mehtab Bagh, but he could well imagine the sight. It would be the ultimate in the symmetry so beloved of the Mughals.

Somewhere between the Aaraam Bagh and the Mehtab Bagh, almost rubbing elbows with the latter, stood the garden that Muzaffar and Akram had seen from the embankment. It was a modest spread of land, with no pretensions to the vastness of the imperial gardens. No more, thought Muzaffar, than a square of about two hundred yards on each side. Some fifteen or sixteen bighas of land, but that well cultivated. The layout of the garden adhered strictly to the accepted style: the square divided carefully into four smaller squares; a stream of water, bounded by stone paving, running through the centre, with intermediate pools of water; a stone pavilion on the north side of the garden, overlooking the flowerbeds. Most of the plants lay dormant, but the roses were exuberant splashes of deep crimson and the jasmine bloomed bravely.

A couple of weeks now, and the mists would not be quite so thick and quite so tenacious. The sun would shine warmer and the dew would not be nearly frost. Then the more delicate flowers would blossom, too: the deep blue delphiniums and the pink hollyhocks, the carnations and the maroon-red cockscombs. The peach trees in front of the pavilion would be covered in a froth of pink flowers, and the nobleman who owned this garden would come, with an entourage of family, friends and attendant slaves, to picnic in the grounds. Tents would be set up, and the guests would play chaupar or chess; eat and drink; listen to musicians; and, when they tired of all that activity, would stroll beneath the cypresses, those omnipresent symbols of mortality that stood in every Mughal garden.

With spring still distant and no picnicking nobility in sight, those who tended the garden were hard at work. In the corner nearest the river, a dalv – a rope and bucket chain – had been rigged up.

Two oxen were plodding, heads down and eyes half-shut, on a circular path surrounding the low wall of a well. The buckets of water they drew up as they moved emptied themselves into a narrow channel that snaked its way through the garden, past the peaches and cypresses, into the mango orchard. One man, stick in hand, was controlling the oxen; another was clearing the water channel of leaves. A couple of sweepers, twig brooms in hand, were sweeping the pathways. Scattered across the garden were more men, gardeners by the looks of them, weeding and pruning and clearing away dead foliage. One, better dressed than the others, was standing under one of the mango trees, talking peremptorily to another, of whom only a pair of spindly legs could be seen atop a ladder reaching up into the canopy of the tree.

Nearest the gate, a gardener sat on his haunches, weeding a patch of screwpine. He had glanced up when Muzaffar and Akram entered the garden; now he got to his feet and came forward, wiping his hands on a rag draped across his shoulder. 'Huzoor?' He brought with him the fragrance of the screwpine; even without its flowers, the screwpine's leaves held enough scent to sweeten the air.

Muzaffar inclined his head briefly. 'We are looking for a horse.'

The man's eyes turned curious; but before he could speak, his colleague – or more likely his boss, Muzaffar guessed – came striding imperiously from under the mango tree. 'Yes, huzoor?' Without waiting for Muzaffar to reply, he ploughed ahead. 'I am the head gardener here. These lands are under my supervision.' Turning his head a fraction, he added, 'You, Afzal. Get back to your work.' When his gaze returned to Muzaffar, it was expectant, blank, ready for anything from a request to be allowed to view the gardens to an accusation that the well was drawing too much water from the river.

'I said we were looking for a horse. A piebald horse, black patches on white.' Muzaffar paused, waiting for the man to respond. Off to the left, beyond the head gardener's right shoulder, Muzaffar could see the gardener back amidst the screwpine, his hands barely moving and his lips compressed. There was one paying a lot of attention to the conversation.

'We were at the riverbank,' Muzaffar added, 'down where the boats come in, when we saw someone going past on the horse. *So beautiful.* I have never seen a horse so fine. Eh?' He turned to Akram with a vacuous grin. 'I even told my friend here' – he addressed the head gardener again – 'that such a horse must surely belong to a very wealthy amir. No doubt it has been imported. Would you know?'

The head gardener blinked. 'I would not know, huzoor,' he replied. 'I am a mere gardener. What would I know of horses?' Behind him, the man tending to the screwpine had left off all pretence of work. He was now looking towards them, his fingers curled idle around the base of a plant, his eyes bright with interest.

His boss continued, oblivious. 'There are no horses here, as you can see, huzoor.' He flung out an arm, inviting inspection of the gardens. 'Just a pair of oxen, and even those aren't especially grand to look at. Why do you look for that horse anyway, huzoor?'

'Perhaps to buy it. I must admit to being something of a hedonist. To see such a superb horse and not own it? That would never do.' He looked beseechingly and long at the head gardener, and said in a whine, 'Are you sure you don't know whose horse that is? Or where it went? I'm sure we saw it headed this way.'

'I regret to say you must be mistaken, huzoor. Or perhaps we here have just been too busy to pay attention to who passes by. *We* have not seen any horse of the type you describe. The rider may have taken some other road, not past here. Who knows?'

'And you don't know who owns such a horse?'

'No, huzoor. I do not.'

Muzaffar heaved a sigh of deep disappointment. 'Ah, well. Come on, then,' he said to Akram. 'Let's go.' As they moved off, he noticed from the corner of his eye that the man among the screwpine was looking straight at them. His mouth was half open and his eyes were wide as he nodded his head once.

Ten minutes later, Muzaffar and Akram, standing behind a clump of bushes, saw a lone figure sidle surreptitiously out from a wicket gate in the wall of the garden. The man moved swiftly away from the gate, closing it behind him. A quick glance to the left and the right, and he spotted the two noblemen further down the riverbank. 'I have to get back in before anybody discovers I'm missing,' he said in an urgent whisper as he joined Muzaffar and Akram in the shelter of the bushes. 'You were looking for a horse, huzoor. Black and white, you said?'

Muzaffar nodded. 'Probably went by earlier this morning. Perhaps half an hour back. I'm not sure.'

The man bobbed his head in agreement. 'Yes. I saw it. I've been working near the gate. I didn't see who was riding it; he went by too fast – but I saw the horse all right.'

'Do you know who owns it?'

The man glanced over his shoulder nervously. 'The master. The man who owns this garden.' His voice had dropped to an almost inaudible murmur.

'His name?'

'Mirza Sajjad Khan.'

'Does he live nearby?'

The man shook his head vigorously. 'No. Khan Sahib lives on the opposite bank; his haveli is between the fort and Kinari Bazaar. Anybody will give you directions. He is well known.' The man looked expectantly at Muzaffar. Muzaffar reached into the pocket of his choga and drew out a couple of coins to slide into the man's eager palm. The gardener barely waited to tuck the money into his waistband before he had begun to move out from behind the bushes.

'Wait!' Muzaffar grabbed his arm and hauled him back. 'If your master lives on the other side of the river, then what was his horse doing on this side of the river? Surely if your master had crossed the river, he'd have visited his garden? Does he have other lands or properties close at hand? Another house, or a stable? Something? Do you know?'

The man tugged madly, his voice rising in panic as he tried to break free from Muzaffar's grip. 'Allah is my witness, huzoor! I have told you all I know – how do I know why Mirza Sahib did not enter the garden? If it *was* him; I told you I did not see who rode the horse. Please let me go, huzoor. If I should be seen, it will go ill with me! Please!'

Muzaffar let go so suddenly that the man, straining against Muzaffar, nearly stumbled and fell. He scrambled up quickly, and without even a last look at his interrogator, was gone, racing back towards the garden. Muzaffar did not spare him a second glance; he was already striding away, retracing their steps from earlier that morning. Akram, caught by surprise, clucked with annoyance as he ran after his friend.

6

A SHRIEK, WORDLESS, not very loud, but startlingly intrusive in the mournful quietness of Mumtaz Hassan's haveli, rang through the halls. Muzaffar, hand outstretched to take the scrap of paper from Basheer, shuddered visibly. Akram jumped and cursed under his breath. Basheer winced, and placing the paper in Muzaffar's palm, said in a sheepish tone: 'It's the ladies. My mother, and Abba's other begums. They've not taken this well, you know.'

'Of course.' The paper, a fragment torn from perhaps a much larger page, had been left behind by the hakim. He had explained to Basheer that he had other work to attend to; he could not hang around all day long at Hassan Sahib's haveli waiting for the young nobleman from Dilli to return from his headlong chase after Allah knew who. In Muzaffar's absence, the hakim had carried out somewhat of a more detailed examination of Mumtaz Hassan's corpse. The cadaver had yielded up little in the way of further information. Dead, by garroting, as the hakim had first diagnosed. A man past middle age, but in fairly good health. A couple of old scars on his back, which seemed – and this was a surprise, considering that everybody had believed Mumtaz Hassan to have always lived in the lap of luxury – to be the result of a whipping. Years ago, said the hakim. Probably when Mumtaz Hassan was in his early twenties.

And there was this, what seemed an accidental bit of evidence. Clutched tightly in the dead man's fist had been a scrap of thin paper, highly perfumed. The body had already turned stiff, the hakim had grumbled as he struggled to prise Mumtaz Hassan's fingers apart; but he had eventually managed to get the paper out, and handing it to the dead man's son, had expressed a desire to be permitted to leave. He was gone now, and Basheer, having fulfilled his duty by handing the paper over to Muzaffar, was droning on, talking about how badly the women of the harem had taken Mumtaz Hassan's death.

The children – Basheer's siblings and half-siblings – had been cooped up in the mahal sara since the morning, and the more energetic of the lot were getting restless. From Basheer's somewhat incoherent ramblings, Muzaffar gathered that the rest of Mumtaz Hassan's offspring were much younger than Basheer. Of those above twenty years of age, there were only two, both females: one already betrothed, the other on the verge of being married. That marriage would have to be put off for a while, mourned Basheer. Ah, the troubles that bore down upon a man suddenly turned the head of his household...

'Well, Muzaffar?' Akram butted in. 'Is anything written on it?'

Muzaffar did not look up from the paper. Instead, he lifted his palm a little higher, bringing the scrap up almost to his nose. He closed his eyes momentarily, then glanced at Akram. 'Something, though I'm not sure what. Tell me, Basheer: do you know of any enemies your father may have had?'

Basheer, so unceremoniously interrupted by his cousin, had fallen into a petulant silence. Muzaffar's question appeared to add fuel to the fire; with a derisive snort, Basheer reached forward to lift an apple from the platter lying before him. 'Enemies? If you began suspecting every man who was his enemy, you could line them up from here to Dilli. Enemies!' He polished the apple briskly against his chest – Muzaffar heard Akram sniff disapprovingly – and bit into it.

'Why do you say that?' Muzaffar asked, his tone carefully low, neutral.

Basheer chewed for a while before answering. When he spoke, his mouth was still working, his cheeks bulging with fruit. 'Isn't it obvious? A wealthy man, wealthy beyond even the dreams of most people. And not wealthy in a generous philanthropic way. You wouldn't have caught *him* digging wells and building sarais and laying out gardens where weary travelers could ease their aching limbs.' The snort again, this time with a bitter laugh thrown in. 'No. That wasn't his style. He liked the good life. You can see, can't you?' He waved his hand, with the half-eaten apple still clutched in it, indicating the inlay of the dalaan, the fine painted plaster, the carpets, even the gleaming silver of the platter that held the apples. 'Wealth.'

'Mere wealth isn't enough to antagonize the world,' Muzaffar observed. 'It may make a lot of people jealous, but few are so consumed by jealousy that they will resort to murder.'

Basheer swallowed. 'Mere wealth, perhaps not. But when you take into account how that wealth was obtained? Then, who knows?' He inserted the fingernail of his little finger between his two front teeth and worked it briskly, up and down. 'If you'd been done out of your fortune by a man who then went about flaunting it – and in your face too – you might be driven to kill him, no?' He stared at his nail, rubbed it against his thigh, and took another bite out of the apple.

'Whom do you mean?'

'Nobody in particular. My father wouldn't go around parading his misdeeds in front of his offspring, would he, now? He may not have been an exemplary father, but he had his pride... one hears things, you know. Tidbits of conversation, something here, something there. Enough for me to guess that a lot of this is ill-gotten gains.' The hand waved about again in an expansive gesture.

'Basheer, will you mind that apple?' Akram snapped. 'If you aren't careful, it'll land in my lap and ruin my choga.'

His cousin leaned forward, deliberately holding the apple above Akram's lap. 'I'll buy you a new choga, Akram,' he murmured. 'I am a wealthy man now. I can afford all the chogas in Agra. Probably in Dilli too,' he added as he sat back. 'Abba may not have left me anything else, but he left me his trading concerns, didn't he? He made me a rich man, too.' For a moment, the sullen man who listened to his father's jibes at the dinner party was gone. And with him, too, was gone the arrogant newly-minted owner of all this wealth. Even as he boasted of his wealth, Basheer appeared to Muzaffar to be pouring scorn on that very wealth.

Basheer patted Akram's thigh, then turned to look at Muzaffar. 'I'm not the person you should be asking about my father's enemies. Talk to Taufeeq. Or my mother, or one of the other wives. There are two of them, besides Ammi. They will know. Taufeeq will know if my father did a man out of his fortune, and Ammi will know – perhaps – if he did a man out of his wife. She invariably got wind of whom he was cuckolding in town.'

From the mahal sara came another wail, starting low, building up into a desperate crescendo, and then melting away into an eerie sobbing, an echo of the grief that had prompted the keening. Deep in the cloistered and perfumed depths of the women's quarters, a lady was mourning for Mumtaz Hassan as if mourning for the loss of her own soul. As if, with the passing of the man, life itself had bade her goodbye. The three men sitting in the dalaan – Akram, his fingers still splayed across his lap, ready to shield his choga from whatever Basheer may drop on it; Basheer, still clutching the now yellowing apple; and Muzaffar – sat in silence, careful to avoid each other's gaze.

When the haveli had lapsed once more into its usual comfortable calm, Basheer sighed. 'And how they weep! As if there's nothing left on earth or in paradise after his death.' He reached for the enameled spittoon beside the window, and spat into it.

Muzaffar and Akram remained quiet.

Basheer put the spittoon down. 'Of course, you won't be able to meet the ladies today. Perhaps not for a few days, what with the state they're in. Will that be a problem? It'll delay your investigation, won't it? If you wish, I could speak to Ammi. Try and persuade her to talk to you.'

'I would not wish to impinge on her at this time. Let that be, for the time being; I will try to see what I can do without having to bother her, or the other ladies. But you mentioned someone called Taufeeq. Who is that?'

'My father's secretary. An old fogey; he's been around since I was a child. But he's got all his wits about him, all right. He'll know the ins and outs of what my father has been up to all these years. Mind you, he may not be very forthcoming: he has a sort of warped loyalty that's bound to make him say my father never did a crooked thing in his life.' Basheer broke off to call out to a servant, who entered the dalaan, was ordered to fetch Taufeeq, and responded with the news that Taufeeq was not in the haveli. 'He has gone to meet the imam, huzoor.'

Basheer nodded. 'Ah. Yes. I had forgotten. All right, go on.' He waited until the servant had left the room, then looked at Muzaffar. 'I'm sorry; I had forgotten. Taufeeq had been sent to the imam to make the arrangements for the funeral. There is so much to do, I'm losing my mind.' He shut his eyes, squeezing them tight, his mouth turning down at the corners and the mask of good natured pamperedness sliding away to reveal a face careworn and fatigued.

Muzaffar had not seen many deaths in his life, but the death of his own father ten years earlier had occurred at a time when Muzaffar had been old enough to know what death meant, old enough to feel real grief. Mirza Burhanuddin Malik Jang had been a fond but singularly neglectful father, leaving his only son to be brought up by a much older sibling. Zeenat Begum and her husband Farid Khan had been, to Muzaffar, his true parents, the people who had taught him everything from his letters to the difference between truth and falsehood. They had also made it very clear to a young Muzaffar that his father, absent though he may be and chasing about the countryside on one campaign after another, was still his father. And worthy of the respect and devotion due to him, even if his son did not remember his progenitor's face.

The news had been brought to Kabul by a dusty rider one hot, sunny day in 1056 of the Hijri calendar, 1646 AD. Mirza Burhanuddin Malik Jang, wounded and with a raging fever, was being brought from Balkh. The hakim who was accompanying him had voiced a fear that they would have to bury the old general somewhere along the way between Balkh and Kabul. For a man in the condition Jang Sahib was in, the 130-odd kos from Balkh to Kabul was an impossible distance.

It had all begun with the ambitions of an emperor with too much wealth to squander. Shahjahan, eager to regain the territories of Balkh and Badakhshan, beyond the wind-torn Khyber Pass, had sent his armies out under his son Murad. 60,000 men had lugged field artillery as they marched through the mountains and into Balkh, sweeping aside the Uzbeks who controlled the region. Murad and his men had settled firmly in Balkh. Firmly, but not entirely comfortably. The Mughal musketry and field artillery were formidable; they were not infallible. As Murad's brother Aurangzeb – ordered out from Gujarat by Shahjahan to boost the forces at Balkh – discovered to his chagrin, the Uzbeks were not cowed down. They continued to launch skirmishes, attacking, withdrawing, ambushing, and snapping at the heels of the comparatively unwieldy Mughal armies as they made their way to Balkh. The orchards and grain fields of Balkh had already fallen prey to the war Murad's forces had waged; Aurangzeb's men found themselves floundering for food, weary and war-sick. It came as no surprise that a veteran officer, already weakened by lack of food, age and the long ride to Balkh, should lay down his arms before a fever brought on by a well-aimed arrow.

Against the hakim's direst predictions, Mirza Burhanuddin Malik Jang had hung on to life tenaciously enough to be able to gasp out his final words – 'La ilaha ilallah' – in the presence of his family. *There is no God but Allah.* Muzaffar could still remember the shuddering hoarseness that marked his father's whispering of the Shahada, the waxy greyness of that unfamiliar yet well-loved face, the perspiration on the lined forehead. And the sudden look of triumph as Jang Sahib, having summoned up the strength to affirm his faith, smiled weakly and died.

'Muzaffar?' Akram's voice was gentle. 'Are you all right?'

He was, of course. A mere reverie, brought on by the confusion and the sorrow that prevailed in the house.

'Where is Basheer?'

'Gone off to attend to the ghusl. The funeral will take place in the afternoon.'

Muzaffar nodded. The hakim, before leaving Mumtaz Hassan's haveli, had bound the dead man's jaw and covered the corpse with a clean sheet. It was now up to the family to ensure that Mumtaz Hassan's mortal remains were administered the rites required by the faith. Basheer, along with other male members of the family, would carefully wash the body, again and again if needed: three times, or five, or seven, all it took to wash off the stains and taints of earthly life. With clean water, one rinse mixed with lotus leaves and another with camphor. The ghusl would end with a towelling, before the three winding sheets that formed the kafan or shroud were wrapped and tied around the body.

It would take time, but there were sufficient hours yet to go before sundown.

Muzaffar stretched and breathed in deeply. 'Shouldn't you be there too?'

'Basheer thought I would be of more use looking after you. There are enough men there to help him out, never fear.'

'Come, then; if you're supposed to be looking after me, nobody is likely to raise an objection if you come out into the garden with me. We'll stroll about in the mango grove a while.'

7

'YOUR COUSIN DOES not appear to have had much affection for his father,' Muzaffar remarked as they walked under the mango trees between the gatehouse of the haveli and the main door. The soldiers that had swarmed the gatehouse while the Diwan-i-kul had been visiting were long gone. There were a couple of servants around, going about their business: a guard at the gatehouse, and a man sweeping the paved path that led to the haveli. Quiet, subdued men, with the carefully long faces and lugubrious expressions of men who thought they were expected to mourn even if they felt no genuine regret at the passing of a man they barely knew. Even if the man's own son felt little, if any, grief.

They had walked on a few steps before Akram answered. 'You saw them together, Muzaffar,' he said. 'You saw how Mumtaz Hassan treated Basheer, didn't you? There wasn't much liking on either side, I think. The father ridiculing the son, the son hitting back.'

'Yes. I did wonder. Why was that, do you know?'

Akram shrugged. 'It's one of those things I've noticed, but never bothered to dig deeper into. Surely you know how it is? You meet relatives for a few days, maybe once or twice a year. At a wedding, at a funeral, at Id. Perhaps once in a blue moon, when they're on their way somewhere and stop by for a couple of days at your house. Or you stop by at their home. Just a few days, and all is camaraderie; sometimes even amongst people who otherwise fight like cats and dogs. If you're a child, the last thing that occurs to you is to try and understand why people behave the way they do.'

He grinned suddenly, eyes twinkling as a wave of nostalgia hit. 'When Mumtaz Hassan and his family visited us, I'd be more interested in seeing how much taller I'd grown than Basheer, or what skills he had learned in the time we had been apart.' The grin vanished, to be replaced by pensiveness. 'But yes, now that I think of it, even back then, there seemed to be very little affection between Mumtaz Hassan and Basheer. He never patted his son on the head and told the other relatives how proud he was of Basheer. And Basheer never crowed about the hunting trips his father took him on, or the things his father bought him – or *anything*. I suppose I noticed that, but I never really thought about it. It seemed merely odd, that's all.'

From somewhere in the dark glossy leaves of the mango trees, the mad hooting of a brain fever bird broke out, growing increasingly louder and more frenzied with every escalating note. Muzaffar tilted his head, his eyes searching the trees. 'Yes,' he murmured, half to himself, still looking up. 'I should have realized you would not know. Do you think your Abba would be able to tell me something?' He glanced back, down at Akram.

'I don't know. You can ask him yourself. Abba will be there at my uncle's funeral today.' Akram's eyes widened with sudden enlightenment as a thought struck him. 'Allah,' he breathed. 'You – you are thinking Basheer killed Mumtaz Hassan, isn't that so? That was why you were so evasive about that note, the one the hakim found in Mumtaz Hassan's hand! I thought there was something wrong. You were trying to make Basheer think you didn't think it of any importance! But there must be something in that note that incriminated Basheer. What –'

'Not so loud!' Muzaffar pulled Akram behind the bole of an old tree, even as he shoved a hand into the pocket of his choga and drew out the note. 'You will have to admit that Basheer *could* be a suspect. If he did indeed murder his father, it won't serve my purpose to go about airing my suspicions and putting him on the alert. Here, look at this; I was going to show it to you anyway, so stop glaring at me.'

He held out the scrap of paper, and Akram took it a little gingerly. It was fine, smooth paper, roughly triangular with two clean straight edges joined by a rough, ragged one. Only a few words remained of what had probably been a letter. 'You hold my.' Akram glanced up at Muzaffar with a lopsided smirk. 'You hold my what?'

Muzaffar chuckled. 'Letter? Or were you thinking of something more interesting?' Still grinning, he added, 'Or a maund of musk? That paper smells as if it's been steeped in the stuff. Whoever wrote it must be rolling in wealth, to use musk so liberally.'

Akram lifted the paper to his nostrils. Muzaffar saw a look of puzzlement dawn on his friend's face; then, with a snort, Akram lowered the paper. 'Hardly. That isn't musk. It's musk mallow.'

Muzaffar lifted an eyebrow. Musk mallow, a wild relative of the humble okra, was grown for its seeds, the perfume of which strongly – and much more cheaply – resembled that of the musk produced by the musk deer of Kashmir. The seeds of musk mallow were scattered between folded garments to keep them free of moth. Those who could not afford genuine musk used musk mallow to scent everything from their breath to their coffee. And noblemen with gardens like the one near the Mehtab Bagh invariably set aside a part of the land in which to grow musk mallow. Along with roses, which could be used to distil rooh gulab, or attar of roses, it was a valuable crop.

'Are you sure?'

'Of course I'm sure. Call me whatever you wish, but don't call me unfashionable, Muzaffar. I can tell the difference between real musk and a poor substitute.'

'Hmm.' Muzaffar nibbled at his lower lip. 'Which means,' he muttered, thinking as he spoke, 'that the person who wrote that may not be wealthy at all, just trying to appear wealthy.'

'I don't see that being very effective. My uncle was hardly a country bumpkin – oh, no offence meant! Not that you are one, Muzaffar – but he certainly would have known the difference too. One whiff and he'd have guessed that someone was trying to fool him into thinking they could afford musk.'

'Then I can't understand it,' Muzaffar said. 'Unless the writer of that letter didn't realize that Mumtaz Hassan would know it wasn't real musk. Or didn't care either way.'

Akram looked at the paper one last time and handed it back. 'Well? So it seems my uncle was corresponding with a lady. And not just corresponding; holding things for her too.' He grinned lasciviously, eyes twinkling.

'That's what you say. Perhaps the missing word was heart. *You hold my heart.*' Muzaffar tucked the paper back into his pocket. 'It may have been, for all we know, but I doubt it,' he said, moving on, the smile now gone from his face. Somewhere in the mango trees nearest the gatehouse, the brain fever bird began calling urgently again. 'Someone wrote a surprisingly informal letter to your uncle. No preamble, no flowery and formal salutations. Just straight off: *You hold my* whatever.'

'This may not be the start of the letter.'

'It looks like it. It's the top right corner of a sheet of paper. And I noticed that the first few strokes were thicker, as if too much ink had pooled onto the paper. It looked to me like a pen had been picked up, freshly dipped in ink, and put to paper.' They had reached the path that led from the gatehouse to the haveli. The sweeper was now cleaning the steps leading up to the mansion.

'It may have been a continuation of a longer letter,' Muzaffar conceded. 'But even then, those words by themselves seem rather too intimate.' He stood on the earth bordering the path, hands clasped behind his back, frowning thoughtfully down at the star-and-diamond pattern of the red sandstone beyond his feet. After a moment, he looked up at Akram and added, 'Actually, we can't even assume that it was a woman who wrote that, or that she wrote it to Mumtaz Hassan. Men use musk too. And it could have been that the letter was addressed to someone other than Mumtaz Hassan, and that it just happened to come into his hands.'

Akram's face fell. 'Then we've been barking up the wrong tree. It perhaps has absolutely nothing to do with Mumtaz Hassan's death.'

'Oh, I don't think so,' Muzaffar said, stepping on to the path as he did so. 'Because someone snatched it out of his hand. And now that I think of it, I did overhear instructions that a certain note was *not* to be left behind.'

Basheer may have harboured little affection for his father, but there was no faulting the diligence with which he fulfilled his duties at Mumtaz Hassan's funeral. The imam, leading the congregation in the funeral prayers, had mumbled a few private words of consolation to the bereaved son and had assured himself that the young man was behaving exactly as prescribed: with decorum and dignity. There was none of the weeping and wailing here that had prevailed in the women's quarters of the haveli. But Basheer, thought Muzaffar as he stood among the men lined up behind the imam, would not have cried for his father. Akram's aunt may have wailed loud and ostentatiously through the day, but Basheer had shed not a single tear. There was too much hurt there, accumulated through years of being unappreciated – perhaps even neglected, if Akram's childhood memories were accurate – for Basheer to forgive his father. The pain had gone too deep, the wound had festered too long. It would take time for it to heal. And that, if the Almighty was merciful. Muzaffar felt a pang of pity for Basheer.

With a final prayer and an assalam aleikum, the imam signaled the end of the funeral prayer. Akram's father, Abdul Munim Khan, stepped forward with a nod to Basheer and Akram. Other members of the congregation – a couple of burly middle-aged men, and a small frail man whom Akram had whisperingly identified to Muzaffar as Taufeeq, the dead man's secretary – moved out of line and forward, to join Khan Sahib, Akram and Basheer. Muzaffar, gaze wandering as the men bent to lift the pall, stiffened. Past the now wavering lines of men, the orderly ranks breaking up into a crowd, he had noticed a face. Against the backdrop of the triple-arched mosque, its bright white domes gleaming in the afternoon sun, there were many faces, bearded and moustached and even occasionally clean-shaven. The dead man's associates, the men he had called friend or family during his life. And among those shifting faces, Muzaffar had seen one that was oddly familiar.

The funeral procession, led by the pallbearers, surged out of the mosque's courtyard, the last few men lingering to whisper a word of consolation to Taufeeq, who, on Abdul Munim Khan's persuasion, had agreed not to help bear the pall all the way to the graveyard. Muzaffar, stepping out through the gateway of the mosque, looked over his shoulder to see Taufeeq nodding to a man who had stopped to offer condolences. Already Taufeeq was moving, edging forward towards the gate. Muzaffar walked on.

Ahead of him, the procession had moved on, the shuffling of the men's feet the only sound that marked their passage. The graveyard was perhaps a quarter of a kos from the mosque, the path to it meandering between trees of neem and khirni bordering fields of chickpeas and the occasional hut. A woman, cooking in the courtyard of a dilapidated mud hut, looked up at the passing concourse, the curiosity in her eyes giving way to sudden comprehension as the pallbearers came into view. Where the path curled around a well, the procession slowed to make its way around a group of toddlers playing in the dust.

Muzaffar, striding to catch up, searched the crowd for the man he had noticed. Among the turbans and skull caps, there was one he thought he knew: a white turban of plain unadorned cotton, keeping in mind the sombreness of the occasion. Muzaffar twisted between two old men and whisked ahead, reaching forward to grab the shoulder of the man in the white turban, just as the pallbearers reached the gate of the graveyard. The man, startled, whirled around and looked up into Muzaffar's face.

There was a moment of mutual consternation, of looking into a face that was familiar yet not familiar enough to merit instant recognition. The recognition dawned a moment later for Muzaffar. 'You! I met you at the nakhkhas yesterday morning! You were trying to sell me that palomino. Shakeel Alam – that is your name, isn't it? What are you doing here?'

He had said it in as low a voice as he could manage without being inaudible, but several heads turned immediately, eyes curious or downright accusing. An elderly man tut-tutted and whispered something to his companion about disrespect to the dead. A few men slowed, waiting to see what was happening. Ahead, the pallbearers had disappeared into the graveyard.

An officious-looking man was pushing his way through the crowd towards Muzaffar. He arrived, bright-eyed and panting, and Muzaffar recognized Haider, the steward of Mumtaz Hassan's haveli. 'Jang Sahib – huzoor, is all well?' He glanced meaningfully towards the horse trader, trying to size up the man's potential as a troublemaker; then he looked worriedly towards the graveyard. 'The funeral is about to start,' he murmured, his eyes already distracted, as if his mind had switched from this seemingly minor incident to the larger issues of his duties: the need to ensure that his late master's body was interred properly; that the men who had come to the funeral were not inconvenienced in any way; that all was dignified yet comfortable when the family and its acquaintances returned to the haveli.

Muzaffar and the horse trader looked at each other, Muzaffar wary and curious and suspicious, all at once, the other man expressionless. Then letting go of the man's arm, Muzaffar shook his head. 'It is all right. There is nothing wrong.'

Haider was gone, an indistinct murmur of acknowledgement hanging in the air behind him, even before Muzaffar had finished speaking. The men who had stopped to watch moved away into the depths of the graveyard. At the western end, under a gnarled and twisted ber tree, the pallbearers had put down their burden. The imam had begun speaking, his sonorous voice carrying across the square yard.

Muzaffar, revising his opinion of the day before – was it only a day? One sunrise and one sunset, and so much gone awry in the passage of those few hours? – decided that the horse trader's face was not so much that of a saint, but more that of a consummate actor. At the nakhkhas, he had been the seller, silken-tongued and smooth-voiced, his eyes sparkling with the joy of looking upon the horse he had convinced himself was the very best money could buy. A few moments earlier, when Muzaffar had tugged at his sleeve and he had whirled around, the initial surprise in his eyes had settled swiftly into a careful watchfulness. Now, with Haider gone and the other men drifting off towards the grave, Shakeel Alam's face too slipped into a properly mournful expression. Eyes hooded and dull looked out of a drawn face, the corners of the lips curving down into the beard. It passed Muzaffar's mind that a man such as this did not need ashes and sackcloth; every line of his face, every contour and every dip spelled sorrow. Who knew whether he really felt any? Did he himself know?

'Mumtaz Hassan was a good friend of mine,' Shakeel Alam said softly. 'I have known him for many years now. Surely one is permitted to attend the funeral of a dear friend?' One eyebrow lifted in sarcasm.

Muzaffar bit his lip. 'I would like to talk to you once the funeral is over,' he said, finally. 'Meet me here, at the gate.'

The man did not nod or show any signs of agreeing to Muzaffar's suggestion. Those melancholy eyes looked steadily into Muzaffar's face for a moment, then he turned and was gone, walking with swift steps towards where the pallbearers were now lowering Mumtaz Hassan's body into the grave dug for it. Muzaffar stood all by himself at the gate, then made his way to the grave.

It was neatly done. Neatly and with a dignity, a sobriety that Muzaffar thought at odds with the loose-lipped luxury-loving sybarite that Mumtaz Hassan had been during his lifetime. His body, carefully wrapped in its white shroud, had been positioned against one wall of the grave, lying – as dictated by the faith – on its side, so that even in death the man's face may be turned towards the holy city of Mecca. Prayers were offered for the repose of the soul.

Flowers were scattered over the grave, and then earth. The grave was speedily filled up, and Mumtaz Hassan was covered up, once and for all, sins and all. The imam intoned one last benediction, and Muzaffar, with an absently murmured 'Amen', glanced around, looking for Shakeel Alam. But among the few men who remained in the graveyard, there were only a few he recognized: Basheer, Taufeeq, Haider, Akram and his father. Muzaffar hurried to the gate and looked out, searching the surrounding area, the fields of green chickpeas, the quiet lanes of the village nearby, the path that wound its way towards the domes of the mosque.

But there was no sign of Shakeel Alam.

The sun had set by the time Muzaffar reached Qureshi Sahib's haveli. A wisp of cotton clouds, its edges pink and gold, lent colour to the sky. Other than that, it was a clear, cloudless dusk. No fog, no damp, none of that softly enveloping blanket that had cloaked the town the previous evening. It was going to be a harsh, cold night.

Muzaffar stood at the entrance of the room that had been given to him for his stay in Agra. With the Diwan-i-kul's peremptorily assigned task hanging over his head, and no idea of when he would succeed – or if he would –he had no way of knowing when he would be able to leave Agra. It was not fair on Zeenat Begum, who had left husband and household behind in Dilli only to make a brief pilgrimage to Ajmer. A long sojourn in Agra had not been part of her plans. For Muzaffar, there was no option. For his sister, there was no need. It was his responsibility to provide an escort for her to return to Dilli while he stayed on, for however long it took to unravel the mystery of Mumtaz Hassan's murder.

Muzaffar sighed and turned away, moving towards the mahal sara.

The eunuch on duty outside the women's quarters nodded in a deep, obsequious dip of his head in response to Muzaffar's request. 'If huzoor will take a seat,' he murmured, indicating the stone bench that stood outside. Muzaffar, with a small wordless shudder at the thought of that cold stone, remained standing.

It was a few minutes, no more, before the eunuch emerged from the mahal sara. In his wake came a feminine figure, slender and swathed completely in silk and soft pashmina. Muzaffar, who had stepped forward, halted in his tracks as he realized, even without being able to see the woman's face, that this was not his sister.

'Jang sahib,' she said, 'Good evening. Khursheed here said you wanted to meet Zeenat Begum.' It was Shireen. In their brief acquaintance so far, he had been the one doing most of the talking; yet he realized, with a sudden start, that he recognized her voice. Soft, mellifluous, and yet neither timid nor quavery nor in any way weak. 'She has not been feeling well, I'm afraid – a mere touch of cold, but we thought it best to let her rest a while. She is asleep now. Is there a message I can perhaps give her from you when she wakes?'

He bit his lip, undecided and unsure. 'Or if you would like to write a note for her?' Shireen suggested gently.

Muzaffar came to a decision. 'That will not be necessary,' he replied. 'Thank you. But if you could tell her that I am obliged to stay on in Agra for a few days more – or rather, for an indefinite period; I do not know when I will be free to return to Dilli.' He paused, wondering how much he should confide in Shireen. She was a woman, after all. And women, in Muzaffar's admittedly limited experience, tended to interest themselves in clothing and jewellery, household and family. Their world was the mahal sara. Zeenat Begum was an exception. An eccentric old lady, some called her behind her back. If she had been here, Muzaffar could have told her all that had happened. He could have depended upon her discretion and her sense, even have asked her for advice.

But Shireen was not Zeenat Aapa. She would not understand. She would be bored, just as Ayesha had been.

Muzaffar blinked, trying to rid himself of Ayesha's memory. The pause in his sentence had elongated into a silence. He did not offer any further explanation to Shireen, and with a brief dip of his head, turned to go.

'It is something to do with Mumtaz Hassan Sahib's death, is it not? Have you been asked to find out what happened, Jang Sahib?'

Muzaffar, his back to the young woman, halted in his tracks. *How could she have guessed that?* He frowned, perplexed, then turned back. His eyes were wary but his voice expressionless when he said, 'And why should you think that?'

'Zeenat Begum had enquired about you this morning. I was with her when the maid came to say that you had been called away to Hassan Sahib's haveli very early this morning. Even before the sun had fully risen. That would mean an emergency...' her voice trailed off into a pensive pause. She moved to the stone bench nearby, and smoothing out her skirts, sat down. 'And then, later in the day, we heard about Hassan Sahib's murder. A woman selling glass bangles had come by, and she told us. My aunt will probably go tomorrow sometime to offer her condolences. One of Hassan Sahib's widows is an old friend of hers.

'He was a well-known figure in Agra, Jang Sahib. Powerful too, and wealthy. Enough to play host to the Diwan-i-kul himself; we know that much. And if the Diwan-i-kul, on his way to the Deccan to wage war against Bijapur, takes the time to call on Mumtaz Hassan Sahib – it must be something important. Then Hassan Sahib gets murdered, and you get an urgent summons to his haveli at an unearthly hour.' She lifted her head, and even though she was fully veiled, Muzaffar could imagine her looking up at him, daring him to deny that what she had said made a lot of sense.

He could not deny it. He had a strange feeling that this odd young woman would probably see right through him, even if he attempted it. 'Yes,' he admitted, with a sigh. 'The Diwan-i-kul has ordered me to investigate the death. I have to report to him when he returns. And if I don't have the culprit by then – Allah alone knows what will become of me.'

Shireen remained silent for a moment; then, in a small, husky whisper, she said, 'If there is anything we – I, I should say, for I cannot vouch for the rest of this household – can do to help, will you let me know?'

The ghost of Ayesha reared its head again. Enticing him, drawing him in, in the guise of another woman, perfumed and beautiful. Offering herself to him, even if only in this seemingly pragmatic style.

'No,' he said, in as forbidding a voice as he could manage. 'Thank you, but there is no need.'

She lowered her head. 'Very well. But' – her voice quavered a little, and Muzaffar's heart sank, fearing more pleas, embarrassing appeals – '"*in this city, the headstrong men pursue their trades of avarice and greed. Resignation and Temperance are the citizens of fame and virtue; Lust and Wantonness the thieves and pick-pockets.*" I fear the thieves and pick-pockets outnumber the citizens of fame and virtue in Agra, Jang Sahib.' He realized, with a sudden start, that the quaver in her voice had been amusement. He also realized that what she had said had sounded very familiar.

'I know those sentences,' he blurted out. 'Is that from Sa'adi?'

'Yes, from *Bostan*. I do not care for Sa'adi much – he prates on too much, at times. But some of his poetry is sublime.' Again, he heard the smile in her voice. When she spoke again, though, her tone was grave. 'Be careful whom you trust, Jang Sahib. In an unknown city, you can never be too cautious, can you?'

She rose to her feet, pulling her pashmina shawl closer about her. Her bangles clinked gently. 'Zeenat Begum has become a dear friend of mine in these few days. I – I beg you, will you ask *her* what *she* would prefer, regarding the journey to Dilli? Whether she would like to return to Dilli, or stay on in Agra until you have finished your investigation? I think she might feel safer travelling in your company, even if it means a delay. Perhaps the decision should be left to her.'

Muzaffar, who had to concede the wisdom in this suggestion, agreed that he would meet Zeenat Begum sometime the next day, when she was feeling better.

'I shall talk to Basheer about accommodating us in their haveli,' he added in a stifled tone. 'We have stayed long enough in your uncle's house for us to be now considered an imposition.'

'As you please. But I am quite sure that my uncle does not consider you an imposition. Far from it.' And on that ambiguous note, Shireen dipped her head, murmured a brief good night, and was gone, whisking back into the confines of the mahal sara. Muzaffar returned to his chamber, where he sat, staring into the dancing flame of the lamp beside his bed, for nearly a quarter of an hour. When he finally blew it out and lay down, sleep did not come. When it came, it brought with it no relief.

The next morning, the eunuch from the mahal sara knocked at Muzaffar's door, bearing a note from Zeenat Begum. She was better now, and had been told that Muzaffar had wanted to meet her. After breakfast, then. In the khanah bagh. Muzaffar went, frowned in sympathy at the pallor of his sister's countenance, enquired after her health, advised the drinking of hot water mixed with honey and lime juice – and was shushed by an irritable Zeenat Begum, who hated to have anyone fuss over her. 'As if you know better than me,' she said in a mock grumpy voice. 'Let that be, Muzaffar, and tell me what you have been up to. Why did they call you to Mumtaz Hassan's haveli yesterday, all so suddenly? Shireen thought it had to be something to do with his murder, and I think so, too. What happened?'

Muzaffar had not meant to hide any of it from his sister – and experience had taught him that her wisdom could often show him the light, or at least the way to a candle, when all was dark. So he told her all – all about Mumtaz Hassan's murder and the Diwan-i-kul's dictatorial assignment. Then he went on to relate all that had followed: his suspicions of Basheer, of the mysterious scrap of musk-scented letter that had been found in Mumtaz Hassan's fist, and of the piebald horse that he and Akram had chased so unsuccessfully across the river.

Zeenat Begum listened, as Muzaffar had known she would,

attentively. She murmured encouragement, she expressed curiosity and surprise; and, when his tale finally came to an end, she took his hand and held it between her own. 'You *will* be able to find the culprit, Muzaffar,' she said. 'I am sure you will. And' – her eyes brightened in sudden defiance – 'I refuse to go back to Dilli in the company of Allah knows who – someone smelly and uncouth, or maybe even the type who'll make off with my jewels one night. *No.* I will wait for you to find out who murdered Mumtaz Hassan.'

'And what if I cannot find the murderer?'

The indignation in Zeenat's eyes flickered into something approaching fear. 'Then you will need me by your side even more,' she said quietly. 'Go now, Muzaffar, and do not worry. Not about me, and not about Qureshi Sahib and whether or not it is prudent – or proper – for us to be staying on here.' She squeezed his hand. Her own were warm, reassuring. Muzaffar's cold fingers instinctively curled, drawing as much from the welcome heat as from the comfort she offered.

Muzaffar regarded her with affection as he drew his hand away and stood up. 'I must go now, to the nakhkhas,' he said. 'I'm sure that horse trader knows something.'

'He wasn't there,' Muzaffar said to Akram later that morning. 'Nobody around had seen him there today, and nobody knew whether he was likely to come.'

'You think he's made himself scarce?'

Muzaffar nodded as he looked out over the garden, past Akram's shoulder. The morning was beautiful, with the crisp, clear freshness that is possible only on a sunny day in the deep of winter. Mumtaz Hassan's household bore the signs of mourning: the hushed voices, the downcast eyes of the servants, the absence of laughter or music or anything that might be considered frivolous.

'Which could mean he knew something,' Akram said.

Muzaffar shrugged, then frowned to himself. 'And here I was, thinking how pointless his reticence was, yesterday. *So what if he disappeared from the graveyard?* I'd catch up with him at the nakhkhas today and ask him some questions.' His lip curled in self-derision. 'Stupid. So utterly stupid. I should have guessed. A man who was so quick to vanish yesterday would hardly turn up today at the one place where I would go to find him.'

Akram maintained a diplomatic silence. Muzaffar, with a muffled oath, swung around to look towards the main doorway of the haveli. 'Do you know if Basheer is in?'

'He isn't. He sent a note to me to say that he would be going out after breakfast to have a look at Mumtaz Hassan's tomb.'

Muzaffar lifted an eyebrow. 'So soon? Mumtaz Hassan has not been in the ground one day, and Basheer has the land bought, and the construction of the tomb begun? That *is* fast work. Or did Basheer know in advance when a tomb would be needed?'

'You don't let go of an idea easily, do you?!' Akram shot back. He saw the faint glimmer of embarrassment in Muzaffar's eyes, and shrugged. 'No, Basheer did *not* have a plot of land in mind, or any thought of buying it to build his father's tomb. I happen to know, because I was taken to see the tomb myself, a few days back. The day before I met you at the nakhkhas, I think. Haven't you heard of the emperors and the noblemen, the high and mighty of the land, who build their own tombs? My uncle considered himself in no way inferior to the best of them. He selected the land and bought it a few years ago. Designed the building himself, procured the material, and chose each of the men working on it – down to the lowest water-carrier – himself. It's still a long way from completion, but they're making good progress on it.'

'And now that Mumtaz Hassan is dead, Basheer is supervising the work? That sounds a little uncharacteristic. The devoted son, and all. Not what I would have expected of Basheer.'

'Aren't you being a bit harsh on him, Muzaffar?' Akram said quietly. 'Granted, he did not like his father. I wouldn't have, either, if I had a father like that. My uncle could be a heartless man – and he was, to poor Basheer. You saw that, too. But I know Basheer; I've known him since we were children. He wouldn't hurt a fly.' In almost the same instant, he shook his head. 'No, that is exaggeration, of course. Basheer *could*, if needed, kill. I think so. Any man could. In the heat of battle, to protect his own life, or whatever and whoever he values. But in cold blood? His own father?'

'A father who was not worth being called a father. Let us not discuss it any more just now, Akram. I was stupid to leap to conclusions.'

Akram looked a little disconcerted, but eventually grinned. 'And when it comes to the supervision of the construction of Hassan Sahib's tomb, I don't think Basheer's doing his bit out of any filial feeling. More, probably, because he's genuinely interested in things like that. In architecture and stone carving and all things beautiful. He doesn't have the depth of knowledge or experience that his father did, and he isn't the type to get his own hands dirty, but he's passionate about it in his own way.' He squinted up at the sun, already high above the horizon and bathing the garden in its warmth. 'Plus, there's the fear that if he doesn't keep a weather eye open, the men working on the construction will line their own pockets or make off with handfuls of turquoise, or something... Basheer wouldn't want his new inheritance going down the drain.'

He glanced at Muzaffar. 'So Basheer isn't here. What now?'

'The secretary? Taufeeq? Do you think it would be possible to meet him? We could begin by putting some questions to him.'

Akram nodded. 'Let's ask Haider.'

But Taufeeq was not at home either – he had, in fact, as Haider informed them, accompanied Basheer to the site where Mumtaz Hassan's tomb was being constructed. Muzaffar waved the man away, waited till he was out of earshot, and then turned to Akram. 'It appears today isn't our lucky day. But since I can't afford to waste any time, I'll go out and try to find the haveli of that Mirza Sajjad Khan, the owner of that garden. Perhaps I'll be able to discover something about that piebald and what it was used for.'

Akram gazed at his friend through narrowed eyes. 'You will go to Sajjad Khan's haveli? And what shall I do in the meantime? Walk about in the garden? Twiddle my thumbs? Go into the mahal sara and tell the ladies not to cry quite so much?' His voice rose in indignation, and Muzaffar gave a small smile, self-conscious but placating.

'I don't think it would be a good idea for you to come along to Sajjad Khan's haveli,' he explained. 'We would certainly be asked to identify ourselves, and what would happen then? A Muzaffar Jang, the guest of Abbas Qureshi, is unknown, unthreatening. An Akram Khan, nephew of the recently murdered Mumtaz Hassan – and staying in his haveli, too – would be instantly suspect. If Sajjad Khan or any of his household are involved in your uncle's murder, they'll clam up as soon as they discover who you are.'

'They needn't. I can give a false name, can't I? Say I'm so and so. No relative of Mumtaz Hassan at all. Besides, if they're guilty of murder, they're hardly going to admit it. Not to anyone, whether or not he's related to Mumtaz Hassan.'

'And I would rather you stayed here and tried to work your charm on your aunt a bit. Ask her why she thinks anybody would have wanted to murder her husband.'

Akram rolled his eyes. 'If you think she's going to stop crying simply because I say so... don't be naïve, Muzaffar. Even if the Qu'ran forbids it, she will cry her eyes out for the full four months and ten days she must mourn my uncle.'

With a deep sigh, Muzaffar surrendered. 'Very well, then. Come along.' He glanced down at the deep blue choga, rich with embroidered paisleys, that Akram wore. His gaze travelled up, past the triple row of pearls, all precisely graded, that hung down on Akram's chest, and the magnificent sapphire that formed the centrepiece of a flamboyant turra, a turban ornament topped off by a snowy aigrette on the side of a brocaded turban. 'Hmm,' he said. 'For once, I do think you may be more appropriately dressed than I am.'

8

A KINARA IS an edge: the edge of a road, or the bank of a river. A kinari too is an edge, but of a different nature – not merely the feminine equivalent of a kinara, not perhaps a more diminutive kinara.

Muzaffar, gazing wide-eyed at the shops past which he rode, marvelled at how it could be that even having seen wares like these a thousand times, he was still dazzled by the spectacle. Agra's Kinari Bazaar, like its newer counterpart in Dilli, specialized in the sale of kinari, edging for the extravagant clothes of the wealthy. While in Dilli kinari was just another of the goods on sale, here in Agra it was part of a flourishing industry. The city was known for its embroidered stuffs and its metallurgical work. Zardozi – the fine, originally Persian embroidery that combined sequins and metallic thread, tiny beads and more, was one of the city's most famous products; but so, too, was kinari. Heavy glittering loops of kinari hung on pegs and nestled in bundles in the shops of Kinari Bazaar. Just beyond Akram's shoulder hung a border, as wide as Muzaffar's palm, composed of minuscule flowers: tiny but precise coronas of orange and blush-red, with little green leaves and golden arabesques. Beyond was a slimmer pattern, with paisleys in blue and purple and silver. And simpler, less extravagant designs, some made just of silk thread and glass beads.

The shopkeeper poked his head out, his face breaking into a smile of welcome. His gaze darted from Muzaffar to Akram and back again. Muzaffar could sense the anticipation in the man's expression, the happy realization that these two young noblemen were fashionable enough to have halted outside the shop to buy something. 'Just stopping to ask for directions,' Muzaffar said by way of greeting. 'A Mirza Sajjad Khan? We were told his haveli stands between the fort and Kinari Bazaar.'

And so it did. The shopkeeper, his smile now vanished, gave directions. The haveli was not exactly, as the crow flew, between Kinari Bazaar and the fort. More on the way to Hing ki Mandi, the wholesale market for asafoetida. Down that way, through the second lane off to the left – 'Not a very fine area for a wealthy man to live in.'

And it was not. Mirza Sajjad Khan may have the means to lay out a large garden in the vicinity of the Mehtab Bagh; he may own stables full of the most splendid horses to be found east of Isfahan; he may be the owner of a haveli the address of which was known to every street urchin of Agra. It did not follow that that haveli and those horses would be housed in a neighbourhood of requisite grandeur. Perhaps Mirza Sajjad Khan did not care for anything beyond the thick stone walls that surrounded his mansion. Perhaps the shabbiness of the surroundings – the wattle-and-daub huts, the bony cattle grazing amidst the thistles, the hollow-cheeked porters and labourers at work in the fields and the narrow lanes – perhaps all of that remained hidden behind the curtain of the palanquin in which Sajjad Khan sat whenever he ventured out. Perhaps he clutched a muslin handkerchief, reeking of rooh gulab, to his nostrils when he stepped out, to block out the smells of dung and sweat and poverty. Perhaps he kept himself and his family locked in, secluded and safe inside the scented luxury of the haveli. Perhaps Sajjad Khan himself had last set foot outside his house at the Baadshah's coronation.

'The master is not at home, huzoor,' said the sharp-eyed steward who came to the gate to meet the visitors. He stood, arms folded across his chest, in the doorway of the narrow door that he had opened in the gate. 'He is not expected back before the day after tomorrow.'

Muzaffar blinked. 'Oh? But I saw a horse –' he glanced at Akram, as if seeking confirmation. 'A beautiful horse, white and black. I was told that it belonged to Mirza Sajjad Khan, and that he had bought it recently.'

The steward regarded Muzaffar with interest. He did not say anything, however, and it was Muzaffar who continued, in the high-pitched, half-disappointed, half-excited tone of one who had come a long way on what was fast revealing itself to be a wild goose chase. 'But you don't understand, I think,' he burst out, 'how important it is for me to talk to Sajjad Khan about this horse! It's a beautiful horse, one in a million. And I saw it gallop too. It would leave the wind behind. I want to buy it, can't you see? If Sajjad Khan isn't around, surely the man who minds his stables is here? I can talk to him?'

'He is not here either, huzoor. Nor are any of the stablehands.' He paused. 'They have all been gone, with Khan Sahib, for the past three days. Out duck shooting with some guests of Khan Sahib's.'

'Duck shooting? But I saw that horse just yesterday morning! Near Mehtab Bagh – Sajjad Khan has a garden there, does he not? – well, I saw the horse close by, and I was told it belonged to him. How could he and his men be away shooting ducks and his horse – prize horse too, I'll wager – be wandering about that side of the Yamuna?'

The man shrugged. 'Whoever told you the horse was Khan Sahib's was mistaken, huzoor. Surely there cannot be only one piebald horse in all of Agra. That huzoor saw one near Khan Sahib's garden does not mean that it must be the one Khan Sahib bought.' He levelled a glance at the horse on which Muzaffar had arrived. It was a muscular roan that Basheer had ordered equipped for Muzaffar's use while he was in Agra. Muzaffar, uncomfortable that Shireen's uncle had provided his best horse under the impression that Muzaffar might reciprocate by marrying his niece, had graciously returned the horse to Qureshi Sahib. 'My stay in Agra has been extended because of Mumtaz Hassan's death,' he had explained. 'As it is, I would have shifted to his haveli by now, had it not been for my sister. She has made friends with your ladies, and will neither leave for Dilli, nor move to Mumtaz Hassan's haveli.'

Qureshi Sahib had looked stricken and had done all he could – short of falling at his guest's feet – to persuade Muzaffar that he and all his kin were welcome to stay as long as they wished. To use whatever resources his humble household could offer. To mount his best horses, to eat him out of house and home, to – but Muzaffar had stemmed the flow with a businesslike smile, and had taken himself off.

Sajjad Khan's steward was now looking at the roan with a shrewd eye. 'That is not a bad horse, by the way,' he said. 'A man with a horse such as that might consider himself adequately mounted.'

'Another man might,' Muzaffar agreed. His nose flicked up in a markedly supercilious sniff. 'Not me.' His fingertips skimmed down the brocaded collar of the choga, moss-green embroidered in tendrils of crimson and muted gold, a showy coat which he had borrowed from Akram along with the matching cummerbund. An archer's ring, also borrowed, its ruby glittering large and ostentatious, shone briefly on Muzaffar's thumb.

The obvious display did not impress the steward. His eyelids drooped, as if from boredom. 'I cannot help you, huzoor,' he said flatly. 'I am deeply sorry. Now, if you will excuse me –' he turned to go, then glanced back over his shoulder, as Muzaffar's hand fell on his arm. 'I have work to do, huzoor. I have already told you, I fear I cannot be of any assistance. Either come back at the end of the week, when Khan Sahib will be back, and see if you can persuade him to part with the horse; or go to the nakhkhas and see if you cannot find another horse to suit your fancy.'

'I want a piebald,' Muzaffar insisted. 'I think it'll look beautiful with my crimson choga – red, white and black: what a striking picture that will make, eh?' – He directed the question at Akram, but did not wait to see the amusement on his friend's face before he turned back to the steward. 'Come, come. Surely you can help me with *that*? Which horse trader in the nakhkhas did your master buy the piebald from? Perhaps he's got another piebald tucked away somewhere.'

The steward heaved an impatient sigh. 'I do not know, huzoor. Goodbye.' And, briskly dislodging Muzaffar's hand from his sleeve, he stepped back, closing the door behind him. Muzaffar stood looking up at the weatherworn gate, its heavy wooden planks rubbed and polished by years of sunshine and rain and dust-laden wind. The door, a man-wide strip of wood studded with iron knobs, looked newer, an afterthought. From behind the shut door drifted the barely audible sound of footsteps. A muffled voice asked a question. Another, even more muffled, responded. Muzaffar, straining to hear and failing, shook his head in disgust.

'Let's go,' he murmured. 'I've had enough of looking like a rooster dressed for the table.'

'And what's even more frustrating,' he added as he mounted the roan, 'no diners in sight.'

'A friend of Basheer Sahib's had come by,' said a man at the construction site of Mumtaz Hassan's tomb. 'Basheer Sahib took him around, showed him the progress. They went along that side' – he gestured towards the right, where, beyond a fallow field rose a low hillock, its crown darkened by a small grove of ber trees – 'and then down to the river, where the gentleman had come, in a boat. Basheer Sahib accompanied his friend back, across the river.' The man paused, as if wondering whether it would be circumspect to add anything to what he had revealed. 'I think the gentleman wished Basheer Sahib to note certain details at the tomb of Itimad-ud-Daulah,' he said finally, and left it at that.

Muzaffar nodded. With Mumtaz Hassan dead, the completion of his tomb fell to his son. And Basheer was not one, from what Muzaffar had gauged of his personality, to recklessly spend on what he did not hope to benefit from. *His* money was being spent; he would have a say in how it was spent. Muzaffar had a sneaking suspicion that Mumtaz Hassan's tomb could well turn out to be far less magnificent than its future occupant had intended it to be.

As of now, though, work seemed to proceed unhindered on the tomb. The construction site was on the west bank of the Yamuna, perhaps half a kos north of Mumtaz Hassan's haveli. The tomb – or, to be precise, the shell of the rauza, which would house the cenotaph – stood on a promontory that bulged over the river, vaguely reminiscent of the bend in the river in which the Empress's mausoleum stood. Mumtaz Hassan's ghost, if there were such beings on Allah's Earth, thought Muzaffar, could look across the plain, down the river and see the haveli it had occupied in its lifetime. Which Basheer, having inherited, would no doubt soon stamp with his own individuality.

Muzaffar frowned as a thought suddenly came to him. There was the question of escheat. According to law, all Muslim noblemen who were the subjects of the Mughal Baadshah were, by default, subject to the principle of escheat: when they died, all their wealth passed to the state. Houses, mansions, lands, jewellery, coin – all were included. The state did as it pleased with such property: gifted it to other mansabdars, gave it to princes, or, in a fit of benevolence, gave part of it to the offspring of the dead man. Rarely did the offspring receive – or expect – anything more than a mere fraction.

The only property exempt from escheat was that which was for charitable purposes. Sarais, wells, baolis or step-wells, gardens, mosques, public baths: these remained with the owner's family. So did tombs.

Muzaffar squinted as he looked towards the site. He did not know if escheat would apply in the case of Mumtaz Hassan; the man, after all, had been a merchant, not a courtier. And even among the courtiers, those who were none too prominent, or none too wealthy, often passed away without the state paying the slightest attention to who inherited whatever possessions had been left behind. In Mumtaz Hassan's case, there was wealth aplenty to be picked up. And his proximity to the Diwan-i-kul might mean that Mumtaz Hassan *had* held a rank at court, even if mostly nominal. It may well be that the exchequer would appropriate most of his wealth, and leave Basheer with only this tomb.

Muzaffar blinked and looked around.

The skeleton of the rauza was already built. A few months now, and the polished stone, plaster and tile that formed the exterior would be cemented on. After that would come the decoration: the inlay work, the carving, the careful patterns in coloured tile. If Basheer wished to stint on that, he could. But to leave a father's tomb looking shabby – that would not do. Muzaffar doubted that Basheer, even if the state took away most of Mumtaz Hassan's wealth, would actually be bankrupted. Surely there would be trading concerns, other business that would now fall to Basheer's share and from which he would derive the profits. Basheer, even if only to save face, would do well to bow to convention and let his father be interred in as grand a tomb as the dead man had envisaged for himself.

It was an octagonal rauza, of which all that could be seen was the red brick dome rising above the bamboo scaffolding that surrounded the building. Sturdy ramps criss-crossed the scaffolding, carrying a stream of workers, men and women with baskets of building material perched on their heads. There were the thin, kiln-baked lakhori bricks, which were the main substance of the structure. There were the ingredients for the mortar: the stone dust and gravel, the mud and the sand. There were also the many varied additions that made it tensile and pliant, mortar that breathed and expanded or contracted with the passage of the seasons: lentils, fenugreek, yoghurt, molasses, cow dung.

And there was the stone for the cladding. A team of labourers, sweat pouring down their faces despite the chill of the day, were pulling up along the ramp, a slab of white marble, wide as a door and at least half a foot thick. Somewhere, in one of the many little workshops that had come up around the construction site, the marble would have been prepared, separated from a block brought perhaps from the marble quarries at Makrana, which had also yielded the stone for the Taj Mahal. It would have been smoothened, increasingly finer grit rubbed over the surface of the marble under the hard, flat head of a trowel. It would have been worked, patiently and painstakingly, with hammer and chisel, the edges progressively thinner and the strokes progressively finer, until no flaw and no coarseness remained.

The team of marble-carriers hauled, inch by inch, their burden up onto a landing of reinforced scaffolding. A man, probably a mason, took over, supervising the untying of the ropes that held the slab. Muzaffar turned away to look at the man who had been talking to him. 'Do you know when Basheer Sahib will be back?'

The man wagged his head apologetically. 'I do not know, huzoor. Perhaps Taufeeq Sahib would know.' He smiled in greeting as Akram – who had absented himself for a brief while on arriving at the tomb site – returned, looking more debonair and less dusty.

'Ah, yes. Taufeeq. Is he here, then?'

Taufeeq was at the construction site. Had been, it transpired, through most of the morning, and had been hard at work. Muzaffar and Akram's self-appointed guide, a man who appeared to have been placed in charge of the policing of the site – 'Just to make sure nobody walks off with anything' – chatted comfortably with Muzaffar and Akram as he led the two men to the shed north of the tomb. Like the tomb itself, the shed was of lakhori bricks, but bare, unadorned and unintended for posterity. A few months from now – a few years, even – when the tomb was finally ready, this shed would be torn down, its bricks carted away by the inhabitants of the nearby villages to reinforce their own huts. It would be a windfall for them. The huts of the poor did not boast of bricks. Sheets of dry reeds, woven together and slathered with wet clay, formed the walls; and rough thatch formed the roofs. It was the norm, even in the imperial capital of Dilli. Fire was a constant threat, and Muzaffar knew of noblemen who went through great trouble to build their havelis as far away from the ubiquitous clusters of huts.

At this stage, the functions of the little brick shed were many and varied. It was apparently used as a dumping ground of sorts. Thin panels of white marble, a couple of them already carved into delicate lattices, leaned against the southern wall. In the corner beyond were blocks – of what, Muzaffar could not see but guessed was stone – wrapped in sacking and secured with heavy ropes. Along the eastern wall, and occupying about a quarter of the room, were bales of jute, probably left over from what had been used to reinforce the foundations of the building; lengths of bamboo; odd bits of wood; and a wooden chest, its iron bindings rusty.

In the western half of the room, an attempt had been made to maintain some semblance of order. True, the mattress looked lumpy and moth-eaten, and the sheet that covered it was long past the day on which it should have been laundered. But the mattress *was* there, and it was covered. One half was crowded with scrolls and sheets of paper, scribbled over or covered with drawings. On the other half was a mango wood desk, standing on inch-high legs, with a built-in drawer under the sloping top. Taufeeq, sitting at the desk with a reed pen in hand, looked up when the three men entered the room. For a moment, there was puzzlement in his rheumy old eyes, the look of a forgetful man who knows he should recognize the face he sees before him, but cannot. Then, with a sudden glimmer of relief, he put the pen down next to the inkwell that stood on the desk, and rose to his feet, knotted-knuckled hands resting briefly on bent knees. The man who had been sitting beside him, a length of paper in his hand, rolled it up and placed it with the other scrolls lying on the mattress.

'Mahmood,' Taufeeq said, 'we shall continue in a while. Perhaps you can go and have a look at the work on the site? I shall join you later.'

The man nodded as he reached under the mattress and pulled out a rumpled sheet. He stayed just long enough to gather the scrolls into the middle of the sheet, tie its ends into a bundle, and deposit the bundle next to the desk. 'I shall send one of the men to stand guard outside,' he said in a slightly hoarse voice. He ducked his head and was gone. The man who had led Muzaffar and Akram to the shed followed, leaving the two visitors alone with Taufeeq.

'There are some questions I wish to put to you,' Muzaffar said, after a moment's silence. 'Mainly about Mumtaz Hassan. I believe you had been secretary to him for many years?'

'Twenty-five years, give or take a few.'

'Long enough to know him well?'

For a moment, the old man looked as if he was going to disagree; then he shrugged and said, 'As well as one man can ever know another, I suppose. Or as well as a servant can ever know his master.'

'A servant would perhaps know his master better than an acquaintance or a friend would, or even a close relative. Most men do not bother to wear masks in front of their servants.'

'That depends upon the servant, huzoor,' Taufeeq said. 'And on the master. Would you like to hold your conversation here? Or would you prefer to go outside?'

'In here. We will have more privacy, I think. And there will be less chance of being disturbed. Does that suit you?'

In response, Taufeeq gestured towards the mattress. 'Please sit. Would you like a hookah? I cannot offer you any other refreshment, and the hookah is likely to take some time, but that *is* available, should you want it.' He noted Muzaffar's shaking of his head, declining the hookah, then seated himself on the mattress. Akram glanced in turn at Muzaffar and at Taufeeq, before sitting back, leaning against the wall.

Muzaffar cleared his throat. 'Tell me about Mumtaz Hassan,' he said. 'What sort of a man was he? What sort of a master?'

Taufeeq's eyes narrowed. His lips twisted, and when he spoke it was with a slight sneer. 'Those are two separate questions, huzoor,' he said. 'The man he was, and the master he was. Which do you wish to know?'

Muzaffar, disconcerted by the remark, took refuge in bluster. 'Can we get on, do you think? I have no time to waste, and the Diwan-i-kul will not take kindly to being told that we have spent more time arguing over semantics than finding Mumtaz Hassan's murderer!' He frowned, winced, and continued in a more level tone: 'How was he as a master, first.'

Taufeeq nodded, his face bland, as if he had not just a moment before disagreed with Muzaffar. Muzaffar, watching the old man, marvelled at his self-confidence. Taufeeq was stooped and round-shouldered, his limbs looking as fragile as the dry reeds that lay in bundles at the other end of the room. But the eyes, even if short-sighted, were intelligent. The hands, though knotted with age and what looked like chilblains, had held the reed pen with sufficient capability. And Mumtaz Hassan – a man of considerable calibre – had trusted this man to the utmost. Taufeeq may be old; Muzaffar doubted very much that he was senile.

The old man rubbed at an ink stain on the edge of his forefinger. 'He was a good master,' he said. 'Considerate, not cruel or brutal, as some masters can be. He treated me as a human being, not a possession.'

'And was that how he treated his other servants? Was your long association with him perhaps the reason for his kinder treatment of you?'

A shrug accompanied Taufeeq's reply. 'Possibly. But then, he was always good to me. From the very beginning, from the day I first came into his service.'

'And how did that happen? How did you become Mumtaz Hassan's secretary?'

From the site outside, sounds drifted in: workmen calling to one another, the rhythmic tok-tok-tok of hammer and chisel and stone, the scraping screech of a heavy load being pulled up the ramp. Taufeeq chewed his lip briefly before answering. 'I met Hassan Sahib about the time the Empress passed away. Just after that, in the winter. The Baadshah had her body disinterred from where he'd buried it, in the Deccan, and he brought it to Agra in a golden casket – it was buried beside the river, you know, while the Taj Mahal was being designed and built.' He pulled a voluminous muslin handkerchief from the pocket of his dowdy gravel-grey choga, and wiped his face. When he had replaced the handkerchief, he said, 'Hassan Sahib had been living in Bijapur. He was a well-travelled man, of course; he had to be, in the trade he dealt in. Wandered with the caravans, upcountry and down, wherever gemstones were to be either mined or sold... when the Empress died in Burhanpur, he heard the news. He also heard all the rumours that soon began floating about, about how the Baadshah was going mad with grief, how his beard turned white overnight. Most importantly, about how he planned to build a mausoleum that would surpass all others.'

'Work on the Taj Mahal didn't begin till a year after the Empress's death, I thought?' Muzaffar remarked.

'It didn't. But the Baadshah had acquired the land that very winter, and the designing of the rauza began around the same time.' He paused to gather his thoughts, and took up the thread again where he had left off. 'So, Hassan Sahib realized that a massive building project was in the offing. Who does not know the Baadshah's love for fine marble and semi-precious stone? Of course he would use both – and in prodigious quantities – in the Empress's mausoleum. Here was Hassan Sahib's opportunity to make a name for himself, and make a good deal of money too. He left Bijapur and came away to Agra, to present himself at court and make himself known to those who had a say in things.'

He rubbed his hands together and blew on them. 'That was a cold winter too,' he muttered, in a surprising departure from the matter of fact tone he had adopted so far. 'But when you're young, it is easier to bear the cold.'

A sharp glance, as if taken aback at his own familiarity with the visitors, and he was again the impassive narrator. 'I was in Agra, working for a merchant. He was a bad master, vindictive, malicious. Not satisfied with anything I did, always finding fault. One day Hassan Sahib happened to visit the merchant and noticed me. He

needed a secretary. Two days later, he sent a note, asking me to
come and meet him. That was it; by the end of the week, I had left
the merchant's employ.'

Muzaffar nodded. 'I see. And you have never had cause to
regret that decision? Mumtaz Hassan was *never* anything but the
ideal master?' When Taufeeq did not respond, by word or gesture,
Muzaffar added, 'Never a word of admonition? Never a demand
that was even slightly unreasonable? In twenty-five years, not one
word, not one deed that could be held against him?' Taufeeq sighed,
shrugging as he did so. 'Who can ever be absolutely and always
patient and good? It is not in human nature. Even saints have their
moments of weakness. Of course there were times when Hassan
Sahib did things I did not agree with.'

Muzaffar waited for elucidation, but it was not forthcoming.
Taufeeq tucked his hands into his armpits. 'But, on the whole, he
was a decent master, the sort of man any servant would be glad to
serve.'

'Would you say – coming back to what we were discussing earlier,
about Mumtaz Hassan's treatment of his other servants – that he
treated all his servants well? Or are there those who would have
hated him?'

The old man smirked. 'So you think one of the servants did away
with the master? I doubt it, huzoor; I doubt it very much. Other
than I, very few servants or slaves had anything much to do with
Hassan Sahib. You cannot begin to harbour a murderous hatred
for another human being if you only see him when you serve him
his dinner or present his hookah, or clean his room and wash his
clothes.' He paused to clear his throat. Before he could resume, the
door swung open and the man who had been with Taufeeq a while
ago – Mahmood – poked his head in. His smooth, slightly fleshy
face looked troubled and his lips – full and sensuous – were curved
down at the corners. Short bristly hair stuck up at odd angles on
his bare head, as if he had run his fingers through it in despair.
He had smiled pleasantly at Muzaffar and Akram when they had

first arrived; now he did not even acknowledge their presence, but addressed himself only to Taufeeq.

'I have to go,' he said. 'A passing peasant stopped by to inform me; Abba's not feeling well.'

'Oh?' Taufeeq looked concerned. 'What happened? Did he say?'

The younger man shook his head, his vivid brown eyes worried under their sharply etched brows. 'It must be the same old problem. I'll see; maybe send for the hakim, if need be. I've stationed Zulfiqar at the base of the ramp to keep an eye on things. I'll try to be back as soon as I can, but I can't be sure when that will be. Could you go out onto the site for a while?'

'Of course. You get along; and don't come back if your father needs you. I'll come by and look him up in the evening.'

'If you need to ask me any more questions, huzoor,' Taufeeq said to Muzaffar when Mahmood had gone, 'you'd better come out onto the construction site and walk about with me.'

'Mahmood may be Basheer Sahib's favourite, but he isn't a patch on his father when it comes to talent,' Taufeeq said in a voice made indistinct by a mouthful of areca nut. He chewed on, areca-reddened mouth working rhythmically, jaws moving up and down and sideways, as he stared at Mumtaz Hassan's tomb, the workers moving about across its scaffolding like ants on a hill. There were more workers now than when Muzaffar and Akram had arrived: more skilled workers, busy chiseling and polishing and carving; fewer labourers, lugging loads about for the others to work on. Perhaps the labourers were elsewhere, assigned to another part of the site. Digging pits for the water channels and the fountains, or breaking blocks of stone into the rubble that would go into the walls surrounding the tomb. Or doing some other task that required brute force, not finesse and skill.

'Mahmood can carve stone as well as the next sang taraash, but Ibrahim?' The old man spat, a dark red stream that left a spatter of

vivid drops across the dusty earth. 'Ah, Ibrahim was a class apart.'
He smiled dreamily. 'Give him a chisel and a piece of stone, and he
could create magic out of it. Flowers that looked as if they had been
plucked fresh from a garden. I remember one maulvi who nearly
threw a fit when he saw some of Ibrahim's work. He said that such
precise mimicry of nature was against all the tenets of the faith. He
insisted that Ibrahim deliberately carve an imperfection into each
piece. "*Otherwise, on the day of Resurrection, you will be told to breathe
soul into what you have created.*"' He laughed, his suddenly wide open
mouth revealing a tongue and gums vividly crimson, half the teeth
long fallen out. The next moment, his expression changed, the light
winking out of his eyes, the smile vanishing and leaving behind only
a crestfallen old man. 'Perhaps that is why he is in this condition,'
he whispered.

Akram cleared his throat. Catching Muzaffar's eye, he lifted
an eyebrow as if in query. Muzaffar dipped his head in an almost
imperceptible nod, and addressed Taufeeq. 'You said you did not
think Mumtaz Hassan could have been murdered by a servant. Then
who do you think *did* murder him?'

Taufeeq blinked, disconcerted. For a few moments, he stared
across the construction site, looking unseeingly at the workers, as
if Muzaffar's question had not registered. He called out an abrupt
'Zulfiqar! Get that scaffolding shored up on that eastern corner! It's
sagging so badly, someone will fall if it isn't attended to!' He sniffed
loudly and shoved his hands deep into the pockets of his choga.
Finally, he looked at Muzaffar. 'Who murdered Hassan Sahib? How
could I tell, huzoor? If I knew, would I not have told the Diwan-i-kul
that very morning?'

'I'm not saying you know; I'm asking if you have any suspicions.
If not a servant, then who? Do you know of anyone who harboured
an enmity for Mumtaz Hassan?'

Taufeeq stared down at the toes of his worn shoes. Muzaffar watched
him. Away in the background, he could hear the sounds of Zulfiqar

– the man who had initially escorted him and Akram to Taufeeq –
mobilizing a group of labourers to repair the scaffolding. Through
the hum and bustle of the moving workers rang the hammers and
chisels of the sang taraashes, the stonecarvers. Unsychronized,
unorchestrated, yet never discordant. There was a soothing rhythm
to it.

'A man as successful as Hassan Sahib is never completely without
enemies,' Taufeeq said. 'There will always be those who grudge him
his success. Those who are jealous, or those who feel that he trod on
their toes while climbing the mountain...' his voice trailed off.

'And? Can you name some of those?'

Taufeeq looked shocked, as if the invitation to tell tales was
unexpected, even immoral. 'I – I cannot say, huzoor,' he said in a
stifled voice. 'When I say that there are men who did not like Hassan
Sahib, I did not mean that they were necessarily men who would
resort to murder. It is a big thing, to take another life. To kill a man
simply for profit? I would not impute that sin to anyone, even if I
knew him to be hostile to Hassan Sahib.'

'Very well. Do not name men as Mumtaz Hassan's murderers.
Name them as his enemies. Tell me who his enemies were.'

Taufeeq glanced at the mausoleum, as if seeking permission from
the spirit of the man whose body would come to occupy the building
someday soon. He looked at Muzaffar with miserable eyes. Muzaffar
stared back, expressionless and unrelenting.

'You understand, huzoor,' Taufeeq said eventually. 'The names
I take may well be of men who are innocent. It may be that it is
only I who am under the impression that these men hated Hassan
Sahib. Perhaps I am mistaken. Perhaps there is some terrible
misunderstanding –'

'Go on.'

The old man heaved a sign of resignation. 'Very well. Abdul
Hafeez, for one. He is a merchant, a trader in various goods. Precious
stones, gold and silver thread, silks. He has considered himself
a competitor of Hassan Sahib's for many years now, though my

master did not think so – *he* regarded Abdul Hafeez with contempt; an upstart, he would say, who could not tell the difference between a garnet and a ruby.'

'And why do you think this Abdul Hafeez would kill Mumtaz Hassan?'

Taufeeq bristled. 'I did not say that!' Spittle flew, and Muzaffar backed away a step. 'I did not say that Abdul Hafeez murdered Hassan Sahib. Just that he could be an enemy.' He took a deep breath to calm himself, and swallowed. 'Business rivalry. There have been, over the years, numerous occasions when Hassan Sahib has stolen a march over Abdul Hafeez. The Taj Mahal, of course, but also other lucrative commissions. When the money involved is small, it is easy to forgive. When, year after year, one finds that all the juiciest contracts are being gobbled up by another: it rankles.'

'And how do you know that Abdul Hafeez hated Mumtaz Hassan for that? Did he ever say it?'

Taufeeq shook his head. 'Not to Hassan Sahib's face, no. But just as Hassan Sahib had his network, so do I. I know servants, secretaries, clerks in households and shops and workshops across the city. I hear things. Snatches of conversation reach me. *This man said this to that man.* Abdul Hafeez has not been careful about when and where he spews venom.'

'What did you hear?'

'Nothing with my own ears. But I heard of things he had said. Maligning Hassan Sahib, talking of how – how corrupt Hassan Sahib was. How indecent, how full of vices.'

Muzaffar's eyes widened. 'He sounds very bitter.'

'Hmm.' There was a moment's silence, then Taufeeq said, 'And then there was Khush Bakht Khan; I suppose you could call him inimical. He certainly made no attempt to hide his dislike for Hassan Sahib. But that was some years back; I do not know if he still holds a grudge.'

Muzaffar spread his hands, palms facing upward, in a silent gesture of query.

'Khush Bakht Khan is a trader too. Diamonds. They used to be at daggers drawn once upon a time, years ago, when Hassan Sahib lived in Bijapur. Khush Bakht Khan still lives there. Hassan Sahib's coming away to Agra diluted the battle somewhat. I do not even know if they have had any interactions ever since.'

'But you would still count him among Mumtaz Hassan's enemies?'

'You asked me to list them, huzoor. I am listing them, whether or not they may be responsible.' He looked up, towards the eastern section of the tomb, where the team of men assigned to the repair of the scaffolding was making slow, careful progress. Rope was being wound around bamboo that had fractured; more bamboo, thicker and stronger, was being added as reinforcement; and Zulfiqar was supervising the carriage of a bale of jute sacking up to the sagging scaffolding.

'Taufeeq,' Muzaffar prodded gently. The man looked back at Muzaffar and said in a tired voice, 'You ask much of an old man, huzoor. The years are catching up with me. I cannot stand on my feet as long, and I cannot remember as well, as I once did.' He squeezed the bridge of his nose between the tips of his forefinger and thumb, shutting his eyes tight as he did so. His eyes looked bleak and exhausted when he opened them. 'I think Khush Bakht Khan was an enemy of Hassan Sahib's. But who is to say how ruthless an enemy? I will not pass judgement.'

'Very well. Who else?'

Taufeeq peered intently into Muzaffar's face for a few moments, then shook his head. 'No one else that I can think of.'

'No one? But surely – you gave me to understand that Mumtaz Hassan probably made a lot of enemies in his lifetime.'

Taufeeq smirked, the fatigue suddenly giving way, the weary old man reverting to the cocksure secretary who knew the ins and outs of his master's business. 'I said it wasn't unheard of for a man like him to have made enemies. And enemies are of different kinds, aren't they? A beggar whom Hassan Sahib kicked out of his way would have cursed him and wished he were dead, but he wouldn't have tried to kill Hassan Sahib. And then there are the men whom Hassan Sahib reconciled with, or the men who have since died, well before they could get around to exacting vengeance.'

'So there are no others?'

'None that I can think of.'

'What about Mirza Sajjad Khan?'

Taufeeq's eyes narrowed. 'Mirza Sajjad Khan? Why would you think of *him*?'

'Just answer the question, please.'

Taufeeq rubbed his chin, his forehead creasing into a frown as he thought. 'Perhaps,' he replied finally. 'But I don't see any particular reason for Mirza Sajjad Khan to hate Hassan Sahib. I don't even think they knew each other very well, besides perhaps having met occasionally at a banquet or at court in the good old days when the Baadshah lived here in Agra.' He shook his head resolutely and said, 'Mirza Sajjad Khan is one of those grand old nobles. More grandeur than wealth. He may have envied Hassan Sahib his money, but I don't see him slaying Hassan Sahib for it.'

'In any case, slaying Hassan Sahib for his money would make sense only if one were to inherit that money,' Akram said, his voice unnaturally shrill in the silence that had followed Taufeeq's pronouncement. Almost as soon as he spoke the words, he flushed, and wincing, added hurriedly, 'No – I don't mean that Basheer had anything to do with it –'

Muzaffar came to his friend's rescue. 'Tell me, Taufeeq,' he said, 'I assume you would have dealt with Mumtaz Hassan's business correspondence; I would like to have a look at that sometime – but what about his personal correspondence? Do you have access to that?'

'His letters should be in his bedchamber, I suppose. But I would not be able to allow you to see them without Basheer Sahib's permission. You understand that?' The last sentence was said in a hesitant tone, as if Taufeeq had realized, a little late in the day, that Muzaffar Jang had after all been assigned the investigation of

Mumtaz Hassan's death by the Diwan-i-kul, one of the highest in the land. To be treating him like he was simply an inquisitive young man wanting to dig up the dirt in Mumtaz Hassan's life was rash.

Muzaffar nodded. 'And when will you be heading back to Mumtaz Hassan's haveli? I could come with you, obtain Basheer's permission, and pick up the letters. That way, I can start to go over them tonight itself.'

'All right. But I had thought I would go visit Ibrahim and see how he's doing. It will not take long, and his home is just over there,' Taufeeq replied, indicating the southern end of the construction site, beyond which Muzaffar could just about make out the shape of what looked like a wattle and daub hut standing beside a mango tree. 'It won't take long. If you are willing to wait, I am willing to have you come with me.'

Muzaffar had turned to Akram to ask his opinion, when a noise – a loud cracking, growing louder by the moment – drowned out the usual sounds of the site. Amidst the screams of terror of those up on the scaffolding, and of those racing away to safety on the ground, the bamboo scaffolding that was being repaired crashed to the ground.

9

'IT IS THE work of jinn.'

The room was rectangular, the short side double the length of an average man's height, the longer side a few hand-breadths longer. The walls had been made, not as Muzaffar had initially thought, out of wattle and daub, but of rubble; perhaps Ibrahim's skill as a stone carver had won him certain privileges. No other man, a mere worker, could have afforded anything better than a hut of reeds and dried sticks, plastered over with river mud mixed with cow dung. The house – though small, it could hardly be called a hut; no building made of stone and mortar should be demeaned with that appellation – stood under the canopy of a mango tree. It would be pleasantly cool in the summer. In winter, the shade of the tree added to the chill in the room.

On the outside, mud plaster had been used to cover the walls. On the inside, the rubble of the walls could be seen. The floor was stone slabs, well fitted and with the roughness chiseled away. In one wall, a wooden door hung ajar, leading out into a small courtyard from which drifted the sounds of a hammer and chisel being used on stone. Muzaffar, following Taufeeq into Ibrahim's home alongside Akram, had caught a glimpse of a yard bordered by waist-high thorn bushes. Mahmood, having welcomed them into the house, had retreated into the yard, murmuring something about work that needed to be finished.

The room in which Muzaffar and Akram now stood was the only chamber. At the other end of it was a confused mass of utensils, a couple of bundles, what looked like a rolled-up mat of woven grass, and a large earthenware waterpot, its brick-red belly catching the sunlight from the window opposite. Nearby was a charpai, a rope-bed, covered over with an old, worn quilt. An almost exact replica of the charpai stood at the other end of the room; the only difference was that this bed was occupied. Beside it, sitting watchfully up on its hind legs, was a dog. A pale brown mongrel, clean and bright-eyed, thin but obviously healthy. And, equally obviously, devoted to the man who lay on the bed.

Ibrahim was not as old as Muzaffar had thought he would be. Perhaps sixty or sixty-five, Muzaffar realized. He must have been, in his prime, a thick-set man. The shoulders were still wide, and must once have been powerful. The chin was firm, determined. The eyes were bright. It was only the right side of the body and the face – immobile and useless – that gave some indication of the affliction that had struck Ibrahim down. When he spoke, the words were faintly slurred, so that it took the first-time listener some time to understand what Ibrahim was saying. The hands – one clutching the quilt, the other lying still on Ibrahim's chest – were marked with long-ago scars. Of slipped chisels, stone chips that flew too close? Muzaffar wondered.

'The jinn are displeased,' Ibrahim said. 'When the days were brighter, I would sit outside. All day long, under the mango tree.'

He took a deep breath. Taufeeq, seated on a small cane stool that Mahmood had brought for him, patted Ibrahim's hand. Muzaffar and Akram, obliged to stand because there were no other chairs or stools, and because they had no wish to seat themselves on the cold stone floor, stood nearby, looking on. Ibrahim, huddled on the bed under a pile of blankets and a quilt, continued. 'I would look at Hassan Sahib's rauza coming up, and I would wonder if it would be completed without interference.' He swallowed, painfully. 'There are jinn in these parts, you know.' His gaze wandered and came to rest on Muzaffar, to whom Taufeeq had briefly introduced him. He gave a small, lopsided smile before continuing. 'Good jinn, perhaps; I don't know. But bad jinn, yes. I have known that for years. They have dwelled here, along the riverbank, for very long now. Perhaps they were here before the Baadshah's forefathers came to Agra. Perhaps they were here before men first came to Agra.' He coughed, and Taufeeq rubbed his chest and made some soothing noises.

'Be quiet, Ibrahim,' he said, after the stone carver's cough had died down. 'Your stories will keep. You should rest now.'

'Stories?!' Ibrahim spluttered, his outburst setting off another fit of coughing. The dog sitting beside the bed cowered and whined, distressed. When Ibrahim finally fell back on the thin pillow, his face had gone pale and sweat beaded his forehead. 'Taufeeq Sahib, I am not seeing things! I – I know what I know. They are here, around us. Up in the mango tree, there lives a genie who takes the form of a vulture, except when he goes into town and looks like a man, so that nobody will recognize him... there were jinn at the Empress's tomb, too, when it was being built.'

'Hush, Ibrahim.' Taufeeq was squirming now. His fingers tightened around Ibrahim's hand.

'Why hush?! I am saying this so that you and Mahmood, and everybody else who is concerned with the building of Hassan Sahib's tomb, can be more careful in future.' The left hand whipped out and caught the collar of Taufeeq's choga with surprising strength, pulling Taufeeq down so that his face nearly touched Ibrahim's own, distorted one. 'Listen to me, Taufeeq Sahib! They don't like us men. Allah made us from clay and them from smokeless fire; you know that. And clay and fire don't mix. Perhaps if you throw clay over fire, you can stifle it for a while; but there has to be a lot of clay for that, and the fire has to be weak –'

'Ibrahim, you're exciting yourself,' Taufeeq said, gripping the other man's hand and pulling it away, trying to lay it on the quilt. It was a struggle; the ill man was not one to give up easily. 'You had a fit today, didn't you? Thank Allah that you did not fall and hurt yourself. But rest, now. We will talk later. I will come tomorrow. Yes?'

For a few moments, it looked as if Ibrahim's stubbornness was going to win. But the seizure he had suffered earlier in the day had left him weaker and more disoriented than he had seemed when Muzaffar and Akram had arrived with Taufeeq. Fatigue and dizziness were catching up with him. He heaved a deep sigh and shut his eyes. His good hand moved off the edge of the bed, groping, searching – and finding the head of the dog. Ibrahim's fingers curled affectionately through the thin fur, tickling the animal's ears, stroking its forehead. He smiled; the dog moved closer.

'Let me call Mahmood for you,' Taufeeq said.

The eyes flickered open again. 'Mahmood? Let him be. He is at work; it is not good to disturb a man at his work.'

'You aren't well, Ibrahim. You need someone to sit by you.'

Ibrahim shut his eyes. 'I need nothing. If I do, I will call my son. Do not worry, Taufeeq Sahib. This is not the first time this has happened. We have had long experience of this. We will cope with it.'

'Very well,' Taufeeq said unhappily. 'Goodbye, Ibrahim, and Allah grant that you may be well very soon.' He nodded to Muzaffar and Akram, and the men, by mutual consent, moved towards the door that led out onto the dirt track. At the door, Taufeeq turned to look back at the man lying on the bed. Ibrahim's eyes were again open, staring at Taufeeq. He looked troubled, distressed despite the weariness that must be weighing down on him. His hand still stroked his pet, but absently now.

'You mark my words,' he said in a low voice. 'The jinn are angry. That is why they are doing this. All of this – Hassan Sahib's death, and the accident today.'

Whether it had been the work of incensed jinn or a simple accident brought on by carelessness or sheer bad luck, the collapse of the scaffolding had been a bad blow to work at the construction site. The falling stacks of bamboo had pulled down adjacent sections too, destroying nearly all of the scaffolding on the eastern side of the rauza. On the section closest to the broken scaffolding, workers had been in the process of fitting on the cladding that would cover the brick skeleton of the rauza. A marble slab, heavy and polished to a high gloss, had lain ready to be cemented onto the building. That had been the first to react to the sudden instability. It had tilted, slipped, and crashed, taking with it the two men who had been working beside it, plastering mortar onto the wall. It was not a very long way to the ground. One man landed awkwardly, his foot twisting at an unnatural angle beneath him. The other was more unfortunate; the sharp edge of the slab came straight down on the fingers of his left hand, slicing them off with surgical precision.

His fellow workers had been equally, or even more, unlucky. Six of them had plummeted to the ground, screaming and clawing in vain for a handhold. One had survived, having had the good fortune to fall on a large heap of sand. The others had died, necks broken, skulls crushed. Alive one moment, dead the next.

On the ground below, the first signs of impending disaster – the ominous cracking and creaking, the falling of a few shards of bamboo, the shout of warning from Zulfiqar – had had an instantaneous effect. Workers had abandoned loads and equipment and had fled for their lives. Some, working further away, or with a clear, level path ahead, had escaped without too much difficulty. Some, tied down by loads too unwieldy to be easily abandoned, had tried to run with the load. Of these, several had collapsed under the burdens they had been carrying; not crushed by the falling scaffolding, but injured nevertheless. Around the base of the shattered scaffolding, an old woman had been skewered to the earth by a hefty bamboo plunging from above. Of a group of boys directly below the fractured scaffolding, three had not been able to outrun it; they had been caught, crushed under the bamboo and wood, stone, and falling bodies.

A few yards away, the confusion had resulted in a minor stampede. The more frail had been pushed and shoved; a few had fallen. The worst injuries, fortunately, had been mere bruises and scrapes.

An hour had gone by. Those who had been lucky enough to

survive intact, or nearly so, had begun patching themselves up. Clothes already little more than rags had been torn to produce makeshift bandages. Some who prided themselves on knowing about folk medicine were dispensing advice. Muzaffar had heard snatches, now and then: 'Turmeric; that is the thing. Sprinkle lots of turmeric on that cut, and bind it down. You'll see, the bleeding will stop as if it had never been.' Or, 'My father told me there was no better way to knit a broken bone than a broth of trotters, drunk three times a day.' Or, 'Remember to give him lots of milk. It's *so* nourishing.'

All theoretical, of course, in this case. Turmeric and trotters were for the rich; and milk was a luxury if one did not own a cow or a buffalo. And who did, amongst these labourers? Their wounds would be bound up crudely, their bones fitted together by an experienced friend or relative. Perhaps they would rest a day or two. And then they would be back, working on Mumtaz Hassan's rauza.

Muzaffar had wondered, for a moment, if the dead were perhaps better off. Better to die outright than thus, slowly and painfully, over years of a hopeless existence.

But was it? He had seen the women wailing over the torn bodies that had been plucked from the rubble. He had seen an old man screaming as a younger one tried to pull him away from the corpse of the old woman. A wife gone, a father, a husband, a son. These had all been breadwinners, even if the bread had been meagre. At least misery shared had been misery lessened. Now even that was gone.

Muzaffar had turned away, suddenly sickened.

He now waited with Akram as Taufeeq stepped across to the thorn fence and called to Mahmood. A brief conversation ensued. *Taufeeq was going home for the day, Zulfiqar was still at the site, but work had been halted for the day. The next day – well, Allah alone knew what the next day would bring. Hopefully all would be well.* Mahmood said he would come to the site if his father was feeling all right.

Muzaffar watched in silence as the two men talked. He saw Taufeeq reach across and pat Mahmood briefly on the shoulder, as if commiserating with him. Expressing a hope, no doubt, that Ibrahim would soon be well. Mahmood smiled, his eyes – too close together to be proportionate – twinkling momentarily.

Muzaffar looked away with a frown, his mind groping for an elusive thought, a memory that hovered just out of reach, like something in a dream. Something – he did not even know what – bothered him. He was still lost in thought, still staring into space when he heard the polite clearing of a throat behind him.

'Shall we go, huzoor?' asked Taufeeq.

They walked back together, the young noblemen and the old secretary, to the construction site. The rauza looked a far cry from what it had been just a couple of hours earlier. The hum and buzz of industry was gone. The glimmer of approaching grandeur, glimpsed in the lakhori bricks and the still-naked dome, had been extinguished by the collapse of the scaffolding. It looked as if, with the falling of a few bamboos and a slab of marble, the work on Mumtaz Hassan's tomb had come to a standstill. Muzaffar had been present when Taufeeq had declared work stopped for the day; he had sensed the palpable relief of the workers as they moved away. Not just those whose kin had been killed or injured, but everyone, even those who had escaped without a scratch. It was as if the accident had frightened the workers into not wanting to work anymore. At least not today. Half a dozen men remained, clearing up the area. Sweeping, cleaning away the debris, brushing sand and dirt over the blood.

'They're a superstitious lot,' Taufeeq said. There was a note of apology in his voice, as if he held himself responsible for not just the work, but also the beliefs, of those whose work he supervised.

'So is your friend,' Muzaffar observed, after a moment.

'Ibrahim?' Taufeeq walked on a few more steps before replying. 'He isn't superstitious; just – just unhappy, I think. And embittered. Life has not been kind to him, huzoor.'

When Muzaffar did not comment, Taufeeq added, 'I have known him since I began working for Mumtaz Hassan Sahib. Hassan Sahib was one of the merchants who supplied gemstones for the decoration of the Taj Mahal; Ibrahim was one of the stone carvers who fitted those gemstones into the Taj. He was the best – I told you, didn't I? – there was none better than him. Big and strong and proficient in his work.'

He fell silent. They were now within stone's throw of the shed where Taufeeq and Mahmood had made their office. Zulfiqar was standing outside, talking to the driver of a bullock cart stationed next to the shed.

'What happened?'

'Eh?' Taufeeq's head jerked up and he looked at Muzaffar, blankly at first and then with dawning comprehension. 'Oh. Ibrahim, you mean? Things fell apart... suddenly, in the space of a few days. First, his wife disappeared, then the next day, his best friend died. Then Ibrahim was struck by some strange malady. One day he was well; the next, he was the way you see him now, but worse. He has improved with time, but then, it was terrible. He could barely speak, and then not well enough for people to understand. One eye remained shut. And his right side had gone completely useless.' He drew in a deep, shuddering breath. 'He had been in his prime, huzoor. Forty years old, with a wife and son, a pair of skillful hands, an envied profession. Within the space of less than a week, he was a wreck, unable to even wash himself, let alone earn a living. The only relative he had left was a seventeen-year old son who was still just an apprentice. Wouldn't you be embittered?'

At the haveli, the chest inside Mumtaz Hassan's bedchamber had yielded a bundle of letters, wrapped in a sheet of unbleached cotton. The sheet was so large that the bundle had been wrapped and rewrapped, again and again. It was a bulky shape, a distorted cube that was so padded it revealed nothing of its contents. Basheer, applied to by Taufeeq, had raised an eyebrow and said, 'They were my father's letters, and he's gone. Jang Sahib is investigating Abba's murder; if the letters can be of any use to him, he is welcome to them. Why ask me for permission?' He had wandered off after a few minutes of desultory chitchat with Muzaffar, who found himself taken aback by Basheer's lack of interest in how the investigation was progressing.

'You've seen it yourself, Muzaffar,' Akram had said as he walked with his friend to the drum house where a groom stood, holding Muzaffar's horse. 'There was little love between father and son.' The sun had set over an hour ago; the smell of woodsmoke hung on the air – in the small settlements along the river, fires had been lit for dinner, and whatever a poor peasant or labourer could scrounge was being cooked. Rice and lentils cooked together into a khichri, or some wild amaranth leaves picked from the wayside.

'Even if there was little love between them, I would have expected some curiosity.' Muzaffar tucked the bundle of letters more securely under his arm. 'Your cousin seems disinterested in the details of his father's death.' He shrugged. 'But, as time goes by, I'm beginning to wonder if, had I been in Basheer's place, I would have felt any differently. I think not. Anyway, let's see if these letters reveal anything. Perhaps we'll discover that Mumtaz Hassan was blackmailing someone. Or maybe the wealth was all a façade, and he had got into trouble in his attempts to make some money.'

'I hope and pray you're not being unduly optimistic,' Akram said with a wry half-smile.

They stood at the drum house for a few minutes, watching the sun sink. 'What happens if the Diwan-i-kul does not return from Bijapur, Muzaffar?' Akram murmured. 'What if he is killed in battle? What then? This was a task he had set you; nobody will question you if you haven't been able to unearth the murderer.'

Muzaffar took the bridle from the groom, and nodded to the man in a gesture of combined thanks and dismissal. 'My conscience would question me. My curiosity, too, I suppose.' He stroked the horse's neck. 'But there's an equally good chance that the Diwan-i-kul *will* return. I thought his forte was court politics, intrigue; will he actually mount up and lead his troops into battle? I would think that would be more the Shahzada Aurangzeb's style.'

The horse lowered its head, rubbing its nose against Muzaffar's shoulder. Akram did not say anything. 'That is Aurangzeb's strength, isn't it? His skill at warfare. He's a seasoned campaigner. If it comes down to it, I doubt he'll have much trouble getting rid of Dara Shukoh and crowning himself the emperor.'

'Muzaffar!' Akram, as always more circumspect – and more inclined to shy at shadows – snapped at his friend. 'Are you out of your head? Don't even say such things!'

'There's nobody around, and this horse, wonderful though he is, cannot be bothered with politics, I think. Don't you see where we're headed, Akram? The Baadshah may have proclaimed Dara Shukoh his heir, but he has, in reality, done all he can to actually prevent Dara from being an effective ruler' – he saw the protest rising to Akram's lips, and shook his head to pre-empt it. 'Oh, yes, I agree Shahzada Dara Shukoh is erudite and broad-minded and wise, in his own way. But with the state of the empire being what it is, an emperor would also have to be a good general, don't you think? And that is what Dara is not. Very definitely not. He's been cosseted and kept close to the throne, and it's always been Aurangzeb who's been sent out on the most difficult campaigns. If push comes to shove, Aurangzeb will win in a battle for the throne.'

'Shh. *Please*, Muzaffar. Go on home. And keep quiet. The Baadshah is alive and well, his heir is in a powerful position and by his father's side. Nothing will happen; you'll see. Aurangzeb and the Diwan-i-kul will defeat Bijapur and come back north with tributes and wealth unlimited.'

Muzaffar merely smiled knowingly and mounted his horse.

Three hours later, having ridden back to Qureshi Sahib's haveli, eaten dinner and begun reading through Mumtaz Hassan's correspondence, Muzaffar was inclined to share Akram's scepticism. The letters were a bit of a jumble. Akram's uncle, it appeared, kept in frequent contact with his friends and relatives. There were letters here from all across the land – from Bijapur, from Bengal; from Kandahar and Kabul and up in Kashmir. Missives scrawled untidily on coarse paper; thin, elegant paper covered in exquisite calligraphy; even a few sheets of parchment. There were letters giving all the news: so-and-so was getting married; someone's servant had decamped with a valuable piece of jewellery; a long-lost cousin, once wealthy and handsome, had come back from who knew where, now penurious and decrepit and unrecognizable. There was court gossip, hush-hush stories of libidinous princesses sneaking lovers into their apartments at night, and less scandalous tales of political alliances made and broken and remade. There were tales of woe and requests for money.

By the time midnight came, Muzaffar was yawning. He had ploughed through approximately three-fourths of the correspondence, and had found nothing that sounded suspicious. Where there had been gossip potentially dangerous to know, it was either too far back in the past to have repercussions now, or Muzaffar would have thought the letter-writer more at risk than Mumtaz Hassan. There seemed nothing amidst all that he had read which could have led to the murder of Mumtaz Hassan.

He straightened, rolling his shoulders and stretching to ease the kinks out of a stiff back. The brass chiraghdaan, a lamp on a circular base with its oil bowl atop a carved pillar the length of a man's forearm, had enough oil left to feed for an hour the seven cotton wicks around the rim of the bowl. Muzaffar pressed his palms to eyes squeezed shut. Outside his room, the haveli had fallen silent. Even the last sounds of the servants – cleaning utensils, locking doors, packing up for the night – had died down. He was alone with the life of a dead man.

Muzaffar opened his eyes and blinked as he reached for the letters that still remained. There were a couple of handfuls still in the bundle, sheets of paper folded into rectangles, some so old and perused so often that they were falling apart. And at the bottom of the bundle, there was a surprise: another bundle, wrapped in white silk and fragrant with musk. Or was it musk mallow? Muzaffar drew out the bundle and undid the knot in the blue cord that held the silk together.

Unlike the hotchpotch of the rest of Mumtaz Hassan's correspondence, these letters were uniform: on fine cream paper, each sheet with a thin border of tiny painted flowers, deep pink and gold, with curling green stems and minute green leaves. The ink was black, the writing flowing and neat. Muzaffar glanced at the topmost letter.

You hold my heart.

He stared, his mouth gone dry. Then, with unsteady hands, he put the letter aside and reached for the next letter, and the one beneath. Each began the same way. *You hold my heart.*

Muzaffar carefully put the letters on one side, clear of the chiraghdaan, and rose to his feet, letting the thin quilt he had draped around his shoulders slide off. Beside his bed, on a small stool, lay Muzaffar's pen box. He opened it, and taking out the scrap of paper that the hakim had found clutched in Mumtaz Hassan's fist, brought it back to the chiraghdaan for comparison.

The paper was as smooth and as fine, though the scrap the dead man had been holding had no decorative border on it. And the handwriting was different; also neat, but different. Muzaffar gave a sigh of disappointment and gathering the quilt around him, settled down once again to read the letters.

An hour later, having finally read through the remaining letters, Muzaffar extinguished the flames of the chiraghdaan and lay down to sleep. But sleep would not come, even though his eyes were gritty and his body yearned rest. His mind refused to stay still long enough for sleep to overtake it. There was the question of Mirza Sajjad Khan and the piebald horse; there was Basheer, a man Muzaffar was beginning to like, but who could not yet be cleared of all suspicion; there were the letters... and there was a young woman, sleeping in this very haveli, less than a hundred yards away, who had offered to help. He needed help.

'I thought you did not want to have anything to do with Shireen,'

Zeenat Begum said, with a slightly smug smile, when Muzaffar met his sister in the khanah bagh after breakfast.

'This is not personal. She had offered to help, and right now, she is the only one I can think of. I need the help of a woman who knows high society in Agra. She seems the most obvious choice.'

'And she is intelligent.'

Muzaffar shrugged and refrained from commenting. 'Will you ask her first?' he said. 'Tell her all the background – all that I have told you – and if she agrees, I shall talk to her uncle and obtain his permission. This must be done correctly.'

'Of course it must,' Zeenat Aapa said with eyes sparkling so bright with mischief that Muzaffar shuddered and took his leave.

A self-respecting nobleman, and a good Mussulman to boot, would have balked at letting a young woman of his household meet a man who was not a relative. Many would have disapproved of her even meeting a relative. Qureshi Sahib, to Muzaffar's surprise, was not just willing, but it seemed even eager, to let Muzaffar meet Shireen. Muzaffar, having received a favourable answer – from Shireen, but through Zeenat Aapa – had gone to great lengths to explain the circumstances to Qureshi Sahib. He had made it abundantly clear that he required the help of Shireen in his investigations of Mumtaz Hassan's murder. He had also explained that Shireen would, at the moment, only be required to read some documents and give her opinion on them. Nothing more.

Assured that Zeenat Begum would be present at the meeting – and at any subsequent meetings, if any – Qureshi Sahib had nodded. 'Yes, yes. I trust you wholeheartedly, Jang Sahib; you know that. I will have a servant inform Shireen. She will be glad to be of help.'

Shireen came, clad in a long silk skirt, fashionably patterned in stripes of green, crimson and gold. She probably wore a close-fitting smock above that, with the waistcoat that most ladies donned when venturing out of their rooms; Muzaffar could only see the drapes of the voluminous pashmina shawl, delicately embroidered in muted red, that she had wrapped around her. Her hands, smooth and slim, were the only part of her that was visible. Bangles of enamel, bands of pearls and of filigreed gold, jingled gently as she spread her skirts on the mattress on which she sat.

Zeenat Begum seated herself after what seemed to be much thought: close enough to be the chaperone she had been appointed, in case someone should barge in during the meeting, yet distant enough to let Muzaffar conduct the conversation with Shireen, not with both women. Muzaffar waited for the women to settle down, and then seated himself on the mattress near Shireen. They were sitting at right angles. She was near enough for him to see the fine tracery of blue veins on the pale hand that rested on one shimmering silk-clad knee. For a moment, his mind was a blank, and then a sudden coldness gripped him. Was he mad? A woman – a fashionable young woman, with her mind probably right now occupied with her jewellery and her clothing – what was he doing, putting his faith in her? In the dark of the night, and in the first flush of dawn, it had seemed like a good idea. Zeenat Aapa had assured him that Shireen was enthusiastic and eager to help. But would she be able to help? Or was she looking forward to this as a means of entertaining herself? Would she grab the letters and spend hours over them, looking not for clues, but for gossip to share with her friends?

Zeenat Begum cleared her throat ostentatiously. 'We are ready, Muzaffar, whenever you are.'

It would be unforgivably rude to back out now. And he had no other option, either. Zeenat Aapa, ignorant of Agra's society, could not help.

There was no help for it. He squared his shoulders and got ready to begin. Before he could speak, Shireen spoke up. 'Zeenat Begum has told me that you need – pardon me for being presumptuous – that you need help.' Her voice was soft, faintly hesitant, as if she feared he would consider her offer an affront to his male superiority.

Muzaffar was startled into a moment's silence. 'Yes,' he said finally. 'Yes, I do need your help. I believe Zeenat Aapa has told you about Mumtaz Hassan's murder' – he glanced towards his sister, who nodded – 'and about the scrap torn from a letter that was found clutched in his fist.' Shireen inclined her head, and Muzaffar, gathering courage from that simple gesture, continued, telling her about the personal correspondence he had ploughed through. He skimmed over the letters from cousins and aunts and uncles; those were of little consequence. What he did dwell on were the letters that had been wrapped separately in silk. The letters, embellished with painted flowers, scented with musk, and beginning inevitably with that now hauntingly familiar sentence: *You hold my heart.*

'But wasn't that what was written on the scrap that Hassan Sahib held? Or at least part of it?'

'It was. That is why I was immediately interested in these letters. That sentence, and the fact that that too was scented with musk – though Akram said *that* was musk mallow; I don't know about these.' He glanced down at the small pile of sheets, each page neatly aligned, that he had placed on the carpet between the two mattresses. Shireen reached a hand out and lifted the topmost sheet. She hesitated, caught between curiosity and propriety, one hand holding the page, the other hovering near the draped edge of her dupatta. She murmured something to herself – about it not being the first time? thought Muzaffar – and drew her dupatta up, unveiling her face for the few moments it took to raise the letter to her nose and sniff.

A fleeting glimpse, and that was it. She was as striking as Muzaffar remembered her, from the one time he had seen her accidentally unveiled during the trip to and from Ajmer. High cheekbones splashed with a warm flush of red, large eyes the colour of rich, polished teakwood. A full pink mouth – and he was looking at the curtain of her dropped dupatta. Shireen was veiled again, decorous as ever. Muzaffar looked down at his hands, clenched in his lap. Ayesha would never have been that matter-of-fact, that swift, about something like raising her dupatta in front of a man. She would have teased, pretending to be shy and demure, until he would have been silently begging her to do him the honour of letting her catch a fleeting glimpse of her face.

'It is musk,' Shireen said. 'No doubt about it.' She replaced the letter on top of the pile. 'Whoever she is, she's a rich woman.'

Muzaffar nodded. 'And a careful one. She seems to be discreet even when she writes to her lover. There is no signature, and the letters contain no names – ever. Not hers, not Mumtaz Hassan's, not of her family or friends.'

'You are certainly setting Shireen a hard task,' Zeenat said drily. 'Are there any clues to go on, other than that this woman is wealthy and likes to use musk on her letter paper? There could be a hundred such women in Agra.'

Muzaffar gathered up the pile of letters and shifted it onto his lap. 'The lady may have been discreet, Aapa, but she isn't a completely closed book. Every now and then, she lets drop a piece of information that could help identify her.' His voice trailed off as he riffled through the letters, searching for a familiar phrase. 'Ah! Here's one.' He read from a letter. '"*I had gone to Jauhari Bazaar yesterday, to buy a necklace that an acquaintance had described to me. It is the most exquisite guluband I have ever seen, seven gold roses strung on threads of golden silk, each rose with a little diamond in its heart – but you shall see it for yourself when we meet next. I had just about agreed to the jeweller's price when I suddenly began feeling dizzy and so sick that there was no choice but to climb into the palanquin and come straight back home. Thankfully, the streets were not very crowded, so we made good time. I was back home within a quarter of an hour.*"'

'She lives not far from Jauhari Bazaar,' said Zeenat Begum.

'And she owns a distinctive guluband,' added Shireen. 'I have never seen one like what she describes.'

Muzaffar set the letter aside and picked up another. 'From what I gather, she lives in her brother's household. There are occasional mentions of an old auntie who is supposed to be a chaperone of sorts, I think – though she appears to be too infirm to keep a strict eye on her ward. The lady seems to go about pretty much where and when she pleases. Listen to this: *"Do you remember the wonderful time we had in the Aaraam Bagh last summer? Auntie was saying yesterday that the narcissi must be blooming there now, and we should go for a picnic. I had a hard time keeping a straight face, because I happened to be wearing the attar of narcissus you brought me from Kashmir two years ago!"* She goes on a bit about how the auntie is so frail that they would need to include a hakim in the retinue if they were to go on a picnic... and then there's this bit: *"You will be going to Kashmir again this summer, will you not? Can I plead for some more of that narcissus attar? I had asked my brother to get some when he went in the spring, but he has been in such a sulk since his begum miscarried that that request came to naught."* Pleasant woman.'

'She sounds frightfully self-centred,' Shireen said. 'But attar of narcissus – that too is uncommon. I hope she still uses it.'

'She also has a brother whose begum miscarried sometime before the spring. And the brother went to Kashmir in the spring.'

There was a silence, while Muzaffar re-read the letter he held and Shireen and Zeenat sat, lost in their own thoughts. It was Zeenat who said, in a voice low enough to sound as if she were talking more to herself than to the other two people in the room: 'I wonder why the brother was in such a sulk that his wife lost her child.'

Muzaffar looked up at her, astonished. 'Wouldn't any man be?'

'Some men would, yes. Your brother-in-law, for instance. Or you. A man who is caring and sensitive, and who truly and deeply loves his wife.' She sighed and pulled her shawl closer about her. 'But not many men are cast in the same mould as you. I am more inclined to think that this lady's brother had been trying desperately for an heir, and that was why the miscarriage went down so badly with him.'

'I shall keep it in mind,' Shireen murmured. 'A brother, either devoted to his wife, or badly needing an heir – which means he has no sons yet – or maybe even no daughters?'

She was shrewd, thought Muzaffar, not just a pretty face. But how shrewd? Even Ayesha had been shrewd, in her own way – shrewd enough to milk him of all that he had to give, and fool him all the while into believing that she loved him.

Muzaffar gritted his teeth and forcibly shoved the thought of Ayesha out of his mind.

He picked up the stack of letters again and set his mouth in a grim line, forbidding enough for the most determined of flirtatious women. Or so he hoped.

They worked their way through the letters, Muzaffar reading out excerpts he thought pertinent. There was a description of a grand banquet hosted by the princess Jahanara on a visit to Agra; the writer of the letter described in exuberant detail the iced juices, the fragrant pulaos and biryanis and kababs, the dresses of the ladies who attended the banquet, the costume of the princess herself – and gave a somewhat pompous description of her own clothing, all fine muslin and gold thread, so delicate that a *'whiff of your breath would whisk it away'*. The princess had distributed gifts to the ladies as tokens of her affection and esteem; the writer had been given a pair of earrings, jade and gold with tiny rubies. *'Not as fine as what some other ladies got,'* was the peevish comment, *'but certainly better than what my brother's begum found herself taking home.'*

'She is not just wealthy, she is a lady of rank,' Shireen remarked. 'I remember the party the princess hosted; only the very cream of Agra society was invited. If this lady got an invitation, she is either from a well-respected aristocratic family, or – it may be – a family of merchants that has clawed its way into a position where it commands a great deal of respect.'

'The latter,' Muzaffar said. 'I saw a reference to her brother being summoned to Dilli for some goods the Baadshah wanted purchased.' He had been searching through the letters as he spoke, and pulled out one. 'Here it is... yes, this is it: *"I shall be free of my brother's gimlet eye for the next two weeks. An associate of his had come from Dilli, and told him that the Baadshah is interested in looking over some goods for purchase. He had recommended my brother's name to the Baadshah, so the Baadshah* has told him to come to Dilli with samples of what he can supply. He will be gone at least two weeks! I can easily hoodwink Auntie and meet you – even every day, if we should so desire. Shall we begin with tomorrow? Outside the Mehtab Bagh?" The brother is a merchant.'

'Oh,' he said, after a moment. 'And this lady seems to have been followed from that rendezvous at Mehtab Bagh, back home.' He flicked through the pages, his gaze flitting down each sheet, until he reached the paragraph he had been looking for. 'I had not noticed it – I was too engrossed in admiring that lovely bracelet you gifted me – but when Auntie and I were on our way home in the palanquin, Auntie said she thought we were being followed. She was already a little upset that I got late meeting her near the Mehtab Bagh; then she started off talking about this man whom she thought was trailing us. Very silly!' He glanced up. 'I don't think the auntie was actually being silly, though. Someone definitely seems to have entered the lady's chambers a few days later.'

He had been leafing through the pages as he spoke. Now he read out another excerpt: 'You will not believe what happened! I was in the middle of writing to you and had left the letter on my pillow, along with the reed pen and ink on the table beside – when auntie called me to come and see the wares of a bangle-seller who had stopped by. When I got back to my room, the letter had disappeared! I searched everywhere for it, even under the bed, but it was nowhere to be found. So I have had to write this all over again.'

On the surface of it, that was all there was. 'But if you will not take offence, I would like to keep the letters and read through them myself,' Shireen said. 'Who knows, there may be some little detail there that would make sense only to a woman, or only to someone who knows Agra and its people?'

When she was leaving the room a few minutes later, the little package of letters tucked under her arm, she stopped in the doorway and turned to look over her shoulder. Zeenat Begum, already outside in the corridor, walked on a few steps before coming to a halt. For one bizarre moment, Muzaffar wished that Shireen would lift her veil so that he could see her face again. But she did not; she only spoke.

'*Entrust jewels to treasurers, but be the keeper of thine own secrets,*' she quoted, her voice so soft that Muzaffar thought she was speaking to herself. Her voice became a little louder as she continued. 'These *are* secrets, Jang Sahib; I recognize that. And I know the need to keep them safe.' She lifted her head, still veiled. Thank you for putting your trust in me. 'I will do my utmost to uphold it.'

Muzaffar stood staring at her, wondering what to say and do. Thank her. Reassure her of the rightness of that trust. Bow politely and say he was grateful for her help. Beg her to once again lift that dupatta and let him see her expression. Thank her for having given him that one glimpse of her face. He was still floundering when she said, 'It may take me a couple of days, but I hope to be able to find the lady for you. Allah help you in your endeavours, Jang Sahib. Goodbye.'

And then she was gone, moving briskly down the corridor in a swirl of striped skirt and embroidered shawl. Zeenat Begum walked at a more sedate pace behind her. Muzaffar smiled to himself as he watched them go: Shireen, business-like and determined; Zeenat, calm and collected, secure in the competence of both Shireen and Muzaffar. The women in his life.

He swallowed abruptly and shook his head, physically trying to shake off the thought. Where had *that* come from?

Basheer was talking to the steward of his haveli, Haider, at the drum house when Muzaffar reined in. A groom stood outside the drum house holding the reins of Basheer's horse; Basheer broke off in mid-sentence to walk over and take the reins from the man so that the groom could take Muzaffar's horse to the stables. 'I assume you will be here at the haveli for a while,' he said to Muzaffar. 'I won't, because I have to go and see how things are at Abba's rauza. But Akram is here, he'll help you out. So is Haider. Here, Haider: come here.' He bobbed his head a little apologetically at Muzaffar. 'Just give me a moment, will you? Some instructions – oh, and I have to give you something we found.' He shoved a hand into the pocket of his choga, scrabbled about and drew it out, still empty. Muzaffar heard him mutter an almost inaudible 'Where has it disappeared?'

Haider, standing next to his master, said quietly, 'Has something been misplaced, huzoor?'

'Yes, yes – that letter, which you handed over to me. The one you had found tucked away in Abba's clothing.'

'I had given it to huzoor at breakfast. Perhaps huzoor left it behind in the dalaan? Shall I go and have a look?'

Basheer nodded. 'Yes, do. And give it to Jang Sahib when you've found it. I don't have the time to wait; I must leave now. Oh, and listen, Haider: send one of the servants out with a stick to beat the shrubbery outside my window. I'm sure I heard a hissing there last night. I wouldn't want a snake crawling in and making itself comfortable.' He signaled to the groom, gesturing to the man to help him mount. 'I will send Mahmood in the bullock cart sometime in the afternoon; have the blankets packed and ready by then.' He hesitated, brow crinkling in thought. 'That's it. Off you go. Give Jang Sahib that letter.'

'Haider found a letter addressed to my father,' he said. 'It should have been in that bundle of personal correspondence you took away with you yesterday, but Abba must have received it recently and not had a chance to put it away. Anyway, Haider will give it to you and you can see for yourself. I'm off to see how things are at the rauza. What with yesterday's mishap and the bitter cold, the workers are in a dismal mood. Ammi's been after my life to give something to charity – donate blankets to the beggars so that they will pray for Abba's soul. So I thought, why not kill two birds with one stone? I'll give the blankets to the workers; that'll cheer them up, and Ammi won't be any the wiser.' He grinned. 'I shall see you later, then. Come to the site sometime while I'm there; I'll give you a guided tour.'

He rode off, leaving Muzaffar to make his way to the house. He was halfway up the path when the quilted curtain hanging at the main entrance of the haveli was lifted and Akram stepped out, resplendent in a rich maroon brocade. Behind him came Haider.

'Muzaffar! Haider told me you had arrived. Beautiful day, isn't it? All nice and sunny. Such a change after the fog we'd been having.' He beamed at Muzaffar. Muzaffar grinned back.

'Yes, it is a lovely day. Would you like to come out for a ride with me?' he asked. 'I have much to discuss with you, and it would be a crime to stay indoors on a day such as this.'

With a quiet 'Huzoor', Haider pressed a folded sheet of paper into Muzaffar's hand, and went off to the stables to instruct the grooms to have the horses fetched. Muzaffar slipped the letter into his pocket, and turned to talk to Akram, who wanted to know whether Muzaffar had discovered anything interesting in Mumtaz Hassan's letters.

'Shireen has said she'll try to identify the woman for me within a few days. Let's see if she succeeds,' Muzaffar said as they rode their horses out on to the riverbank, leaving Mumtaz Hassan's haveli behind. A sharp wind was blowing off the water, and Muzaffar winced as his horse topped a hillock. 'Whew, it's cold out here.' He tugged the end of his turban out, and wrapped it around his ears and face. 'Shall we go down, towards those rocks? It might be less windy there.'

'As I see it,' Muzaffar said a while later, a little more comfortable now that they were sheltered behind the bulk of a large riverside boulder, 'there are a lot of possible clues floating around. But whom they lead to is anybody's guess.' They had scraped together some dry driftwood and ignited a small fire; Muzaffar picked up a stick and poked meditatively at the fire as he spoke. 'First of all, there's the piebald horse, which belongs to Sajjad Khan. It seems almost certain that the horse – or rather, its rider – was involved in the killing of Mumtaz Hassan. I don't know whether that means Sajjad Khan himself is implicated.'

Akram listened quietly.

'Then there's this mysterious lady who seems to have been carrying on an affair with Mumtaz Hassan. And, no matter how careful she might have been, it seems someone knew of the liaison.'

Akram lifted an interrogative eyebrow.

'It stands to reason. Someone sent Mumtaz Hassan a bad forgery – a letter, scented with musk mallow, and beginning with the same words Hassan's ladylove used as a salutation for him, *You hold my heart.* Someone, I think, used that forged note to kill Mumtaz Hassan.' Muzaffar broke the stick in half and then into quarters, before feeding it to the flames. 'You remember, I said I'd heard somebody outside early that night on the riverside, mentioning a note? And there were pebbles on the floor of Mumtaz Hassan's room when we entered the next morning.' Absently, he gathered a handful of pebbles from the sand around – 'Someone threw pebbles up, from the riverbank below, through the jharokha and into the room' – he chucked a couple of pebbles into the fire – 'to attract Mumtaz Hassan's attention.'

'Obviously, he couldn't pass the note to Mumtaz Hassan at that distance, so he probably begged Mumtaz Hassan to allow him to throw up a rope, which your uncle would tether to the chest. Then the messenger could climb up and hand over the note. Or that was what your uncle believed.'

'It all sounds very hole-and-corner.'

'It was. Your uncle was probably carrying on an affair with an unmarried woman of wealth and position, under the protection of her brother. Naturally he'd want it kept under wraps. I'd think he was used to meeting her clandestinely, and exchanging letters and notes on the sly. This cloak-and-dagger business would not be anything extraordinary for him.'

'So while my uncle was reading the note, the messenger slunk up behind him and garroted him?'

Muzaffar nodded. 'It looks like it.' He let the remaining pebbles, now warm from the heat of his palm, slide into the sand beside his boot. A few moments went by in silence, broken only by the crackling of the flames and the raucous call of a paddy bird as it took off over the water in a flash of white feathers.

'Then there's the horse trader,' Muzaffar said. 'Shakeel Alam. Allah knows where he's disappeared.' He sniffed, a little glumly. 'Things look bleak, Akram, don't they? There are too many threads, and I'm getting the feeling I'm pretty useless as a weaver.'

The next moment, he sat up, reaching into his pocket. 'And – I just remembered, there's something else. There's this letter Haider gave me,' he said, pulling it out and unfolding it as he spoke. 'Though, of all Mumtaz Hassan's correspondence, the only letters that seem to be any use are the ones his lady friend wrote to him. And this isn't from her, so it's unlikely –' he broke off, eyes widening.

'What is it?'

'Ya Allah,' Muzaffar whispered. 'Another thread to add to the mystery. How many people could have murdered Mumtaz Hassan?!'

10

THE WORKERS HAD returned to Mumtaz Hassan's rauza. When one's next meal – or the absence of it – depended upon whether or not one had worked during the day, fear and superstition were easily put aside. There was a certain hesitation in venturing near the eastern part of the tomb, but elsewhere, work was back to normal. On the western wall, workers were fitting the marble cladding. For the southern wall, an archway of pierced stone, a network of six-pointed stars, had been towed right up to the foot of the wall. It lay on the ground wrapped in sacking and ready to be lifted into place. On the eastern side, under the supervision of both Zulfiqar and Mahmood, new scaffolding was being erected. Basheer and Taufeeq stood below, Taufeeq shouting occasional instructions, nearly all of them unnecessary.

In the bustle and noise, the arrival of the two horsemen went largely unnoticed. A couple of the men digging the water channel looked up at the sound of hooves, but that was all. Akram and Muzaffar's horses had almost reached the shed when Basheer, glancing over his shoulder, spotted them. The two men dismounted at the shed and tied their horses to a tree nearby. Basheer was still standing, turned halfway towards the shed, when they left their horses and walked towards him. Muzaffar saw the expression on Basheer's face: mild surprise, a sort of bored interest, but not much more.

'You are here sooner than I would have expected, Jang Sahib,' he said with a lazy smile. 'You are welcome, of course. But I'm afraid all of us are somewhat occupied at the moment. Once we've got the scaffolding up on the eastern side, things will be better.'

Muzaffar dipped his head in a gesture partly of acknowledgement, partly of apology for the intrusion. 'I just have a question or two for Taufeeq here; if I may?' He waited just long enough to see Basheer's nod of assent before turning to Taufeeq. 'It is a matter of some confidentiality. Would you prefer we went to the shed?' He glanced back at Basheer. 'You too, please, Basheer Sahib. It is important.'

Basheer looked as if he was going to protest, but then, with a frown to register indignation, he fell into step behind Muzaffar and Akram. Taufeeq led the way.

Once they were inside the shed, Muzaffar waved aside Taufeeq's invitation to sit. He had pulled the letter out of his pocket, and unfolding it, thrust it into Taufeeq's hand. 'Read that out aloud, please.'

Taufeeq's gaze skittered – from Muzaffar to the letter, from the letter back to Muzaffar, to Basheer, and then to Muzaffar again. Indignation. Curiosity. Bewilderment. Muzaffar, looking on at the old man, wondered where those last two emotions had come from. Or whether he had read them incorrectly. 'Go on,' he said. 'Read.'

'"Hassan",' Taufeeq read. '"My son Omar bears this letter. He comes to you as my emissary. You and I both know that we do not hold each other in high esteem. This, however, is on a matter of great urgency, and one that will require the laying aside of rivalries that have cost us both dearly. I trust you will have the foresight to listen to what Omar has to say to you. He speaks with his voice, but my words. Pay heed."' Taufeeq licked his lips. 'There is a signature and seal below, and a date.'

'What?' Muzaffar's voice was menacingly low. His narrowed eyes flashed, his moustache almost bristled with rage. Akram, watching in rapt fascination, looked grateful to not be at the receiving end of that cold fury.

'It is dated – a month back. The signature and seal are those of Khush Bakht Khan.'

Muzaffar extended his hand, palm upwards, for the letter. 'And you told me,' he snapped, 'that you did not think there had been any interactions between Khush Bakht Khan and Mumtaz Hassan since Mumtaz Hassan shifted to Agra. You gave me to understand that that was an enmity that existed twenty-five years ago and may well be long dead! And here I find that the enemy's son came bearing a letter – and possibly had a long conversation with Mumtaz Hassan! Why did you keep quiet about that? Why didn't you speak up about Omar having visited Mumtaz Hassan?'

'Allow me, Jang Sahib,' said Basheer. Taufeeq was looking a little pale. 'I think I know more about that than Taufeeq does.' He took the letter from Muzaffar, glanced at it, and handed it back, all with an air of supremely dignified tranquility. 'Omar came, with that letter and two companions, about a week back. Taufeeq was not in Agra then. Abba had sent him to Fatehpur Sikri to transact some business.'

Muzaffar turned to Taufeeq. 'When did you go?'

It took the old man a few moments of thought; then he replied, 'I left Agra ten days ago. It took me a day and a half to get there. I stayed there for two days, then headed back.'

'So you were gone – what? – five days?'

Taufeeq nodded.

'During which time Omar visited Mumtaz Hassan. And Mumtaz Hassan never mentioned the visit?'

Taufeeq shook his head.

'I apologize, then. I should not have assumed that you had lied.' Taufeeq, eyes wide and mouth hanging open, gulped, fumbled for words and tried to mutter something, but could manage nothing beyond a vague 'No, huzoor – there is no need.'

Muzaffar, looking a little deflated, directed his next question at Basheer. 'Since you seem to know more about this business than Taufeeq, do you know what it was that Omar discussed with your father? Why had he come to Mumtaz Hassan? As an emissary, says Khush Bakht Khan – but to talk of what?'

Basheer shrugged. 'Who knows? I only happened to know that a man named Omar had come from Bijapur because he arrived when

Abba and I were sitting in the dalaan. Haider came in to announce this Omar, and I took myself off. I didn't meet him, and Abba never said a word about what they discussed.' He stroked his neat little moustache, then added, 'Are you finished? May Taufeeq and I go back to the rauza now? After yesterday's accident, it's not good if both of us stay away from the site for long. Not good for the morale of the workers, at any rate.'

He noted Muzaffar's quick nod, and moved to the door, beckoning to Taufeeq as he did so. Muzaffar watched them go. When he turned back to Akram, his face wore a look of bitter amusement. 'I'm beginning to understand why so many of the omrah we know keep a low profile. Go riding, go hunting, go shopping for jewels and horses and pretty slave girls; but turn a blind eye if anything resembling crime comes anywhere near you. If you or your family suffer because of the crime, crib a little and leave it to the kotwal to find a culprit. But don't get ensnared in it. There's no end to the bloody business.' He grunted with exasperation and walked briskly out of the door and into the sunshine outside.

Akram, sauntering out on Muzaffar's heels, said quietly, 'You don't believe any of that, Muzaffar. And you never will.' He glanced around, looking at the workers flitting about the site, and at the figures – one stout and flamboyant, the other frail and dull – of Basheer and Taufeeq, as they walked to the rauza. 'Now what?'

Muzaffar, instead of answering, was looking towards the south; Akram heard him mutter, 'Now what could *he* be up to?' A tall figure, thin but broad-shouldered, wrapped in a dark, shapeless garment, was making its way towards the construction site. It bobbed and hobbled in an awkward fashion, now down, now up, lurching as if unsteady on its feet. The garment ballooned briefly in a gust of wind, and Muzaffar realized that it was a blanket. It whipped back, and the long, thick stump of a crutch was exposed. There was a little flurry of movement, and a dog came, lolloping along, from behind a thicket of bushes. It came up to the man, prancing cheerfully along in his wake, as he limped onward.

'It's that Ibrahim, isn't it?' asked Akram, standing beside Muzaffar and looking on. 'Mahmood's father. And he's coming here, to the shed; not to the rauza. I wonder why.'

'Perhaps at this distance he hasn't recognized us. Maybe he thinks one of us is Mahmood.' Muzaffar set off at a brisk walk towards the man limping along the path. 'I'll go let him know before he goes through the trouble of coming any further.'

'If you're looking for Mahmood, he's up there, at the rauza,' Muzaffar called to Ibrahim. The old man continued to hobble along for a few more steps, bringing him close enough for Muzaffar to see that though one eyelid still drooped, Ibrahim's eyes were bright and clear, the exhaustion of the previous day gone. 'He's getting the scaffolding put up again,' Muzaffar added. Akram, striding along, had joined them. Ibrahim smiled his lopsided smile at them and murmured a soft salaam. Then he turned away, looking out towards the rauza. There were too many figures milling about along the scaffolding for any one of them to be pinpointed as Mahmood, yet the old man kept staring, eyes narrowed, for a long time.

'They will anger the jinn again,' Ibrahim drawled, just as Muzaffar was getting ready to bid farewell.

Muzaffar exchanged a glance with Akram. Ibrahim paid them no heed; he was still standing, his crutch tucked under his arm, looking out over the site towards the rauza. Or, actually not, realized Muzaffar; he was not looking at the rauza, he was staring into space. The glassy look in the old stonecutter's eyes was of a man physically in one place, but otherwise absent. Far, far away. Drifting along in his own thoughts.

'And why should that be? Do the jinn not want Mumtaz Hassan's rauza to be built? Does the building of the tomb anger them so much?'

The vacant look in Ibrahim's eyes vanished in a trice. His head snapped around, eyes boring into Muzaffar's. There was something disconcerting about the man: broken and maimed, yet with a virility about him that almost frightened Muzaffar. Instinctively, he backed away a step. Ibrahim leaned forward, shifting the crutch. 'You think this is all superstition, don't you?' he whispered. 'Stupid superstition, that only the poor believe in!' For a moment, he looked furious enough to swing out with that crutch and hit Muzaffar. But he mastered himself quickly enough; a deep gulp of air, and he turned away, tugging the crutch expertly around, his left hand reaching to swivel his right leg the few inches it needed to turn his body away. A moment, and he was facing the way he had come. The dog growled at Muzaffar and Akram, and stood its ground, refusing to follow Ibrahim.

Ibrahim hobbled forward a few steps, then turned his head and called out to the dog, 'Come on, let's get back!' He glanced at Muzaffar, and said, in a more controlled voice, 'Mumtaz Hassan was evil. He did not endear himself to the jinn. Why should they accept anything that glorifies him?'

And with that, he moved away, down the path that led to his hut.

'He's taken leave of his bloody senses,' Akram said heatedly, once they were astride their horses and heading away from the site of Mumtaz Hassan's tomb. 'Jinn and all, my foot! If there are jinn around here, I'm sure they have better things to do than expend their energies on concocting petty mishaps at my uncle's rauza. You should have given him a talking-to, Muzaffar, for spouting such bilge.'

'It wasn't my place to do anything of the sort, and you know it.' Muzaffar's tone was mild as he handled the reins. 'And I feel a little sorry for him, don't you? He's an old man, Akram, crippled and ill. He's had a hard life, too. He can be forgiven for being bitter at times. I would be too – much worse, perhaps – if I had been through what he's had to bear.' He glanced across at his friend. 'Let it be. Ibrahim said nothing that causes us – or anybody, for that matter – any harm. Let him say what he wants; he's old enough and seemingly senile enough to merit that.'

Akram gave a grunt of disgust before asking, 'Now what? You know that Khush Bakht Khan sent his son Omar to meet my uncle. But we have no idea why, and we don't know where Omar is now. For all we know, he may have gone back to Bijapur.'

'I have a good mind to write to the Diwan-i-kul and tell him that since he's in Bijapur, he might as well make himself useful and track down Omar for me,' Muzaffar replied with a rueful grin. 'Don't look so worried, Akram. I won't. But you're right; we don't know anything about Omar and his whereabouts. Basheer doesn't know, and Taufeeq doesn't know. The two people most likely to have some knowledge of what transpired between Mumtaz Hassan and Omar – and they don't know. Do you think your aunt might know?'

Akram shrugged. 'You'll have to ask her.'

'Haider could be another possibility,' Muzaffar mused. 'After all, he announced Omar. He probably showed him into the dalaan to meet Mumtaz Hassan. Perhaps he overheard something... come on, let's return to the haveli.'

Of Mumtaz Hassan's widowed wives, Akram's aunt had taken on – with a macabre sort of enthusiasm – the role of chief mourner. She had spent the last few days in almost incessant crying during the waking hours. Now, it seemed to have dawned on her that weeping could not be sustained indefinitely. It made one's eyes swell and hurt, it resulted in a sore throat, and those who were initially sympathetic had drifted off, back to their own lives. Even the other begums had reconciled themselves to their fate and returned to the routines of the household. She had been left crying to herself, with nobody to applaud her devotion to her dearly departed lord and master.

She had therefore stopped wailing, and apart from the occasional sniffle, was now in control of her emotions. She did not, however, agree to meet Muzaffar in person. Akram, by virtue of being her brother's son, could not be refused without causing offence. She allowed him to be ushered into her presence. But there was nothing she could contribute to their knowledge of Omar, his mission, and his whereabouts: she had not even known that Khush Bakht Khan's son had come visiting her husband.

Muzaffar, sitting down to lunch with Akram, settled himself against a bolster and said, 'Another hope gone down the drain. I can only pray that Haider heard or saw something. I have no wish to go all the way to Bijapur on Omar's trail.' His voice trailed off as a small but impressive procession of servants filed into the room, carrying silver salvers and bowls, pitchers, and, at the end of the line, a large fruit bowl filled to overflowing with grapes, apples, pears and oranges. Till a day earlier, in keeping with the tradition of not consuming any flesh after a funeral, Mumtaz Hassan's household had abstained from eating anything but grain and milk, fruit and vegetable. The meat was back, Muzaffar noted. While one servant came forward with the sailabchi for them to wash their hands, the others put down the dishes and removed the covers. There was a simple khichri, rice and lentils still steaming and fragrant with cinnamon and pepper; there were succulent kababs and a dish of lamb cooked with turnips. In earthenware bowls were dishes of fried aubergines, and of mellow pumpkin tempered with mustard seeds, fenugreek and cumin. Haider beckoned to a servant, who came forward to place little bowls of pickled ginger and limes and of tart, sweet, preserved carrots – a murabba – in front of the two noblemen.

Naans and rotis were set down, and sweets to be consumed midway through the meal: balushahi, flaky and rich; and dar bihisht, made with milk cooked long with rice flour.

All of it food either bought from the shops in town, or sent by friends and family, for no food could be cooked in a house of mourning for forty days.

'Haider,' Muzaffar said as the rest of the servants withdrew, 'please stay back. I have some questions for you.'

The food was served, the Bismillah was intoned, and Muzaffar asked Haider what he remembered of the visit of Omar. The steward looked puzzled; then enlightenment dawned and he nodded. 'He had come with two other men, huzoor,' he said. 'All three in their late twenties, I think, and all three very similar. Rich young men, used to having their own way. But it was the gentleman who presented the letter – the gentleman who introduced himself as Omar – who did all the talking. I think.'

'You *think*?' Muzaffar paused in the act of conveying a morsel of naan and kabab to his mouth.

'I was not present throughout the conversation, huzoor. I showed the gentlemen into the dalaan when Hassan Sahib bid me usher them in; then I went off to see to the serving of refreshments. I came back to the dalaan only long enough to supervise the servants as they laid out the food. Hassan Sahib told me to leave along with the servants once that was done; the guests wanted to be alone with him. I had to stay within earshot, of course, in case anything was required.' There was a significant pause.

'So you were within earshot. What did you hear?'

Haider stepped forward a pace and bent to pick up the bowl of murabba to offer to Muzaffar, and then to Akram. Muzaffar shook his head. Haider replaced the bowl on the white sheet, the dastarkhan, on which the food had been spread out. He spent several moments fastidiously aligning the bowl of murabba with the bowls of lime and ginger pickle on either side; it was unnecessary, but, Muzaffar guessed, Haider's way of buying some time for himself. He remained silent, waiting for the man to speak.

Haider finally straightened. 'Very little of consequence, huzoor. When I was in the dalaan, in their presence, Omar Sahib was talking about Bijapur. He was telling Hassan Sahib about all that was going on in Bijapur. The rumours circulating in the bazaars, and how those rumours were beginning to affect trade. He was still talking about that when all of us – the servants and I – were dismissed from the dalaan.'

'But you yourself admit that you remained within earshot. You heard something even when you weren't in the room.'

The steward looked uncomfortable. He shuffled his feet and stared fixedly down at his hands, fingers knitted together below his stomach. 'I heard snatches, huzoor,' he said finally, with the guilty air of one giving away a secret. 'Omar Sahib was saying something about loyalty, that Hassan Sahib owed it to his people.'

'Owed what? Loyalty?'

Haider shrugged helplessly. 'I do not know, huzoor. He kept his voice low, and they were sitting at the far end of the dalaan, well away from the doorway. It was only now and then, when he raised his voice, that I heard something.'

Muzaffar indicated that Haider should continue.

'Hassan Sahib grew angry. I heard him ask Omar Sahib what Bijapur had ever done for him, for Hassan Sahib. He said –' he swallowed – 'that all he had to thank Bijapur for was a few scars and some vile lessons that had lasted him a lifetime. He sounded very bitter. And then he laughed and told Omar Sahib to take his pleas elsewhere. He said he would do what *he* wanted to, not what others tried to coerce him into doing.'

'Wait. What was that about those scars and those lessons?' Muzaffar helped himself to the creamy dar bihisht, wondering idly why anyone should make this summer favourite now, in the depths of winter. Beside him, Akram reached out to break a balushahi in half.

'I do not know, huzoor.'

'Anything else? Did you hear either of them – Mumtaz Hassan, Omar, or maybe even the two men who had accompanied Omar – say anything else?'

'They did not stay after Hassan Sahib said that bit about taking their pleas elsewhere. I think they rose immediately and stormed out of the dalaan. Omar Sahib looked pale and very angry.'

'And the other two men?' Muzaffar put down the bowl of dar bihisht and started on the khichri.

'They too.'

'So you heard nothing else? Not from them, and not from Hassan Sahib?'

'No, huzoor.'

It was while Haider was offering the besan, the chickpea flour used to clean greasy hands, that Muzaffar said, 'Did you hear anything that could indicate where these men were staying while in Agra?'

Haider had taken, from the servant deputed to wash diners' hands, the equipment for ablutions: the sailabchi, the pitcher of warm water, and the neatly folded napkin draped over the forearm. He poured a stream of water carefully over Muzaffar's hands, his mouth puckered up and a frown creased his forehead. Akram's hands had been washed and dried, and the bowl of fruit presented to the two young men, when Haider finally answered.

'I escorted them out to the drum house,' he said, 'where their horses had been tied. Just as they were about to mount, one of the men – not Omar Sahib, but one of his companions – looked down at his choga and uttered an oath. Something about having stained his clothing with turmeric while eating. "I'll have to make sure I give it to a washerman as soon as we get back to the sarai," he said.' He bent again, placing small plates before Muzaffar and Akram for the peels and pips of the fruit. 'The other man said, "By the time we return to the sarai, that turmeric will have dried well and proper. Better gift the choga to the washerman, my friend." They chuckled a bit, until Omar Sahib looked at them with anger. Then they rode off.'

Akram picked the pith off a segment of orange. 'So whichever sarai they were staying at, it was at a substantial distance from here,' he remarked.

'Or they were intending to go elsewhere before heading back to the sarai,' Muzaffar said. 'But, since we do not know if they were going elsewhere' – he glanced towards Haider for confirmation – 'it would seem that the best place to continue our enquiries would be the sarais of the city.'

At the first sarai they visited, nobody knew anything of a Bijapuri named Omar, accompanied by two of his countrymen. The man in charge of the sarai said, 'He sounds wealthy. All these merchants from Bijapur are. If he's as rich as all that, he wouldn't stay at a place like this; the moneyed like to stay with their own kind. Of course, that allows them to forge alliances and transact deals even during meals and in between,' he conceded. 'Why don't you try at the Sarai Nur Jahan? The man you're looking for may have stayed there.'

On the eastern bank of the Yamuna, between the Bagh-e-Nurafshan and its neighbouring Buland Bagh, spread the vast caravanserai built by the Empress Nur Jahan in the early years of the century. Nur Jahan had been granted the land as her jagir – her fiefdom – some forty-five years earlier, in what the Europeans knew as 1612 AD. With the canniness she was renowned for, Nur Jahan quickly assessed the worth of the jagir she had acquired. That the jagir could be used to generate an income was obvious; that she could enhance its value by investing some money and effort was the result of Nur Jahan's business acumen. She had built a sarai on the land, a large inn that could accommodate up to three thousand people and five hundred horses at a time. The building of the sarai entitled Nur Jahan to collect customs duties on goods prior to their being shipped across the Yamuna at that point.

Nur Jahan had been dead nearly twelve years now. The imperial capital had been in Dilli for some six years before that. But Agra still flourished as a centre of trade, and the old empress's sarai was still important, still large, still popular.

Muzaffar and Akram, riding past the Buland Bagh – the garden named after Sarbuland Khan Khwajassara, a eunuch of the Emperor Jahangir's court – could hear the sounds drifting across the walls of the sarai: the coming and going of horses, bullock carts and many men; the clanking and jangling of cooking pots and carpenter's tools, of chain mail and weaponry; the thuds and bumps of the shifting of bales of cloth, baskets of spices and sacks of grain; the shouts and laughter, the anger and exasperation, the triumph of a deal pulled off. 'If Omar is as committed a trader as Taufeeq makes his father out to be, I'd wager he stayed here when he was in town,' Muzaffar remarked as their horses passed under the shadow of the octagonal Battis Khamba, the thirty-two pillared tower that stood at the northern edge of the garden and acted as lighthouse and watch tower. A few paces further, and they turned in through the Buland Bagh gate of the sarai.

Akram drew in a sharp breath. 'Allah! Look at the – the *chaos*! And this, when we've entered through the smaller gate. I shudder to think what it'll be like at the eastern gate; we'd probably have been crushed to death before we ever managed to step in.'

It was not chaotic, though. Merely terribly busy, frighteningly so to anyone unused to the clamour and din of commerce at its peak. The sarai was built as a massive hollow square, constructed of stone. A row of single-storeyed rooms, each with its own dalaan, fronted by a dripstone overhanging the huge central yard, formed the living quarters for those who stopped by. At the western end was the mandatory mosque. There were wells and stables, living quarters for the servants and slaves who travelled with their wealthy masters; and the cells for the soldiers who remained in residence at the sarai.

The noise that had filtered through, over the walls and outside, was a fraction of what hit their ears now. It was a din, a maddening assault on the senses. There were bullock carts trundling in and out, the neighing and clip-clopping of horses, the sound of many feet. There were a thousand conversations in progress; fights, brawls, loud guffaws of laughter. From the shed of a blacksmith at one end sounded the rhythmic thudding of a heavy hammer; from almost directly opposite his shop drifted the sound of ankle bells and music, dancing girls either practising or performing.

Muzaffar reined in his horse, just in time to stop the animal colliding with a couple of labourers who were lugging a load of jute towards a storeroom. Off to the left, a merchant – not wealthy enough to have his servants handle such matters – was bargaining with a seller of grass and straw. 'It's a madhouse,' Muzaffar said.

'What?' Akram leaned forward, straining to hear. 'Speak up, I can't hear!'

Muzaffar drew his horse closer to Akram's and leaned towards his friend. 'I said it's a madhouse! If Omar stayed here, I doubt if anybody will even remember. Thousands must pass through here every day!'

But Omar, as luck would have it, was remembered. Muzaffar and Akram, having stabled their horses, were directed by the officer in charge of the sarai to a harassed man sitting in a small one-room office near the mosque. The office was small, but packed to capacity and overflowing into the yard outside. Merchants and their servants stood about, the more belligerent or impatient yelling out their demands or their complaints, the more placid waiting their turn. There were men here, complaining of dirty rooms or of noisy neighbours; men railing against washermen who had shredded their clothes to bits; men wanting to know why there were so few barbers around, when every man needed his face shaved or his moustache trimmed, men enquiring about boats that had not yet arrived or consignments that had not yet been cleared by the customs officials.

Slowly, minute by patient minute, the officer and his assistants handled the barrage of queries and complaints. Apologies were made, even when there was no call for them. Assurances were given, information was passed on, servants were sent out on errands, instructions were written down. Finally, Muzaffar and Akram found themselves standing in front of the officer, who sat on a mattress spread on a platform high enough for him to be nearly at eye level with anyone standing in front of him. Splatters of ink, mud stains and the remains of a meal had soiled the sheet on the mattress. A servant was picking off scraps of paper from next to the small tabletop desk that stood at one end of the mattress, beside a pile of ledgers. A clerk was sitting cross-legged at the desk, writing in one of the ledgers.

'Omar? Omar who?' The officer snapped, voice and face a mixture of harassment and irritation.

'Khan, I suppose. He's the son of a prominent merchant of Bijapur named Khush Bakht Khan. Omar would have come to Agra perhaps about a week ago, maybe a little earlier than that, though I –' Muzaffar was cut off in midsentence by the officer's abrupt 'Yes, yes! We don't have time for all that; move over there, please.' He indicated the clerk who was bending over the desk. 'Here, Usman!' he called, even as Muzaffar and Akram moved off and some half a dozen men behind them pushed forward, a couple of them already beginning to speak. 'They want to know about somebody who stayed here!'

Usman looked marginally less harried than his boss; the complainants and petitioners referred to him, though a substantial number, were obviously just a fraction of the total. Muzaffar repeated his question, and was met with a frown. A frown of concentration, though, not annoyance; Muzaffar held his tongue.

'Omar? From Bijapur, you say?' The man chewed on his lip as he put his reed pen down along the spine of the ledger he had been working on, and closing the ledger, placed it on the desk. Still sitting, he twisted around and reached for the pile of ledgers beside the desk. He pulled out one ledger, and still frowning and chewing his lip, flipped through its pages. Off to the right, an argument had broken out over which man had first right to speak to the officer.

'Ah!' The clerk looked up in triumph, his tired face transformed by a grin. 'I knew there was something familiar about that. He happens to have left some instructions.'

Muzaffar leaned forward eagerly. 'Instructions? What were they about? Can you tell us? My friend's uncle' – he tugged Akram forward by the arm as he spoke – 'had received a visit from Omar and his friends, but they left no address where they could be found. We're out looking for them.'

The man read through the scribble in his ledger, and then glanced up again at Muzaffar. 'It's a little complicated. It seems Omar Sahib was expecting someone to leave a package here for him – what, he does not say. It was to have arrived sometime either yesterday or today. He had intended to stay here till he received the package, but he happened to meet a friend in the city who persuaded him to leave the sarai and go stay at this friend's haveli. So Omar Sahib went off there, leaving instructions that the package, whenever delivered, was to be held for him.' He closed the ledger. 'Then, a couple of days after he went to stay with his friend, Omar came by with another request: that the package may have to be held a few days longer, since he was going out of town for a few days with this friend. He said he would come by to collect the package when he returned to town.'

'And when would that be?'

The clerk shook his head as he opened the ledger he had been writing in when they had interrupted his work. 'He didn't say. Maybe within the week? I don't know.'

'Has the package arrived?'

'Not yet.'

Muzaffar, turning to go, halted. 'One more question: Omar had two companions with him. Are they still here?'

The clerk was back at work, his reed pen flying across the page. He did not even look up. 'No. They went with him, to stay at his friend's haveli.'

It was not yet six hours past noon, but the sun was about to disappear beneath the horizon. The crowd in the sarai had increased, with more travellers coming in for the night. The smoke and smell of burning wood and cow dung began to permeate the air in the yard. Soon, when the fires were well and truly lit, the cooking of the food would begin: the frying and the broiling, the quick roasting in the tandoor. Right now, the sound of spices being pounded was the only indication that dinner was under way. Even the smells of the place, thought Muzaffar, marked it as an abode for the wealthy. Out in the villages, or in the neighbourhoods of the poor, the fragrances that arose from cooking pots were simple ones that spoke of frugal meals:

plain rotis, a dish of lentils. Here, the air was imbued with all the aromas of the rich: the spices, the ghee, the finest of game.

'So?' said Akram. 'Omar and his friends are still in Agra, but we don't know where. What do we do now?'

Muzaffar glanced around at the milling crowds. Most were headed towards their own rooms. Some, the more devout, had begun to congregate at the mosque in readiness for the evening namaz. 'Let's go out on to the ghat and sit there for a while,' Muzaffar said. 'I can't think in all this commotion.'

'It's going to be equally crowded on the ghat,' Akram pointed out as they made their out of the sarai and towards the riverside ghat, the long rows of wide steps that led down to the Yamuna. The ghats fulfilled many purposes. They acted as a convenient landing stage for the boats that came, laden with merchandise, along the river – bringing raw silk from Patna, cotton from Bengal, and innumerable other goods. They were a platform for the washermen who took the laundry from the sarai down to the river and used the steps to scour, scrub and pound before rinsing. The ghats provided easy and safe access to the pious Hindus among the sarai's residents, who went down to the sacred river to offer prayers, flowers and coins. And, occasionally, they were a place for people who just wanted to sit and watch the sun go down.

'The ghats will be crowded,' Muzaffar conceded, 'but at least they won't be enclosed, like this place is. Here, I'm feeling as if the people are closing on me.' He took a deep, relieved breath as they reached the ghat.

The sun had set, leaving the few clouds in the sky a vivid orange and gold, fast merging into the greyness of the evening. The river, where it was visible through the prows and oars, shimmered in the reflected light of the sunset and the lamps being lit along the riverfront. A nobleman's long, sleek boat, its brightly coloured oars dipping in unison, its snowy white yak tails and its flags floating in the breeze, went gliding silently by, a delicate maiden among the muscular masculine hulks of the cargo boats around it.

They walked on, along the ghat, past the far wall of the sarai. It was less busy here, with only a few boats – too late to find a berth in front of the sarai – having docked. There were several porters around, a couple of boatmen attending to the unloading of the boats, and some labourers lighting small fires further inland on the shore to either warm chilled bones or cook dinner. Or both, thought Muzaffar.

He looked out across the river towards the flickering lights of the city. 'We seem to have run up against a wall,' he said in a terse, tense voice. 'Those letters, that woman – Shireen will need a few days to identify her. If she is able to. As for the piebald horse that probably belongs to Mirza Sajjad Khan, we cannot do anything until Sajjad Khan returns from this hunting trip he's gone off on. And now, just as I thought we'd struck gold... it turns out even Omar is out of town.' He grunted with annoyance, so loud that a porter passing by with a large wooden box on his bent back looked up in surprise.

'I suppose the one thing we *can* do is to try and find the horse trader Shakeel Alam. He was a friend of Mumtaz Hassan's, and he vanished most unexpectedly. I am inclined to think there is something the matter there.'

'So?' Akram said. 'How do you propose to set about finding Shakeel Alam? You've already been to the nakhkhas and asked about him, haven't you?'

'Yes, I asked if anybody had seen him or knew where he was. They hadn't, and they didn't know. Maybe now I should ask if anybody knew where he was staying in Agra. Perhaps we'll be lucky again.'

11

THE NAKHKHAS WAS the same steaming, seething mass of humanity and cattle that it had been the last time Muzaffar had visited. The enclosure where Shakeel Alam had been selling his horses had been occupied by a rotund Afghan horse trader who had sold off most of his horses and was now getting ready to pack up his ample earnings and head for home. He tried to sell Akram one of the remaining horses – a bad-tempered roan with a penchant for snapping at people's ears – and condescended, with ill grace, to answer their questions when informed that his visitors wanted information, not mounts.

'I'd seen the man around, spoken to him now and then,' he admitted. 'But I don't know where he stayed. Why don't you check at one of the sarais?'

'There are over fifty sarais in Agra, my friend,' Muzaffar said with a wry smile. 'Do you know of anyone who might know where Shakeel Alam stayed?'

The man stroked the roan's neck with a pensive expression on his face, his head darting expertly away when the animal tried to nip him. 'Ayub might know,' he said suddenly, and jerking his head up, yelled to a stable hand who was sweeping out the far end of the enclosure. 'Ayub! Leave that and come here!'

Ayub shook his head when Muzaffar put the question to him. 'I don't know, huzoor. Maybe he stayed at one of the sarais in town. He never said.'

Muzaffar exhaled, deeply disappointed. 'Come, Akram,' he said, as Ayub turned away to return to his work. 'We should –' a thought struck him, and he called Ayub back. 'Do you know where his horses were stabled?'

The man shrugged, shaking his head. He waited for Muzaffar to say something, and when the nobleman kept silent, he went back to the end of the enclosure and picking up his twig broom, resumed his sweeping. The plump horse trader had collared a potential buyer and was extolling the virtues of the roan to him. Muzaffar stared fixedly at the tableau, hearing the man praise the beauty and the speed of his horse. Just as Shakeel Alam had praised, to the skies, that palomino to Muzaffar.

He whirled and grabbed Akram by the arm. 'If we can find out where Shakeel Alam stabled his horses, we might be able to find out where he stayed – because his horses might still be there, at the stables. Probably his servants, too, whoever helped him with the horses. Maybe the servants will be able to offer some information on where he could have gone. Or if we find out where he stayed –'

'Muzaffar,' Akram said quietly, 'It's a long shot. Very long. Besides, how will you go finding his horses? There must be thousands of horses in Agra.'

'Yes,' Muzaffar's voice rose in excitement, as he tugged his friend along with towards the other end of the enclosure. He strode towards Ayub, busy sweeping the floor, completely oblivious of them. 'Yes, there must be thousands of horses in Agra, but I hadn't ever seen a horse like that palomino of his. If he hadn't sold it when he disappeared – we might have a chance.'

'A palomino, huzoor?' Ayub looked puzzled. 'The black and white horse?'

'No. A golden-brown one. Like polished bronze, with a cream tail and mane. This one was a mare.'

'Oh. Oh, yes. I remember that one. A nobleman going back to Lahore bought her.'

But Muzaffar was barely listening; he had latched on to the man's earlier words. 'A black and white horse? Did Shakeel Alam have a black and white horse too?'

The man nodded. 'Yes. That was one of the first horses to be sold. A local amir bought it.'

'So what do you plan to do?' Basheer said, sprawling against a silken bolster and chewing a paan. 'You have to wait, whether you like it or not. Come with me to the Taj Mahal instead. We were talking about it last night at dinner, and Akram told me you've never seen it since it was built. That is shameful; we cannot have you stay in Agra and not see the Empress's mausoleum.'

Muzaffar chuckled, too amused to be able to contain it. 'And if the Diwan-i-kul should come to know that I am gallivanting around Agra like a tourist? When I should have been investigating the murder of your father?' The astonishment he felt at Basheer's unselfconscious dismissal of the circumstances surfaced. 'He was your father. Surely you would want his killer to be brought to justice?'

Basheer did not respond immediately. His gaze shifted to the paandaan lying near his feet; then beyond, to the patterns of the Persian carpet on the floor; and then to his hand, playing absently with the areca nut cutter lying beside the paandaan. When he looked up, it was with a blend of bitterness and accusation in his eyes. 'You think I'm a poor excuse for a son, don't you, Jang Sahib? Abba thought so too.'

'I never implied –'

Basheer waved aside Muzaffar's words. 'It's all right, I don't mind. Why should one mind the truth?' He picked up an areca nut from the small octagonal silver container next to the paandaan, and fitted it between the strong brass jaws of the cutter. 'And I do admit, I'm not especially interested in finding out who did Abba in. What difference will it make? If it brought back Abba and made my mother stop crying, I could see the sense in it. But other than that? I won't gain, will I?' He had been working the cutter, swiftly and precisely decimating the areca nut. He now glanced up from the shreds of areca nut that lay on the silver platter. 'Don't look so shocked, Jang Sahib,' he said, with a sarcastic laugh as he picked up another nut. Hidden, not too far below the surface of that sarcasm, was sadness; Muzaffar could sense it. A sorrow had to cut deep indeed into a man's soul to show its gloom even when he was trying to hide it behind anger. 'I am the way I am because of what my father taught me. Look at nothing but money, he said. Human relations are all very well, but it's money that eventually matters. Nothing but money.' He put the nut down intact. After a moment's steady, unbroken silence, he flung the cutter away with a force that was vicious in its intensity. The cutter clattered noisily as it hit the paandaan, then thudded across the thick carpet beyond.

It was Basheer himself who broke the awkward silence that fell across the room. He heaved a sigh – of regret or resignation, Muzaffar could not tell – and picked up the silver platter, offering the slivered areca nut to Akram and Muzaffar. 'I can tell you this: my father would not want me to mourn him to the extent that the family's fortunes suffered. He would rather I went back to the trade right after the funeral, than that I wept and grieved and went hunting for his killer.'

Muzaffar and Akram both having declined the areca nut, Basheer slipped a few pieces into his already reddened mouth. 'Which brings us back to what we were discussing. You are hunting for his killer; the Diwan-i-kul has entrusted you with that task, and I am not one to interfere with that. I know better than to come in the way of government work. But seriously, what do you hope to achieve today? What do you have planned?'

'I've already told you –'

Again, Basheer butted in. 'Yes. You've told me. There's the question of the piebald horse, which now appears to have been sold to Sajjad Khan by none other than Abba's friend Shakeel Alam. But you don't know where Shakeel Alam is. You don't know where Omar is, or when he will return to the sarai. You don't know when

Sajjad Khan will come back home – and I don't suppose you even know what you'll do once he's back in town, do you? If you go and ask him if he was the one who got Abba killed, he's hardly going to say yes, even if he did.' Beside the mattress stood a brass spittoon, its flared rim decorated with engraved lotuses. Basheer picked it up and spat into it. 'Well?' he said, looking up. 'What then?'

His host, thought Muzaffar, was turning out to be an interesting man. At first glance, at that fateful and awkward dinner party the night Mumtaz Hassan was killed, Basheer had struck him as being a put-upon but sullen glutton. A slighted son, who had – and perhaps understandably so – no affection for his father. This was the same man; this man, who skillfully supervised the building of his father's tomb, and had so shrewdly summed up Muzaffar's investigation. Mumtaz Hassan's had been a sharp intellect; his son's possibly equaled it. And perhaps was tempered with a little more morality.

'I'd probably need to spy on Sajjad Khan,' Muzaffar said. 'I don't know yet; too many pieces are missing. There's that mysterious woman, too. We don't know yet who she is.' He sat back, leaning against the bolster, looking despondent. 'I thought it might help if I knew when Sajjad Khan is going to be back. He and those three guests whom he's taken –' his eyes, dull and despairing, suddenly snapped open and he sat up with a jerk. 'Allah,' he breathed, turning to Akram. 'Could it be?!'

'*What*?'

'Sajjad Khan went out of town hunting with three guests. He won't be back for some days yet, perhaps. Omar and his two friends – three men in all – left the sarai and went to stay with an acquaintance of Omar's in town. And from there, they went off somewhere else, out of town. And will not be back for a few days yet, perhaps. Is that mere coincidence? Or could Omar and his two companions be Sajjad Khan's three guests?'

Akram wagged his head, acknowledging the logic of the statement. 'It could be.'

'And if Omar had had a quarrel with Mumtaz Hassan, that might have led eventually to murder – and who better to connive with, than another enemy of Mumtaz Hassan's? In any case, Omar was from Bijapur, an outsider in Agra; hiring an assassin to enter Mumtaz Hassan's room may not be as easy for an outsider as it would be for a man who lived in Agra. It just may be...' his voice dwindled into a murmur and died down as he puzzled over the ramifications of the theory that had suddenly sprung out of nowhere.

'Still,' Basheer said, 'you can't do anything much today, can you? Neither Sajjad Khan nor his guests – if they *are* Omar and his men – are in Agra. Until they come back, what can you do? And you don't know when they will be back.'

'I can go to his haveli and find out. In disguise, perhaps, because I doubt if that suspicious steward of his will give me any information if he sees me like this.'

'I have a better idea,' Basheer said, gathering up a few more pieces of areca nut and putting them in his mouth. 'Let me send a man with an innocuous note for Sajjad Khan. The man will be given instructions that the note is to be handed over to Sajjad Khan only; and if Sajjad Khan is not in residence, then the man is to find out when he will be back.'

'And where he has gone,' added Muzaffar, with a nod of approval. 'Yes, that might work. But what note will you write? What if Sajjad Khan has returned this morning? Wouldn't he get suspicious if he received a note from his enemy's son? Especially if the enemy had recently been killed? Even more so if Sajjad Khan *is* the killer.'

Basheer chewed on, looking pensive. 'I could say I'm organizing a small feast in honour of Abba,' he said after a while. 'And that I'm inviting all the important men in Agra. Even Abba's business rivals. That should lull his suspicions.'

'I hope so.'

Basheer got to his feet, brushing his choga down with plump hands. 'And I sincerely hope that Sajjad Khan is not back in town to see that note and accept an invitation to an expense I have no intention of incurring,' he said drily. 'Wait here while I write out the note and send my man off. Then we'll go see the Taj Mahal. You'll like it, Jang Sahib; mark my words. You'll like it.'

Basheer had been right, thought Muzaffar with a small, private sigh of contentment. He *did* like it. All the way from the Jilaukhaana, where they dismounted, to the gate, with its splendid inlay of jasper on white marble – and through, into the vast walled garden in which stood the Empress's rauza. Muzaffar's memories of it had been piecemeal, a fragmented glimpse here, a half-forgotten recollection there. He had remembered it as being large, large to the point of obscenity, or so he had thought when he had first seen the naked brickwork rising high above the Yamuna. Now, clear and clean as moonlight, perfectly symmetrical and looking more fragile than a dream, it seemed to him nothing short of exquisite.

But yet large. It took them a good quarter of an hour to walk the distance from the gate to the rauza. That, of course, was not just because the garden was so large, but because Basheer was so enthusiastic, so eager to share his passion for the building and its gardens. As they walked along the bank of the water channels, he told them how the flowers of the gardens – the roses and irises, the tulips, crown imperials and chrysanthemums – were duplicated in the carvings and inlay of the rauza. 'And you know, of course, the legend behind the tulip,' he said, and waited only to note Akram's wide-eyed look of blankness. Muzaffar, looking past the fountains, towards the cypresses and fruit trees of the garden, did not react. From somewhere in the recesses of his memory arose an image of dozens of gardeners and labourers, hard at work planting trees. That had been years ago, he recalled; Khan Sahib, Zeenat Aapa and their entourage – Muzaffar included – had stopped by in Agra on their way to Lahore. They had made their almost-mandatory trip to the site of the Taj Mahal, and Muzaffar had been struck by the trees. All ungainly saplings yet, but holding within their spindly branches the promise of much shade and abundant fruit in the years to come. 'There will be no dearth of water for irrigation,' Khan Sahib had said with satisfaction, indicating the river beyond. 'This will be a fine garden.'

But Basheer was talking about the tulip, that flower so beautiful, but so short-lived in the brief winter of Agra.

'It is derived from the story of the lovers Shirin and Farhad. When Farhad heard that his beloved Shirin had died, he mounted his horse and rode it over a hill, plunging to his death. From each of his wounds, wherever a drop of blood fell to the ground, a tulip blossomed.' He smiled with self-satisfaction.

'What a ghastly story,' Akram said. 'It's brutal to assign such a hideous origin for such a pretty flower.' Basheer looked affronted, as if he had been personally insulted.

They walked on, past the square pool, its shimmering waters reflecting the rauza. It was a reflection both broken and enhanced by the lotuses and the goldfish in the water. The twenty-four fountains along the periphery of the pool gurgled soothingly. Basheer, all of a sudden fired with a zeal to hurry up the steps to the rauza, pushed past the few travellers who were idling beside the pool. 'Come on, Jang Sahib; hurry up, Akram! Once this rabble gets to the rauza, we won't be able to see a thing,' he hissed.

'Just about a month left for the Empress's urs,' said Basheer with a sigh of relief as the three noblemen ascended the short flight of steps up to the rauza. Mumtaz Mahal, having died in childbirth, was considered worthy of veneration. Her urs, the anniversary of her death, was therefore observed as an annual event, with thousands – including the bereaved Emperor – coming to pray for the soul of the lady who lay buried here. 'It will be a hundred times more crowded then. Come. This way.'

Like a connoisseur keeping the best for the last, Basheer led them first of all to the mosque, off to the left. Muzaffar was used to seeing mosques at the tombs of the rich and powerful; those who came to visit a tomb were encouraged to spend a while in prayer for the departed soul. But most mosques at tombs were small, nondescript ones – often just a wall with the direction of prayer, the west, marked by a decorative closed arch.

The mosque at the Empress's tomb overshadowed all the others. Its three domes, of white marble, topped a façade of red sandstone, adorned with inlays of white marble and intricate painting. Directly above the imposing central arch leading into the mosque, a recessed inset held a painting: a vase of flowers, spreading out in a flamboyant display of petals and leaves, the vase itself flanked by two stylized Taj Mahals. Beyond, the interior of the mosque was appreciably colder than the outside. Not just because they were no longer in the sunshine, but because this was darker, dimmer – a place, even though there was nobody on their knees right now, of prayer and quietude.

Even Basheer, so bustling and brash outside, seemed suitably subdued. 'The musallas,' he murmured, in a mere whisper. 'Don't miss the musallas.' The floor, Muzaffar noticed, was polished red sandstone. But not merely red sandstone; across that floor had been created a pattern, the precise shape and size of musallas or prayer rugs. Strips of white marble, black marble and golden Jaisalmer stone formed dozens of ready-to-use prayer rugs for worshippers. You could come in here, kneel next to your neighbour, and say your prayers without fearing that you would intrude in his space or he in yours.

'Ibrahim did some of the inlay at the Mehmaan Khaana,' Basheer said as they made their way, walking across the front of the rauza, to the guest house – the Mehmaan Khaana – that mirrored the mosque. The Mehmaan Khaana was proof of the Mughals' incurable love for symmetry. A mosque had to be built next to the rauza, but erecting a building on one side of the rauza and leaving the other side bare would have resulted in an unpardonably asymmetrical arrangement. Therefore the Mehmaan Khaana. Visitors to the Empress's tomb could stay here, had been the logic. They need not, if they came to pay their respects to the dead queen or to offer prayers for her, stay in the city and trudge all the way here. No, they could stay right here. It gave Shahjahan a good excuse to create a building on the other side too, right opposite the mosque.

It looked very much like the mosque in its essentials, too: the same red sandstone and white marble; the same trio of white domes. The floor did not have musallas, though, and of course there was no beautifully carved mihrab, the sealed arch denoting west. Muzaffar glanced up and gasped at the sight of the vaulted ceiling, white painted on red in a brilliantly precise network of interlocking triangles and stars and pyramids. At one end, where all the triangles tapered off, was a circular mass of white painted flowers: a garden caught in a spiderweb.

'Here,' Basheer said, 'this way.'

He led them along the inside of the Mehmaan Khaana, then out again into the sunlight, pointing out, as they walked, the flowers carved into the red sandstone façade of the Mehmaan Khaana. 'Ibrahim helped on some of those,' he said. 'Just by the way. It wasn't his main work at the Taj Mahal, though,' he added, with a smirk, a combination of self-satisfaction and almost childish glee at knowing something his companions did not.

They walked, from the Mehmaan Khaana, along the edge of the colossal platform on which the rauza stood. The marble was cold, cold as the now dead empress who had lived and laughed and brought the palace to life while she had been alive. Now she lay buried, thought Muzaffar, deep below this extravagant tomb; was it really, as everybody said, an ostentatious symbol of the Baadshah's deep love for his wife? Or was it, as some cynics said, really just an excuse to indulge in his favourite hobby, building great monuments to his own everlasting glory?

As if he could read Muzaffar's mind, Akram said, 'The Baadshah surpassed himself with the Taj Mahal, didn't he? What do you think, Muzaffar? Back in Dilli, the Jama Masjid and the fort *are* beautiful, but there's no comparing them to this. This is like a little bit of paradise brought down to earth.' He turned to Basheer. 'Is it true, that he had the hands of all the artisans chopped off? So that they could never create anything as beautiful for anyone again?'

Basheer halted, almost in mid-stride, jaw dropping open in surprise. The next moment, the surprise was gone, replaced by a blend of scorn and annoyance. 'Akram, if you weren't my cousin, I'd have hit you for that,' he spat out. 'Have you left your brains behind in Dilli? Ah, but you never did have any to start off with, now that I think of it –'

'Here! There's no call to be rude. It's not as if I'm the only one who's saying that. It's a common enough belief!'

'A thousand people believe a falsehood, and it becomes a truth? Don't be stupid! Do you know how many men worked on the Taj Mahal? And how much the Baadshah paid them? *Millions.* And some of the best stone carvers around today are men who learned their trade as apprentices to the stone carvers working on the Taj. What do you think? After investing that much, the Baadshah would simply chop off their hands? And they'd keep quiet about it, too? If he had, wouldn't all the *other* stone carvers in the realm flee immediately? To Persia, or Arabia, or even down into the Deccan? No! *You* think they'd just sit around waiting for the Baadshah to call them up to work on his next project – obviously he'd have to get fresh workmen, since he'd already incapacitated the ones who'd worked for him earlier? And when *that* project was over, they'd wait patiently for the Baadshah to hand over their wages and line them up to chop their hands off?'

Basheer had said it all in one mad, indignant rush, the words almost running into each other. He now stopped to draw in a huge gulp of air, and before anybody could interrupt, carried on. 'Really, Akram. Who do you think did the carvings at the fort in Dilli? Or at the Jama Masjid? Amateurs? Have you seen the carving there? And the carving here' – he swept his arm in a flourish, indicating the dados along the outside of the main rauza. 'Or the inlay work? Is there much difference?'

He moved off, briskly for a man of his size, towards the rauza. 'And look at this! All of this – the gardens, the buildings, the calligraphy. What will you say next? That the Baadshah dug out the brains of the men who designed them, so that they could never think up anything so wonderful again?!'

'I'm sorry, Basheer,' Akram said in a small, plaintive voice. 'I suppose it's all a rumour.'

'Don't listen to rumours,' Basheer snapped back. 'Use your head. That's why Allah gave you one.' He turned away, striding off towards the parapet that overlooked the river beyond. Akram and Muzaffar followed, Akram looking stricken, Muzaffar amused. Behind them, a little trickle of visitors – drawn by Basheer's vociferous tirade – had latched on to the heels of the noblemen. There were whispers and a few stifled giggles; Basheer had, it seemed, attracted an audience with just that one impassioned speech. They kept their distance, though. Every commoner knew that it was safer to not linger too close to an amir. Who knew when an amir, catching a faint whiff of sweat from an unwashed body, would hit out at its owner?

Basheer walked on, oblivious. 'Look at the minar,' he said, waving a hand in the direction of one of the four white towers that surrounded the rauza. 'See the black mortar marking each block of the marble? *See it?*'

Muzaffar, looking out over the Yamuna, did not respond. Akram nodded.

'Ah, but it's not black mortar, you see.' The smile, the smug look of the pedant, flickered. 'It's black marble, and it doesn't mark the blocks of marble; it just pretends to. It's parchinkari!'

But it was on the rauza itself that the parchinkari – stone inlaid in marble – was truly awe-inspiring. Basheer led his two guests across the platform, and to the outside of the rauza. The dadoes here were a garden replicated in marble: an expanse of flowering plants – tulips, daffodils, crown imperials, irises – all carved exactly as they were in real life. The same size, the same shapes, the same imperfections. As if they had been captured in ice, frozen and frosted white for all eternity. Above and below were bands of parchinkari: more flowers, but stylized. Garnets, carnelians, agate and jasper had been used here to depict swirling vines and geometrical leaves, neat buds and perfectly symmetrical three-petalled blossoms.

'Artists used to draw the patterns on the marble with henna first,' Basheer explained. 'And then the stone cutters – the parchinkars – would carefully chisel away at the pattern, creating grooves and hollows into which they'd fit the gemstones. Abba was one of those who used to supply the stones, you know; he'd come to Agra from his travels, bringing the stones that went into all of this. Not the marble or the sandstone; that was for the others, the Emperor's men who were entrusted with the quarrying and carting of that heavy, dangerously difficult stone – one slip, and a block could crush a man into oblivion. As far as the overseers were concerned,' – his smile turned sarcastic – 'what was worse, one slip and the block could develop a crack that would render it useless.'

He let his outstretched hand drift across the surface of the parchinkari. 'I would accompany him occasionally, because I loved seeing the building take shape. I loved watching the men at work. Especially the parchinkars and the sang tarashes, the stone workers. *Their* work was the most fascinating.' Basheer paused. 'Let's go in; there's no point trying to tell you things that you had best see for yourself.'

The little crowd of hangers-on had fallen behind; some were looking out over the river, admiring the view of the Yamuna from the platform surrounding the rauza. Others had drifted off towards the Mehmaan Khaana, or the mosque. Basheer led Akram and Muzaffar through the arched doorway and into the rauza.

Inside, the Empress's cenotaph stood directly below the dome of the rauza, surrounded by an octagonal screen of white marble. The screen was a net of flowers, a filigree so fine that Muzaffar wondered at the immense patience and sureness of hand that must have gone into its crafting. Along the top of the screen – six feet above the ground, Muzaffar's own height – were more flowers, carved and inlaid. Pretty tendrils, rich green leaves and flowers with red petals and large stamens.

'The Baadshah had originally commissioned a golden railing, inlaid with precious stones, to surround the cenotaph,' Basheer said. His voice echoed eerily in the chamber, losing itself under the vastness of the dome. Despite the softening effect of the Persian carpets on the floor and the silken hangings on the walls, this was a huge, empty chamber that emphasized the grandeur of the rauza, and the comparative insignificance of the three men. 'But then he changed his mind,' Basheer added. 'He guessed, I think, that it would be too great a temptation for some people.'

The sang tarashes, the parchinkars, and the artists had reserved their best work, their finest and most intricate display of parchinkari and carving, for the cenotaph of the Empress. The flowers here, a veritable sheet of them covering her cenotaph, were a thousand times more delicate than those that decorated the exterior of the rauza.

The three men passed through the gateway of blood-red jasper that pierced the screen, hanging on gold hinges. In silence, they crossed the floor, with its pattern of six pointed stars, worked in thin lines of black marble inlaid in the white of the floor. At the Empress's cenotaph, topped with the symbolic takhti or writing tablet that signified the grave of a woman, they came to a standstill, looking down in awestruck wonder at the profusion of flowers that had been inlaid on the surface of the cenotaph.

'This is exquisite,' Muzaffar whispered, after a few moments. 'It's – it's matchless.' He bent, peering at one of the flowers. 'There are so many shades in this,' he muttered, voice low with something approaching disbelief. 'It's almost as if it really were a flower, the petal tinted different shades, the sunlight falling here but not there, one edge frayed but the centre still fresh and newly blooming... one would think you could pluck the flower and put it in a vase, it's so real.'

'The hues and tones are because of how they used the stone,' Basheer said. 'Stone has shades too, you know. Like lapis lazuli; it can be a bright, vivid light blue, like the morning sky. Or it can be a deep, rich midnight blue. And it can be a hundred shades in between. That was what the artists and the parchinkars took advantage of, you know: they would use copper wires to cut each block of stone into thin slices, sometimes each slice a different shade. And then they would put it together, one slice here, one slice there, combined for the best effect. I have seen – see, here – a flower that is only an inch across, but has more than fifty different pieces of stone in it.'

'You have good eyes, then,' Muzaffar said with a shaky laugh. 'To be able to count the number of pieces in that.'

Basheer looked reproachful. 'I saw the parchinkar working on that, Jang Sahib. I saw him put that flower together.'

He turned and walked away, out beyond the screen and through the arch into the sunlight outside. Muzaffar heaved a sigh and glanced towards Akram; his friend shrugged and then winked and shook his head. 'The high and mighty are swift to take offence,' he murmured, and strode off in Basheer's wake. 'Was that Ibrahim?' he asked, when he caught up with his cousin outside. 'The artisan who did that fabulous bit of parchinkari?'

Muzaffar emerged in time to hear Basheer's reply. 'No, no. Ibrahim didn't do that; I don't remember who did. Ibrahim was mainly a sang tarash; a stone carver – not a parchinkar. The parchinkari is very specialized work. Some sang tarashes did parchinkari too, but not all. Ibrahim could do it. In fact, he did help in the parchinkari on that screen. Abba was very impressed with Ibrahim's work. So impressed that he wanted it to be replicated on his own – Abba's – rauza. But Mahmood isn't that skilled.' He had calmed down now. Arms slung loosely behind his back, fingers clasped, he strolled along towards the steps leading down to the gardens. A few visitors were making their way up, a couple of them carrying flowers to be placed on the Empress's cenotaph. Basheer waited for them to pass, then went down the steps.

'Abba used to visit the building site often,' he said as they began the walk back towards the gate. Now that the day had advanced, the sun high in the sky and the air as warm as it could get on a winter's day in Agra, more visitors were streaming in to see the Empress's tomb. People from across Hindustan, of course; but also foreigners: Turks and Persians, and a few light-haired, fair-skinned Europeans. Mostly traders, thought Muzaffar; men who had come to Agra with horses, pearls, coffee, oddities and luxuries produced only in far-away European cities. Men, too, who came to buy the goods that Agra produced: indigo, saltpetre, vermilion, quicksilver, jewellery, brocades. These were men on business, men with probably little time to spare on sightseeing. But the Taj Mahal was no mere sight; it was a marvel.

'It was Abba who first told me of the calamities that struck Ibrahim,' Basheer continued. 'I was very young, so he didn't tell me everything. But I do know that all of a sudden, everything went wrong for Ibrahim. His wife disappeared, his chisel broke – what could be worse for a sang tarash? – his best friend died in an accident, and then he fell ill.' He nibbled unhappily at the inside of his cheek. 'His hand became so useless that he couldn't even lift a hammer and chisel any more.'

'It's not just his hand that's useless,' Akram retorted. 'His mind's gone too. We met him the other day, you know. He was babbling on about jinn and whatnot. Kept saying that the jinn were angry, that was why the scaffolding collapsed.'

Basheer ducked his head sheepishly, as if by dint of employing Mahmood, he also became responsible for the ramblings of Mahmood's father's mind. 'Yes, I've heard that too. This isn't the first time – but believing in jinn is no sign of madness,' he said, his voice growing gruff with a defence he did not himself seem to have much faith in. 'The Qu'ran itself says that Allah created jinn. Would you refute the Qu'ran?' The last sentence rang with a half-hearted defiance.

Muzaffar, trailing behind a few steps, found Akram looking back pleadingly at him. The two cousins had come to a halt, and a couple of paces down the path brought Muzaffar beside them. 'I don't think that was what Akram meant,' he said soothingly. 'But belief is one thing, obsession quite another.'

Basheer looked long into Muzaffar's eyes, his own clouded with something between lugubriousness and indecision; Muzaffar could not say what. Finally, with a shake of his head, he mumbled, 'As you say. Come, let us be going. We can fit in a visit to Abba's rauza before we go back to the haveli for lunch.'

They were not, however, to leave the Taj Mahal so soon; between the gate and the Jilaukhaana, Basheer met an old friend.

'Basheer Sahib!' The words were half drowned in the hubbub of visitors coming and going, but they were loud enough to make Basheer whirl around, his head turning this way and that, searching for the voice that had called to him. Jostling his way through a large party of Afghan travellers came a man dressed in threadbare pajamas and a long jama of thickish cotton, covered over messily with two coarse shawls, one a dull blue and the other beige. The man must have been in his fifties; his jaw had not been shaved for at least a week, and his greying hair was long enough to brush against his cheek despite the turban wound untidily around his head. The smile, though, was genuine, the eyes gleaming brightly with sincere joy at having noticed Basheer.

'Mangal!' Basheer caught the man by his forearms, and Muzaffar, looking on, was surprised at the warmth in the nobleman's greeting for a man who was obviously not of the first rank. That Muzaffar himself would not have thought twice about having a friend so down at heel was nothing unusual, but that the fashionable Basheer, always so fastidious, should have made a friend such as this... and was not ashamed to admit the friendship in public, too. Passersby were glancing over their shoulders towards the two men, now chatting animatedly, Basheer's hands still gripping Mangal's arms. It made Muzaffar think better of Basheer. He realized, with sudden pleasure, that he had been thinking better of Basheer for a couple of days now. This was an intelligent man, a sensitive and sincere one, even if he was given to getting overly emotional about matters that he held close to his heart. Perhaps the lack of emotion when it came to Mumtaz Hassan's murder stemmed from deep emotion, too – the hurt and humiliation of being made the object of a father's contempt.

What if Basheer had been the one behind the killing of Mumtaz Hassan? Muzaffar doubted it; the clues did not seem to point that way. But if he was... this growing liking for the man would make it very difficult for Muzaffar to hand him over to the Diwan-i-kul.

Basheer had brought his friend over to where Muzaffar and Akram stood. Mangal, it turned out, had been a watchman at the site where they now stood. 'Years ago,' he said, somewhat cowed by the presence of the two strange noblemen. 'I was here all the while the rauza was being built.'

'But where now, Mangal? Are you still working here?' Basheer butted in. 'The last time I came – two months back – I didn't see you. Come to think of it, not even any time over the past couple of years.'

Mangal shook his head, his smile benign. 'I don't work here anymore, Basheer Sahib. My son is married now, and has two little children who like to be pampered by their grandfather. We have a small patch of land that we till and farm, on the way to Sikandra.'

A few minutes passed in more questions, more answers, more sharing of old memories. Muzaffar gathered that Basheer had been a boy, visiting the building site of the Taj Mahal, when Mangal – a young man then – had been one of those patrolling the grounds and keeping vandals and thieves at bay. An unlikely but strong friendship had sprung up between the two, and it appeared to have endured. Basheer mentioned the death of Mumtaz Hassan, and Mangal expressed his grief. 'I wish I had known,' he said. 'I would have liked to pay my respects. But living out there, away from the city, we get little news. Do you know, this is the first time I have been able to return to the lady's mausoleum since it was completed?'

'It is a coincidence that I should have met you here,' Basheer said, the momentary embarrassment caused by the news of Mumtaz Hassan's death now blown away, his smile back in place. 'We were just now talking of the days when the tomb was being built. I was telling my friends here about Ibrahim and his ill luck. Remember? One misfortune after another.'

Mangal's face had lit up briefly when Basheer had smiled; now his expression changed. Not grief, exactly; not even pity, but something like regret. Regret at a life wasted. He nodded. 'Yes, that was sad indeed. He was a very good craftsman, wasn't he? I remember you pulling me along to see some of his work.'

'I was a great admirer of his.' Basheer's smile was sunny. He chuckled the next moment, clapping Akram suddenly and unexpectedly on the back. 'And my cousin here says Ibrahim has gone off his head!'

'I never –'

'Oh, yes, you did! I ask you, Mangal, can a man be said to have lost his mind simply because he believes in jinn? Ibrahim told Akram and Muzaffar that the jinn are angry, that is why they are harming Abba's rauza. And now Akram and Muzaffar think that Ibrahim is mad. What do you say, Mangal? Eh?'

Mangal maintained a diplomatic silence, regarding Akram and Muzaffar in turn with a curious but respectful interest. 'Go on, Mangal! I know you wouldn't jump to conclusions like that about any man, least of all Ibrahim. You knew him slightly, didn't you? Back in the good old days? Did you think him mad?'

Mangal shook his head. 'Not then, no. I have not met him since. Perhaps there is something other than his belief in jinn that makes huzoor think him – ah – unstable?'

'He claims to have seen jinn!' Akram spluttered.

'I have too,' Mangal said gently.

12

THE BROKEN SCAFFOLDING at Mumtaz Hassan's mausoleum had been repaired; the labourers appeared to have recovered from their fear of further injuries – or, worse, death – and work was proceeding at what looked, to the untrained eye, a smooth, efficient pace. Basheer, having told Muzaffar and Akram that he would be back soon, had taken himself off to the rauza, where Zulfiqar was in charge. Akram had been inclined to sit in the shed that functioned as an office; Muzaffar, who had been restive and laconic ever since their visit to the Taj Mahal, wanted to stretch his legs. Akram acquiesced.

'I didn't realize you wanted to walk over to Ibrahim's hut,' he said, when Muzaffar's wanderings – conducted almost entirely in silence – brought them near the mango tree sheltering the stone cottage. 'Does this have anything to do with what Basheer's friend said?'

Muzaffar came to a standstill, but did not immediately answer his friend. 'I don't know,' he said eventually. 'It *is* strange, I think. Mangal seemed like a sensible man. And then he suddenly tells us that he saw jinn, and that too at the Empress's tomb. And what did he see of the jinn? Lights dancing about above the ground, the night after Ibrahim's wife vanished. Why should any man automatically assume that those are jinn? It could well have been men.'

'Doing what? At a construction site? And that too an imperial one, patrolled constantly by watchmen?'

Muzaffar frowned. 'I don't know. Perhaps they were stealing something – stone? Even slabs of marble can be precious if they're of the quality that was used at the Empress's rauza. They could be worth stealing. Especially if one could pretend to be a genie and scare off any watchmen who happened to be in the vicinity.' The frown changed to a grin, his expression lightening immediately. 'We seem to have stumbled on to an old crime, Akram!'

Akram did not smile back. His face was uncharacteristically grim as he said, 'An *old* crime, Muzaffar. Don't forget that. You have a new crime to solve, and a promise the Diwan-i-kul will hold you to. Don't let your attention be diverted.'

'That can hardly happen,' Muzaffar commented, as they resumed their stroll. 'An old theft? And one that was probably never even noticed? Why should it make any difference now, twenty-five years later? And what difference should it make to me?' He shook his head, as if literally shaking the thought from his mind. 'No, it's just all this talk of jinn. It makes me – not uncomfortable, precisely – but just a little curious. Why is Ibrahim so obsessed with jinn?'

'You can ask him yourself. Here he comes.'

And there he was, the old stone cutter, limping towards them. They were a stone's throw from the cottage, and Ibrahim, it seemed, had noticed them. He was not effusive in his welcome; this man, thought Muzaffar, could never be effusive. A man whose emotions revealed themselves only infrequently, and that too in ways that could be frightening. The memory of Ibrahim, clutching the quilt and wrestling with a frustrated Taufeeq, insisting that jinn were responsible for the collapsed scaffolding, came back vividly to Muzaffar. This man could go to extremes when it came to expressing emotion. Right now, thankfully, the ruling emotion appeared to be a lazy complacence, as if the warmth of the sun had mellowed him. He gave a half-smile, dipped his head in turn at Muzaffar and Akram, and murmured 'So what are you doing *here*, huzoor?'

Muzaffar told him of Basheer's visit to Mumtaz Hassan's rauza. Ibrahim, listening with only half an ear, looked about him, and finding a convenient fallen tree, hobbled over to it and settled himself down. His pet dog, which had appeared in the meantime, trailed along in its master's wake. Ibrahim was a good five or six paces away from the two noblemen; Akram glanced enquiringly towards Muzaffar. 'Shall we take ourselves off?' he whispered. Muzaffar nodded and was about to bid farewell to Ibrahim when the man said, 'I came away because it is painful for me to stand long. Surely you see that, huzoor? I cannot stand long, even with the crutch to support me. Come here and sit a while, if you have nothing else to do.' His dog had come to his side and was burying its nose in Ibrahim's hand.

Muzaffar turned to Akram and said in a low voice. 'I will spend some time here with Ibrahim. Would you like to stay?'

But Akram preferred the relative comfort of the office shed near the rauza. He, declined and left, promising to wait for Muzaffar at the rauza. Muzaffar walked over to the fallen tree and having tested its stability with a well-placed hand, sat down beside Ibrahim. The dog glanced up at him with its brown eyes, assessing Muzaffar. And probably realizing, with the uncanny sixth sense that dogs seemed to possess, that here was a potential friend. Muzaffar patted the creature on its head, and it whined blissfully. 'I met an old acquaintance of yours today,' Muzaffar said. 'Mangal. Basheer told me he used to be a watchman at the Taj Mahal when it was being built.'

'Ah, Mangal.' Ibrahim smiled again. At first glance, that twisted smile had been unnerving. Now, it was merely different. Even endearing, when you saw the affection in the man's eyes as he looked down at his dog and stroked its thin flank. Ibrahim may be superstitious; but then, so were millions of others, thought Muzaffar. He could also be highly emotional and devoid of all emotion, by turn. He was a man, and like any other man, there were things to like about him, and things to hate. Muzaffar liked the fondness he saw in those keen old eyes now.

But Ibrahim had not reacted to Muzaffar's latest remark.

'He told me he had seen jinn at the Taj Mahal when it was being constructed,' Muzaffar said. 'Lights hovering about outside the mosque at night.' Somewhere off to his left, a small group of babblers, sharp-eyed and fluffy-feathered, came flying down from one of the taller trees and alighted below a ber tree. Muzaffar watched them a while, and then, when Ibrahim did not say anything, he turned back to look at the older man. 'It seems a little unusual, this – this fascination with jinn. Many people believe in them; but not many can claim to have seen them. But you do. And so does Mangal. And you know each other, somewhat.'

He waited, with increasing impatience, for a response. Under the ber tree, the babblers started a squabble, cackling madly as they pounced on the overripe fruit scattered at the foot of the tree. The dog, which had sunk into a dozy sprawl, sat up and let loose a volley of sharp barks. Ibrahim stroked it, murmuring soothingly all the while. He let the barking – and the squawking of the birds – die down before he replied. 'He saw what he saw. I saw what I did.' He had laid his crutch alongside his right leg, which he had stretched out in front. Now he lifted the crutch with his left hand and pulled it towards him, standing it up, leaving a furrow in the dust. Muzaffar, sitting on Ibrahim's left, found himself looking at the man from beyond the crutch. A bar, separating the two men, shielding Ibrahim from Muzaffar's questions.

But Ibrahim did not give Muzaffar the opportunity to ask another question. Even as he pulled the crutch upright, he said, 'I met Taufeeq Sahib yesterday. I had gone down to the rauza to see how things were, and he was there too.' He cleared his throat and spat in the direction of the ber tree. The more timid of the babblers flew up on to the branches of the tree. 'He told me that the Diwan-i-kul appointed you to investigate the murder of Mumtaz Hassan Sahib.'

Muzaffar nodded, cautious.

'And have you discovered anything yet?'

Muzaffar stared, dumbfounded for an instant before he grinned. The gall of this man! The average commoner would not have dared ask an amir a question so impertinent. But it was refreshing, too, the candidness of this old man. 'No,' he said. 'Not very much.'

'And what if I were to tell you who killed Hassan Sahib?'

Muzaffar's head jerked up. Ibrahim looked the same as ever, eyes clear and bright, the face unsmiling but languid. He must be joking, Muzaffar supposed. Or this was another manifestation of the senility that seemed to have gripped Ibrahim before his time. 'What do you mean?' Muzaffar asked. 'Do you mean to tell me that you suspect someone?'

An expression finally dawned on Ibrahim's face: amusement, almost a smugness. He was pleased to know something more – if he did, that was – than Muzaffar. An old, crippled sometime-worker getting ahead of a nobleman, a man whom the highest in the land had commissioned for a task. It was something to be smug about. He smiled at Muzaffar, a smile that had not a jot of happiness or goodwill in it. Just self-satisfaction. 'I did not say that. I do not suspect anyone. I *know* who killed Hassan Sahib.'

'Who?' Muzaffar's voice emerged almost as a croak.

'Mahmood.'

'His own son?! But why on earth – and why on earth did Ibrahim tell you?' Akram was as, if not more, confused as Muzaffar had been.

Ibrahim, his revelation made, had pulled himself up onto the crutch and was already moving towards his cottage when Muzaffar, jolted out of his shock, had risen and hurried after the old man. Ibrahim had not been forthcoming; his explanations and his answers to Muzaffar's questions were disjointed and illogical. Muzaffar had pursued him to the door of the house, and then – reluctant to force his company upon a man who obviously did not want to welcome him in – had taken himself off. His rendezvous with Ibrahim had been dramatic but brief; Basheer was still at the rauza, chatting with Zulfiqar. Akram was pacing impatiently outside the shed, and it was to him that Muzaffar went with the news.

'I don't know,' Muzaffar said. 'He did answer my questions, but he didn't make sense. At least, not that I could see.' He rubbed a palm along the back of his neck, peering up into the sky as he did so. 'Ibrahim says that Mahmood killed Mumtaz Hassan because he knew that though Basheer favours Mahmood, Mumtaz Hassan didn't. While Mumtaz Hassan was alive, Mahmood wouldn't get an opportunity to succeed.' He lowered his head, squinting in the direction of the rauza. 'See what's happened now that your uncle is dead. Basheer has made Mahmood in charge of the work here. That would have been a mere pipe dream a few days back.'

'It sounds like a flimsy reason for a murder.'

'Exactly. And Mahmood, from what little I've seen of him, doesn't quite strike me as an ambitious man. Quiet, obedient, willing to remain in the background. But that is no guarantee of his innocence, of course... perhaps my impression of him is all wrong. What I can't understand is why Ibrahim would tell on him. Even if Mahmood is the culprit, why would his own father say so?'

He clasped his hands behind his back. 'I asked Ibrahim that, actually,' he added. 'And he said, "There are some crimes too heinous to be hidden".'

Basheer's work at the rauza appeared to have finished. He was walking back, coming at a brisk pace, towards where Muzaffar and Akram stood. Akram glanced at Muzaffar. 'What do you think? Do you think Mahmood did it?'

'I don't know what to think. I was almost certain that Mirza Sajjad Khan was involved. And now this.' He heaved a sigh of frustration. 'I'm going to have to start all over again. Come along, let's break it to Basheer. I don't think he's going to be very happy to hear about the doings of his protégé.'

'Ibrahim's gone off his head,' Basheer said flatly when informed. 'Mahmood wouldn't kill a fly. *Couldn't* kill a fly.' He tilted his head up, squinting at the sun. It had climbed overhead, and had now begun its journey down to the western horizon. 'Let's go back to the haveli. I'm hungry.'

Of the three men who sat down to lunch, Basheer turned out to be the only one who actually enjoyed the meal. Muzaffar was too distracted to pay attention to what he was eating. Akram was too busy asking Muzaffar questions and airing his own opinions to utter even one word of praise for the dishes laid before them. Lunch over, Basheer, yawning prodigiously, excused himself on the pretext of taking a nap. Akram bestowed a look of disapproval on his cousin, and when he was alone with Muzaffar, remarked, 'Basheer doesn't seem to be terribly perturbed about Mahmood having murdered my uncle.'

'That's probably because he doesn't believe it. Neither do I.'

The servants, under the supervision of the steward Haider, had cleared away the dishes; all that remained was a large fruit bowl crowded with oranges and apples. Akram leaned across and picked up an orange. 'And how logical is this belief of yours? Is there any proof? Or do you believe that Mahmood is innocent simply because he does not seem the sort to murder a man in cold blood?'

Akram peeled the orange and pulled apart each segment in silence. 'The second,' Muzaffar admitted after a while. 'I don't think Mahmood is the kind to kill a man in cold blood. But that's only a feeling of mine, and I wouldn't use it as a basis to condemn or absolve any man.' He accepted a segment of fruit from Akram's hand. 'Besides that, there's the fact that there seems to be no logical reason for Mahmood to have killed Mumtaz Hassan. Just because you're favoured by a man and not by his father is hardly reason to slay the father.' He swallowed. 'On the other hand, there is the fact that Mahmood is too short to have killed your uncle.'

Akram frowned, puzzled.

'Don't you remember?' Muzaffar said. 'The hakim who examined Mumtaz Hassan's corpse said that Mumtaz Hassan had been killed by a man as tall as him, or taller. He said that if the man had been shorter, the marks of the garrote around Mumtaz Hassan's neck would have been angled downwards. Mahmood is a good bit shorter – at least a head shorter, I'd say – than your uncle had been. He didn't kill your uncle. Unless he hired someone to do it. I've heard Mahmood speak; and I heard the man who gave the murderer his instructions. It wasn't Mahmood; I'm quite sure of that. He had an odd accent, now that I think of it.' Muzaffar reached across and took another segment of orange from Akram's hand. The corners of his mouth drooped and a furrow had appeared between his eyebrows. 'In any case, I doubt if Mahmood would be able to afford to hire a killer,' he said, after a moment's thought.

'And you can't go interrogate Mahmood for the next couple of days anyway,' Akram pointed out. 'Basheer said he's been sent to Mathura, right?'

Muzaffar nodded, still half-lost in his own thoughts. Akram, orange finished, was wiping his hands on a clean napkin when Muzaffar suddenly got to his feet. 'Let's go wake up your cousin,' he said. 'I need to ask him for directions.' He was already striding towards the doorway when Akram, scrambling to stand, tripped over the fruit bowl, stumbled, and caught his foot in the edge of the carpet. He fell with a thud muffled by the carpet, twisting his ankle under him.

Sikandra, it was said, had been named after the sultan Sikandar Lodhi, a man who had spent much of his energy in trying to annex Gwalior to his empire. And, since Gwalior was too, *too* far from Dilli to allow frequent toing-and-froing between the two cities, he had made Agra a mid-way halting place, a subsidiary capital, so to say. A place from where he could, with not too much travelling, launch attacks on stubborn Gwalior; and a place which was also close enough to Dilli to allow the Sultan to go back when he was fed up with being held at bay. He had laid out a garden here, they said, outside the city.

Now the most prominent building in the area was the magnificent tomb of Akbar, Shahjahan's grandfather. He had renamed Sikandra Bihishtabad – abode of paradise – and had designed and erected here his own mausoleum, of red sandstone and white and black marble, as Rajasthani in its little domed pavilions as it was Mughal in its slender towers and arched gateways. Akbar's tomb stood just off the main highway that connected Agra to the north, to Mathura and Dilli, and way beyond, to Lahore and Kabul and faraway Kandahar. Travellers coming along the route stopped for a glimpse, marvelled at the splendour of the rauza, and went on to Agra, to marvel all over again, and with deeper sighs and wider eyes, at the Taj Mahal.

Muzaffar had seen Sikandra. It had been built over fifty years ago, so when he, towed along by Farid Khan and Zeenat Begum on their perennial marches across the land, had been in the vicinity, he had gone along with his brother-in-law to see it. He still remembered the wildly exuberant beauty of the gate's inlay: the massive flowers, white and black marble sketched into a background of red sandstone, flanked by long and unbelievably intricate panels of calligraphy carved out of marble. And panels of chessboard-like decoration, crafted from white marble, black marble, golden stone, deep red sandstone. A jumble, perhaps, and not as fantastically elegant as the Taj Mahal. But it was certainly a tomb worthy of a king.

He could see its silhouette on the distant horizon; Mangal's small home was closer to Agra than it was to Sikandra. This was a hut, wattle-and-daub with a thatched roof, and a few small fields beyond. There were other, similar, huts nearby. Huts from which, as from Mangal's, there came the sounds and smells of families preparing for night. The pungency of burning fuel – dry sticks, cow dung cakes – mixed with the earthiness of simmering lentils. The muted murmurs of mothers putting children to bed, of wives welcoming home husbands who had been out in the fields all day long, of women who had worked all day long and whose work was not yet done.

Unlike many of the other Mughal noblemen, Muzaffar did not confine himself to a luxurious, perfumed cocoon of wealth. He had friends – as Akram had once said – in 'low places'. He had visited their homes, seen how they lived, seen the dire poverty they survived in. These were the millions whose only possessions could often just be tied up in a ragged bundle and hoisted onto one's back.

He could smell that poverty around him, in the fetid air heavy with smoke and the lingering stench of garbage. He could hear it, in the wails of a baby somewhere near, crying for milk that was not to be had. He could see it in the patched clothing, the lack of any jewels on the women, in the dark dimness of these homes. He could feel it. All around him, surrounding him and silently accusing him of being an intruder.

Somewhere inside Mangal's hut, the old watchman's daughter-in-law too was cooking the evening meal. Perhaps his long stint as an employee at the Taj Mahal had made Mangal a relatively wealthy man; that would account for the fields he owned. It would also be the reason why his hut seemed just a trifle more prosperous than those in the neighbourhood. Muzaffar could hear the pounding of mortar and pestle, the clank of vessels and the sound of water being poured. He had caught, out of the corner of his eye, a glimpse of a billowing orange odhni, a woman's veil, as she moved past the door. Once, her children – a little boy about four years old, another barely able to toddle – had peeked out, their shyness overcome by curiosity. The younger one had finally plucked up his courage and come out, running along unsteadily on tiptoe on fat little legs that looked as if they would land him in the dust any moment. Mangal laughed, holding his grandchild in his arms and lifting him up into his lap.

'So you have escaped, have you?' he grinned, tickling the infant and eliciting a joyful giggle. He shifted the child on to one thigh and smiled at Muzaffar, one hand still fondly stroking the downy little head resting against his ribs. 'This compensates for having to leave Agra,' he said quietly. 'I had thought I would be miserable away from the city. But I have adjusted. It is good here, more peaceful than in Agra. And I have these two to keep me very happy indeed.'

He whispered something into the child's ear. Muzaffar looked on. He wondered if the child really understood what was being said to him; surely he was too young? The giggle that followed was probably because Mangal's breath tickled, not because Mangal had said something amusing.

With a small sigh – satisfaction at having enjoyed the company of the child, and resignation at having to return to the world of adults and their problems – Mangal lowered his grandchild to the ground and gave him an affectionate pat on the bottom. The child, after one admiring gaze in his grandfather's direction, toddled off towards the hut. His elder brother emerged, and caught one pudgy little hand in his own. From inside, a woman's voice said something, cautioning the children, telling them not to go far.

'I only knew Ibrahim slightly,' Mangal said, returning to the subject of their conversation. 'I had spoken to him a few times, but I was not a friend of his. Of course, all those tragedies that struck him – one after the other – created quite a furore. *Everybody* knew about that.'

'Everybody seems to mention it, at any rate,' Muzaffar commented. 'Taufeeq told me about it, and Basheer. You too, when we met you at the Taj Mahal. But nobody has said very much about it. What actually happened? His wife vanished, did she? And some friend of his was killed?'

Mangal nodded, his face grim. 'It all happened around the same time. Within a few days, in fact. I think a week; perhaps less. It's been a long time.' He hesitated, eyes narrowing and tongue licking nervously at dry lips. 'The gossip was that Ibrahim went home one evening and found that his wife was nowhere to be seen. He went around, to the neighbours' and elsewhere, waited for her through the night, but there was no sign of her. She just vanished.'

'Didn't she leave any note for him? Anything to say where she had gone?'

Mangal gave a small, patently patient smile. 'An educated woman, among the likes of us, huzoor? Ibrahim's wife couldn't read and write. I don't think he can, either.' He waited for Muzaffar to say something, and when Muzaffar maintained an embarrassed silence, he continued his story. 'Nobody had seen her since the afternoon. I think a neighbour's wife had come by just after lunch for a chat, but after she left, nobody saw Ibrahim's wife – not in her own home, since nobody came by; and not outside.'

'Did anyone see anybody coming to Ibrahim's house?'

Mangal shrugged. 'I do not know, huzoor. Remember, I am simply telling you all that I know. I am a poor illiterate man; I was one then too. I did not know what questions to ask. None of us did, not even Ibrahim. He did search, I know that. Perhaps he asked his neighbours if anybody came.' He rubbed a palm on the rough blanket draped across his thigh. 'In any case, who was I to ask any questions? My job was to ensure nobody stole anything or killed anyone at the construction site of the Empress's rauza.'

'And Ibrahim never found his wife?'

Mangal shook his head. 'Not that I know. Who knows what passes between a man and his wife, huzoor? Perhaps they did meet someday years later in the marketplace, she disgraced because of the way she had deserted her husband, and he all distorted and crippled because of his illness – and perhaps they decided they were happiest without each other. Who knows?'

Muzaffar was not inclined to enter into a discussion on a state of which he knew nothing. Besides, he was running out of time; the sun had nearly set. He was running out of time in other ways, too. The Diwan-i-kul could be marching on Bijapur by now, with Aurangzeb's armies hand-in-hand with his own, ready to rout Bijapur and pin her to the ground at the feet of the Baadshah.

'What of the friend who died? In an accident, I think, someone said?'

'Fakhruddin,' Mangal said. 'He was a sang tarash too. He was Ibrahim's friend and colleague *and* neighbour. They used to invariably work together, and then when the day ended, they would head home together. Two days after Ibrahim's wife went missing, Fakhru fell off a rickety bit of scaffolding and plunged to his death. Ibrahim had been working right next to him – they were putting up the cladding of the mosque at the time – and he leaned out, trying to grab Fakhru as the scaffolding tilted. But it was no use. Fakhru fell, twisting onto the slabs of the paving below. He might have survived if he had fallen straight, but he fell head first. It was terrible, blood all over the place and Fakhru's head a mass of gore.' He shuddered. 'That was the day after I saw the jinn, the lights hovering about at night,' he added, a ghost of a smile on his face. As if he knew Muzaffar did not believe him.

'I think it was a day or so later that Ibrahim was taken ill. At the site itself; he was up on the scaffolding when he began shivering and shaking. He couldn't speak, and when they brought him down and put him on a charpai, he began to bleed from the nose. They brought a hakim to have a look at him, but the hakim couldn't really treat him.' He pulled a stray thread from the edge of the blanket, and wound it around his forefinger. 'That was the last I saw of Ibrahim; he couldn't work anymore. His son Mahmood was an apprentice, so I used to see *him* now and then, but we never spoke.' Mangal shivered and gathered the blanket closer about him. 'It's growing cold. Excuse me; I will get some sticks and light a fire.' He rose to his feet and walked across to the back of the hut, returning with a bundle of spindly sticks and one dead branch, enough to keep off the chill for an hour or so.

Muzaffar watched as Mangal arranged the sticks, then went inside the hut to get a burning stick with which to ignite the fire. When he had finally sat down on his haunches and started – with much patient blowing, and the help of a burning coal which his daughter-in-law had given – to get the fire started, Muzaffar spoke up. 'Tell me, Mangal. Did you ever see any signs of Ibrahim hating Mahmood?'

The watchman looked up from his task. The last remnants of the day's light were almost gone now, and the light from the fire was fitful, at best. Muzaffar could not see the expression on Mangal's face, but he heard the surprise in the man's voice when he spoke. 'Ibrahim hating his own son? Why do you ask that, huzoor?'

'Just tell me, please. Did you notice anything of the sort?'

Mangal went back to coaxing the fire. Inside the hut, the younger child began a tantrum, his bawling echoing in the small dwelling. A loud clang rang out; some vessel or the other had been flung, in a childish rage, at one of the walls. A woman's voice, commanding obedience but not getting any, murmured in the background as the wails increased. The older child came out of the hut and went towards the buffalo that was tied with a rope to a short pole in the corner of the yard. The wall behind the buffalo was plastered with round discs of dried cow dung; the boy peeled off three of the cakes and took them back into the hut.

'It is odd that you should ask that question,' Mangal said. The fire had finally caught. It was still only a smoulder, but it would spread to the sticks on its own now. Mangal rested his hands briefly on his knees as he got to his feet. 'Because along with all these disasters that struck Ibrahim, there was also the inexplicable way in which his attitude changed towards his son. Before his wife disappeared, Ibrahim was the fondest of fathers. He was proud of Mahmood, doted on the boy. When the other stone cutters took a break to eat lunch or to stretch their legs – Ibrahim would go and check up on Mahmood, see if he needed help, or give him a quick lesson. Or just go and stand, watching his son.'

'Taufeeq told me Mahmood was never as good as Ibrahim.'

Mangal lowered himself onto the charpai on which Muzaffar was sitting. 'I wouldn't know, huzoor. I have not the eye to distinguish between good work and bad. My eye was meant to see where a thief could enter, and to stop him.' He extended his hands, palms out, towards the small fire, the warmth of which was already beginning to spread. 'After his wife vanished, in fact from the very next day, Ibrahim changed completely. He was disturbed. Anyone could see that. But to turn against the one person who was closest? It can happen, of course – perhaps Mahmood was the only one to whom Ibrahim could truly reveal his grief and his frustration. He may have felt awkward talking about such things to others. But still; it was strange. I saw him snap at Mahmood, yell at the boy for some trivial fault. You could see the anger in every line of his body, in every look he gave Mahmood.'

'And what about Mahmood? Did he snap back?'

Mangal shook his head. 'Mahmood wasn't the type to snap back; he was always very quiet. No, he bore it all quietly. I think he was very puzzled. Maybe he asked Ibrahim what was wrong; I doubt it. It didn't look as if the relationship between the two of them was any longer the type where the son could ask questions of the father and get satisfactory answers. If Mahmood asked something, he probably got abuses in return.'

'And then the friend died in the accident, and Ibrahim himself was stricken?'

'Yes.'

Muzaffar stood up. 'That will be all, I think. I had better be heading back for the city.' He bent to warm his own hands on the fire, then recalling something, said: 'You mentioned that Fakhruddin was a neighbour of Ibrahim's. Do you know where they lived? And did Fakhruddin leave behind any family?'

'Fakhru may have had children, I don't know,' Mangal replied. 'But there was a widow, certainly. She came once to meet the overseer and plead with him for compensation – I think she was having problems living on whatever savings they had. *If* Fakhru had been able to save. I don't know where they lived, but maybe you could go and ask the overseer.

'Mohammad Hussain. Like me, he too has retired; but unlike me, he lives in great style. He has a grand house near Taj Ganj, many servants and much luxury.'

Muzaffar listened while Mangal explained how to get to Mohammad Hussain's house. Then, with a few words of gratitude by way of farewell, he mounted his horse. 'If you are able to talk to Mohammad Hussain, you're likely to get answers to a lot of your questions,' Mangal said encouragingly. 'His is one of the sharpest minds I have ever seen. He should be able to help you, huzoor.'

The small gate of Qureshi Sahib's haveli – brick, plastered over and painted in a pale yellow wash – had lamps already burning in the two small arched niches on either side of the entrance. The servant who acted as guard, groom and general dogsbody came forward to take the reins from Muzaffar when he dismounted. 'No, let it be,' Muzaffar said. 'I am headed for the stables to look at my horse; I'll take this one there.'

The stables smelled pleasantly of straw, a little less pleasantly of manure. Akram would probably have turned up his nose and refused to enter; Muzaffar merely nodded at the man in charge, handed over the horse he had been riding, and strode towards the far end of the stables to have a look at his own horse. He had been coming to meet his stallion faithfully every morning since they had arrived in Agra; but the previous morning and this one had plunged him into so unexpected a welter of clues, confusion, leads and wild goose chases that he had forgotten briefly about checking on the animal.

The chestnut whinnied in welcome when Muzaffar arrived, pushing its nose into his hand and nuzzling. The stall in which it stood was clean and dry, the earth dry and carpeted with clean fresh straw. The awful stench of the thrush was gone, too. Muzaffar bent and had a look at the hoof that had been affected. It was clean and odourless, the hoof of a healthy horse.

He sighed, relieved of one burden. If only the others could be taken care of with such little effort on his part.

Behind him, one of the stable boys came in with the horse's dinner. Cooked lentils, roasted gram, an armload of straw. He salaamed Muzaffar and said, 'Huzoor, there is a eunuch at the stable door. He has a message for you.'

It was Khursheed, the eunuch who acted as guard and messenger for the ladies of Qureshi Sahib's mahal sara. The note he extended to

Muzaffar was from Zeenat Begum, a short crisp couple of sentences that required Muzaffar to come to the dalaan nearest the mahal sara – the dalaan where he had met Shireen and his sister only the other day. At once, before he could even wash or change. Muzaffar tucked the note into his cummerbund and dismissed the eunuch with a message for Zeenat Begum: her brother would be at the dalaan *after* he had washed his hands and face. He refused to socialize – even if it was only with his sister – smelling of the stables.

Zeenat Begum was sitting ramrod straight, the skirt of her pearl-gray peshwaaz discreetly pooling about her legs. 'You must have been very dirty indeed,' she said when Muzaffar stepped into the room, 'I thought that eunuch had given me the wrong message, and that you were not going to come after all.'

Muzaffar seated himself on the mattress beside his sister. 'Were you looking out for me?'

She gave him a sharp look, then nodded. 'Yes. I – I had to speak to you, Muzaffar, as soon as you got back. Preferably before Qureshi Sahib got around to speaking to you. Not that he will, I think. But still.' She played nervously with the edge of her pashmina shawl, rubbing the soft cloth between her fingertips. 'From one of the windows near my room, I can look out onto the road and see who's coming and who's going –'

'What is it?' Muzaffar asked, his sister's unaccustomed edginess rubbing off on him. 'Why did you want to speak to me so urgently?'

Zeenat Begum did not respond at once. She did look up at her brother, her eyes so full of apprehension that Muzaffar was moved to repeat his question in a gentler tone. 'What is it, Aapa? Is something wrong?'

The words came out all in a rush. 'The seniormost of Qureshi Sahib's three begums passed a very broad hint today. We were sitting outside in the khanah bagh after lunch, eating paan and basking in the sun. The other begums were inside the mahal sara, and Shireen and the other girls were at the other end of the bagh – playing a game of chaupar or something. They weren't paying any attention to us. The lady began asking me about life in Dilli, society and court and things like that. Before I knew it, she was asking me about you. Whether you lived with us or had your own haveli; what was your income, did you have lands near Dilli, whether you were married, and when she discovered you weren't – why not, and did you have a young woman in mind.'

'That's hardly any of her business,' Muzaffar butted in, heatedly. 'Why didn't you –'

'Yes, yes. I tried to, but she's a persistent woman, Muzaffar. She doesn't give up easily. She then began telling me how worried they are about Shireen. Already old enough to have been married thrice over, but stuck at home, a burden on their consciences. She was very quick to say that she didn't mean they grudged the fact that Shireen was staying here; no, she was like a daughter to them. But as foster parents, it was their duty to have arranged her marriage long before this.'

'So why don't they?'

'That's just what Begum Sahiba was trying to do, Muzaffar.'

Muzaffar stared at his sister for a moment, then let out a deep breath in a whoosh of annoyance. 'Again! It all comes back to the same thing! Why on earth, Aapa? Why didn't you tell her off? And why do you go on trying to get me married?'

Zeenat Begum placed a gentling hand on her brother's knee. 'Will you at least listen to me if I tell you?' she asked. 'I don't expect you to agree with me, or to not lose your temper at me. Just listen. All right?'

A little grudgingly, he nodded.

'Good. I am not trying to push you into anything; I want you to know that. Both your brother-in-law and I have regarded you as an adult ever since Abba died and you became his heir. We have believed you to have the understanding and the maturity of an adult. We have respected your decisions – including your decision to not get married all these years. Most men of your age are fathers a few times over, let alone husbands. That you did not get married is your business, as you say.'

She ran a fingertip down the seam of Muzaffar's fitted pajama and murmured, 'There's a thread loose here. Give it to one of the servants to have it mended.' Her head tilted up, a look of shy contrition in her eyes. 'I beg your pardon; I could not overlook *that*.'

Muzaffar grinned, a bitter smile that contained no mirth. 'You do not trust me to notice a rip in my garments, Aapa; how can you trust me in greater matters? You betray yourself.'

Zeenat Begum took her hand away from Muzaffar's leg and folded her arms under her shawl. Muzaffar sensed the hurt in her demeanour; she had been offended by his words. 'You are a man,' she said after several moments. 'And men tend to not notice things like this. *Little things*. Men can be blind when it comes to little things, but have the eyes of a hawk when it comes to matters of import. Abba was like that. So is your brother-in-law. And you.

'Do you mean never to marry?' she asked, after a pause. 'No, don't answer just to keep me quiet. Think about it, then say – say exactly what you feel, even if it may cause me pain.'

Muzaffar obeyed. When he spoke, it was with a candour that surprised even him. 'No,' he said. 'No, it's not as if I don't intend to ever get married; that wouldn't do. At the very least, I need heirs. Sons and daughters to inherit all that Abba passed on to me.' His lip curled in disgust. 'That is what most people marry for, isn't it? Just to keep mankind going. I will not be any different, then.'

There was a long, awkward silence. This was the man she had created, with her nurturing and care, her scoldings and her tears and laughter, from the motherless baby who had been left twenty-five ago in her lap. They had been mother and son, sister and brother, friends, confidants. There had been silences before in their relationship, comfortable silences of being at ease in the company of the other. Never a silence like this, troubled and tense.

Finally, Zeenat Begum sighed. 'It *is* Ayesha, isn't it?' she said in a low voice. 'So many years, now. How long has it been? Seven years? Eight? And you haven't forgotten Ayesha.'

Muzaffar's head had jerked up at the very first sentence. His sister looked weary. Sympathetic too, as if she understood what was going through his heart.

He did not respond. Instead, he picked at the loose thread she had pointed out, pinching the gaping edges of the seam together between thumb and forefinger. His eyes were far away, the distress in his face apparent to one who knew him so well.

'Do you still love her so much?' Zeenat Begum said quietly. 'After all these years, after she left you so summarily and ran away – do you still love her?'

Muzaffar looked up finally, his hands coming to rest, clasped loosely in his lap. 'No, Aapa,' he said. 'No, I thought I did, but I know now that I don't. Perhaps what I felt for her all these years was just a heady fascination, some sort of lust that is better left behind with one's adolescence than carried into adulthood. Ayesha did not love me. I know that now. I see no reason to pine away for a woman as faithless as she.'

The sentence hung in the air, while Zeenat tried to interpret it. 'Shireen is not Ayesha,' she said eventually.

'True. But I dare not put it to the test.'

She sat, motionless, for the time it took for a servant to enter, bringing in a chiraghdaan to illuminate the dalaan, till now lit only by a single sputtering oil lamp. The servant placed the chiraghdaan on the floor, well away from the hangings and the mattress, away too from the draught whispering in through the window. He reminded Muzaffar in a gentle voice that dinner – that of the men in the household – would be served in a quarter of an hour. He bowed himself out, and Zeenat rose, shaking out her skirts as she did so.

'If you say *that*, Muzaffar, you may well find that you have already put it to the test. No – hear me out, please.' She stared down at her hands, her right hand twirling and twisting the ruby ring she wore on her left. 'I did not say anything to you when you imagined yourself in love with Ayesha; perhaps I hoped she would turn out to be not as shallow as I believed her. Perhaps I thought she actually felt for you as you did for her. Perhaps, also, I knew it was useless; you would not listen if I tried to warn you.' She fell silent, but the ring continued to turn, the glow from the chiraghdaan reflecting off the facets of the wine-red stone.

'What are you trying to tell me?'

She looked at him steadily for the space of a few heartbeats. Then she drew her shawl closer about her shoulders. 'Nothing. You are a grown man; you know your heart – and your mind – better than when you were a youth. Remember to use both of them when you take a decision.' She left the room, her passage making the flames of the chiraghdaan dance.

13

QURESHI SAHIB HAD either not been told by his wife of her conversation with Zeenat Begum, or he was too tactful to broach the subject with his guest. Dinner passed in conversation that was boringly mundane, the aimless chitchat of people who had been thrown together by virtue of their circumstances. They wandered into the realm of politics; who could not, with the Diwan-i-kul and his army headed south, and the destiny of the empire probably balanced on the outcome of the Bijapur campaign? If the Baadshah's armies won, Bijapur's vast resources would be his to command.

'And win he will,' Qureshi Sahib had said, leaning forward to pour himself a goblet of sherbet. 'I do not know about the Diwan-i-kul, but the Shahzada Aurangzeb is a seasoned general.'

'He has the advantage of numbers, too,' Muzaffar had remarked. 'And possibly better artillery, or so I've heard.' He had paused, waiting to see if Qureshi Sahib had anything further to say. But Qureshi Sahib had been busy drinking sherbet, and Muzaffar had simply said, 'Who knows, it all may well be a repeat of what happened at Golconda.'

Qureshi Sahib had glanced up, his eyes cautious above the rim of the goblet he still held to his lips. When he had lowered the goblet and spoken, it was to talk of other things: of the weather, and how beautiful the Taj Mahal was, and whether Jang Sahib had liked it. It was Akram all over again, Muzaffar had thought; Qureshi Sahib too was wary of delving too deep into politics. Here, tucked away in the former capital, far from court and the many intrigues that raddled it, it was easy to forget that something as distant as a battle in the Deccan could have disastrous consequences. Men would die, in thousands. Even more would be injured, perhaps crippled. The countryside would be ravaged – irrespective of victory or defeat, for armies on the march typically lived off the land, and were not above raiding fields and villages along the way. Trade would suffer. Nobody would remain completely unaffected. But Qureshi Sahib, like Akram, preferred to close his eyes and look away.

For one thing, though, Muzaffar was grateful: Qureshi Sahib had made no reference to a possible match between Muzaffar and Shireen. Qureshi Sahib was enough of a gentleman to not give in to his curiosity and ask how Muzaffar's investigation of Mumtaz Hassan's murder progressed. He was also enough of a gentleman to realize that one cannot force a man to marry one's niece by passing unsubtle hints.

So Muzaffar had sat through the meal, picking at his food and trying not to think of Ayesha and Shireen and what Zeenat Begum had said. He had made small talk as and when a lull in conversation required him, if only for the sake of politeness, to do so. He had made certain that the conversation steered clear of anything remotely approaching matrimony or death. He had been a good guest, if a trifle abstracted, to Qureshi Sahib's good host.

Dinner over, he had retired to his bedchamber and had spent the rest of the night tossing and turning, unable to sleep. Where the previous nights had been restless ones because of his anxiety for the murder investigation, this one was quite different – and caused him as much worry. More, he thought, as he finally crawled out of bed with the first weak light beginning to filter through the curtains. This was a matter of his entire life.

He had just begun his breakfast of roti and spiced minced lamb when the eunuch Khursheed entered with a note. Muzaffar glanced down at the signature. *Shireen*. She had, she wrote, something urgent to ask of him, before he left for the day. It would take no

more than a few minutes; would he be so kind as to come to the
khanah bagh once he had finished breakfast? Zeenat Begum would
accompany her.

As it was, Zeenat Begum did not come. 'I'm sorry,' said a somewhat
breathless Shireen, hurrying down the six steps leading from the
corridor that connected the mahal sara to the khanah bagh. 'She
was all ready to come with me when my aunt was stung by a wasp.
There was quite a hullabaloo – everyone was shouting and screaming,
and Zeenat Begum was the only one who seemed capable of keeping
her head and getting things under control. So I had to leave her in
charge and come away. But I have brought Khursheed with me, as
you can see.'

Muzaffar glanced briefly at Khursheed, who was standing, head
discreetly lowered, hands clasped below his waist, at the top of the
steps. Close enough to keep an eye on the rendezvous, far enough
to not hear much.

Shireen pulled the coral-hued dupatta down a bit and draped
her shawl more securely about her head and shoulders, as if veiling
herself more thoroughly. 'I had to talk to you before you rode out
today,' she said.

'So I believe. What about?'

She drew in a deep, fortifying breath. 'It is about those letters
– Hassan Sahib's letters, from which you wanted me to try and
identify the lady.'

Muzaffar's heart sank. Had she looked through them, and come
to no conclusions? 'Oh?' he asked. 'And do you know who it is?'

She shook her head. 'I only think I know. I suppose I should admit
that I am almost sure who it is, but one can never be sure unless
one has absolute proof, is that not so?' It had all poured out in one
torrent of words, unrelieved and nervous. She paused just long
enough to take a breath, then carried on. 'I will be going to meet
the lady today. I wanted to know if you would allow me to confront
her with it. Will you let me ask her if she indeed was Hassan Sahib's
– um – mistress? I know her well, you see; I do not think she would

agree to meet *you*, so you would not be able to talk to her. But I could ask. Do you think –?' She left the question half-spoken.

Muzaffar stared. This woman, whom he had doubted would find anything useful in the letters, was almost certain of the writer's identity. She must be, or she would not have posed such a question. He frowned to himself, caught in a dilemma. His mind desperately wished that Shireen had solved the riddle for him. And yet, in his heart, there was the suspicion that she was merely trying to entice him by pretending to be of help.

She had asked him a question, and was waiting for an answer. Instead of replying, he asked another question.

'What is to stop her denying it to you, if you should ask her?'

For a moment, she seemed flummoxed. Then the pashmina-clad shoulders lifted. 'I do not know. I suppose she could, but I do not think she will. Mumtaz Hassan is dead, after all; nothing can really come of it, even if her affair with him is revealed now. Yes, her brother will certainly be furious and is likely to either marry her off to the first man who offers for her next – or he will exile her to some half-forgotten little town where she can spend the rest of her days vegetating in the company of the auntie.' A muslin handkerchief, probably clutched in restless hands under the shawl, floated down to the ground. She bent, picked it up – what a lovely, delicate hand she had, thought Muzaffar, and then scolded himself silently – and continued. 'But I think her brother would not hear of his sister's exploits from you, unless that were absolutely necessary. I do not imagine you are a man to take pleasure in spreading malicious gossip.'

Muzaffar inclined his head in acknowledgment of the compliment. 'I would not,' he agreed. 'But have you considered one thing: what if the lady herself were involved in Mumtaz Hassan's death?'

She took a while to answer. But when she did, it was with straightened shoulders and her head held upright. Had she flung back that pink-orange dupatta of hers, her face would have no doubt been all defiance. Those vivid brown eyes flashing with triumph, the lips parted in a smile that was only partly the result of joy. As it was, all he could perceive of her reaction was in her words and in the self-confidence with which she spoke.

'That seems unlikely,' she said. 'Didn't you yourself tell me that Hassan Sahib's murderer probably distracted him by presenting a letter that purported to come from this lady? And that while Hassan Sahib was reading the letter, this man garroted him? Yet the scrap you found clutched in Hassan Sahib's fist was a forgery, at best. The letter paper was not the same; the fragrance was of musk mallow, not musk; and the handwriting was not the same. If this lady were involved in the killing of Mumtaz Hassan, why did she not use her own letter paper, her own musk and her own writing?'

Muzaffar nodded, suitably chastened. And very impressed. He had thought Shireen a less flamboyant version of Ayesha, but a woman nevertheless, and more interested in her body than her mind. Like all the woman he had ever known, with the possible exception of Zeenat Aapa. But Shireen was proving different. Enticingly different, and totally unaware that she was enticing him with the sharpness of her intellect.

He cringed inwardly; what sort of man was he, to give more credit to a woman who awed him with her intelligence, than to one who flaunted her charms before him? A misfit. And Shireen seemed to be as much of a misfit among the women as he was among the men.

'So I may ask her?'

For a moment, he did not know what she was talking about. Then he remembered. 'If it pleases you. I have no objections to offer. But what if she should refuse to tell you? Will you still withhold your suspicions? Or will you be willing to tell me then who this lady is?'

'I will tell you. But I think I will be able to convince her to tell me the truth.'

'I hope so.'

He said a few formal words of thanks and was turning to leave when she said, 'Jang Sahib, may I say something?'

Muzaffar froze. 'Yes?'

'My uncle is old-fashioned, Jang Sahib. He believes that the heir to the throne can do no wrong. I heard that you expressed a fear that – well, that there may be a repeat of the Golconda fiasco this time around. I agree with you; but my uncle is deeply offended.' She cleared her throat. 'I suppose I am being a disloyal niece by saying this, but Qureshi Sahib can be a little – um – *petty* when it comes to things like that.'

Muzaffar had paid little attention to the last sentence. 'You say you agree with me,' he said in an undertone. 'About what?'

She leaned back slightly, as if taken aback. 'About what might happen at Bijapur, of course. That the Sultan and his noblemen might send petitions – duly oiled with personal gifts – to Dilli? That was what happened at Golconda, didn't it? The Shahzada Dara Shukoh was flooded with tributes and a plea for help, and he prevailed upon the Baadshah to have the siege called off.'

Her head was tilted up now, and Muzaffar could imagine her watching him through the veil that hid her face from him. From her tone, he could even sense a growing confidence as she spoke.

'It could happen again. Dara Shukoh is not immune to bribery, even if it comes disguised. And the Baadshah will never say no to his favourite son. Aurangzeb had to taste humiliation at Golconda; everybody knows he was itching to conquer it. If that happens once again...' her voice trailed off.

'...Allah alone knows what will ensue.' Muzaffar hesitated. 'Yes, that is what I fear, too. But nobody seems to be willing to admit the possibility.' He grinned suddenly, a quick smile at the realization that somebody – not Akram, not Qureshi Sahib, not any of the other men he had spoken to – had actually articulated what he had been trying to say. And had agreed, too.

'I understand,' Shireen said. 'But my uncle does not. Keep your mealtime conversations with him free of politics, Jang Sahib. He prefers horses.' A soft chuckle drifted on the breeze as she swept him a brisk but graceful salaam and went up the steps, towards the mahal sara.

There were a surprising number of old men in this story, thought Muzaffar. Or perhaps not surprising, really, since the man who had been killed had been past his prime. It was not strange that most of his associates had been men of his own age. The men whom Mumtaz Hassan had trusted and depended upon – or, in some cases, distrusted and even hated – seemed all to be in their fifties and sixties. Old men by the standards of the day, when most men could not hope to even live twenty-five years. But many of these, Mumtaz Hassan and the men who had been his rivals, were wealthy men, well-fed, well-housed, and well looked after by skilled hakims. Their chances of survival past their middle years were high.

Mumtaz Hassan had been a luxury-loving man. Still vigorous, still virile, still fond of the good things in life. His secretary Taufeeq was a different kettle of fish altogether: dour and humourless, stubbornly loyal to his dead master and sometimes even insolently so. Then there was Mangal, all friendliness, open and apparently honest. And Ibrahim. Superstitious old Ibrahim, who talked of jinn and had accused his own son of murder.

Mohammad Hussain was more the sort of Muzaffar hoped he would be when he grew old: kind, somewhat avuncular, but by no means doddering and simple-minded. He was obviously still the much-loved and well-respected head of the small house he inhabited. A brazier with smouldering wood kept warm the plain plastered dalaan in which he received Muzaffar; it was topped up once by a servant in the course of the meeting. A string of delicacies – fruit, samosas stuffed with spiced meat, kababs – was served up, hot from the kitchens. A teenaged boy came to ask, in quietly respectful tones, if grandfather would like the hookah to be brought. A much smaller child, a little girl whose blue dupatta trailed from her shoulder, came running in, wailing about a lost doll before she was hauled back by a blushing maid.

No wonder Mangal had been certain Mohammad Hussain would be of help; Mangal, after all, probably identified himself with Mohammad Hussain. The two men were in many ways very similar.

'I wouldn't have remembered something like that offhand,' Mohammad Hussain said, leaning against a bolster and sucking on the hookah. 'But that particular string of events was so remarkable that I can recall almost every single thing that happened in those few days. Down to things that weren't even connected to it all. What I ate, how much we managed to build, what bits of carving the sang tarashes accomplished. It's still all here, even after all these years.' He tapped the side of his forehead with a forefinger.

His story was the same as Mangal's, though the words were different. And he knew where Fakhruddin's widow lived. 'Or *had* lived then,' he amended. 'She may have died by now. Allah alone knows how she survived; it isn't easy to be poor.' He gurgled at his hookah. 'She came to me a couple of times, during the first month after Fakhru died. She was having a hard time and hoped that there would be some provision for a pension of sorts.' He fell silent, and pulled so deeply at his hookah that it resulted in a fit of coughing. Muzaffar waited until Mohammad Hussain had regained his composure, then said, 'And? Did she get it?'

The old man shook his head. 'No. There was no such provision, not for a worker like Fakhru. I had thought I would perhaps be able to give her a small sum of money on my account, but I couldn't manage it right then. There were too many matters demanding my time and attention: personal matters, and official. There was the matter of the paving stones; that was never resolved, but it was very awkward while it lasted. They said I hadn't been keeping the books properly.' Some long-forgotten sense of being ill-used surfaced momentarily. Mohammad Hussain flung the end of the hookah aside and sat back, his normally good-natured face twisted into a black scowl.

'One clerk who was acting as an auditor had the cheek to tell me that I must have been seeing jinn too! Or that the jinn were the ones keeping the books, not me! I tell you!'

The jinn again. Muzaffar waited for the tirade to abate before asking a question. 'What was that about? The matter of the paving stones?'

The old man huffed and grunted irritably for a while longer. Then he drew the end of the hookah back into his fingers and pulled at it, drawing the smoke deep into his lungs. 'The workers used to be paid daily, on the basis of the work they had done during the day. So, for example, if they were paving an area, they would be paid according to the number of slabs they had put in through the day. The other overseers and clerks – and I, of course – would move around the construction site through part of the day, ensuring that the work was done. And then one final round towards the end of the workday, to check on how much had been done and to calculate the payments due. Our assistants would then dispense those amounts to the workers.'

A servant came in bearing a silver tray of shakkar para, crisp little golden cushions of deep-fried pastry, dipped in heavy syrup and allowed to crystallize. Mohammad Hussain waited until the sweets had been offered to both his guest and himself, and the servant had left; then he continued with his tale. 'At the end of every week, an inventory would be taken of all the material. At the end of the week in which Fakhru died and Ibrahim fell ill, the inventory showed up something odd. Four slabs of red sandstone were missing. You've seen the type used for the paving in front of the mosque? Those. We checked and rechecked, but we couldn't understand how it could have happened. According to the inventory – the number of slabs that still remained in the storeroom – ninety-two slabs had been used during the week. According to the books – how much we had paid the men for putting in the slabs – they had put in eighty-eight slabs.'

'Someone broke into your storeroom and stole those four slabs.'

'Yes, but here's the odd thing. I went out and counted, one by one, each slab that the men had used in the paving through the week. It wasn't difficult, since they'd begun the paving only that week. We knew exactly where they had started and where they had stopped at the end of the week. I counted those slabs, Jang Sahib; once, and once again. And once, one last time, with another of the clerks, just to make sure my brain wasn't fooling me. But we got the same result each time: ninety-two slabs. Each slab exactly the same in look and quality.

'Someone stole those four slabs from the storeroom only to use them in the paving. But why? It's no simple task to pave an area; it doesn't require much skill, but there's time and effort needed. And there's the effort that must have gone into stealing them in the first place. Besides the fact that you run the risk of being caught and flogged as a result. Why go through all that trouble only to do work for which you could have demanded money?'

Fakhru's widow was certainly alive, though no one in the neighbourhood knew her any longer as Fakhru's widow; she was Rashid's widow. 'How long is a woman with just one son, and that too a baby, supposed to survive on her own?' she said to Muzaffar. 'And how? I'm an honest woman, I wouldn't do the things some do.' She was sitting cross-legged on a charpai, picking through a large platter of wheat. Against one leg of the charpai rested a half-full sack of wheat – the 'dirty' wheat, full of chaff and tiny pebbles, perhaps a clod or two of earth. On the charpai was another sack, considerably less full, of wheat that she had cleaned over the course of the morning. The charpai was rickety, the woman's clothing patched and ragged at the hems. In comparison to Fakhru's – or Rashid's – widow, Mangal and his family appeared to live in near-luxury. Muzaffar wondered how long the wheat she was picking was meant to last. Would it be rationed out, one precious fistful at a time, eked out with more easily available, if barely edible, things? Wild greens picked from the edges of a forest? Fruit stolen from a tree leaning too far out over a wall?

The few wisps of hair that had strayed from beneath the dupatta covering the woman's head were grey. Her forehead was deeply lined, the mouth curved down in a permanent scowl. An old woman, and not just old but also embittered. Muzaffar felt sorry for her.

She did not invite him to sit. Not that there was much space on the charpai anyway, and there was nowhere else to sit, except the packed earth floor of the courtyard. 'So Mohammad Hussain Sahib sent you here,' she said after a while, not even looking up at Muzaffar. 'If it hadn't been for my second husband, I would have been begging in the streets. Or worse. And no thanks to Hussain Sahib! What do you want?'

Muzaffar told her. She looked up then, her gaze unblinking. Muzaffar found it disconcerting. 'And why should I tell you anything?' she said finally. 'How do I know you won't find some pretext to execute me? What if you say I killed my husband? I know imperial officers; if you can't find a culprit, you find a scapegoat. That's your philosophy. I open my mouth, and the next thing I know, your men will be pinning me down in front of the elephant that comes to crush me to death!'

She talked too much, thought Muzaffar with an inward groan. If only she would consent to tell him what she knew – and tell him in as much detail as she seemed to say everything that came into her head.

'Why should I?' he retorted. 'I know too that you couldn't have killed Fakhruddin. He died on the construction site, falling from the scaffolding. I had that from both Mangal and from Mohammad Hussain. But you used to live near Ibrahim's house; you knew his wife, didn't you?'

'So?'

'So, surely you must remember something of what happened. After all, Fakhru was also Ibrahim's friend. When Ibrahim's wife went missing, did the two of you not even talk about it? Did you not help in the search for her?'

Her fingers, thin and long and with the joints swollen out of all proportion, stilled. She remained hunched over the platter on her knees, though, and did not say a word for so long that Muzaffar wondered if she had fallen asleep. Then the fingers began moving again, slowly and methodically picking the chaff out of the wheat and throwing it beside her, onto the ground. '*Fauzia.*' The single word hung in the air, spoken with something close to reverence. Deep affection, Muzaffar realized when Fakhru's widow lifted her head and looked up at him. Her eyes were soft and something close to a smile lit up her face.

'Was her name Fauzia? Ibrahim's wife?'

She looked startled, as if she had forgotten that she had company. The head dipped again, the fingers went back to their work. 'Yes,' she mumbled. 'Fauzia.'

'Tell me about her, if you will.'

'She is long gone,' Fakhru's widow snapped. 'Why dig up the past?'

'There is no harm in remembering an old friend. And perhaps one may make amends for the past. A little, wherever and however it is possible.'

She seemed to mull over that for a few moments, before she heaved a long sigh – Muzaffar could hear exasperation in it – and reached over to pour a platterful of cleaned wheat into the sack on the charpai. The empty platter was then plunged into the other sack, and another load of polluted grain hauled out. The monotonous business of picking through the grain began all over again.

'Fauzia was very unlike Ibrahim,' the woman said once she had settled down again. 'You have met him? Fauzia's disappearance and his own illness did make him a bitter man, but not much more than he already was. Ibrahim was always a grim, quiet man. Not nasty, but not vivacious and cheerful like Fauzia was. He kept to himself. I think the only person he really loved was Mahmood. Even for Fauzia he had very little love. He didn't beat her or anything, but it always seemed to me that he didn't feel anything for her.'

Somewhere in the neighbourhood, a cow lowed and what sounded like an entire herd of goats began bleating. A dog was barking frantically, its yelps contributing largely to the cacophony. Fakhru's widow called to someone, to go and see what the matter was. 'Children up to no good, of course,' she said, half to herself. 'They have nothing better to do, and their parents don't have the time to look after them.' She hummed irritably for a moment or so. 'Fauzia was not from here, you see –'

'Where was she from, then?'

She scowled, annoyed at the interruption. 'Bijapur. She came from a good family. Not well to do, she said; but I think they were, to some extent. I had heard her tell of servants, of good clothes, and jewellery. Perhaps they weren't *really* wealthy, but they were certainly nowhere near as poor as Ibrahim.'

'How did she end up married to him?'

Outside the courtyard, the clamour had stilled.

'How do such things happen?' Fakhru's widow said in a sour voice. 'Sheer ill luck. Her father and brother were ambushed by bandits while they were travelling. Everything they carried was stolen. Worse still, both men were killed. Only one servant made it back to tell Fauzia and her mother. Things went badly for them after that. It turned out her father had been in debt. Deeply. They had to sell off just about everything they possessed.

'Then her mother fell ill. It must have been the strain; she was always a fragile thing, Fauzia said. All the calamities that had visited the family took their toll. Fauzia turned to some of their relatives for help, but it wasn't forthcoming. Nobody wanted to take on the burden of looking after two destitute women. Fauzia was very young then, only about fifteen or so, and not set in her ways like her mother. She went out looking for work – and found it. A young merchant employed her as a maid in his household. She worked there for a couple of years until the man got married. His wife was a jealous sort; she did not like to have young women as maids in the house.'

The story was somewhat tedious; it traced Fauzia's history, from one employer to the other, from the merchant's house to that of an aristocrat and then to a sarai where she worked briefly as a washerwoman. 'Who would have imagined,' Fakhru's widow said softly, regretfully. 'That lovely young thing – I knew her when she was much older, of course; but I could well imagine what she must have been like when she was that young. And fallen so sadly in life! Her mother died somewhere along the way, unable to take it anymore. Fauzia was strong as iron, though. She bore it all stoically enough. It was at the sarai that she met Ibrahim. He was in Bijapur to work on a haveli some amir was building... he saw Fauzia, and wanted to marry her. Probably thought, since she was all alone in the world, or at least for all practical purposes, he wouldn't have to cough up a bride price.'

'And she married him because that was better than being on her own?'

The woman sniffed and wiped her nose on the back of her hand. 'Wouldn't you, if you were in her place?' She picked a clod of dried mud out of the wheat and flung it far out into the courtyard with a muttered oath. 'Anything was better than wearing your fingers to the bone washing the clothes of strangers day in, day out. That's what she told *me*. So she married Ibrahim, and went on one last round of Bijapur before they set out for Agra. She told me she went back, one last time, to meet the merchant who had first given her employment, and he gave her a wedding gift. A bracelet, gold inlaid in some black metal. She showed it to me later; it was like nothing I had ever seen before, but it was very fine. That was the only valuable thing she ever possessed after the death of her father.'

'But she wasn't very happy being married to Ibrahim, was she?'

The woman laid aside her platter of wheat and yawned, rubbing her eyes as she did so. 'The aim of marriage is not happiness, you know,' she said in a serious voice, as if imparting a lesson to one young enough to be her son. 'Some say a marriage is meant so that children can be born who will take care of us in our old age. I say it is so that we will not have to go through life alone. If you have to shoulder every burden all by yourself, it can be very difficult indeed.' She had leaned forward as she spoke; she looked at him narrowly and then straightened, blinking self-consciously as if realizing that she had been rambling. 'No, Fauzia wasn't happy. But at least she didn't have to work for other people to keep body and soul together. And at least Ibrahim didn't beat her. That's more than a lot of wives can boast of.'

'And then there was Mahmood?'

'Yes. He came along pretty soon after they were married. She was already with child when they set out from Bijapur for Agra. And once he was born, there was no stopping Ibrahim from being the good father.' She picked up her platter and got back to work. 'We came here when Mahmood was about eleven years old, I think. Ibrahim doted on him.'

The sun was warm on his back and neck. Deliciously warm and comfortable. So comfortable that if he wasn't careful, he might just go to sleep standing on his feet. Muzaffar cleared his throat and tried to draw the conversation back on track. 'What happened on the day she disappeared? Had you seen her? Spoken to her?'

Fakhru's widow nodded, but grudgingly, reluctant to change the topic. 'Yes.'

'And? Had you noticed something wrong? Did she – for instance – seem agitated? Upset? Did she say anything that might indicate that she was thinking of running away?'

The woman shook her head. A long curl of wiry grey hair tumbled down the side of her forehead and hung over a gaunt cheek. 'No. Nothing. She wasn't upset. On the contrary. She seemed excited; happy about something, I don't know what. She wouldn't say. I asked her, but she refused to tell me.' She reached a hand up and tucked the tendril of hair behind her ear, pulling the dupatta firmly over it. 'She did say she was going out, but that she would be back soon. And she did. I saw her going, all dressed up in her best blue clothes and with her black and gold bracelet on her wrist. She came back later in the afternoon. I was busy inside my own house, but I saw her through the window, walking home.' She trailed her fingertips through the clean wheat in the platter, leaving parallel furrows in the grain, waving and twisting and looking like an artist's depiction of a turbulent sea. 'If Fauzia meant to run away, she should have fled with her best clothes on and her most valuable possession on her wrist. Why did she come back?' She looked up and Muzaffar saw bewilderment in her eyes.

'Did you meet her after she had come back?' he asked.

She had begun sifting through the wheat again, back to work after those few moments of careless meandering. She did not even look up at him when she answered, 'Not to speak to. I didn't have the time. I was out in the courtyard doing something – sweeping, perhaps, maybe giving the goat something to eat; I don't remember. I looked up just as Fauzia was passing by, because I saw that brilliant blue peshwaaz of hers out of the corner of my eye.'

She flicked a tiny pebble out of the wheat. 'I was busy, and she seemed to be listless. I called out a greeting, just to ask how her outing had been. She waved to me and said it was all right. That was it. She went on her way, and I went back to my work. We didn't meet.'

'But did she seem as excited and happy as she had appeared before she was setting out? You said that was how she had been.'

The woman shook her head. 'No. That happiness had gone. She looked – well, not devastated or distressed or anything, just a little melancholy.' She glanced up at him, a frown creasing her forehead. 'If you think she went and drowned herself in the river out of unhappiness, you can kill that thought. Fauzia was not that sort.'

Muzaffar restrained himself from saying that it was possible that Fauzia's unhappiness – in stark contrast, moreover, to her earlier joy – may have had something to do with her vanishing. Instead, he put another question to his unwilling hostess.

'What about later in the day? You did not see her leave her house later that day?'

The woman shook her head. 'I did not. But then, I wasn't standing at the window or outside my house all day. Maybe she stepped out again when I wasn't looking. Or maybe she went some other way, not in front of my home.' She bit her lip, thinking. 'But later,' she said after some thought, 'when Ibrahim raised the alarm, I went around with my husband, asking about her. A few people said they had seen her in the early afternoon – when I had seen her too – but not since then. On the other side of their house, a boy had been keeping an eye on a herd of goats. He swore he hadn't slept a wink or looked away from the path. And that Fauzia hadn't come that way.'

Muzaffar frowned, perplexed. 'Did she take anything with her? Was anything missing?'

Fakhru's widow's patience seemed to suddenly snap. She had been sitting cross-legged with the platter in her lap; now she shifted the platter onto the charpai and surged to her feet. The effect was ruined by the fact that her knees had gone stiff and she lost her balance, so that Muzaffar had to grab her arm to prevent her falling. She pulled herself free from his grasp and glared up at him. 'How much do you think I remember, eh? And what do you think I am? One of those stylish ladies of yours, who do nothing all day long except dress themselves up and gossip? I have work to do! I can't sit around indefinitely, answering your stupid questions!'

Muzaffar was taken aback, but he rallied swiftly. 'You liked Fauzia, I thought,' he said quietly. 'Don't you want to know what happened to her?'

'I know what happened to her! She got fed up of staying with that cold fish of a husband of hers! She decided she'd had enough, and she ran away! That's what happened. You don't need to carry out an investigation to find that out! Not now, so many years later!'

'But what if she hadn't run away? Nobody seems to have seen her leave the house after you saw her return.' He stopped as another thought struck. 'Tell me: how did she feel about Mahmood? Ibrahim loved him once upon a time, but what about Fauzia?'

'How would a mother feel about her own son?' The woman snarled at him. 'Of course she loved him. Doted on him, much more than Ibrahim ever could. She would have given her life for him!'

'And you think she would have left this son, whom she loved so very deeply, and gone away without a word?'

The woman's eyes widened, the anger dissipating and leaving behind it bewilderment. She looked away from Muzaffar. He could almost see her grope desperately for a reason to account for her long-lost friend's inexplicable behaviour. It would be easy, he thought, for Fakhru's widow to say that Fauzia, perhaps, had found a new life for herself. A new beginning with another man, a better existence and a happier one. One for which she was willing even to make the sacrifice of losing her son.

She looked up finally, and all the fight had gone out of her. The irascible old woman of a minute ago was now just an old woman, somewhat pitiable in the way she glanced up at him, searching his face for an explanation.

She heaved a sigh. 'Yes, I hadn't thought of that. Fauzia would not have left Mahmood and run away. Not for anything. She would have borne – *was* bearing – all the tedium of an existence with Ibrahim, for the sake of her son. She loved him that much.'

'I heard Mahmood was an apprentice at the time. He must have been – how old?'

'A youth. Sixteen, maybe? Seventeen? No more.'

'Perhaps Fauzia thought he was old enough to fend for himself? That he didn't need her anymore?'

Fakhru's widow shook her head so vigorously, her dupatta slid off her hair and she had to tug it back on. As if physically giving up her former anger, she lowered herself onto the charpai again. 'No. Not Fauzia. His growing up made no difference to her. She loved him as much as ever.' She reached for the platter and placed it in her lap, looking dumbly down at it. Finally, as if she could not bring herself to go back to her work, she put the platter back on the fraying plaited hemp ropes of the bed and began wringing her hands. Her shoulders shook, her chin tipped down until it nearly rested on her chest. She wept.

Muzaffar stood, embarrassed and unsure of what he should do. Had it been Zeenat Begum who cried, he would have enfolded her in his arms and given her his shoulder to cry on. He would have whispered words of consolation. He could hardly recall any other woman crying in his presence. Ayesha's tears, so crystal-pretty that they added to her beauty, had been limited to when she was being petulant and wanted her own way; both of them had known it. Last summer, he had been called to investigate a murder. There, a slave girl, lover of a murdered catamite, had wailed horrifically over the boy's corpse – but there had been other people around, and her grief had been so dramatic that one had not felt especially awkward about it, just a little awed. It had not been like this, this nearly silent sobbing. This was unnerving.

After what seemed an eternity, the woman wiped her eyes with the corner of her dupatta. She did not look up. 'If Fauzia did not go of her own accord – are you saying that someone carried her off? Kidnapped her?' Her voice was hoarse, blurred by her tears. She swallowed noisily.

'Perhaps. But there *were* other people about, weren't there? Neighbours like you. If Fauzia were being abducted, surely she would have raised the alarm? And even if she didn't – let us say, she was gagged or bound, or both – somebody may have seen her. It's difficult to kidnap a grown woman and take her through a populated area in the middle of the day. Someone is bound to hear or see something.'

The woman shook her head. 'No. Nobody did. We asked. The last anybody saw of her was when she came back, wearing her bracelet and her fine blue clothes. Not after that.'

'Did you happen to go into Ibrahim's house that evening?'

Muzaffar said, after a while. 'Whether she left on her own or was kidnapped, there were likely to have been some signs to indicate where she may have gone. Were all her clothes there? Was anything missing?'

'No, nothing. Ibrahim showed me the chest in which Fauzia used to keep all the family's clothing and bedding, full up to the top, her blue peshwaaz – the one she had worn that day, the one she liked so much – spread over the top. I didn't see her bracelet. I didn't think about it then. But if her peshwaaz was there, I suppose the bracelet would have been, too.'

'And the house itself? Were there any signs of a struggle, perhaps? Things knocked down, or spilled –'

The woman did not even let him finish the sentence. 'No. The house was exactly as it always was. Nothing was different.'

'Nothing?'

She glared at him, defying him to get her to take back her own words. Then, suddenly, as if she had recalled something, she bit her lip. 'There was something, but hardly a sign of a struggle...'

'What?'

'I don't know if it meant anything – I thought it didn't. Ibrahim said he didn't know either.'

'What was it? Please tell me.'

'There was a sort of crack in the wall, fresh, like a gash. As if someone had flung an axe at the wall. I'd have expected a lot of loose earth on the floor, spilled from the crack, but there wasn't. Instead, the floor had been newly wiped. You could see the streaks of wetness in the mud floor. I was surprised; Fauzia was never a very good housewife, you know. If something was spilled, she'd more often than not just pull a mat over it and hide it up. And if it was merely dry earth that had spilled onto the floor, why, there wasn't any need to mop it up anyway – any woman would have simply swept it out the door.'

And that was all Muzaffar was able to get out of her. She clammed up after that, telling him in a tight-lipped way that she would have got all the wheat cleaned a good half-hour back if it had not been for his incessant questions. Muzaffar apologized and asked that he be allowed to visit her again if he needed more information, but she neither acknowledged the apology nor granted him permission. 'I have told you all I remember,' she said in a dismissive tone.

14

AKRAM, LEANING BACK against two fat bolsters piled one on top of the other, was looking sorry for himself. Although his sprained ankle had not deterred him from dressing up – he was sporting a particularly fine turban, a pale dull gold embroidered in cream – it had played havoc with his usual ebullience. He was showering curses on a slave boy, barely fifteen years old, who was holding a salver with a silver tumbler on it. 'And you can tell the cook what I said! He can take that concoction and – oh, get lost! Out!'

Muzaffar, entering the room, passed the slave as he was bowing his way out. His expression was one of longsuffering; this was apparently not the first time Akram had vented his frustrations on the youth. A wisp of steam arose from the tumbler. Muzaffar caught a whiff of something fragrant, both earthy and spicy – and then the slave was gone, bearing his salver back to a kitchen which would still be relatively cold, still not functioning in deference to its late master.

Akram perked up at the sight of Muzaffar. 'It *is* good to see you,' he said, gesturing to his friend to be seated. 'I am heartily sick of seeing the servants come by with one remedy after another. All at my aunt's instigation, of course. My sprain seems to have come as a godsend for her; she's taking a vicarious pleasure in thinking up new remedies for me. Two hakims have been here to examine my foot and prescribe for it. The first one put some sort of poultice with myrrh in it. Not bad, since it smelled all right too. But the second hakim said myrrh was outdated and its efficacy in question, so the thing to apply was turmeric ground with saltpetre and lime. That's what you can smell right now.'

'It doesn't smell bad,' Muzaffar pointed out, soothingly.

'That's because you haven't had it smeared liberally on to you,' Akram growled back. 'And you haven't had to drink and eat things calculated to churn your stomach. My aunt remembered that sheep's trotters are supposed to be very good for broken bones, so my last two meals have consisted only of trotters, with rotis. I *hate* trotters, Muzaffar. I hate them with a vengeance. And in between meals, I'm being dosed with milk cooked with ghee and gram flour. It's supposed to be good for colds and chest infections. Allah knows I have neither – nor do I have broken bones – but I am expected to have all of these ghastly things for the sake of my ankle.'

'I hope you get well soon.'

'I sincerely doubt that I will, at this rate. But leave that be. Tell me what you have been up to.'

So Muzaffar, sitting beside his injured friend, told him all that he had done and learned over the past day. 'I have a feeling that Fauzia, after she returned from wherever she had gone in her blue clothes, never *did* go out anywhere else.'

Akram frowned, puzzled. 'I don't understand. If she didn't go out, how could she be missing? And your ladyfriend did say that she went inside Ibrahim and Fauzia's house when they were looking for Fauzia. I can wager anything you like that Ibrahim's home wasn't large enough for Fauzia to have been away in another room, unaware of all the hullabaloo –'

'That's not what I meant. I'm quite certain Ibrahim's house was small enough for Fakhru's widow to have seen all of it in just one glance. But perhaps Fauzia had been just too well hidden away?' When Akram, still looking bemused, did not comment, Muzaffar made an effort to explain. 'See, it seems highly unlikely that she was abducted, because nobody heard or saw anything. Even if one assumes that the walls of the house muffled any sounds – it would have been well-nigh impossible for somebody to drag her away from the house without anybody else seeing or hearing something.'

'In a large basket...?' Akram ventured. 'Or piled into the back of a cart and covered over with bales of straw, or something of the sort?'

Muzaffar grinned. 'Before you know it, the Diwan-i-kul will be assigning investigations to you, Akram! But yes, I did think of that, when I was on my way out of the area. I went back and asked Fakhru's widow. She nearly burst a blood vessel when she saw me returning. She reminded me of that goatherd she had mentioned; he said he hadn't seen anything suspicious. Not Fauzia, not anybody towing along a woman or anything large enough to be a woman. Nobody else had seen anything of the sort, either. And the lanes of the area are too narrow for carts; the huts are too close together.'

'In any case,' he said, 'if she had been kidnapped, then that begs the question: why? It cannot have been for material gain; Fauzia and her husband were too poor for anybody to hope for ransom. She had no other close relatives who would be willing to pay up, either.' He paused for thought. 'Someone could have kidnapped her for other reasons, of course. Perhaps she knew something that could be damaging for another; but in that case, why kidnap? Why not simply silence her? Either with money, or by killing her? If we assume that the culprit had scruples about murdering as opposed to kidnapping – well, then, if Fauzia is alive and well, then why has she not in all these years tried at least once to make contact with the son she loved so much?'

He broke off as a thought occurred to him. 'And here I am, jumping to conclusions,' he muttered angrily. He glanced at Akram. 'Sorry. Consider that last sentence unsaid. I do not know for sure. Maybe Mahmood *has* heard from his mother, and has simply kept the information to himself. We will know only when he is back in town and I can speak to him.'

'Which reminds me,' he said, 'what of that man Basheer had sent to Sajjad Khan's haveli to find out when he would be back? In all the confusion, I nearly forgot about that. Was there any news?'

Akram nodded. 'Sajjad Khan and his guests are supposed to return to Agra this evening. Basheer's man ended up waiting for three hours at the haveli; the steward had gone out on some errand across the river.' He stretched out his arm and lifting the thin quilt that had been laid over his legs, he gently felt his swollen ankle. He winced. 'Both hakims agreed on one thing: it would be best for me not to walk for at least another month. So you will have to go racketing about Agra on your own. While I sit here, getting bored and drinking my aunt's frightful decoctions.' He made a face. 'What do you plan to do now?'

Muzaffar did not answer at once; he was too deep in thought. 'It depends,' he said. 'There are too many clues, leading in too many directions. Mirza Sajjad Khan's piebald horse has a definite link to the murder, as far as I'm concerned. Or at least to the covering up of the murderer, which could mean the same thing – why try to remove evidence if you weren't connected in some way to it? And if Omar and his two companions *are*, as I suspect, Sajjad Khan's guests, then – well, it would be too much of a coincidence, wouldn't it? A man, son of one of Mumtaz Hassan's enemies, comes to Agra to meet Mumtaz Hassan and ends up quarrelling with him. Then he leaves, but doesn't leave Agra; he goes off, instead, to stay with another enemy of Mumtaz Hassan's. And shortly after, Mumtaz Hassan is killed.'

'*If* Sajjad Khan's guests are Omar and his friends.'

'Well, Haider will have to identify them, then.'

Akram raised his eyebrows. 'You'll go calling on Sajjad Khan and take Haider along? Get Sajjad Khan to present his guests?'

Muzaffar chuckled. 'And you think he will, if I ask him to? For a mere steward? He's more likely to throw both of us out of his haveli. I'll think of something.' He leaned sideways, glancing out of the window and up at the sky, gauging the time. 'Perhaps I'll go and talk to Ibrahim in the meantime,' he said as he straightened and stood up.

'Ibrahim? You think he's involved in this?'

Muzaffar had bent to dislodge a burr that had sunk its hooks into the fabric of his pajama. He tugged off the tenacious little thing and pitched it into the small brazier that stood near Akram. It flared up in a sudden burst of fire, sizzled for a few moments, and then was consumed. 'No,' Muzaffar replied as he rubbed the cloth, getting rid of the last few bits of dried thorn that still stuck to his clothing. 'No, I don't think Ibrahim is involved in this. Not in your uncle's murder, at least. Though he does manage to make his way around fairly well, he's still not capable of strangling anyone – and he seems too much of a recluse to have connived with someone else, even Sajjad Khan, to do it. But there *is* something in Ibrahim's past. Something that makes him hate Mahmood enough to want to send him to his death, if possible.'

Akram's eyes widened. 'Is that why you've been going all over the place – Sikandra and all – asking about Ibrahim? I thought you'd gone a little berserk. Or that you'd found some odd, long-ago connection between Ibrahim and my uncle.'

Muzaffar glanced up, looking oddly at Akram as he sat on the mattress, his leg stretched out in front of him, resting on a cushion. 'No,' Muzaffar said. 'I haven't found out anything of the sort. And there *is* a connection between Ibrahim and Mumtaz Hassan; his son is making your uncle's rauza, after all. And the two men knew each other from when the Taj Mahal was being built.' He straightened, dusting his hands as he did so. 'No, Akram; I don't know what it is yet, but I have a feeling there is something very fishy in Ibrahim's past.'

'Related to my uncle's murder?'

'I doubt it. Yes, yes; I know – you're going to warn me that I'm wasting my time on something that happened ages ago, instead of concentrating on solving Mumtaz Hassan's murder. And that the

Diwan-i-kul will have my hide when he discovers that. Put it down to curiosity. Put it down also to the fact that I was going through a period of enforced waiting. Omar is not in town. Sajjad Khan is not in town. And Shireen needs time to search for that mysterious lady.'

'But Sajjad Khan will be back in town tonight.'

'Exactly. And I will be back on the job, trying to find out how Sajjad Khan – or at least that piebald of his – is connected to the murder of Mumtaz Hassan. Right now, though, since Omar and Sajjad Khan are still not available, I can go and meet Ibrahim. Do me a favour, Akram, will you? When you meet Basheer at lunch, will you please let him know that I would require Haider for a brief while this evening? I want him to come with me to Sajjad Khan's haveli. Thank you.'

Ibrahim was at home, reclining on a charpai outside in the warm sunshine. Muzaffar, having stopped along the way to eat a quick lunch of greasy and tough kababs with rotis at a vendor's, arrived about two hours after noon. The old man had been lying down with his eyes closed. He must have heard the muted clip-clop of Muzaffar's horse, because he opened his eyes and raised his head. There was no word of greeting, but the trademark lopsided smile flickered briefly on the old man's face. Muzaffar was not surprised; he knew Ibrahim well enough by now. It did not even come as a surprise to find that Ibrahim was not eager to discuss the past.

'It's dead and buried,' he said gruffly, when Muzaffar shamelessly sat down on the edge of the charpai without being invited to do so. 'I thought you were supposed to find out who killed Mumtaz Hassan, not what happened one generation back. Leave it alone. It is none of your concern.'

'But it does concern *you*, doesn't it? And Mahmood, since it was his mother who went missing all those years ago. And Mahmood, from what you tell me, is the man who killed Mumtaz Hassan. So perhaps there *is* a connection.'

Ibrahim was adamant; there was no connection. Mahmood's hatred of Mumtaz Hassan had nothing to do with the disappearance of Fauzia. Fauzia had vanished – a bad thing for a mother to do, leaving behind a son who was so deeply attached to her – but that was it; it was done, and Mahmood had forgotten about it. So had Ibrahim. It had been a long time ago. They had learned to live without her. It had been a hard lesson, but they had learned it, and they did not need the past raked up again.

Muzaffar interrupted the soliloquy. 'I believe that was a very eventful period in your life. Traumatic, even. You must remember it very well. What happened?'

Ibrahim stared at Muzaffar, and then, without any warning, swung out with a vicious swipe of his crutch. That it did not hit Muzaffar was thanks to his own swiftness. He scrambled out of the way and stood up, well clear of the range of that crutch. Ibrahim's foul temper had had its effect on Muzaffar as well; the two men glowered at each other, Muzaffar standing a good three yards away from the charpai, the old man half-sitting, supporting himself on his good elbow, his entire body quivering with agitation.

'Listen, you,' Muzaffar grated out before Ibrahim could get his breath back. 'I haven't come here to pass the time of day with you. I have no more liking for your company than you have for mine – but I'm not going away until you've given me some answers. So let's get that over and done with –'

Ibrahim burst in even before Muzaffar could end the sentence. 'I'm not giving you any answers! I have more than done my duty by telling you who killed Mumtaz Hassan! Go away!' He swung the crutch again, ineffectually this time, only to have it go flying out of his hand and land beyond the far edge of the charpai, well beyond Ibrahim's reach. Muzaffar glanced at the old man, the eyes filled with a petulant anger, one side of his face still and expressionless, the other so angry that it looked as if it would disintegrate under the force of its own emotion. Muzaffar sighed and walked across to the crutch. He bent, lifted it from the ground, and brought it back to the charpai.

'I wasn't making empty threats when I said I wouldn't leave until you'd answered my questions,' he said quietly. 'I won't. You can throw things at me, you can abuse me all you want. But I won't budge.' He stared fixedly at Ibrahim, who had now collapsed back on the bed. 'Yes? Will you tell me what happened the day your wife disappeared?'

The fight went out of Ibrahim. His eyes continued to smoulder with irritation, but it was a resigned irritation, tinged with the knowledge that it was useless. 'She disappeared, what else?' He drew in a deep breath, steadying himself. 'I apologize, huzoor,' he said. 'I should not have said the things I did, or behaved the way I did. I beg your pardon for that. But it is pointless, this questioning of yours. If I knew anything more than what I have already told you, I would not have withheld it from you. Why should I? Go, huzoor; go. You waste your time with a cripple like me.' He looked away.

'If I waste my time,' Muzaffar said, 'then that is my foolishness, and I will pay for it, no doubt. But I see you are not busy; surely you can spare the time to answer a question or two. Tell me about that day your wife disappeared, Ibrahim. What happened?'

When Ibrahim still did not react, Muzaffar continued. 'Had she said anything about going somewhere? Had someone come to visit her? Did you have any notion that she might be thinking of going away?'

The old man shook his head. He did not say anything.

'And when did you find that she had vanished?'

Ibrahim answered after some hesitation, as if he disliked the very idea of satisfying Muzaffar's curiosity. 'When I came home from work. She wasn't home.'

'Was she always home when you returned?'

Ibrahim shrugged. 'Where would she go? Shopping? She may have been a wealthy lady once upon a time; not any longer. A poor man's wife spends her days at home.'

Coming from someone who had, less than a minute earlier, refused to utter a word, this was volubility indeed. Muzaffar blinked, taken aback. 'You hadn't known her when she was a wealthy lady, had you?' he asked, conversationally. 'Did she sometimes speak to you of the days when her family did have riches?'

Ibrahim grimaced. 'That one? You couldn't get a word from her if you tried to beat it out of her with a stick. She may have lost all her wealth, but she still had all the airs of a lady. It was a surprise to me that she even consented to let me consummate the marriage!' He spat out the last words, so intensely acrimonious that Muzaffar could not help but feel a twinge of sorrow for that man, all those years ago, who had married above his station and none too wisely.

'Why did you marry her, then?'

'Any man with his manhood intact would have wanted to marry her,' Ibrahim replied after a while. There was a grudging softness in his voice, the glimmer of a long-ago lust, thought Muzaffar. 'She was a beauty, all huge eyes and long lustrous hair and a figure you could appreciate even when she was clothed.' The softness was replaced by defiance. 'And she encouraged me, I could see that. She never smiled at any of the others who hung around her, trying to win her over with gifts and sweet words. It was *me* she liked, *me* she accepted.

'Or so I thought,' he added after a moment. Muzaffar, watching him silently, marvelled at how suddenly and without warning human emotions could change. Ibrahim's defiance was gone now; what was left was bitterness. Muzaffar could sense, in that flat voice, the regrets of an old man for the more gullible days of his youth – for the time when he had let his life be ruled by a passion that had been one-sided. A ghost flitted through Muzaffar's mind, of Ayesha – beautiful, capricious Ayesha, who had led him on too, and then deserted him. It was an eerie coincidence, he thought. And in the next moment, realized that it was not the same, not at all. He had left Ayesha behind; she was only a memory. Vivid, yes, at times; but not strong enough to hold him any more. Fauzia, on the other hand, seemed to live on. Cold and distant to her husband, and now missing for so many years, but still smouldering in Ibrahim's being, feeding his anger.

He was still talking of her, of her perfidy and deception. 'I suppose she simply needed me as a means of getting out of Bijapur. Perhaps she was sick of Bijapur; it was the place where her family had been ruined, after all. Maybe being there brought back memories she didn't want. Maybe she hated the thought of running into people she had once known, but who were now so vastly superior to her. I don't know.'

'So, she changed after marriage, did she?'

Ibrahim nodded, listless now. 'Indifferent. She didn't shirk her work, no. She would do the housework, everything a poor man's woman could be expected to do. But there were no smiles, no laughter or joking or coquetry. Who would want to live with a woman like that?'

There was no answer to that. Muzaffar let a moment or two pass in silence, then asked, 'And you saw nothing unusual at home when you got back, that day when she vanished?'

Ibrahim shook his head. 'She was missing, that was all. First I thought she had gone out, perhaps visiting a neighbour, or maybe to the well or down to the river. But when she didn't come back for an hour – more – I went out looking, asking people around. Those who had seen her said they saw her when she was returning from somewhere, all dressed up.'

'Where could she have gone, wearing all her finery?'

The old man shrugged. 'I don't know. Perhaps she took it into her head to go to the market.'

Muzaffar raised an eyebrow. 'Dressing up to go to the market?' The question was implicit; a woman of Fauzia's financial status would not see any need to dress well to go and buy coarse flour or onions or salt. Ladies dressed up in fine silks and pashminas and muslins when they went out to purchase jewellery or slavegirls, or to visit their friends and relatives.

Ibrahim said nothing.

Muzaffar tilted his head, looking narrowly at Ibrahim. 'Fakhru's widow said you showed her the chest in which your wife kept her clothing, and that it was full up to the brim. She said Fauzia's blue clothes – what she wore when she went out earlier that day – were in it too. Was her bracelet there?'

Ibrahim shook his head. 'I didn't see it.'

'Didn't you even look for it? I would have thought you would want to; it was valuable, after all.'

Ibrahim gazed coldly at Muzaffar. 'The first couple of days, I was too busy trying to get a hold on myself. Looking for her, and trying to keep the house in order. Then this happened' – he swept his left hand along his side, indicating the comparative uselessness of his limbs – 'and then where would I have gone searching for anything? Perhaps whoever took her away also took the bracelet.'

'Perhaps.' Muzaffar stood looking down at the bitter old stone carver. Ibrahim had lain down, and shut his eyes. He was lying high up on the charpai, the top of his head hanging off the upper edge of the bed. His mouth hung half-open.

'Goodbye,' Muzaffar said after a moment. 'The next time I come, I hope you will have remembered a bit more.'

Haider had admitted to Muzaffar that he had spent all his life in Agra, never having been out of the city in all the many years of his existence. Muzaffar, an incorrigibly enthusiastic traveller, privately thought it a boring existence; but it had its advantages, one being that Haider knew, or knew of, just about everybody worth knowing in town. He had a passing acquaintance with the staff of Mirza Sajjad Khan's haveli – 'it is not unusual, huzoor; though I must confess we do not get along well, since Hassan Sahib and Sajjad Khan Sahib' – he lapsed into a tactful silence, leaving Muzaffar to make what he would of the relationship between Mumtaz Hassan and Mirza Sajjad

Khan. Muzaffar also made a mental note to ensure that Haider was not spotted by Sajjad Khan's servants.

More importantly, Haider knew the shops, the tradesmen and merchants in Kinari Bazaar. He knew where the best filigree work was done, where to buy emeralds and wear to buy pearls. He knew which men had a reputation for honesty and which would have robbed their own grandmothers to make an extra rupee. He had, he told Muzaffar with a quiet self-satisfaction, imbibed it all over his many years in Agra. He knew it better than Hassan Sahib had, if he did say so himself.

He listened carefully to Muzaffar's instructions as they walked through Kinari Bazaar and then beyond, through the lanes and into the increasingly squalid surroundings of Sajjad Khan's haveli. They looked a pair, these two: a lean, round-shouldered man, neatly but simply dressed; and a tall man, as simply dressed but with the end of his turban wrapped securely around his face and covered with a large shawl. Muzaffar was taking no chances; he did not want anyone – not of Sajjad Khan's household, and not even a chance passerby who might talk later – to be able to put two and two together and realize that the two men who had been loitering around in the vicinity of Sajjad Khan's haveli had been closely associated with Mumtaz Hassan. He had insisted, therefore, that Haider too made some effort to cover his face. The steward had agreed readily, producing a voluminous grey shawl, so large as to be almost a blanket. He had wrapped it about himself, draping the cloth over his head and shoulders so that all that could be seen of his face was his chin, his mouth and the tip of his nose.

They had made their way from Mumtaz Hassan's haveli into the bazaar by bullock cart; a horse, normally affordable only by the wealthy, would draw attention that Muzaffar had no wish to attract. The cart driver had dropped them off near a small but busy sarai near Kinari Bazaar, from where the two men had walked to the bazaar. There, Muzaffar stood at a corner, trying to make himself as inconspicuous as possible, while Haider walked away, deeper into the market.

A quarter of an hour later, Haider returned, this time accompanied by a short, rotund man carrying a bulging sack over one shoulder. His eyes gleamed with curiosity when he saw Muzaffar, but he did not ask awkward questions. Haider did not bother to tell the man who Muzaffar was; the man was simply told what he was expected to do in exchange for the rupee Muzaffar would give him.

'Do you understand?' Muzaffar asked. 'You are to ask for Mirza Sajjad Khan, *nobody* else. Say that a tradesman you met somewhere – Dilli, Lahore, whatever – recommended Khan Sahib as a man who would appreciate the wares you sell. Don't let them tell you to hand over your bundle to a servant to go and show Khan Sahib, if he is in. And don't let them take you to someone else. Khan Sahib, or nobody. And if they say he is out and not back yet, come right back here and let us know.' He paused, eyes searching the peddler's face. 'You do have something decent to display, don't you? Just in case Sajjad Khan should be there, and you get called in?'

'Who on earth is he?' Muzaffar whispered to Haider a while later, as they watched the peddler walk down the road leading to Sajjad Khan's mansion. 'No man in his right mind would go about carrying such fine brocades in a sack over his shoulder. What if he should get caught in a storm? What if he should slip and fall in a puddle?'

But Haider had full faith in the peddler of brocades. A good salesman, said Haider; and a man who could be trusted – both to do what he had been commissioned to do, and to keep his mouth shut about it. 'He likes to be on the move,' he explained to Muzaffar. 'Sitting in a shop is not to his liking. His brother does it, but this man likes to go from house to house.'

A quarter of an hour later, the peddler was back. He brought with him welcome news: Mirza Sajjad Khan was not at home. He had been away from home several days now, but was expected back later this evening. The peddler, if he insisted on being a nuisance, should come back tomorrow; perhaps Khan Sahib would look at his wares.

'Good,' Muzaffar said, and handed over the promised rupee. 'You can go now.'

There was at least an hour to go before sunset. If Sajjad Khan and his contingent were to arrive while there was still light, they would undoubtedly notice Muzaffar and Haider loitering around near the haveli. True, their faces were adequately hidden, but Muzaffar's height was unusual enough to make him easily recognizable. 'Come along,' he told Haider. 'Let us get closer to the house, and find some sort of shelter from which we can look out. It wouldn't do to be seen.'

They did find shelter, in an empty cowshed standing at the edge of a field just beyond Sajjad Khan's haveli. Not a disused shed, Muzaffar realized as the smell of cow dung hit him hard in the gut; merely empty. The cows had probably been let out to graze, under the supervision of a youth, as was the usual practice. They would come home when the sun sank below the horizon.

The same thought, it seemed, had occurred to Haider. 'What happens when the cows are brought back?' he whispered. 'We can hardly peer out at Khan Sahib's haveli while the cows are nudging us and chewing the cud. Maybe even trying to gore us, if there are any belligerent ones among them.' A note of anxiety had crept into his voice.

Muzaffar peered out of the small window let into the wall of the shed. 'The light's fading fast,' he said. 'And I can't see any cows raising any dust for as far as the eye can see, in any direction. I'd think by the time the cows get here, it will be dark. We can move out then.' He indicated three stunted mulberry trees which grew in a cluster next to the cowshed. The branches of one tree brushed against the wall of the shed. 'Between the trees and the wall, we should be sufficiently hidden.'

'I only hope it isn't too dark by the time they arrive,' Haider muttered, the quintessential worrier. 'Otherwise I won't be able to see their faces.'

But the Almighty was kind. By the time Sajjad Khan's well-illuminated cavalcade came trotting wearily down the road, it was dark. The sun had set over an hour earlier, and with the startling speed of a winter evening, night had fallen. The first stars were already out, the moon had breasted the horizon and the cows had been brought back to the shed by a boy who had clucked sleepily at them as he slapped their rumps and urged them into the shelter of the shed. The shed had a rickety door hanging from hinges made of twisted rope; the boy had pulled it into place, tied another rope from one door post to the other, and gone away, dragging his feet and yawning prodigiously. Muzaffar, who had been keeping a lookout for the cows, had slipped out of the cowshed along with Haider as soon as he had seen the cows approaching.

They spent a cold half hour huddled between the mulberry trees and the shed. Then, simultaneously, both of them whispered, 'There they are!'

The servants – the sweepers and attendants, the cooks and their helpers, the men who would attend to such sundry tasks as the pitching of the noblemen's tents, the laying out of the noblemen's bedding, the carrying and washing and dusting and cleaning – would probably be following behind, in bullock carts that came at a languid pace. Some, perhaps, not as indispensable as the others, would have preceded the party and already arrived sometime during the day. The hunters and beaters, and the men who looked after the falcons used for hunting birds, would be trailing somewhere behind, as fast as they could follow on foot.

But the most important section of the group, Mirza Sajjad Khan and his three guests, was the one that now approached. The noblemen had the finest mounts, but the men who carried flaring torches also rode. They were strung out along the length of the small procession: two men in front leading the way, two bringing up the rear, and two along the way.

'That is Sajjad Khan Sahib,' Haider murmured, as the rider just behind the leading torch-bearers came into view. The man sat like a half-filled sack of grain atop his horse, slumped and slouching.

Muzaffar had seen many riders exhausted from day-long rides looking as if they would fall off their horses at the slightest jolt; never had he seen a man who looked as if he would need to be physically removed from his mount.

The two torch-bearers at the head of the cavalcade had reached the doorway of Sajjad Khan's haveli. The gate had been opened, and servants had appeared to welcome the master and his guests, to relieve them of their horses, to help them down. Sajjad Khan *did* need help, Muzaffar noticed with a private grin; he leaned so heavily on the shoulder of a brawny servant that the man lurched visibly. More torches had been brought out. The gate of the haveli and the area around it were awash with the flickering yellow light.

The men riding behind Sajjad Khan had walked into the pool of light now, dismounting stiffly. One of them stretched his arms high over his head, tilting his chin up as he did so.

'It's him,' Haider hissed. 'That is Omar, huzoor. And I am sure that other man – that one off to the left – is his friend. Oh, and there's the third of them, that man who's getting off his horse now.'

But Muzaffar was barely listening to Haider; his attention was focussed on the last of the men who had ridden his horse up to the gate. He looked, if the ease with which he slid off his horse was anything to go by, to be more used to riding very long distances. A man who was thin and almost delicate-looking. A man who patted his horse's neck before handing the reins to a servant who had stepped forward. A man who wore a turban that was ridiculously large for the size of his head and shoulders.

'The horse trader! Shakeel Alam.' Muzaffar breathed. 'What is *he* doing with *them*?'

15

FROM NEAR THE gate came an enraged bellow. 'You bastards! Who told you to untie his hands? Get him tied up again!' Sajjad Khan, slumping with fatigue just a few moments earlier, was pushing his way through the men and horses milling about the gate, shoving them aside in his haste to get to where Shakeel Alam was standing. The two torch-bearers who had been trailing at the back of the procession had moved hurriedly forward to grasp the horse trader's arms. They looked sheepish, one of them downright worried. Sajjad Khan must be a hard task master, thought Muzaffar.

He was. The nobleman reached the tail end of the by now disintegrated procession and flung out an arm, slapping the back of the nearest torchbearer's neck with such force that the man lost his grip on Shakeel Alam. He went sprawling across the road, the torch flying off in one direction, his body in the other. One of the servants, hurrying forward in his master's wake, veered off in pursuit of the torch. Flames were already spreading to the dry brush that bordered the road by the time the man reached it and began frantically flinging clods of earth at it. The torchbearer got to his feet, slowly and painfully. Even in the dim light of the single remaining torch, Muzaffar could see that the man's knees were grazed and had begun bleeding.

Sajjad Khan was yelling abuses at the other torchbearer. The man, hampered by the fact that he had only one free hand with which to work, was trying unsuccessfully to pull out a coil of thin rope, one end of which had been tied to the strip of cloth wound round his waist. Sajjad Khan's shrieks of rage were unnerving the man even more. Off to the side, the servant had succeeded in extinguishing the torch, but the spreading flames were licking hungrily at the dry vegetation, flaring up too swiftly for him to be able to control. He turned and called in a panicking voice to the mob at the gate. His words were mostly eaten up by the clamour around, the neighing and screaming of frightened horses, the shouts of Sajjad Khan – who had only now realized that a sudden crisis had erupted – and the startled yells of someone near the gate.

There was confusion confounded.

'Haider,' Muzaffar said urgently, grabbing the other man by the arm, 'Run back to the bullock cart and return to the haveli. Don't wait for me, I'll get there on my own. *Go!*'

Haider was not a man to stand around and ask questions; he was already moving away, still wisely keeping to the shadows beside the road and well away from the dancing, illuminating fire that was now raging across the road. Muzaffar moved at an angle, the mulberry trees and the cowshed behind him – the cattle inside had started up a frenzied mooing – and emerged on the edge of the road, just behind where Sajjad Khan had now caught hold of Shakeel Alam. The nobleman was standing behind the struggling horse trader, whose arms Sajjad Khan had pinned behind his back. Sajjad Khan himself was still screaming, now yelling at the torchbearer to hurry up and get the rope out.

Muzaffar paused just long enough to bend and lift an old brick that lay beside the road. Then he was hurtling forward, an avenging spectre emerging suddenly from the darkness, landing a hefty blow on Sajjad Khan's back and yelling to the astonished Shakeel Alam: '*Run! Follow me!*'

The next moment, with Shakeel Alam's wrist in his grip, Muzaffar was gone, racing madly through the fields, heading for wherever Sajjad Khan's servants would not find him.

'They looked, of course,' a mud-stained and dishevelled Muzaffar told Akram and Basheer an hour later. Haider, who had arrived a little earlier and informed Basheer of Muzaffar's adventures – up to the point when Haider himself had been dismissed so suddenly – had been standing at the drum house, with two other servants in tow, ready to spring to Muzaffar's assistance, should it be needed. A battered, shaking Shakeel Alam, one eye black and with a large and unsightly burn mark across the back of his right hand, had been shown to a bed chamber where he could rest. Muzaffar had asked for a dependable man to be put on guard at a discreet distance from the room.

Muzaffar himself was now sitting in the dalaan with his friend and the friend's cousin. Basheer and Akram had been in the middle of dinner when Muzaffar had burst unceremoniously in on them, looking dishevelled and a little muddy.

The remains of the meal were still spread out on the white dastarkhan, the bowls and platters of meats and rotis and fragrant biryani. But Basheer was looking uncharacteristically uninterested in his food. Akram, eyes wide, stared worriedly at Muzaffar, who was wiping the dirt off his face with a damp napkin. 'I suppose it took them some time to sort themselves out,' Muzaffar continued. 'There had been a lot of confusion, you know, what with the fire and me having felled Sajjad Khan. Some of them must certainly have stopped to help him to his feet – if he hadn't been knocked unconscious. And a couple of them would definitely have had to help prevent the fire from reaching the haveli; it was spreading rapidly.'

He dumped the stained napkin in a shallow bowl standing beside the mattress, and reached for the coffee that had been especially brewed for him. 'Besides which, that chessboard of huts and fields and ditches and whatnot is not exactly conducive to following a trail – not after dark, at least, and not when you're wondering if you will get back to find your master dead and his house gone up in flames. They were too close for comfort once or twice, but more by accident than design, I think.'

Muzaffar and Shakeel Alam – the latter too dazed and bruised to say anything – had managed to hire a palanquin near Kinari Bazaar. The kahaars, the men who carried the palanquin, had complained that the weight of two men – and one of the height and breadth of Muzaffar Jang, too – would be too much. Muzaffar, not eager to waste time and be found bargaining with the kahaars when Sajjad Khan's servants arrived at Kinari Bazaar, had bundled Shakeel Alam into the palanquin and ordered the kahaars to start off. He himself had run along beside them.

'You could surely have hired another palanquin,' Basheer commented.

'And take my eyes off Shakeel Alam? Have him slip out somewhere along the way and disappear again? No, thank you.'

He took a long, grateful swallow of his coffee and licked his lips. 'Did you send someone to Qureshi Sahib's with a message, Akram?' he asked, suddenly reminded of the first instruction he had given Akram as soon as he had arrived at Basheer's haveli. *Basheer's haveli*, he thought; not Mumtaz Hassan's haveli, as it had been till a couple of days ago. Even though Mumtaz Hassan had died, Muzaffar had found himself thinking of these walls as Mumtaz Hassan's haveli. As if the spirit of the flamboyant old trader had poured itself into the brick and mortar and plastered walls, so that it would live on and on... but Basheer was the heir, and Basheer it was who was now the master of this household. It was Basheer's haveli.

Akram nodded. 'Yes. They have been reassured that you are safe and well. And that they are not to wait up for you.' He noted Muzaffar's nod, and added, 'Eat something now, Muzaffar. Coffee is not enough.'

'It is for me.' Muzaffar grinned, but he also nodded. 'All right. Truth to tell, I am ravenous. And I need to be strong and with every sense at its keenest when I go to have a chat with Shakeel Alam. Allah knows what that man has been up to.'

But Shakeel Alam had proven frailer than Muzaffar had imagined him to be. He had, whispered the servant stationed at the door to attend to the horse trader, collapsed on the bed as soon as he had sat down on it. He was now snoring fit to shake the foundations of the house.

'That man is not waking in a hurry,' Muzaffar said disgustedly to Akram and Basheer, who had accompanied him to the door of the chamber occupied by Shakeel Alam. 'And if I try to wake him up, he perhaps won't be in a fit state to have a conversation with.' He drew aside the heavy curtain and peered into the chamber. Then, nibbling on his lower lip, he stepped over the wooden threshold and into the room, walking on soundless feet through it, along the walls, to the window – whose carved stone screen he caught with both hands and tested for strength with a good shake – and around the bedstead on which the horse trader lay asleep under two heavy quilts. Muzaffar cast one final look around the room and came out.

'There seems no way out other than this door. Put a guard out here to ensure Shakeel Alam doesn't wake up and give us the slip. If you think it's necessary, give orders that the guard is to change every now and then. We can't risk a man falling asleep and letting Shakeel Alam escape.'

Muzaffar reached Qureshi Sahib's haveli well after the moon had climbed into the middle of the sky. Assured that his message had been delivered, he had allowed himself to relax a while, to drink another draught of coffee and to listen to Basheer talking about the progress that had been made on the construction of Mumtaz Hassan's tomb.

At the gate of Qureshi Sahib's haveli, he handed his horse's reins over to a sleepy-eyed servant who came forward. Light still spilled out from some of the windows in the mansion; he could hear a woman laughing throatily somewhere in the mahal sara. Though not as exhausted as Shakeel Alam had been, Muzaffar *was* tired. It had been an eventful day. He needed time on his own, time to think over all that had happened. He shook his head at the steward who came forward asking if huzoor would like to be served a meal, or to be announced to Qureshi Sahib, who was perhaps still awake in his bedchamber.

In his own chamber, stripping off his choga and ruefully noting an irreparable gash along the shoulderblade, Muzaffar flung it onto the wide stool beside the bed. The next instant, he leaned down, pulling the folds of the choga aside to get at the flash of white he had seen under the cloth. On the padded cushion of the stool lay a folded note, with his name written on it.

It was from Shireen, and he felt a twinge of disappointment at its brevity.

Jang Sahib, she wrote. *I have an answer to your question. Zeenat Begum and I will come to the khanah bagh tomorrow morning whenever you should find it convenient. Please let Khursheed, at the door of the mahal sara, know when you will be able to meet us.*

So she had an answer, Muzaffar thought as he lay down a short while later, having undressed and washed in a state of distraction. His back ached, the muscles knotted and stiff as a board. Something stung there too; perhaps whatever had ripped his choga had penetrated through the thin layers of clothing below and scraped his flesh too. He turned over onto his side and stared into the moonlit depths of the room. The silhouettes of a tapering pitcher and a goblet dominated the small table beside the bed. He could dimly see the white rectangle that was Shireen's note to him.

Had she come into the room herself to leave the note there? But no; that was not done. She would have sent Khursheed, perhaps – Muzaffar fell asleep.

He had slept deeply and dreamlessly all these nights. This night he dreamed. Dreamed of being chased through fields of waving wheat and chickpeas, through stands of thorny ber trees which reached out to grab him and tear at his clothing. He was chased, by men on horseback and men on foot, shouting and trying to hit him with their sticks, but he was always ahead – until he slipped and fell, sprawling in the mud of the Yamuna's right bank.

And there she was, leaning down and helping him up. Shireen, unveiled and lovely, smiling at him, urging him up, taking his hand in her own. And he was smiling at her, telling her he did not care for

Ayesha any more, that Ayesha had been the longing of a long-ago youth – and then they were there, the men on horseback, racing towards them. The horses' hooves were thudding across sand and mud and gravel, the gravel flying and the horses snorting with exertion, froth dripping from their mouths. There were archers among the men. Arrows were beginning to fly, burning arrows that set fire to anything ignitable that they struck. Shireen was screaming, eyes wide with fear, her azure dupatta billowing about her. An arrow struck and the dupatta exploded in a sudden flaring of flame. As if the sky had been set on fire.

Muzaffar came awake with a start, drenched in sweat. Try as he might, he could not fall asleep after that.

She was all right, of course, when he saw her, standing quietly in the khanah bagh a few hours later. Whole and well and unscorched. And no doubt as beautiful as ever under the dupatta that veiled her. It was blue, like the one she had been wearing in his dream. That disturbed him, but it had been a mere dream, after all.

'It is too damp and foggy out here in the garden,' Zeenat Begum said briskly when Muzaffar greeted the two women. 'Let us go inside and sit in the dalaan. We will be more comfortable.'

'And how are you, Muzaffar?' she said, when they were seated. 'We heard that you were late coming back last evening – Qureshi Sahib sent word that he had received a message that no one was to wait up for you. All is well, I hope.'

Muzaffar told her what had happened. 'Hopefully, Shakeel Alam will have recovered by the time I get to Basheer's haveli,' he concluded. 'I cannot wait to find out what happened. How he ended up being in Sajjad Khan's captivity, and why.' He glanced, cautiously, towards Shireen.

She sat, straight backed and silent, on a mattress pulled up beneath a window that faced the rising sun. The first rays of the sun, fighting against the fog and still weak, filtered through the sandstone lattice of the window. Perhaps a few minutes from now the sun would be stronger, the rays bright enough to pierce the depths of that blue veil. Muzaffar bit his lip, mentally admonishing himself for letting his attention wander. 'Shireen Begum?' he said, 'You have discovered who the lady of those letters is?'

Shireen nodded. 'Yes. I met her yesterday, and confirmed it. She was discomfited, but when I reassured her that it would remain a secret – that you would not tell a soul, as far as it was possible – she did admit it.' From a pocket in one of her garments, she drew out a packet, the size of a small book, wrapped in a piece of white and red brocade. She placed the package next to her on the mattress and continued.

'She said she had first met Mumtaz Hassan Sahib a few years ago, when her palanquin had collided with a runaway horse in one of the markets. Hassan Sahib was nearby; he helped calm the lady down, took charge of her kahaars, and even had them take her to a nearby garden where she could soothe her nerves for a while.' Shireen shifted, perhaps with embarrassment. 'He certainly did help soothe her, somewhat. She is not exactly a shy and retiring female.'

Muzaffar suppressed a smile.

Shireen lifted the package. 'These are all that remain of her liaison with Hassan Sahib. His letters to her, mostly. And a few gifts he gave her.'

'Why did she give them to you? Are you so close a friend of hers?'

Shireen shook her head. 'No. I think – I think her love for Hassan Sahib was not really love, not lasting enough for her to feel anything but a mild regret that he is dead. It seemed to me, when I spoke to her, that what she was most sorrowful about was that his pampering of her had ended now that he was gone.' She paused. 'She does not sound a very nice woman, does she? But she isn't wicked, not *really*. Just shallow, materialistic. Perhaps too attached to things, not enough to people. As long as Mumtaz Hassan was around to give her gifts and say pretty things to her, she was happy. Now that he is dead, she is getting ready to marry the man her brother has chosen for her.'

'And who is this lady, pray?'

'Ah.' He heard the amusement in her voice. He could almost picture her smile, her lips curving up at the ends, that dimple twinkling in her cheek. 'I will not tell you her name, Jang Sahib, because I vowed to her that I would not speak it, not even to you.' She lifted a hand in a gesture to silence the protest she could sense rising to Muzaffar's lips. 'A mere formality, though, because I do not need to tell you her name for you to discover her identity. She is the only sister of her brother. You would only need to go to the household – not even that – to discover who she is. She is the sister of a prominent trader named Abdul Hafeez.'

Muzaffar gaped. 'Abdul Hafeez? Are you sure? But – but Taufeeq had told me that one of Mumtaz Hassan's most bitter enemies was a man named Abdul Hafeez. Can there be two traders with the same name? I cannot imagine Abdul Hafeez allowing –'. He stopped short, realizing the stupidity of what he had been about to say. Of course Abdul Hafeez had been kept in ignorance of his sister's affair with Mumtaz Hassan; she would have been careful to be utterly discreet about that relationship. Not just because Mumtaz Hassan was her brother's most hated rival, but because she was supposed to be a good, decent Muslim lady. A lady destined to be wrapped, from the swaddling cloths of her birth to the shroud of her death, by the stark walls of the zenana. Within the zenana a lady was to live, away from male eyes other than those of her immediate relatives. Within the zenana she was to eat and drink, sing and weep, live and die.

By the standards of the day, Abdul Hafeez's sister's affair with Mumtaz Hassan made her no better than a courtesan. She would be decreed a promiscuous woman, one to be ostracized if her affair became public. No wonder she had been so quick to hand over the last proofs of her late romance to someone who could get rid of them.

'She must trust you implicitly,' Muzaffar said, 'to have given these letters to you. Anyone else would have burnt them long ago. After all, what is to prevent you blackmailing her tomorrow by telling her that you will show the letters to Abdul Hafeez?'

'*Muzaffar*!' Zeenat Begum was looking daggers at him. 'How dare you!'

'I am not casting aspersions on Shireen Begum,' Muzaffar said placatingly. 'I would not ever imagine her capable of something like that. But I wonder why this lady – Abdul Hafeez's sister – was so trusting.'

This time Shireen did not merely sound amused; she actually chuckled, a rich throaty sound that swept away any fear he might have had that he had inadvertently offended her. 'Not so much trust, I think,' she said, 'as the fact that there seems to be nothing much there that I could use to blackmail her, even if I wished to. I looked through these letters yesterday after I had come home; she had given me permission to do so. She may have been unwisely passionate in her letters to him; but Mumtaz Hassan Sahib appears to have been the very soul of discretion when it came to his letters. There is not one word there to indicate whom he is writing to, or who he himself is. Nothing one can use as a clue to discover who the writer is.' She held out the brocaded packet towards Muzaffar, urging him with that gesture to read the letters for himself. 'She has requested that you destroy them once your work with them is done – if you should need them, that is.'

Muzaffar nodded and took the packet. The brocade was an old piece, the fine silk thread worn away and frayed in places. The red silk cord that held the edges together was new, though, and strong. Muzaffar balanced the package on his knee and untied it. The letters were very few – perhaps not even a dozen in all. Mumtaz Hassan had not been the most ardent of lovers when it came to correspondence. Below the letters was something else: a small, heavy bundle wrapped up in muslin. Muzaffar, without undoing it, glanced up questioningly at Shireen.

'The gifts I spoke of,' she said. 'The lady has given some of the gifts Hassan Sahib gave her. Jewellery.'

Muzaffar gave a lopsided grin. 'And I thought she was fond of material things?'

'She is. Surely you do not think that was all Hassan Sahib gave her?' Shireen laughed. He heard the rich, infectious sound and wished with all his heart that he was alone with her, so that he could beg her to lift that veil away and allow him to look his fill at her. But Zeenat Aapa sat by, a stolid figure, the very embodiment of propriety. Even if she had not been there, he would probably not have dared lift a finger to touch Shireen. It was *not* done.

Inwardly, Muzaffar groaned. His mind was wandering down lanes it had no business going. Fragments of his dream flashed through his mind; he remembered the look of fear in the dream-Shireen's eyes, the feel of her hands, the trust –

'He showered her with jewellery,' Shireen was saying.' Most of it gold or silver – she has had no difficulty having it melted. She told me she hurried to her trusted jeweller in Jauhari Bazaar the very day she heard of Hassan Sahib's death, with everything he had given her that could be melted. She said if Basheer or Hassan Sahib's begums discovered he had been giving her jewellery, they would probably want it back. And Allah forbid, if they were family heirlooms – then perhaps the family would even be able to identify them. The best solution was to have them melted and recast in a completely different pattern. That way she'd be able to keep them and nobody would be any the wiser.'

He could hear the sarcasm in Shireen's voice, her almost contemptuous admiration of the woman's insatiable greed. Muzaffar grinned, suddenly relieved, suddenly no longer scared of where he was going. He knew the path ahead, and while it seemed fraught with difficulties, they were not difficulties he would shy from. They looked from this far, like adventures he would enjoy experiencing.

'How *very* ingenious,' he said, trying to bring his mind back to the conversation. 'And this?' he indicated the little bundle of muslin in his hand. 'Is this not jewellery? Or is there another story to this?'

'Untie it and have a look,' Shireen prompted.

He did. It was a large square piece of fine white muslin, the size
of a man's handkerchief. The ends were knotted tightly together,
in multiple knots. It took him a while to undo the first couple of
knots. It revealed an elegant but unusual piece of jewellery: a pair of
earrings, lovely paisley-shaped ones made of some black, dull metal.
Pressed into the inky surface were the finest of gold wires, curving
into tendrils and tiny flowers. It was a work of art, so intricate that
it took Muzaffar's breath away. 'It's beautiful,' he whispered. 'I've
never seen anything like it.'

Shireen nodded. 'Neither had I. She told me it's known as bidri,
from the town of Bidar. The black metal is an alloy of zinc and
copper; they rub it with a special local soil which gives it that
deep black colour. It's popular in Bijapur too, now. Hassan Sahib
was from Bijapur; perhaps that was why he gave them to her – to
build a connection between the woman he loved and the city that
he loved.'

'I'm not so sure he really loved the city very much any more,'
Muzaffar murmured as he kept the earrings aside on the mattress.
Where the earrings had nestled was another knot, pressed down
into the centre of what looked like a large bangle. He could not see
it yet, but the shape was there, all right: thick and perfectly round,
a heavy, broad piece of metal designed to fit a woman's wrist – he
pulled the last tangle of knot aside and opened the bundle. Inside
it lay a bracelet. It too was bidri: black, inlaid in gold in a pattern
of Persian roses. Muzaffar stared.

'She said her jeweller wouldn't take responsibility for melting
those down – the bracelet and the earrings.' Shireen was saying.
'He wasn't familiar with bidri work, and didn't know what would be
the result if he put that into the furnace. Whether the gold would
run into the alloy, whether he would be able to pick out the gold
or not – he didn't know. And she didn't want to keep these pieces;
she said they were too distinctive, too risky. You could hand them

over to Basheer Sahib; they would be the property of the family, I should think.'

Muzaffar nodded, but his mind was already far away.

Shakeel Alam balanced the bracelet on his open palm, as if weighing it. 'The more usual type is made with silver,' he explained. 'Silver wire, or silver sheets that are inlaid in the black metal. But Mumtaz Hassan was not a man for the usual. He would have nothing less than gold.' He looked at Muzaffar. His face was now thin and haggard, not thin and elegant. 'Yes, I can well imagine that Mumtaz Hassan would have given this to a lady he admired. It's beautiful and it's distinctive.'

He held the bracelet out to Basheer, but Muzaffar took it before Basheer could. 'If I may have it,' he said. 'Only for a few hours, no more. There is someone I need to show this to. I will bring it back to you as soon as that is done.' He waited to see Basheer's nod of assent, and tucking the bracelet into his choga pocket, turned back to Shakeel Alam. 'And now: how did you come to be a prisoner of Sajjad Khan's? And why?'

The horse trader winced as he leaned back against the bolster. 'My back is very sore,' he muttered by way of explanation. 'That – that scoundrel had me beaten.'

'That reminds me,' Muzaffar said, startled into a sudden recollection by Shakeel Alam's words – 'You've known Mumtaz Hassan for many years now, haven't you?'

The man nodded, looking a little wary as he did so.

'He had scars on this back. Deep, rough scars, as if he had been lashed at some point in his life. Would you know how that happened?'

For a few moments, Shakeel Alam did not say anything. He did not even meet Muzaffar's eyes; he stared down at his own hands. When he finally looked up, his eyes were disturbed. 'It's a – a story that Mumtaz Hassan did not want revealed. Not to his friends and associates. Not to his own household, even, as far as that was possible.'

'I know. It came as a surprise to Basheer. But I would think the time for secrets is long past. Who knows, perhaps there is something in that secret that has a bearing on why Mumtaz Hassan was killed. Please tell me; it is imperative that I know.'

Shakeel Alam looked briefly as if he might protest; then he sighed deeply. 'It is a distasteful story. Not that my friend was to blame, as far as I could tell. It happened in Bijapur. Years ago – Mumtaz Hassan was a young man then, perhaps a couple of years younger than you. Even back then, he was a canny businessman. He knew how to get ahead in the trade, and that brought with it enemies. There was no dearth of merchants in Bijapur who would gladly have seen Mumtaz Hassan banished or killed.' He drew in a ragged breath. 'One of them spun a web of intrigue – we never did find out all the details of that – but the fact was that he took advantage of my friend's weakness for women. It was put about that Mumtaz Hassan had raped a young noblewoman and then killed her, to keep her silent. A corpse was produced... but any young woman, dead and draped in finery, can be passed off as noble.'

He bit his lip. 'Mumtaz Hassan protested his innocence, but there were enough people to testify against him. In any case, it was no secret that he liked the company of women. And there were sufficient men in the city to malign his character. Not just when it came to women, but in every other aspect too. They said Mumtaz Hassan was immoral, corrupt, evil beyond belief. He was sentenced to thirty lashes.'

'Oh. So that was why.'

Shakeel Alam nodded. 'That was why. It embittered him terribly; it became part of the reason why he eventually left Bijapur. Ostensibly, he remained a Bijapuri merchant for the next twenty-odd years; in reality, he spent only a fraction of those years in Bijapur. The rest of the time, he was wandering through Hindustan, through the world, searching for means to make his fortune even more unassailable than it had been earlier.'

'I see. Anyhow, to get back to the present: how did you end up as Sajjad Khan's prisoner?'

Shakeel's eyes narrowed as if sizing Muzaffar up. Muzaffar was looking not quite his usual self today. For one, he had not shaved, and his jaw was already shadowed with blue. For another, he appeared to have had a restless night – as he indeed had, what with that dream of his – and his eyes looked bloodshot and weary.

'That day at Mumtaz Hassan's funeral, a man came to me,' Shakeel Alam finally said. 'I had seen him hovering in the background when you were speaking to me. When we went into the graveyard, he stayed near me. All through the funeral. Then, when everybody was drifting out, he came up to me and asked to have a word. I didn't suspect anything; he said he had known Mumtaz Hassan.' He shifted, making a face as his sore muscles protested.

'He was a big, broad man, but he walked very slowly, trailing along as if his feet hurt. That made me slow down too. He didn't say much, just commented on how dignified the funeral had been. We were walking past a mango orchard – deserted and getting dark, because the sun was setting – when he leaped at me. He must have hit me on the head, because the next thing I knew, I was waking with a headache and he was tying me up. He had stuffed my mouth full of rags.'

'He must have been strong, to have overpowered you all by himself,' Akram remarked.

'He had the advantage of surprise. And he was much bigger than I am.'

He continued his tale after a break to sip from the tumbler of water beside him. 'He tied me up and bundled me into an abandoned shed in the grove. He went off then, and I must have fallen asleep from the pain and the exhaustion. When I awoke, I struggled hard to get free, but it was useless. And the gag he had put on me was terrible; I couldn't utter a squeak. And the stench made me want to throw up.' He shuddered delicately. Muzaffar was reminded of the first time he had met Shakeel Alam, of the almost fragile, effeminate elegance of the man as he had seemed then.

'The man returned after some time, with two other men. They came in a bullock cart, with one man riding a horse alongside. I was hauled out of the shed and bundled into the cart.'

It had been, by Shakeel Alam's account, a long, wearying ride. The horse trader seemed to Muzaffar to be one of those who revel in revisiting their own sorrows and discomforts. Every jolt and every jerk of the cart as it went into a rut or bounced over a stone was dwelt upon; every bruise that his poor aching body had suffered was described in lurid detail. Shakeel Alam's captors had been, for most of the time, neglectful. But he had been allowed to get off the cart and attend to his bodily needs, always under the humiliatingly watchful eye of one of the men. Thrice, when they were in completely uninhabited environs, his bonds had been loosened and his gag untied so that he could drink some water and eat. 'Some coarse roti and a foul bit of insipid lentils,' Shakeel Alam said, his voice brimming with disgust. 'Even animals wouldn't touch it.'

'A lot of poor people would kill for it,' Muzaffar observed. 'What happened then? How did you end up on the horse in Sajjad Khan's entourage?'

The journey had ended near Mathura, where Sajjad Khan, Omar and his companions, and their retinues were out hunting. Shakeel Alam's captors had arrived at the camp after having spent nearly all the previous night and the entire day trundling along the road from Agra, almost to Mathura. Shakeel Alam, sore and disoriented because of his headache and the bright lamps shining all around, had been pushed into Sajjad Khan's tent, where the man was sitting at dinner with his guests. It had been a horrible experience, with the noblemen staring at first, then laughing as Shakeel Alam – finally let free, so that he could be questioned – had stumbled around, gasping and blinking and eventually collapsing onto the mattress. 'I was in such a dreadful condition that Sajjad Khan had to call for food and drink for me,' he said with a self-satisfied smirk.

Revival had brought with it the inevitable questioning. 'The man who had captured me told Sajjad Khan that he had overheard you talking to me. "It must be something to do with the horse," he said to Sajjad Khan. I don't think Sajjad Khan had recognized me till then. Then, all of a sudden, he said, "Yes, of course. He's the horse trader, isn't he? The one we bought that piebald from." And that sparked off much excitement. The Bijapuris were there all through it, with Sajjad Khan murmuring in their ears, telling them this and that – I don't know what, perhaps how he had murdered my poor friend – and then he began pelting me with questions. Asking me who you were, how much I had told you, how much I knew and how I knew it. Had I followed the horse, and so on. I didn't know what he was talking about. And I was feeling so dizzy and ill and my head pounded so awfully, all I wanted to do was lie down and die.'

His voice trailed away into a whisper. 'I vomited. Almost in Sajjad Khan's lap. It was terrible.'

'What happened?' Muzaffar said. 'After you – um – cleaned up? Were you able to answer Sajjad Khan's questions to his satisfaction? And what did he really want? Did he suspect you of suspecting him?'

Shakeel Alam nodded. 'Yes. He thought I had kept an eye on the piebald horse even after I had sold it to him, or perhaps that I had noticed the horse near the riverbank opposite Mumtaz Hassan's haveli on the night he was murdered. I ask you! As if that could be reason enough to suspect someone of murder!' He gulped noisily from the tumbler, then reached, wincingly dramatically, for the pitcher and poured himself some more water.

'I hadn't known Sajjad Khan was responsible for my friend's death,' he said. 'I am a trader, not a kotwal. Give me horses to breed and sell; I can do that, better than most men. But ask me to catch a thief or a murderer, and I will leave it to the kotwal. I told Sajjad Khan that; but he wouldn't listen. He decided to keep me captive – said it would be till everything had blown over, but who knows? Perhaps he will change his mind now that he knows I have run away, and have probably told others about how Sajjad Khan treated me. Maybe his men are even now searching me out to kill me!' The man's voice quavered and rose into a near-shriek of self-pity and indignation.

Muzaffar got to his feet. 'I doubt if that will do him any good,' he said. 'If you have already told the world the truth about Sajjad Khan – which you haven't, I may add – it would hardly benefit him to kill you off now. He should have done that much earlier.'

16

MUZAFFAR STAYED JUST long enough to ask Basheer for the loan of a servant. 'Just for an hour or so, not much more,' he said. 'I do not know when it will be possible for me to come back to return that bracelet. If you send someone with me, I'll be able to give it to him to bring back to you.' He stemmed the protest that rose to Basheer's lips. 'Yes, I know you are not desperate to lay your hands on it, but still. It might be dangerous for me if that particular piece of jewellery were to be found on me. And I may need your servant's assistance in a small matter.'

Basheer had graciously offered more servants, should Muzaffar need them – and Muzaffar had just as graciously declined.

The man Basheer had called for happened to be the one whom he had sent, a couple of days earlier, to Sajjad Khan's house. Muzaffar, discovering by chance the man's identity, begged regretfully to be allowed another helper. 'Someone whom Sajjad Khan's household is unlikely to associate with *your* household,' he said. 'And – um – if possible, a man about my height? Any man will do, as long as he can be trusted. That is important.'

Basheer gave Muzaffar a long, puzzled look and called for Haider. The steward listened before bowing himself out, his face carefully expressionless. He returned after a quarter of an hour, to request Jang Sahib to step out. Not just from the dalaan, but from the haveli itself. 'The man is not one we would want to introduce inside the house,' he said, leading the way out, through the corridors and into the bright sunshine outside. He held aside the quilted curtain, and

Muzaffar stepped out, drawing in a lungful of cold crisp air. On it came the faint, almost elusive fragrance of roses. In the stone-rimmed parterres flanking the path that led from the haveli to the drum house, the first roses had begun to bloom. Deep pink-red blossoms, using the warmth of the sun in their battle against the winter cold. A couple of weeks from now, and the parterres would be full of flowers. For now, the roses were the vanguard.

And he had not even noticed them when he had arrived at the haveli.

A man was standing at the base of the short flight of steps that led up to the doorway. He bowed as Muzaffar and Haider descended. 'This is Ganga, huzoor,' Haider said. 'He works in the stables.'

He smelled of the stables, all right. Muzaffar felt his heart sink, and then lift just as abruptly. Allah was being merciful, more merciful than a sinner like him deserved. He grinned. 'Excellent.'

'And now, Haider,' he said, drawing the steward aside, 'there is something I wish to speak to you about.'

Haider had, most reluctantly, agreed to let Ganga take one of the mules from the haveli's stables. Horses and ponies were for the use of those who could afford them; a commoner who was neither noble nor rich, used his own two legs, whether he had to go from Jauhari Bazaar to Hing Mandi, or from Agra to Mathura. When obtaining enough food to feed one's family was a daily struggle, a horse was an unheard-of luxury.

Ganga had looked stunned that Muzaffar should insist on a mount for him; Haider had looked as if he suspected Muzaffar of having lost his mind. The mule eventually deemed worthy of carrying a nobody like Ganga was a tatty, scruffy creature with ragged ears and huge liquid eyes. It was generally used by the washerman to take dirty clothes down to the river and bring the clean, dry load back. It was not used to carrying anything heavier than washing, and protested vociferously when Ganga mounted it. The sound – an odd combination of braying and neighing that got on Muzaffar's nerves – continued most of the way to Fakhru's widow's house.

It began again when, a few minutes later, they left the house. Muzaffar bestowed a despairing look on the animal and said to Ganga, 'Do you know where one would be able to buy new clothes for you? The sort of things you're wearing right now? The dhoti, the shawl and turban? Or, if you prefer, a jama and a pajama?'

The man stared at Muzaffar, speechless. 'Go on,' Muzaffar said encouragingly. 'I'm asking you a question. Where did you get these clothes, for instance?'

'My – my wife made them, huzoor.'

'Hmm. But do you know where one might buy clothes like that?'

It took some coaxing before a bewildered Ganga was able to name a shop where one might be able to buy clothing. It was owned by a darzi, a tailor who stitched fancy chogas for some of the most illustrious names in Agra, but who in his spare time also was known to make cheaper clothing for those unable to afford the brocades and the zardozi. 'Or men who do not have womenfolk to stitch their garments,' Ganga said.

There were dhotis and jamas and pajamas and long lengths of cloth, folded and piled in heaps. Men like Ganga, poor by Muzaffar's standards, were still well-off when compared to the bulk of the population. Most men were too poor to wear stitched clothing; because thread and needle was expensive, because their womenfolk had more urgent things to do with their time than sewing garments, and because that was the way it had always been for most of them. Attire, even in the depths of Agra's formidable winter, consisted of one length of cloth wrapped around the head as a turban; another, wider length wrapped around the waist and upper legs as a dhoti; and a hopefully thicker, wider length functioning as a shawl. The knees and calves would remain bare. So would the chest and arms and back, when work made it impossible to keep the shawl firmly wrapped around one's body.

Muzaffar offered a silent prayer of gratitude for granting him the wherewithal to at least clothe himself warmly against the winter.

The darzi's wares were of coarse cotton, rough and obviously meant for those who could not afford to be finicky. The seams were strong but undisguised, and not one stitch of embroidery relieved the plainness of the cloth. Muzaffar ushered Ganga forward. The man looked on, bewildered, as Muzaffar got him to choose a new set of clothing for himself. A turban, a shawl and a dhoti; exactly what he was now wearing, except that this was all new.

'Will your wife be terribly offended if you were to go back home in clothes made by the darzi?' Muzaffar asked, once they had emerged from the shop onto the street.

Ganga stared. 'No, huzoor,' he said after a moment's thought. 'Why should she be?'

'Good. Let us find a secluded place, where no one can see us.'

Further down the lane, past the awnings that stretched from shopfronts, shielding baskets of fruit and vegetables, spices and grain, they found a small alley that led to a temple. It was a very small shrine, containing a stone statue of the sun god Surya, riding out in a chariot pulled by seven horses. Muzaffar glanced around. There was no priest to be seen, although someone had washed the statue and the floor around it just recently; traces of dampness still remained in the paving stones. A streak of vermilion marked the deity's forehead. A little heap of red and yellow petals sat at the idol's booted feet. A smouldering plug of incense protruded from among the flowers.

'Come on,' Muzaffar said, already hurrying past the shrine and behind it, where a sheltering peepal spread its grey-green leaves in a benediction above the temple. He looped his horse's reins around a low branch and was shrugging off his choga by the time Ganga caught up, tugging at his mule.

If any of the shopkeepers, their servants and assistants, or the shoppers in the bazaar had been paying attention, there might have been a few raised eyebrows. A nobleman had gone into the alley, accompanied by a man who looked, despite his great height, to be a servant: his clothes were the worn, plain ones of a servant, and anyone passing nearby would have caught the unmistakable whiff of horse manure. The smell still clung, but to the other man now. And the other man was not an amir. No, by no stretch of imagination could one have classed this man as an amir, though his skin was not as tanned as that of most poor people, who spent their day out working in the sun. A stablehand in a grand household, perhaps.

Ganga had been made to don the new clothes Muzaffar had bought at the darzi's. He looked uncomfortable in them, and scared.

'I will return your clothes to you soon,' Muzaffar muttered. The unbleached cotton in which the darzi had wrapped his wares now held Muzaffar's fine clothes. 'Here,' he said, handing the bundle to Ganga. 'Take these back to the haveli and give them to Akram Khan Sahib. Or to Basheer Sahib. Tell them to keep it. And –' he retrieved the bidri bracelet, which he had tucked into the waistband of his pajamas – 'give this to Basheer Sahib. Tell them I don't know when I will be back, or even when I will be able to send word. All right? Go, now.'

He waited a few minutes, watching Ganga's mule-mounted figure weave its way through the market, past the red and golden heaps of apples and oranges, the vivid green of leaves – spinach and fenugreek, radish leaves and mustard – and the sunlit gold of wheat heaped on a spread blanket. People surged around, moving, stopping, moving on again. Servants and slaves fetched and carried, cane baskets loaded with goods on their heads. Kahaars went hurrying past with palanquins; horses trotted by, one skittish mare suddenly rearing up in fright when a large goat charged.

Ganga disappeared, Muzaffar's horse, which he was leading, stepping docilely behind. The street continued as it was, its people shifting, moving ceaselessly, sometimes meandering, sometimes striding purposefully – but nobody followed Ganga. By the time he reached the end of the street and turned the corner, all Muzaffar could see of him was the white of his dhoti juxtaposed on the chestnut flank of the mule.

But he was not being trailed. At least as far as Muzaffar could see.

Muzaffar took a deep breath, squared his shoulders and set off in the opposite direction.

The roses had bloomed in Basheer's gardens; in Sajjad Khan's gardens near the Mehtab Bagh, loving care and possibly the rich alluvium of the river had helped push other plants into blossoming too. The cypresses that flanked the water channel leading from the pavilion were their usual grim, dark green – so gloomy, so perfectly fitting their role as symbols of mortality – but the parterres below them had begun to burst into defiant colour. There were already some delphiniums there, deep blue and purple. And carnations. Even a solitary lily, blossoming long before its still-sleeping brothers.

Near the white-flowering kachnar trees facing the river, a tall, somewhat stooped man, his legs muddied almost to the knees, was pleading with the head gardener to be allowed a job. He was wrapped in a worn shawl – which had some straw and a few burrs clinging to its fringes – and shivered as he spoke. 'Even if it is just for the day,' he said. 'Surely you can use one man? Someone to pull weeds, or water the garden, or shovel manure? I will do anything.'

The head gardener lifted one supercilious eyebrow and regarded Muzaffar with interest. 'You look sturdy to me,' he acknowledged. 'But why should you be searching for work? By the looks of it, you have been clothed and fed well enough.'

Muzaffar silently cursed the man's gimlet eye. He would have preferred a man less observant. He shrugged. 'Things happen.'

'Really? Then things might happen here, too. Get lost. I have no use for vagabonds –'

Muzaffar fell to his knees in what he hoped was not an overly melodramatic gesture. 'At least give me a chance! I know – I know I said something happened, but please, please don't condemn me without a hearing. Believe me, I was not to blame!'

The man grunted and was turning away when Muzaffar grabbed his leg. 'Please, huzoor! Listen to me. *Please*. I – my father died, and I have four younger sisters to look after. And my mother – I was dismissed wrongly, huzoor. It was not my fault!' The man tugged his leg free, and kicked Muzaffar in the chest hard enough to send him sprawling. He rolled back onto his feet immediately, slightly out of breath but not daunted in the least. 'She was not the one!' he called after the gardener, who was already a few paces away. 'It wasn't her! I was blamed unfairly!'

The man turned. He made an interesting picture, thought Muzaffar: a solid, sturdy man with his hands clasped behind his back. The whole silhouetted against the distant pavilion in a frame that looked as if it had been painted by one of the masters: the Baadshah's favourite Bichitra himself, perhaps. A gentle blue sky above, with wispy clouds sailing by. The still-bare branches of the peach trees. The green of the grass, the towering cypresses, the trees and herbs and shrubs around. The red of the roses and the blue of the delphiniums.

'Who exactly are you talking of?' the man asked. His voice was low, totally without emotion. So was his expression. Muzaffar could not tell whether the man was a voyeur, titillated by the hint of scandal that had been floated past his nose, or whether Muzaffar's persistence had worn him down. Beyond the man, among the flowerbeds and along the water channel, gardeners and sweepers were leaving their work half-forgotten. Muzaffar and the head gardener were the centre of attention.

Muzaffar got to his feet, taking care to maintain the stoop. 'A – a woman I was with,' he mumbled. 'The steward found us behind the cowshed. He thought she was one of the master's daughters. She ran away, of course, but he thought... he refused to listen to a word I said. I told him who she was –'

'And who *was* she?'

'A milkmaid. She used to – um – milk the cows.' He inserted a sheepish stutter to add verisimilitude. 'The steward wouldn't tell the master of his suspicions, but he kicked me out. Just because I am poor!' The stutter rose, changed deftly into indignation. 'If I had been wealthy, I would have had any woman I wanted, and –'

The head gardener cut him off in mid-sentence again. 'Yes, yes. We know. How do I know that if I take you on, you won't start getting under every ghagra you see?'

Muzaffar looked around with an expression of languid interest. 'I don't see any ghagras around,' he said.

The man glared at him, but nodded. 'All right. I need a man to help out in odd jobs. Weeding, hoeing, this and that. But only for a couple of days, you understand? One of the servants had to go home because his mother was dying. He'll be back soon, and when he returns, I'll take him back.'

A wage was mentioned, a pitiful amount that Muzaffar would have cavilled at had he not been so desperate to spend a day or two at the garden. He muttered to himself as he followed the head gardener to the back of the garden, past the cypresses and the peach trees, to the water channel. He did not need the money, of course not; but it was a matter of the principle of the thing. No man should have to work for less than the cost of his blood and sweat.

'This,' said the head gardener, as he came to a halt behind the pavilion. He waved an arm about, taking in the mango orchard that spread across the area. Trees, dark-canopied and glossy-leaved, that would burst into creamy-green scented sprays of flowers in just a few weeks. 'See the weeds? A winter's worth of grass and rubbish growing there, breeding who knows what insects. Begin weeding them. Start there,' – he pointed to the right – 'and mind you do a good job of it. Remember, I don't *need* you. If you don't do a decent job, out you go.'

Muzaffar had hoped that his dramatic exchange with the head gardener had been interesting enough for the other workers at the garden to come by, wanting to chat, wanting to know more. He had hoped that the gardener who had been deputed, some ten days ago, to weed the screwpine – Afzal, if Muzaffar recalled correctly – would be curious enough to come enquiring about this new employee at the garden. Afzal had shown an inclination, the last time Muzaffar had met him, to be chatty.

But the head gardener, it seemed, ruled with an iron hand. He was constantly roaming the garden, now supervising the watering of the orchards, now shouting at a pair of boys who had done a bad job of weeding the flowerbeds, now examining the patches of musk mallow. A busy man. A man with a sharp eye too: a man who would, Muzaffar feared, rip apart any employee who wasted time talking to another on matters that did not pertain to work.

Lunchtime came, with the head gardener calling for one of the boys at the parterres to bring his food. The boy galloped off towards the gate of the garden, and Muzaffar, peering out through the screen of the mango trees, watched as figures began easing up across the garden. Men hunched over parterres uncurled themselves. Men seated on their haunches, huddled close to the ground as they picked out the weeds from among the plants, rose thankfully to their feet. The small group of men and boys in charge of the dalv – the ox-operated irrigation system – unyoked the animals and led them to *their* lunch, the heaps of grass that had been cut just that morning.

From all across the garden, workers were heading towards the water channel, to wash hands and face before sitting down to eat. It would not be a leisurely lunch, if Muzaffar was accurate in his assessment of the head gardener's character. The men would get just enough time to wolf down their few handfuls of food, and that would be it. No time to chat, no post-lunch siesta.

Muzaffar reached for his waistband and patted the double handful of roasted gram which he had bought from a roadside vendor in the market. He was already striding off towards the water channel, eager to wash his hands and eat what he realized, in hindsight, was probably too meagre a meal. But it was all part of his disguise.

The man he had wanted to meet was there, sitting in a pool of mild sunshine at the base of a bare-branched peach tree. Afzal appeared to have finished eating; a small heap of dried leaves, the remains of a makeshift plate, lay in a crumpled heap beside his foot. His head leaned lazily against the rough bark of the tree, his eyes closed. There was a conveniently empty patch of grassy ground beside him.

'Mind if I sit down?' Muzaffar said, dropping to his haunches before the man could even open his eyes and see who this unexpected companion was. Afzal watched, his eyes empty of expression, as Muzaffar made himself comfortable. It was only when Muzaffar had begun chewing his second mouthful of gram – it was coarse, hard as pebbles in places, and very low on seasoning of any kind – that the other man's eyes suddenly narrowed. And widened, the very next moment.

'You're – Allah –'

'That is very complimentary, but I'm sure it would be considered blasphemous too,' Muzaffar corrected him. 'I am not Allah. But you recognize me, do you?'

The man nodded, throat working as if he wanted to say something. But he remained quiet.

The silence was broken by the strident tones of the head gardener. He was walking around, hauling up those who were inclined to rest a while longer. 'Meet me outside the wicket gate on the side,' Muzaffar muttered. 'This evening, when work in the garden is over. It's important. And it could mean a rich reward for you.'

The sun was still above the horizon when the last tools were stowed away and the cattle unyoked and brushed down. Muzaffar made his way to the secluded wicket gate. He had not yet reached it when Afzal joined him. The man had regained his composure somewhat; he glanced about once, as if to make sure that they were not being watched by anyone. 'Why the disguise?' he said, as he fell into step with Muzaffar.

'It was necessary,' Muzaffar replied, 'In order for me to meet you.' He nodded in acknowledgment of the man's expression of surprise. 'I needed to talk to you. If I came dressed up the way I had before,

your boss – my boss for the time being, too – would be suspicious.'
He swung the wicket gate open and stepped through. 'All right,' he
said, as he pulled the gate shut behind his companion. 'I am here
to talk to you because you were willing to talk the last time I was
here. When everybody else clammed up, you spoke up.'

'For a sum.'

Muzaffar inclined his head. 'I expected as much. Yes, for a sum.
And I assume – since I will be asking for more, *much* more than
the mere name of your lord and master – I assume the sum will be
considerably more than it was the last time we transacted business.'
He saw Afzal's eyes light up. 'Therefore, if I am going to have to pay
such a hefty sum, I expect both efficiency and discretion,' Muzaffar
added. 'This is, literally, a matter of life and death.'

17

'EVERYTHING POINTS TO Sajjad Khan and Omar. Perhaps also the companions he brought with him from Bijapur,' Muzaffar said as he rubbed his palm along his calf. He stank. Stank of the stables, of the manure and urine and straw that had no doubt surrounded Ganga's clothes for many months. Stank, too, of the river through which Muzaffar had waded, the muddy water sloshing about his shins. And stank of the earth, of the dirt, mud and horse manure that went into fertilizing Sajjad Khan's gardens beside the Yamuna.

Akram, jolted out of a deep and dreamless sleep by an unexpected intruder who had turned out to be a friend, nodded, inadvertently drew in a breath, and gagged the very next moment. He rummaged about inside the pocket of a choga draped over the chest beside him, and drew out a large muslin handkerchief which he clapped over his nose and mouth. '*Allah*, Muzaffar,' he said. 'The way you smell, I'd think you'd need to spend an entire day bathing – and in attar, too – to get that stench out of you. And I'm not sure it would work, even then.'

Muzaffar shuddered and pulled his shawl closer about him. 'A long bath will hardly kill me,' he replied. 'But if Sajjad Khan, or that sharp-eyed steward of his – or even the head gardener at his charbagh – should suspect that I am *not* a derelict looking for a job, but the man appointed by the Diwan-i-kul to investigate the murder of Mumtaz Hassan: well, that may certainly be the cause of my death.'

'I am not sure I understand,' Akram said. 'You said everything points to Sajjad Khan and Omar. But that isn't so. Didn't Ibrahim say Mahmood had done away with Mumtaz Hassan? And didn't Shireen Begum tell you that Mumtaz Hassan's lady love was Abdul Hafeez's sister? Didn't that bear out the fact that a letter purporting to be from her had been used to entice Hassan Sahib –'

'Easy,' Muzaffar interrupted, '*easy*. There are many other twists to those stories, and I am quite certain that we will discover more scum at the bottom of this pool than the stagnant water above it seems to indicate. But not now; later. Now I am here only to let you know where I'm at and what I'm doing. Who knows, perhaps tomorrow everything will suddenly fall into place and I will be able to pounce on the culprit?'

He did not even wait for Akram to blink blearily in acceptance of what Muzaffar had said. 'On the other hand,' he continued, voice dimming as he spoke, 'everything may fall apart tomorrow, and Sajjad Khan may realize that he is on the verge of being caught out. And since I'm likely to be in his haveli, all alone and having to fend for myself, I imagine it would be to my advantage if there were someone outside who could be relied upon to come to my aid.'

'I have already visited Qureshi Sahib's haveli earlier this evening,' Muzaffar said, 'and have left a message for Zeenat Aapa. I did not reveal who I was to the man at the gate, and I am pleased to say that I was not recognized. All Zeenat Aapa will know from my note is that I have had to stay away from Qureshi Sahib's haveli, on work, all of today and tonight. Perhaps all of tomorrow too. I have assured her that she need not worry about me. Not, at least, till tomorrow night. If I am unable to get a message through to her by this time tomorrow – or if I am unable to go back to Qureshi Sahib's haveli by tomorrow night – then she is to send for you...?' The sentence ended on a question, a request for help that had not been explicitly asked for.

Akram nodded. 'Of course.'

'I spoke to Haider on my way in,' Muzaffar said. 'And gave him some instructions for what he is to do tomorrow for me. It will involve taking a letter to the Kotwal in the morning –'

'The Kotwal! And you never told me! Or Basheer. Haider knows, but you hide it from us –'

'I'm telling you now. Haider has been told to let Basheer know too, but neither Haider nor the Kotwal even will know the details of what is planned. Even I am not sure, Akram. I don't even know whether this plan will succeed or not; there are too many uncertainties here. But I *will* know whether the game will be up, possibly before nightfall tomorrow. Either I will come here myself, or I will send someone to you with a message. Either the message will be for you to come and meet me – somewhere near Sajjad Khan's haveli, I should think – or it will be to request you to go to the Kotwal of Agra and persuade him to accompany you to Sajjad Khan's haveli. Do not fail me, Akram.'

Akram had been insistent that Muzaffar should spend the night at Basheer's haveli. But Muzaffar was adamant. He had no way of knowing that Basheer's household did not harbour a traitor; what if there was someone in the haveli – an inconspicuous servant perhaps – who was actually in the pay of Sajjad Khan, and who would go off to report that the newest worker at Sajjad Khan's gardens had slept the night at Basheer Sahib's haveli? 'Besides which,' Muzaffar said, sneaking a peek out of the window through which he had slid into Akram's chamber, 'there's the matter of practicality. I have been given strict instructions to report to the gardens at dawn. Not once the sun is high in the sky. Not after a leisurely breakfast and an easy boatride across the river. If I have to keep my job and have a go at entering Sajjad Khan's haveli – I had better be there on time.'

He had slipped out, going the way he had entered, seen by no one and sniffed out only by a suspicious cat, which had yowled and gone padding off into the night. He had made his way, shivering and shuddering in the inadequate clothing he wore, to the ferry that plied across the river. Much of Agra had downed its tools and extinguished its lamps for the night. Here, roughly opposite the

Empress's mausoleum, near the sarai that had been built by the woman who had been both her aunt as well as her mother-in-law, there was still traffic on the river. Muzaffar had paid up a coin and jostled his way between an Afghan soldier on a roan, and two burly men towing a large bale of what seemed like jute. He had disembarked at Mehtab Bagh and made his way to Sajjad Khan's now-deserted garden by the time the moon had begun its descent. The shed in which the straw, the tools, and the equipment for the dalv was stored shone silver in its wan light. Muzaffar, who had noted the position of the shed before he left for the day, made his way in and huddled down into the straw for a fitful, uncomfortable night.

He was awake well before sunrise. By the time Afzal – who had promised to arrive before the others, so that the two of them could have a quick chat – had come, Muzaffar was looking a very far cry from the debonair young nobleman who had visited the garden in pursuit of the piebald horse all those days back. His jaw had gone from blue to black. The moustache was ragged, the eyes red-rimmed and bleary. Even Afzal sniffed disapprovingly at the smell that hung around this disreputable-looking associate.

'You will be glad to know I visited Gokul last night,' he said. Muzaffar noticed, in passing, the fact that Afzal addressed him as an equal, not as an aristocrat. 'I handed over the five rupees. Gokul's son will come by to tell the boss that his father's ill and can't leave his bed.' He squinted, looking out towards the east, where the first flush of the approaching dawn was changing the horizon from grey to gold. 'Mind you, that is no guarantee that you will be the one taking the cart to the haveli. There are others who are just as capable of handling the bullocks. Manohar, for example, or his assistant on the dalv. Either of them. The boss would sooner choose them, I think, than you. He *knows* them. He knows he can rely on them.'

Muzaffar shrugged. 'I cannot bribe the world. Some things have to be left to chance.'

He did not, however, leave things to chance. Manohar, who was in charge of operating the dalv, which irrigated the water channel flowing through the garden, had only just arrived when he found himself being accosted by the newcomer. He was busy fitting together the system of ropes and pulleys and chains when Muzaffar wished him good morning. Manohar smiled briefly in recognition and was turning back to his work when his new colleague spoke up.

Muzaffar was swift and succinct. 'I was talking to that man there,' he said, indicating Afzal, 'because I wanted to know if it would be possible for me to go to Mirza Sahib's haveli.' He paused, giving Manohar room to make a comment if he so desired; but when Manohar carried on with his work, Muzaffar continued to speak.

'One of the maids there – well, I have contrived to sweeten her up enough for her to agree to meet me. Nothing fixed, you understand; but – *but.*' He had caught the man's attention; the rope hung slack on Manohar's palm. He was looking up intently into Muzaffar's face. 'That was why I wanted so desperately to get a job here,' Muzaffar explained. 'I had tried to get a job at Mirza Sahib's haveli, but they had no need for me. Then she told me that maybe there would be a place for me here, you know – and if I got a job here, perhaps I could wangle a trip now and then to the haveli.' He pulled himself back to the matter at hand, deliberately explaining little now that he had won Manohar's interest. 'That man – Afzal, yes? – he told me that a cart goes to the haveli every few days. With grass, fruit, straw. Is that right?'

'Right. But I don't drive the cart. Gokul does.'

'Today he won't. Afzal just told me. He met Gokul's son on his way here. Gokul has a fever and can't come to work today.'

Manohar's face creased in a grin. 'Then you have cause for rejoicing.' He bent, systematically looping one rope over the other and knotting the ends together. 'I have enough work to do here, and my assistant cannot be spared.' He straightened. 'Here comes the boss.'

Muzaffar made it a point to be in the vicinity when the head gardener was told by Gokul's scruffy-haired eight-year-old that his

father was quaking with fever and could not stir from his bed. The
man, having given the boy a half-hearted clout on his shoulder and
told him to get lost, was already turning and yelling for Manohar.
Manohar was coming, striding forward, muttering regretfully that
he had too much work to get done in too little time. And there was
Muzaffar, rising to his feet, begging to be allowed a chance. 'I can
handle cattle well enough,' he said. 'I have been driving my father's
bullock cart ever since I was old enough to hold the whip.'

The head gardener was reluctant and suspicious, but he had,
after all, not much choice. The men at the gardens were mostly
gardeners, men who could coax greenery out of the most barren
of soils but were more often than not completely helpless when it
came to animals. Those who could be trusted to handle the bullocks
could be counted on the fingers of one hand – and none of those men
could be spared. He hemmed and hawed and asked many questions.
The bulk of his questions were aimed at discovering the reason for
Muzaffar's volunteering for a task that was bound to be difficult.
Steering the bullock cart across the river on the ferry, then through
the town to Mirza Sahib's haveli was no joke. And Mirza Sahib's
steward at the haveli was feared far and wide. Even Gokul, who was
known and trusted at the haveli, did not like having to go there on
his bi-weekly trips to deliver the produce from the garden.

Manohar, starting the oxen off on their circuit to draw up water,
glanced at Muzaffar. He could hear the head gardener, of course;
the man's voice carried easily, and the gardens were relatively
quiet. Manohar grinned, and Muzaffar, catching his eye, winked
surreptitiously. Later in the day, perhaps, if Muzaffar were to
disappear, Manohar could be counted upon to reveal the young
man's confidences. They would cluck over it, the older and wiser
men, as they wondered at the stamina of the man and his utter lack
of morals. A milkmaid behind the cowshed; a maid in Mirza Sahib's
haveli... where else did he have his paramours?

The head gardener was talking, letting loose a barrage of
instructions. He was not to dawdle along the way. He was to keep

his eyes open, and make sure the bullocks didn't step into holes. He was to keep an eye on the cartload of grass and oranges; sometimes there were beggars or urchins along the way, who would lose no opportunity to grab some fruit and run off with it. He was to behave himself when he got to Mirza Sahib's haveli, not go chasing the maids – an eavesdropping Manohar burst out laughing, and the head gardener turned to look at him – and he was to go clean himself up before he got into the cart. 'Look at your legs!' the boss said. 'All coated over with mud. And you stink! Clean up and come back here.'

It was like walking on the edge of a knife, thought Muzaffar. Too dirty, and the head gardener would take the skin off his back. Too clean, and he ran the risk of being recognized. Eventually, he settled for a compromise. No shave, but he washed and dried his legs. They looked a little too pampered – untanned, unscarred and clean, not the legs of a man who had supposedly spent all his life out in the open – but Muzaffar hoped nobody would notice.

An hour and a half later, the bullock cart had been loaded, about a quarter of its space taken up by produce – oranges and some vegetables – that had been picked the previous evening from the garden. The bulk of the cart was occupied by grass, newly scythed, and piled rich and high. For Mirza Sahib's horses, Muzaffar guessed. The head gardener shouted some parting instructions, and Muzaffar walked on beside the bullocks, patting them on their flanks, encouraging them on.

The cart had barely rumbled out of the garden – the head gardener was still standing at the gate, yelling at him to keep an eye on the oranges – when a palanquin came into sight. Two kahaars carried it at a fine clip; whoever sat inside was not a heavy load, thought Muzaffar. Beside the palanquin was a horse, the rider a manservant, and seated behind him, a woman. Muzaffar stiffened. This was a noblewoman who approached, then. A lady in her palanquin, with an escort and a maid in attendance. At this hour of the morning, and well away from the city, too. A shiver ran down his spine. *It could not be...*

Muzaffar slowed the cart and drew it towards the side of the dirt road, but did not stop. The head gardener, looking on, would not expect a lowly labourer to come to a halt at the sight of a passing palanquin. It would be considered impertinent inquisitiveness; an aristocratic lady would probably take offence at the suggestion of someone – a nobody, at that – gawking at her.

But the kahaars had stopped and put the palanquin down, while a low-voiced order from inside the palanquin had made the horseman pull up. The maid slid off the horse and stepped over to the palanquin, carefully parting the curtain to peer inside. A few moments, and she was coming towards Muzaffar's cart.

It did not surprise him that the woman was polite in her request for him to come to the palanquin. She had obviously been instructed well – and he had been recognized. He had pulled the bullocks to a halt; he got off the cart and accompanied the maid back to the palanquin. The menfolk – the two kahaars, and the manservant – had drawn away to a discreet distance. A light breeze, blowing off the river, lifted the curtain momentarily, long enough for him to see a pair of slender hands resting on a silk-clad lap.

'Begum Sahiba?' he muttered, head lowered, neck inclined, hands clasped below his waist. Anybody looking on from the garden would think that their new colleague had been accosted by a passing lady in a palanquin and was being probably asked for directions.

'Jang Sahib.' Of course it was *her*; Muzaffar had known it in his bones, though he could not fathom how she could have found him, and why. Shireen had somehow discovered him. 'No; please don't look at me; it will only make people suspicious.' She was nervous, the strain apparent in her voice. 'I came because Zeenat Begum received your note last night. It worried us' – he noted the pronoun she used; not *her*, but *us*. Shireen too had been worried, and the knowledge suddenly lifted his spirits – 'and so I went to Mumtaz Hassan's haveli. Your friend Akram Sahib told me where you would be.'

'You should not have come,' he said quietly.

'I had to. Akram Sahib told me what instructions you had given him. It sounded very' – she seemed to fumble for a word – 'dangerous. I came to tell you that my uncle does have an acquaintance with the Kotwal of Agra, so should you need his help...' her voice trailed away. Muzaffar thought he heard a sniff.

'Pray,' he said gently. 'That is all the help I need. And for when I return, promise that you will grant me one meeting, so that I may talk to you.'

And with that, he accorded her a quick salaam, and returned to the bullock cart. A tug on the leads, a loud 'Haaah!' to spur the cattle on, and he was moving off, passing the palanquin even as the kahaars came forward to lift it once again. The maid mounted up behind the rider, and both horse and palanquin moved on towards the garden. Muzaffar looked back once last time, to see the palanquin stopped at the gateway of the garden; then the cart moved on, taking him out of sight of the garden.

It took him over two hours to get to Sajjad Khan's haveli. The riverside stretch, from the garden, past Mehtab Bagh and then on the ferry, was relatively uncrowded, the day still too young for the traffic that would choke the Yamuna later in the day. Further into town, however, it got busier. Around the fort and beyond, near Kinari Bazaar, business had begun. There were other carts, transporting everything from cloth to foodstuffs. There were porters, scurrying along, nearly overbalancing under the weight of their loads. There was shouting and haggling, hoarse altercations and the occasional burst of laughter drifting from a qahwa khana from which wafted the fragrance of coffee, heady enough to make Muzaffar yearn for some.

A guard, his dedication suspect, was on duty outside Mirza Sajjad Khan's haveli. The man's lance leaned forgotten against the boundary wall of the haveli, and he himself was chatting with the boy who was using a twig broom to sweep the area in front of the gate. It was the boy who first noticed the soft tinkling of the bells around the bullocks' necks and turned around. By the time Muzaffar drew the cart to a standstill in front of the gate, the guard had his fingers wrapped securely around the lance, the boy was clutching his broom determinedly, and they had been joined by a water-carrier, his waterskin bulging along his side.

'I recognize the bullocks and the cart,' said the guard, 'but who are you?'

Muzaffar was explaining his errand when a gatekeeper emerged, pushing open the small doorway in the gate at which Muzaffar had first spoken to the haveli's steward. The steward seemed to not be in evidence now; perhaps he had simply happened to be around that day when Muzaffar and Akram had come by. Perhaps Sajjad Khan, gone on his hunt, had taken the majority of his servants with him – including this gatekeeper.

He listened carefully, though, and seemed satisfied that Muzaffar was whom he purported to be. The bullocks and the well-laden cart were proof enough.

It was the sweeper who made friends with Muzaffar first. He was a trusting lad, perhaps about fourteen or fifteen years of age, and still not over his childhood. He it was who scampered off to summon the steward and let him know that in Gokul's absence a new man had brought the produce from the gardens; he it was who helped unyoke the bullocks and lead them to the well. He it was who, when the bullocks had been watered, asked Muzaffar, 'So? Now what? Gokul always stops long enough to come inside and have something to eat before he heads back. In any case, they'll take a while to unload the cart.'

Muzaffar pretended an anxiety to be on his way, but was persuaded. 'A couple of those oranges,' said the boy as he led the way into a small courtyard on the side, 'and a handful of almonds from the kitchen. Perhaps some palm sugar, yes? My sister works in the kitchens. She's good at sneaking things out – not enough to be missed, but enough to be a treat now and then.' They were walking deeper into the haveli with every step, past a man grinding spices on a stone slab, past the well at which another man was winching up, inch by squeaky inch, a large dripping bucket. Past wheat being winnowed and lentils being sorted, past the warm buttery scent of ghee melting in a pan, ready for chopped onions to be thrown in. Muzaffar felt a twinge of guilt as he realized that this was *his* world – a world of comfort, far removed from the cold shed he had slept in the previous night, or the roasted gram he had eaten for his lunch the previous day. There was something unsettling in knowing that one inhabited that minuscule fraction of society which could afford good food and adequate clothing and shelter. He had known it; but he had never experienced the plight of the vast majority. One day of masquerading as a poverty-stricken labourer had left him feeling cold and hungry. And that was just one day. Not an entire lifetime.

They walked on, past what looked like a storeroom, its door ajar – and Muzaffar groaned and caught his companion's arm in a grip of iron.

'What – dear God, *what is the matter*?!'

The boy may be fifteen years old, or whatever he was. He may be strutting around the house with all the self-assurance of one employed by one of Agra's wealthiest men. He may have been showing off to a visitor. But he was, all said and done, still a child, and he did not know how to deal with a man who had gone from normal to what looked like seriously ill in a wink.

Muzaffar's grip slackened, and tightened again as his eyes widened, staring into the boy's panic-stricken face. 'What? What's happened? Are you feeling ill?!' the boy was babbling, trying desperately to steer Muzaffar towards a stone bench outside the storeroom.

'Dizzy –' Muzaffar mumbled. Then, with a graceful limpness, he slid to the ground.

He had been careful to make sure there were not too many people in the immediate vicinity. An old man, bent over double with the weight of many years and many burdens, was picking through a heap of newly washed and dried wheat, off to the right. The smells and sounds of a busy household were all around them, but except for the ancient, there was nobody else at hand.

The boy was hauling on Muzaffar's arm, screeching wildly all the time, calling for help, wailing that a stranger had died on his hands. Muzaffar moaned and his eyelids fluttered open briefly. 'Hush – headache. Quiet. Please.' He lolled artistically, lifting a hand to his forehead and pressing hard on his temples.

'But what's wrong?' The boy's voice had lowered itself instantly. 'You were all right just a moment ago, and then suddenly – poof! – you've got a –'

'*Please.* Please keep quiet. It'll go, I just need quiet. Some sleep.' His eyes rolled up into his head, and with one last wince, Muzaffar sank again. The boy's grip loosened, and Muzaffar, his eyes shut, wondered what the boy was up to. Was he going to leave Muzaffar lying on the ground?

'What's the matter?' It was a new voice, creaky and hoarse. The old man, Muzaffar guessed.

'This man. He's collapsed. He's got a headache, he says, a blinding headache which he says will go if he sleeps a while.'

'But who is he?'

'I don't know his name. But he's come from the gardens, bringing the fruit and the grass for the stables. Gokul is ill, that's what he said. But what will we *do* with him? Should we just shift him to the side, here? Against the wall?'

A grunt. 'Don't be stupid. Pull down that charpai, leaning against that wall. We'll haul him onto that.'

There was the sound of receding footsteps, a thump and a bone-jarring, tooth-hurting screech as the charpai was pulled down and dragged across the courtyard. If he had really been suffering from a headache, thought Muzaffar, that sound would have driven him to murder the boy. He pretended to come to, hauling himself up on one elbow and warily opening his eyes. The old man was sitting on his haunches, peering at Muzaffar. He looked on, impassive and silent, as Muzaffar groaned and made a half-hearted attempt to rise to his feet.

'Lie down, lie down,' the boy urged. He had abandoned the charpai a couple of paces from where Muzaffar lay, and had come rushing over when he had seen Muzaffar come to. 'Do you want to come to the charpai? – I can drag you there. Will you help?' he glanced towards the old man, who had hauled himself to his feet and was moving off towards his heap of wheat.

'He's conscious now,' the old man called over his shoulder. 'Surely he can drag himself to the charpai. Or you can drag the charpai to him. Whatever.'

The boy did drag the charpai closer to Muzaffar, aligning it neatly against the outer wall of the storeroom. Muzaffar, who could not swallow the idea of being dragged around the courtyard, pretended a valiant effort that needed only minimal support from the boy to propel him to the charpai. He sank onto the rope bed, letting his breath out in an almighty whoosh.

'Should I press your head?' the boy whispered.

'No, no. I will be all right. Just leave me alone.' Muzaffar shut his eyes in the hope that it would deter further conversation. It did, but the boy was of a conscientious bent of mind. He leaned over Muzaffar, his somewhat stale breath warm on Muzaffar's cheek. A tentative forefinger and thumb touched Muzaffar's forehead.

Muzaffar half-opened his eyes. 'Don't press my head,' he murmured. 'If someone touches my head when I'm having one of these headaches of mine, I'm liable to throw up.' The hand was quickly withdrawn. 'Could you get me some water to drink?' The boy nodded and had already stood up by the time Muzaffar, racking his brains to think of some other errand on which to dispatch his unwanted well-wisher, finally spoke up. 'And – and could you get me a new paan leaf, perhaps? It helps, sometimes.'

The boy was gone a few minutes, the time it would take the average human being to rush around the inside of a large and busy household, making his way into areas that were generally out of his ken, and thus having to provide explanations. The explanations, in turn, involved sharing the gossip about the newcomer from the gardens who had collapsed. The hunt for a new paan leaf, already washed and neatly stored in Mirza Sajjad Khan's, and his begums', nagardaans, took even longer. A servant who was required to wait on Mirza Sahib in the dalaan had to be pleaded with to smuggle one leaf out. It was not an arduous task, by no means, since Mirza Sahib had not yet emerged from his bedchamber; but it delayed the boy.

By the time he returned to where he had left Muzaffar sprawled on the charpai, it was to discover that his patient had fallen asleep. Muzaffar lay stretched out on the charpai, one arm across his closed eyes, his mouth fallen slightly open. The boy stood beside the charpai, a metal glassful of water in one hand and the paan leaf in the other. He stared down, regarding the supine man, for a full minute. Then, with a resigned sigh, he placed the tumbler on the floor at the head of the charpai. He balanced the paan leaf carefully on top of the tumbler and, with one last solicitous look at the cart-driver who had fallen ill so abruptly, he went off back to his twig broom, to remove the dead leaves that had collected in the gardens near the gate of the haveli.

Muzaffar lay still long enough to hear the flap of wings, followed by the cooing of pigeons and the faint click-click of tiny bird claws as they pattered across the flagstones of the courtyard. Pigeons were a notoriously nervous lot, thought Muzaffar; if there were any other human beings in the courtyard the birds would never have had the temerity to alight here. Warily, carefully, he opened one eye, and then, seeing nobody around except the pigeons, he opened the other too.

Without moving his head, and only very slowly shifting the arm that lay across his eyes, he glanced across the courtyard – or what he could see of it. The pigeons – two of them –were pecking at some stray grains of what was probably wheat, spilled by the old man in the course of his work. He was gone. The heap of wheat, too, was gone. From beyond the low walls of the courtyard, there still drifted the sounds of the household, the thuds and scrapings, the muted conversation, the sound of someone sweeping a floor. Muzaffar, reminded of the possibility that his young acquaintance might take it into his head to return, sat up. The pigeons flew off in a whirr of wings. He got to his feet, and hurried across the flagstones to the doorway that led out of the courtyard. At the doorway, he paused, wondering which way to turn. Off to his right was the wall of what was surely the garden of the haveli; above the wall he could see the branches of mango trees, and a couple of feathery cypresses. Diagonally opposite him was a long, elegant hall: the qutb khana, or library. On the left, lying on the other side of the broad path that led to the gate, was the bulk of the haveli: the dalaan, where the host received his guests; the small household mosque; and the tehkhana or underground chambers, to which the family would retreat during the heat of summer.

Somewhere, far to the left, at a discreet distance from the tehkhana and the dalaan and mosque, would be the stables, thought Muzaffar. Close enough to the gate for horses to be fetched whenever the master or any other member of the family needed a mount; far enough from the living quarters to not be offensive. Muzaffar moved swiftly left, hoping all the while his guess was correct.

It was. The stretch between the stables and the courtyard where he had feigned his sudden illness was perhaps thirty yards, no more. There were a few people around – a servant weeding the edges of the path, another sprinkling the path with water to help the dust settle. Beyond, leading a splendid black mare into a low building – the stables, Muzaffar supposed – was a thin young man wrapped in a large grey shawl. Muzaffar, having toyed with the idea of somehow sneaking across the expanse, flitting from one shelter to the other, discarded the thought. To be surreptitious would only draw attention.

He strode across. The man weeding the fringes of the path looked up once when Muzaffar's shadow fell across the flagstones, but he did not comment. The man with the waterskin, intent on his task, did not even glance towards the passerby.

The building into which the mare had been led was the stable. It was permeated by the strong, distinctive smell of horses, and there was a warmth here, a warmth very welcome after the chill of the outdoors. Muzaffar paused at the doorway, trying to get his bearings; trying to get used, too, to the dim light in the stables. A wide path, strewn with fresh straw, led between two rows of stalls. There were whinnies and neighs, the clip-clop of hooves, the murmur of men talking to horses they were grooming. There was the soothing shush-shush of a brush, gradually turning a horse's coat to glossy velvet. There was a splash as a bucket was emptied. A string of curses, as someone was accidentally drenched by the spill.

'Move out of the doorway!' someone called, off to his right. 'You're blocking out the sunlight.' Muzaffar shifted. His eyes had now adjusted to the gloom of the stables. A head and a burly shoulder poked out of one of the stalls midway down the row. 'What do you want?' the man called to Muzaffar. His voice was deep, with a harshness to it that could have been the last remnants of a sore throat, or the first signs of one.

'Nothing – I was just searching –'

The man backed out of the stall, pulling down a rough piece of cloth draped over his shoulder as he did so. He began wiping his hands, muttering to himself as he walked towards Muzaffar. Somewhere, from near the other end of the stable, came the clatter of a bolt being drawn, the screech and clunk of iron, followed by the sound of doors moving on badly-oiled hinges. A window – a large window, if one could judge by the amount of light it let in – had just been opened. Muzaffar blinked and stepped back involuntarily. Motes danced in the shaft of sunlight that poured through the square opening in the brick wall. A horse whinnied nearby.

The man had finished cleaning his hands and had slung the cloth back over his shoulder. He now stood opposite Muzaffar, staring intently at the visitor. He was a tall man, nearly Muzaffar's height, but a good bit older. The short hair on his head, revealed by the absence of a turban, was grey, even though the thick eyebrows were a stark, emphatic black. The heavily jowled face was florid. Muzaffar's eyes narrowed; the next moment, he was moving hurriedly forward, as if eager to make the acquaintance of the man.

'I've come from Mirza Sahib's gardens,' he explained, as he reached the man. Beyond the man's shoulder, he could see the stall from which the man had emerged. There was a horse there; Muzaffar could hear it whiffle and grunt, its hooves raising a rustle in the straw. But the man was broad – so broad that his shoulders came in the way, hiding the horse, allowing only a glimmer of movement to be seen. 'I've brought the grass and some fruit from the gardens,' Muzaffar added. 'Gokul was ill.'

The man nodded, eyes still watchful.

'I felt dizzy; haven't been too well myself. Had to lie down for a while.'

'You look all right to me.'

'Now I do, yes. But that's because I've slept a while. I was feeling like death – would you know if my cattle were brought in here? I'd seen the men beginning to unload the cart, and then I fell ill. I was wondering where my bullocks were. I guessed they were in the stables.'

The man snorted. 'In the stables?! Bullocks? Sharing a trough with Mirza Sahib's prized stallions, no doubt!' He pulled the duster off his shoulder and vigorously wiped his hands all over again, as if Muzaffar's preposterous suggestion had dirtied them. 'They must be near where you'd left them. One of the men at the gate would have watered them, or fed them if need be. They wouldn't have come in here.'

Muzaffar tried to peer, without seeming to do so, around the man's shoulder. The horse in the stall moved, and a muscular white neck and back was glimpsed. It was just for a moment, and then the horse had shifted again.

'Could you – um – point me towards the gate, do you think? I'm a bit lost; I don't know which way to go.'

The man stared, eyes boring into Muzaffar, then turned and flung the duster over a nail beside the stall. He strode away then, and Muzaffar got a good, clear, unhindered look at the horse in the stall. It was beautiful, a snowy creature, well-muscled and sleek, with large patches of black on the underside of its neck, along its flank and its belly.

They walked out of the stables, the man striding a couple of paces ahead of Muzaffar. At the edge of the path that led to the gate, he stopped, hands on hips, and asked, 'Did you come this way? You appeared at the stable door that opens out here.' He glared at Muzaffar and flung out an arm, waving towards the gate. 'What do you think that is, *hain*?!' His belligerence had tinted his face an even more vivid red than it had been earlier. He was quivering with impatience, annoyed at having been hauled away from his work to go on a pointless errand.

'Oh, I do beg your pardon,' Muzaffar murmured. 'But you should have just told me. Why did you bother to come all the way here? If you'd said –'

With a snort of anger, the man whirled about and walked back to the stable. Little puffs of dust rose round his heels and his jama snapped as he disappeared into the dark belly of the stables. His entrance was marked by a loud bellow as some errant stablehand was dragged over the coals. For no fault of his own, Muzaffar supposed. He stood, alone and still, for a few moments. Then he made his way back to the courtyard where he had lain after the pretended dizzy spell.

'Ah, there you are.' The old man, the one who had been cleaning the wheat, had returned. He was sitting on stringy haunches, on the ground next to a small rough brazier made of clay. Some sticks had been fed into it and a small fire ignited. The old man extended his hands to the fire and gestured to Muzaffar to come closer, an invitation to the warmth. 'The boy came looking for you,' he said by way of conversation. 'Very worried he was, too. Wondered where you'd gone. I think he's gone to search for you.'

Muzaffar sat down opposite the old man and warmed his hands, making up an impromptu story to explain his absence. A muzzy awakening, a sudden and pressing need to relieve himself, the urgency to go find a suitable place – 'I could not wait for you or the boy to come, you see,' he said. 'I didn't have the luxury of time.'

The old man nodded. 'Feeling better now?'

'Hmm. I should be going. I have to get back to the gardens; they'll be thinking I've stolen the grass and fruit and run away with the bullocks.' He rubbed his hands one last time, and got to his feet. Then, deliberately, just as he was turning to leave the courtyard, he turned back and said, 'Oh. I nearly forgot. I had been given a message to deliver. Is there a guest staying here with Mirza Sahib? A Bijapuri gentleman by the name of Omar Sahib?'

The old man shrugged. 'Who knows? I clean the wheat and shift loads and do other menial jobs. I'm not in the know about who comes and who goes.' He blew on his hands and stirred up the already-dying embers with a half-charred stick he had pulled out of the fire. 'A few guests are here, though,' he added, a little grudgingly. 'Their servants throw their weight about. Go ask at the gate; they'll lead you to your Omar Sahib if you ask nicely.' He looked up. 'Mind you, I'd clean up if I were you. And hope that this Omar Sahib has a bad cold. You don't smell all that good, you know.'

The gatekeeper had allowed Muzaffar to be let into the haveli's grounds on what had been an innocuous errand. Now he grew suspicious; the labourer from the garden had not mentioned another errand earlier. What was this about? Why did he want to meet Khan Sahib's guests? Who did he think he was? Muzaffar, by now getting to be an expert at the swiftly-concocted tale, spun a story, adding to the known fact that he was the cart-driver who had brought the produce from the gardens. 'My brother-in-law works at the Sarai Nur Jahan,' he said. 'They've been keeping a parcel for

Omar Sahib – he stayed there for a while before he shifted here. My brother-in-law heard somewhere that Omar Sahib had been seen with Sajjad Khan Sahib, so he asked me to pass on the message. They're getting jittery, I think – who knows how valuable the parcel is, what it contains? Allah forbid it should get stolen, and then the fat will be in the fire –'

'Oh, all right, *all right*! Have you brought the parcel with you?'

'Me? They would not entrust a poor man such as I with something that may very well cost the Earth. Not because I'm dishonest, mind – but what if I were attacked? What if it was stolen?'

'Then what? If you haven't brought it with you, what are you still here for?'

'Just to give Omar Sahib the message, that the men at the sarai would be grateful if he could relieve them of the responsibility of looking after the parcel. It is very trying, I tell you. My brother-in-law used to be a healthy, happy man before this onus was dumped on him; now he's been whittled down to a wraith by the mere anxiety of having to look after it, and wondering when some thief will make away with it and Omar Sahib will hold my poor brother-in-law responsible –'

'Damn your brother-in-law, and damn *you*! What do you want?'

'To meet Omar Sahib and pass on the message.'

He was made to wash up once again, this time from an earthen waterpot that was kept near the gate for the use of the servants. The gatekeeper supervised the washing-up while another servant was sent into the haveli to tell the steward to request Omar Sahib to grant an audience to a cart-driver who had to pass on an urgent message. A thoroughly convoluted chain of command, thought Muzaffar as he poured icy water on already-shivering feet. The gatekeeper, with ill grace, handed over an old piece of threadbare cotton to be used as a towel, and muttered a few words of advice while they waited for the servant to return. Muzaffar was to keep his eyes lowered in the presence of the gentleman. He was to be brief, and not chatter on about his brother-in-law and how his health had suffered because of his worries. Most importantly, he was to keep his distance from Omar Sahib; he was not to hover close enough for Omar Sahib to smell him. 'That water doesn't seem to have had *any* effect on you.'

When the servant returned, it was with the steward. The man looked at Muzaffar, gaze travelling slowly from the top of Muzaffar's scruffy turban and down to his toes. He did not say anything for a few moments. Just stared in that disconcerting way that made Muzaffar wonder if he had recognized in this bedraggled cart-driver the flamboyant amir who had called at the haveli, wanting to buy the piebald horse.

But no; like the gatekeeper, the steward was simply doing his job of keeping out of the house all those who did not conform to certain set standards. If the sniff was anything to go by, he disapproved of Muzaffar and his dirt. 'No,' he said finally, after a long scrutiny. 'No, you can't go in and meet Omar Sahib smelling – and looking – like that. Give me the message, and I'll tell him.'

Muzaffar guessed it would be useless to try and plead. Far from convincing the steward, it would more likely make him suspicious. He therefore gave the message, emphasizing the urgency of the matter. The steward listened, nodded, turned away and went back into the haveli, motioning to the other servant to follow him. A few minutes passed; Muzaffar occupied himself by chatting with the gatekeeper, complaining about the cold and asking him till when the Bijapuri gentlemen were going to stay in Agra, for didn't they find it excruciatingly cold in this part of the world? The gatekeeper, satisfied now that this grubby visitor had been denied entrance into the mansion, was more friendly and forthcoming than he had been earlier. The Bijapuri gentlemen seemed to like it in Agra, he said; they had been here for a good few days, though some of those had been spent away on a hunt. But they were getting ready to leave, he thought; Jamal, the master of the stables, had been instructed to go to the nakhkhas and finalize the negotiations for some horses they had seen.

'Ah,' Muzaffar said. 'Jamal must be the man I saw leading a black mare into the stables. Thinnish man, my age. He looked as if he knew his way around horses.'

The gatekeeper guffawed. 'Jamal? Thin and young? He may have been that twenty years ago, no longer. He's huge – wider than the two of us put together, I'd think. As tall as you are. Grey-haired and red-faced.'

Muzaffar's face lit up as if enlightenment had dawned. 'Oh, I know. I saw a man like that inside the stable. With a beautiful white and black horse.'

The gatekeeper nodded. 'That horse is the pride and joy of Jamal's stables.'

'Likes it that much, does he? Why? Did he negotiate its purchase himself?'

'Hmm. The master trusts Jamal thoroughly. Mirza Sahib was the one who ostensibly bought the horse, but everybody knows that Jamal was the one who selected it and put it through its paces and haggled with the horse trader.' He grinned. '*And* drove a hard bargain, I'll wager.'

'Still, as long as Mirza Sahib is satisfied with the horse...'

'Oh, I haven't seen Mirza Sahib astride that horse yet,' the gatekeeper said. 'It's a wild creature; Jamal is the only one who can control it. He's the one who exercises it, takes it out on rides.'

Muzaffar frowned, as if puzzled. 'But – surely – no, I must be mistaken, it cannot be.' He fell silent, his gaze far away.

It was enough enticement; the gatekeeper was intrigued. 'What is the matter? What were you saying?'

'Nothing, nothing. I must be in error.' Muzaffar cleared his throat, glanced up to check that he still held the man's attention, and took immediate steps to ensure that he did not lose it. 'Only – I was almost certain I saw that very same horse, about two weeks ago. On the other side of the Yamuna, near Mirza Sahib's gardens. I told you, didn't I, that my brother-in-law works at the Sarai Nur Jahan? I had gone to visit him, and it got late. I spent the night at the sarai. The next morning, when I went down to the river, I saw the horse. I could stake my life that it was the same horse – there could not be two like it, so beautiful! – but this Jamal wasn't the rider. In fact, there was no rider. There was a boy, who was trying to keep a grip on the horse. Doing a bad job of it, too.'

The gatekeeper had been nibbling at his lower lip as he listened to Muzaffar. Now his face cleared, his eyes lighting up in sudden understanding. 'Ah! That must be Jamal's son. Jamal takes him along on errands now and then.'

Muzaffar looked dubious. 'An errand? That early in the morning? So far from here? And at a time when only the birds are up and about?'

The gatekeeper shrugged. 'Horses need to be tended at odd hours, too, I suppose. And it may be far from here, but it's close to the gardens, isn't it? Jamal lives near there. He must have taken the horse there the previous night, to give it some exercise by the riverside.' He grinned. 'Or maybe the gardens grow crops that are good for horses. Screwpine?'

Muzaffar was spared the necessity of answering – and deprived of the opportunity of worming some more information out of the gatekeeper – by the return of the steward. 'Get along, you,' he said to Muzaffar. 'I've given Omar Sahib your message. He remembered that parcel; he'll send one of his servants to fetch it today.'

Muzaffar shook his head frantically. 'No, no, not a servant. That will just be a waste of time. They'll never hand over the parcel to a mere servant. What if he should be an imposter? What if they think he's not really Omar Sahib's man, but a thief who's just trying to get his hands on – uff!' He had received a solid clout on the back of the head from the steward.

'Shut up.' said the man 'You talk far too much. If Omar Sahib gives the man a letter, stamped with his own seal, the men at the sarai cannot possibly refuse, can they? Not if they want to lose all the business they get from the Bijapuri merchants who visit Agra.' His eyes narrowed. 'So. Stop being a pest and take yourself off. You've delivered your message and you've brought the produce from the garden; your work's done. *Go.*'

18

MUZAFFAR'S LAST WORDS at Sajjad Khan's haveli were a muttered 'What a waste of time! I'd better be getting back!' – ostensibly to himself, but spoken loud enough for the gatekeeper to hear. Suddenly the young cart-driver, so inclined to chatter and loll about as if without a care in the world, seemed to wake up to the fact that he had been away from the gardens for well over three hours – more than enough time to have completed his errand twice over. He bellowed for his bullocks, begged to be allowed a boy to help him yoke them to the cart, and hopped into the cart with an alacrity the gatekeeper was astounded to see. The next moment, slapping the bullocks on their flanks and flicking them briskly with the thin stick he carried, he was gone, racing the cart down the lane that led between the fields, away from Sajjad Khan's haveli. A cloud of dust hid the cart briefly from view. Then, at the far end of the lane, the cart flashed into view again just for a moment or two before it turned the corner and was hidden from sight.

Muzaffar was tugging at the ropes with all his strength, reining in the bullocks as soon as they were out of sight of the haveli. A few yards beyond the corner stood a spreading banyan tree, its base surrounded by a circular platform of packed earth. A small group of men – a trio, one middle-aged and thin, the other two younger and sturdier – looked up as the cart trundled to an abrupt halt near the tree.

Haider, the steward of Basheer's household, was the first to get up. Following his example, the two other men stepped off the platform too, regarding Muzaffar with curious eyes. Both, Muzaffar noticed, wore leather tunics on top of their regular clothing. Both, too, reached for the lances that had been laid on the platform. Muzaffar gave them a passing glance and a swift nod of approval even as he got off the cart, saying, 'My clothes, Haider!'

Still on the platform around the base of the tree was a large bundle of unbleached cotton. Haider whirled around, and while the two men looked on in bewilderment, he undid the bundle and swiftly began to pull out of it clothing – a jama, a pair of pajamas, a rough but thick shawl, boots, a turban, a cummerbund. They were not Muzaffar's usual clothes, the elegant but subdued raiment of a nobleman who did not care to be bejewelled and fashionable. Instead, these were the sort of clothes that might be worn by a somewhat well-off soldier: unembroidered, unembellished garments made of cloth that was sturdy and inexpensive. A man wearing clothes such as these could be mistaken for a mercenary out to make a fast buck where he could. His horse, glossy and beautiful, would give him away, but Muzaffar hoped that suspicion would be restricted to imagining that the stallion had been stolen, not that the animal's rider was actually a wealthy amir.

Muzaffar threw off the shawl and the dhoti and donned his own clothing while he spoke, in quick uncluttered sentences, to the three men who had rendezvoused here with him. His instructions were precise and uncomplicated. Haider was busy acting as valet, helping Muzaffar with his boots and his turban – 'No,' Muzaffar said, breaking off in the middle of telling the two men how he wanted them to behave in a few minutes' time. 'No, Haider, leave the end loose. I'll cover up my face. I don't want him to be able to identify me. Some of them in there got a good look at my face recently. It wouldn't do –' His eyes narrowed as he turned his head, listening for tell-tale sounds.

He turned back to Haider, eyes alert and voice brisk as he said, 'My horse.'

Haider hurried away, to return a few moments later with Muzaffar's stallion. The two men – from the kotwali, as Muzaffar had instructed Haider – had no horses of their own, of course; but there was little likelihood of swift mounts being needed. If it came to a chase, Muzaffar was confident of handling it on his own. Or, at the very worst, pulling one of the men up behind him. His beloved chestnut, all traces of thrush now gone, strong and sharp and raring to go, could carry two men a long way.

Muzaffar drew the hanging end of his turban up, across his nose and mouth and jaw, and tucked it securely behind his ear. Then, satisfied that it would hold, he glanced towards the men from the kotwali. Both, according to his instructions, had removed the leather tunics that pointed to their official status. Muzaffar gestured to them to follow him. Haider busied himself with gathering up the discarded clothing before he turned to the bullocks, still standing patiently under the banyan.

Half an hour after the cart-driver's message had been conveyed to Omar Sahib, the main gate of Sajjad Khan's haveli was opened to let out a man on a mule. It was a scrawny mule with an ill-fed look about it. The man was equally gaunt, and had the swarthy complexion and clean-cut features of a Deccani. Muzaffar, watching from behind a screening pair of ber bushes, whispered to the two men beside him: 'I should be able to handle him on my own. But I want one of you to come out onto the road with me when I ride out to stop him. Leave your lance behind; it makes you look like a soldier rather than a petty bandit. Better break yourself a sturdy branch, instead: it'll be a decent substitute.'

He had turned his head, addressing the burlier of the two men as he did so. Now he looked towards the other man. 'I want you to stay back here. If anything should happen – suppose someone comes to his help from the haveli, for instance – come on out. And remember to bring those lances if you do; we'll need them. Otherwise, stay here and wait for us to return.'

The man on the mule had turned the corner when the two men stepped out onto the road, Muzaffar on his horse, and the man from the kotwali on foot beside him. This was a deserted stretch of road, and Muzaffar was grateful for it; what he had in mind would not have been possible if there had been people around. The fact that he was mounted – plus with an armed man at his stirrup – would have deterred most people from trying to oppose him, but there was no knowing. Men in a mob give each other courage. Fortunately, there was no mob in the vicinity. No group working in the fields, nobody sitting and chatting in the warming sunlight.

Muzaffar had reined in his horse right in the oncoming mule's path. The man stopped too, pulling on the mule's reins, watching Muzaffar with fear in his eyes.

Muzaffar walked his horse forward, until it was standing next to the mule, the two animals facing in opposite directions.

'That's a useful-looking animal you have there,' Muzaffar remarked. He winced inwardly at his own words and tried not to notice the look of sheer incredulity on the man's face. 'Considering you look like you haven't had a square meal since the day you were born. You're not from Agra, are you?'

The man blinked, caught unawares by the strange question. 'No,' he said finally. 'No, I'm not.'

'Then? From somewhere down in the Deccan?'

'Bijapur.'

'They breed sturdy mules in Bijapur, do they?' Muzaffar asked. He looked down at the man from the kotwali. 'Shall we let him go? Or do you think that mule would be a good mount for you? Better than walking about.' He lunged out as he spoke, reaching for Omar's man's collar.

There was sheer chaos for the next couple of minutes. The man from the kotwali leaped forward, bashing left and right with his branch, with little thought for whom he was hitting. Muzaffar, hanging on to Omar's man with one hand while he tried to control his horse with his other hand, got a few choice whacks from the stick. But he held on doggedly, swerving to avoid the flying fists of the man they had assaulted. For one so thin, he was surprisingly strong. His fists drove into his attackers with the force of a much larger and broader man, and one fist, catching Muzaffar in the ribs, doubled him up, gasping with pain and breathless.

But the force of that blow had also left the man vulnerable for just one precious moment. His guard down, he did not see the heavier end of the stick – a branch broken off from a mango tree – coming flying at his temple. It caught him on the side of the head, and even as he grunted with pain, the man from the kotwali followed up with a series of quick blows. By the time Muzaffar had straightened up, Omar's servant was down. He had been flung onto the road in the scuffle and lay in the dust, unconscious and with his clothes torn and mud-stained. A trickle of blood ran from one temple down to his chin. His mule had retreated, braying-neighing in panic, and now stood on the edge of the road.

Muzaffar swung himself off his horse and hurried over to the fallen man. The man from the kotwali was already bending over him, methodically searching his clothes. 'Here, huzoor,' he whispered. 'There's a silver coin on a string around his neck.' He tugged on the twine, snapping it off.

'Anything else that's valuable?'

The man, who had continued to grope through the other's pockets and folds of clothing, nodded as he pulled out a sheet of paper from the man's cummerbund. The man on the ground was already regaining consciousness, groaning and trying with weak hands to push away the intrusion on his being. Muzaffar took the sheet of paper that was being held out to him. 'Let's see,' he said, loud enough for Omar's man to hear. He read through the brief note that was the sheet. 'It authorizes this man to collect a parcel from the Sarai Nur Jahan. Hmmm... that might be a fruitful expedition.

Come along, take his mule and that coin – you've searched well, haven't you? There's nothing else of value there?'

The man from the kotwali mounted the mule, and even as Omar's servant got to his feet – still tottering and disoriented, the blood dripping onto his shoulder – the two men rode off. They let the animals gallop on for a while, away from the scene of the attack. When they were far away enough for them to be out of earshot, Muzaffar stopped. The man from the kotwali pulled the mule to a halt as well.

'Well,' Muzaffar said, 'That should be sufficient lure. Let's see what it draws out. You had better take that mule on to the kotwali and bring back reinforcements as soon as you possibly can. At least ten men, I think. Omar will probably not venture out with less than half a dozen to keep him safe from highway robbers like us.'

And while the man from the kotwali rode off on the abducted mule, Muzaffar sat in his saddle, re-reading the sheet of paper he had confiscated. Finally, with a sigh of satisfaction, he folded it and shoved it into his cummerbund. Then he turned his horse about and headed back to the banyan tree where he had left Haider and the second man from the kotwali.

On second thought, he realized that the number of men Omar was likely to bring out with him depended on what his priorities were. If, as Muzaffar guessed, Omar was more concerned about the package awaiting him at the Sarai Nur Jahan than he was concerned about the welfare of his injured servitor, it was possible that Omar would merely call for his horse, mount it and head for the sarai himself. Perhaps with a well-armed bodyguard or two, just in case the men who had attacked the servant were still in the vicinity.

If, on the other hand, he was concerned about his servant and spent some time ensuring that the man was made comfortable – well, then it might not just take longer, it might also give Omar and his host Sajjad Khan time to gather a small force, sufficient to ward off even a fairly fierce band of robbers.

To Muzaffar's relief, it was the former, even though the time it took Omar to venture forth was longer than Muzaffar would have imagined. A little over three-quarters of an hour passed after the attack on the man; then the gate of the haveli swung open again, and three horses thundered out onto the road. The first was a splendid black horse, its mane flying as it galloped out. The two animals that followed it were more plebeian, less flamboyant and less well-groomed, but sturdy horses nevertheless that matched the pace of their leader. The horses passed through; a man – whom Muzaffar recognized as the gatekeeper – stepped out. He stood outside the gate for a few moments, gazing after the galloping horses; then he turned. The gate swung shut behind him.

Muzaffar did not stop even to heave a sigh of relief; he was already moving forward on foot, beckoning to the group of men ranged around the banyan tree.

The odds were in favour of Muzaffar's party. There was little doubt about who would win in a skirmish, if it came to that. As the three horses flew down the road and took the curve, they came up short, nearly colliding with the men ranged across the road, blocking the path. Five men on foot, the one in the middle Muzaffar Jang, who directed his temporary staff with the assurance of a man who knew exactly what he wanted to achieve from this encounter. The other five men – and the two who had originally accompanied Haider to the rendezvous – stepped forward, neatly encircling Omar and his men. They were surrounded, and irredeemably outnumbered. Their only advantage was that they were mounted. For a few moments, it looked as if Omar and his party would disregard the ambush and go careening through; then they noticed the iron chain that had been, even as they stumbled in confusion, tied across the road. It stretched from a peepal tree on the left, to a neem on the right. Behind them, already being tied in place between another pair of trees, was another chain.

Omar yelled, urging his men to turn, to take their horses through the fields on either side. But they were too late. In that critical moment of hesitation, chains had been strung across, hemming in the three horsemen. It was a small and crooked rectangle, but it was an effective prison, the chains too high for a horse to jump, too low for it to go under.

Dust, clouds of it, flew up as the three horses whirled around, their riders trying desperately to find an exit. There were shouts of rage, yelled curses and the clattering of swords in scabbards as the realization dawned that a way out would have to be forced – almost certainly on foot. The men from the kotwali were moving forward, an inexorable and daunting force.

They had been given their instructions: the two men accompanying Omar were not important. It was Omar who was important. Come what may, he had to be grabbed and bound and carted off to the safe haven Muzaffar had chosen for him. And, as far as was possible, he was not to be injured in the process.

The men from the kotwali were well trained. It took only a few minutes for them to use their lances and swords to overpower Omar and his companions. A few of them concentrated their efforts on throwing the riders off their horses and then getting hold of the horses themselves, in order to calm them down. The others went for the riders. Omar's two men were obviously soldiers, or had been in the past – and were almost certainly paid to guard Omar's life with their own. They flung themselves into battle with their attackers as only desperate men can do, cutting and slashing with a vigour so mad that it overshadowed much of the skill they possessed.

But they were, after all, only two men, and facing more than ten. Before five minutes had passed, one had been killed, a lance impaling him to the ground. The other, pushed to a far corner with the trunk of the peepal tree behind him and the chain on either side, was felled with a sword cut that left the biceps of his right arm – his sword arm – bleeding and torn. Omar, driven to try and defend himself, did not succeed for long; the flat end of a well-aimed lance caught him across the shoulders, sending him stumbling to the ground. He was swiftly grabbed, his hands bound behind his back, a gag tied across his mouth, and a blindfold added to the ensemble.

'Well done,' Muzaffar said, his voice muffled by the end of the turban draped across his face. 'Two of you can stay back and remove the chains. The rest of you, come with me. Gather up that man who's hurt; we'll get a hakim for him, but it's dangerous to leave him around here. And put that dead body across his horse – it's better we take him away. Leaving him here for someone to find will likely raise the alarm sooner than we would wish it.'

And so they cleaned up, gathering up the dead and the injured, slinging the unconscious Omar across his own horse and tying him down to the animal. Muzaffar flung the discarded shawl which he had been wearing that morning, over Omar. Then, after a moment's thought, he also draped the dhoti over the man. It would not hide completely the fact that there was a man underneath, but hopefully they would not come across anybody on their way to their destination.

'I feel a strange sense of being without direction. Floating aimlessly,' Muzaffar said to Akram. It had been three days since the episode at Sajjad Khan's haveli.

Akram, his ankle now healed sufficiently for him to go out riding, had gone to Qureshi Sahib's haveli after an excited Haider had informed him and Basheer that Jang Sahib had carried out a daring abduction of Omar Sahib. At Qureshi Sahib's haveli, Akram had been told that Muzaffar was not at home – though Zeenat Begum had received a brief message from him reassuring her of his safety and telling her that it may still be a day or two before he could return.

Akram did not receive any messages from Muzaffar; instead, the day after his visit to Qureshi Sahib's haveli, he received a visit from his friend himself. Basheer, who was at Mumtaz Hassan's tomb site, was expected back before sunset. 'He needs to know the details, of course,' Muzaffar said. 'After all, he should know who did his father in.' He noticed the look of irony on Akram's face, and added, 'Yes. Even if he wasn't especially fond of that father.'

'Now that I know what happened – or rather, now that I have proved what happened – I feel relief. *Of course.* The Diwan-i-kul cannot punish me for not having fulfilled the commission he gave me. And I have satisfied my own curiosity about how and why Mumtaz Hassan was killed. And I know, more or less, what secret lurks in Ibrahim's past. But once we've dealt with that, what then?'

Akram blinked at his friend. 'You know what Ibrahim's secret is? I didn't even *know* he had a secret. Just that he accused his own son of Hassan Sahib's murder, and you didn't think that was true. And you've proved it now. Then?'

But Muzaffar simply shook his head, in a non-committal way that told Akram nothing. Haider, still simmering and shimmering with the excitement of the past several days, led a small contingent of servants in with refreshments. Muzaffar and Akram picked at the food and talked of this and that while they waited for Basheer to return. The talk was mainly all of Akram: of how his ankle felt now, of how he had spent his time during the enforced confinement because of his injury. It was not that Akram was keen on discussing himself – far from it – but he could sense that Muzaffar would rather not talk of his adventures right now. Later, when Basheer was present and when Muzaffar would have to tell it all. Just that one time, not again and again.

Even though he had known this maverick amir less than a year, and even though Muzaffar was in many ways his extreme opposite, Akram had come to know his friend well. Muzaffar was not a man to take pleasure in talking about himself. He would *have* to recount all that had happened in the recent past, simply because Basheer, as son to the victim, had a right to know; but he would not relish the experience.

Basheer arrived sometime after sunset. Servants had, long before, come quietly into the dalaan to both replenish the snacks and to light chiraghdaans. Basheer, informed at the gate that Jang Sahib had returned, bustled in, looking vastly more animated than usual. 'The city is all agog,' he said, after a greeting so brief that a man more aware of his consequence than Muzaffar might well have been offended. He sat down on the mattress and called to Haider to fetch more kababs. Then, turning to Muzaffar, he said: 'Tell me, what is it you have done? The gossip everywhere is that the Kotwal and his men swooped down on Mirza Sajjad Khan's haveli and arrested everybody in sight. It is being said that Sajjad Khan and some of his men have been dragged off to the kotwali and clapped into prison, awaiting the return to Agra of the Diwan-i-kul. And all of this because Sajjad Khan had Abba murdered.' He paused to draw breath and pour himself a goblet of sherbet from the pitcher beside the mattress.

When he resumed, it was in a slightly calmer voice. 'People say that the Kotwal is the man responsible, that he was the one who carried out the investigations. I didn't say anything – but how? And – and why did you suspect Sajjad Khan? Only because of that piebald horse? Why not anybody else? Didn't Ibrahim say that Mahmood was the culprit? And you did say that that lady – your sister's friend – that she made enquiries, and it emerged that Abba –' His voice faltered. When he continued, it was in a softer, more weary tone. '... that Abba was having an affair with the sister of one of his own enemies. Wouldn't that have made it obvious? Surely a woman who is a blood relation of one of your enemies shouldn't be trusted!' For a moment, Muzaffar caught a glimpse, once again, of the resentful son who had been scorned and rejected by his father.

Basheer's expression changed, from indignation to an oddly resigned curiosity. 'Tell me,' he said, pulling a bolster and tucking it under an arm as he settled himself on the mattress. 'Tell me all that happened. And why you thought it was Sajjad Khan. And why he did it.'

Muzaffar took a few minutes to narrate the incidents of the

preceding days. The kidnapping of Omar had been the turning point; till then, Muzaffar, though certain he was on the right track, had nothing to prove that Sajjad Khan or his Bijapuri accomplices had been behind the slaying of Mumtaz Hassan. 'They may have been behind it, but they were not the ones who actually strangled your father. That was Jamal, the man in charge of the stables at Sajjad Khan's haveli. They knew they could trust him – he's as crooked as they come – and they had to, because on their own, they couldn't summon up the nerve to kill a man in cold blood. Omar certainly couldn't. That I discovered in the hours the Kotwal held him in that old ruin near the river.'

'You tortured him?' Akram looked shocked.

'Not me, I didn't. Actually, even the Kotwal didn't really need to. Omar was more of a coward than I'd suspected him to be. Oh, he withstood my interrogation all right – just looked taken aback when I began telling him what I knew – but he managed to keep his mouth shut through it all. Wouldn't admit to anything. Not even the obvious, like the fact that Sajjad Khan owned a distinctive piebald horse which only Jamal could handle. He refused even to answer when I asked him about his visit to Mumtaz Hassan.'

He sighed. 'And then the Kotwal got started. I thought he'd get his men to do the dirty work, but I suppose he decided otherwise because Omar isn't your average criminal. He's wealthy and he's got connections. If – just if – I was mistaken, we couldn't afford to have a wounded or dead Omar on our hands.

'So the Kotwal began. It was almost like he was a cat toying with a mouse. He'd put a hand on Omar's shoulder and say, "Omar Sahib, are you sure you don't know *anything*?" and he'd give this quiet, gentle smile, as if he held his own newborn babe in his arms. But at the same time, that hand would move to Omar's collar, and one forefinger would hook itself in that collar. He'd twist. Twist until Omar was flapping about like a landed fish, helpless because his arms were tied behind him. And all the time the Kotwal would keep smiling.'

Akram's eyes were wide with a horrified fascination. Basheer looked merely faintly shocked.

'He did things like that. Nothing that would scar the man for life. Nothing that would mutilate him, or cause him unbearable pain. But just things that would make it very, very uncomfortable for him. I think the Kotwal's tender smile, as if he were playing with Omar rather than questioning him, was what finally defeated Omar. It shook *me* up, at any rate.'

And Omar had finally broken down. Literally, the tears running down his cheeks and his breath coming in great gasps. They had had to wait for him to recover before they could listen to the confession he was now so eager to give.

'It was as I had guessed,' said Muzaffar. 'Mirza Sajjad Khan, on his own, would probably not have proved a threat to your father's life. What upset the balance was the coming of Omar and his companions from Bijapur. Do you remember that letter Omar brought with him, written by his father, Khush Bakht Khan? It named Omar as his emissary. It talked of a matter of great urgency, that would require the putting aside of old rivalries.' Muzaffar glanced up, sharp-eyed and alert as a hawk on the wing. 'What could be so urgent? And – from what Khush Bakht Khan wrote – possibly dangerous?'

When neither Akram nor Basheer did anything other than look blankly back at him, he answered his own question. 'The Diwan-i-kul has gone south. The Shahzada Aurangzeb has left Aurangabad with his armies, to meet him and to march, together, on to Bijapur. Khush Bakht Khan realizes what the result will be. What happens when the Mughal armies invade? Especially now, with the imperial coffers sounding hollow thanks to the Baadshah's extravagance –'

'*Muzaffar.*' Akram's voice held a warning. For the briefest of moments, Muzaffar was reminded of the one person who had not been shocked when he had questioned the infallibility of the Baadshah. *Shireen.* He had not seen her since that morning near the garden, when a noblewoman in a palanquin had conversed with a filthy, smelly man driving a bullock-cart down to the river.

Muzaffar had returned to Qureshi Sahib's haveli earlier this day, worn out and bleary-eyed. He had bathed, letting a servant scrub and massage him till every pore had been well and truly cleansed. And then he had fallen asleep, so long and so deeply that he had come awake just in time to realize that half the day was over. He had promised the Kotwal that he would be the one to break the news to Basheer, and that had already been delayed. With no time to meet Zeenat Aapa, let alone Shireen, he had contented himself with leaving a verbal message for his sister, assuring her that he was well and would be back within a few hours.

'Jang Sahib!' Basheer said.

Muzaffar, looking up, noticed the scandalized look on the man's face. 'You may not agree, Basheer,' he said. 'But it's true. The Taj Mahal is exquisite. So are the Jama Masjid and the fort in Dilli, and all of those massive mosques and sarais the imperial family has built in the city. But they cost millions, and the treasure chest isn't bottomless. The only way to replenish the wealth – at least for a while – is to conquer a land such as Bijapur.

'Which Khusht Bakht Khan, with his many years of experience, guessed soon enough. I can imagine what must have happened. He, being a merchant, must have links all across Hindustan. He would know how things were progressing. He would know, also, that Mumtaz Hassan had connections in high places. That the Diwan-i-kul, coming from Dilli to Agra, was going to stay in Agra with Mumtaz Hassan. It was not difficult to imagine what would happen then. The Diwan-i-kul is known to have no compunctions when it comes to the means to achieve an end. He has already offered bribes to Bijapuri officers; he could well offer a huge bribe to Mumtaz Hassan and win him over. And Mumtaz Hassan, with his knowledge of how things were in Bijapur, could be of boundless use to the Diwan-i-kul. He might even – would almost certainly, in fact – win over other wealthy Bijapuri merchants and traders who would be willing to help the Shahzada and the Diwan-i-kul enter Bijapur, as long as they themselves were assured of immunity from attack.'

'Are you saying my father would have turned traitor?'

'I do not think your father thought of himself as Bijapuri any more,' Muzaffar replied. 'He has lived in Agra long enough to think of himself as one of this land – and therefore answerable only to him who rules *this* area, the Baadshah. And there was the matter of the way he had been treated in Bijapur too, do you remember? Shakeel Alam told us of how Mumtaz Hassan had been whipped. I think your father' – he glanced at Basheer – 'felt betrayed. Most men would do, I think. Loyalty can only stand so much.

'So Khush Bakht Khan, with a view to reminding Mumtaz Hassan of his duty to the land of his birth, wrote to him. *And* sent Omar to him. Omar's mission was to plead with Mumtaz Hassan to stay firm in the face of the Diwan-i-kul's bribery, entreaties and threats.

'The result was what Haider overheard that day, from outside the dalaan. Mumtaz Hassan laughed in Omar's face and told him to take his entreaties elsewhere. He said that all he had to thank Bijapur for were some scars and some lessons for a lifetime. That was what made me think Omar had come to ask for a favour, not for himself or for his father Khush Bakht Khan, but for Bijapur.'

Akram shifted, reaching across to pick a now cold and greasy kabab from the platter. 'And Hassan Sahib refused? That was why he was killed?'

Muzaffar nodded. 'Yes. As it was, Khush Bakht Khan hated Mumtaz Hassan; the overture – not of friendship, really, but more of a temporary alliance – was because matters had become so urgent. It was a case of do or die. If Mumtaz Hassan agreed to throw in his lot with the Diwan-i-kul, it could spell doom for Bijapur. It seems likely that the Diwan-i-kul has already bought over a good number of the Bijapuri army; if, thanks to Mumtaz Hassan, he also bought over many of its richest and most powerful nobility and merchants, Bijapur would fall like a pack of cards. They could not afford to leave Mumtaz Hassan alive.

'But they went to Sajjad Khan. Omar had already known of him,

and had been carrying a letter of introduction to him from Khush
Bakht Khan. Together, they plotted to get rid of Mumtaz Hassan.
They probably considered themselves too well-born to soil their
own hands with blood, so they got Sajjad Khan's stablemaster Jamal
to do the deed for them. One of them – I learned yesterday that it
was Sajjad Khan – brought Jamal here, to just outside the haveli, to
show him which was Mumtaz Hassan's room. They'd kept their eyes
and ears open when they visited your father; they even managed
to find out where his bedchamber was. They were the men I heard
that night.'

'And the note?' Akram, having eaten the kabab, was now helping
himself to an apple. 'Even if you knew that it was a poor forgery,
purporting to be a love letter from that lady – how could Sajjad
Khan and his cronies have known that Hassan Sahib was in love
with her? Her own brother didn't know it, it seems! Then how did
the men of another household know? And how could they have
discovered details of what her letters looked like, and how she
addressed him? And that she used musk? I'll wager even Basheer
does not know!' Akram directed a quick look at his cousin, who was
looking all at sea.

'How they came to know wasn't too difficult to figure out. Do
you remember what I told you about the lady's letters? She had
mentioned a rendezvous at the Mehtab Bagh – which is opposite
Sajjad Khan's gardens. Perhaps he had been at his gardens, and
had noticed the two of them together. He would have recognized
Mumtaz Hassan, of course, and might have been curious about the
lady. She would have been veiled, but why should Mumtaz Hassan
be courting a lady in a garden – and not in the seclusion of his own
mahal sara – if there was nothing illicit about their relationship?

'In one of her letters following that meeting in the Mehtab Bagh,
the lady had mentioned her aunt having come to the Mehtab Bagh to
take her niece home. I suppose the aunt had been fed some tall story
about why the lady in question was at Mehtab Bagh all by herself in
the first place. Anyway, on the way home, the aunt seemed to have

suspected that they were being followed by a man. The lady, the writer of the letters, scoffed at that suggestion. But I think the aunt was right – because, soon after, in another letter, the lady mentions that a letter she had been writing to Mumtaz Hassan, and which had been interrupted, inexplicably disappeared. She says she looked high and low for it, but it was nowhere to be found.

'If we now look at all those incidents, they fall into place, don't they? Sajjad Khan, on a chance visit to his garden, sees Mumtaz Hassan with a mysterious lady at the nearby Mehtab Bagh. He is intrigued, and sends one of his men to trail the lady and find out who she is. The man succeeds. Sajjad Khan doesn't like Mumtaz Hassan, anyway. Perhaps he begins to think up a plot to get rid of Mumtaz Hassan, by trapping him with his own penchant for women. Or perhaps he just tucks the knowledge away somewhere, to be used if and when needed. Perhaps he had blackmail in mind; I don't know. At any rate, he sent a man to sneak in to the lady's chambers. Maybe he gave the man instructions to bring away something unique, something that could instantly be identified as belonging to the lady. Most probably, the bangle-seller who had stopped by just then to display her wares to the lady was all part of the plot.

'Sajjad Khan's man broke into the lady's chamber, but perhaps he was short of time, or everything personal that she owned was stored away. All he could find that may have been of use was the letter she was in the middle of writing – so he stole that, and brought it to Sajjad Khan.' He licked his lips and swallowed, suddenly tired of talking, suddenly thirsty and in need of a drink. A servant was sent for; while he was gone, the three men sat in silence, Muzaffar's throat hurting and the other two too caught up in his story to say anything. The servant returned, bringing with him three goblets of sherbet, which he placed before Basheer, Akram and Muzaffar.

The man retreated and Muzaffar took a long, grateful swallow from his goblet. The sherbet was a blend of oranges and lemons, fresh and sweet, yet with a sharp tang. He glanced appreciatively into the goblet, sipped once more, and continued with his narrative.

'Then – or perhaps it was later, when he met Omar, after Omar's abortive attempt to wean Mumtaz Hassan back to the side of the Bijapuris – then, Sajjad Khan decided to use that letter as bait. I don't know why he didn't use it as it was, instead of a copy. Possibly because he did not want that it should, if things went wrong, be somehow traced back to –' He reddened and broke off, stopping himself on the verge of revealing the identity of Mumtaz Hassan's lover. 'I suppose Sajjad Khan held no grudge against *that* household; all he wanted was to entice Mumtaz Hassan. So he created a copy – not an especially good copy, either – but enough at first glance to interest Mumtaz Hassan. Long enough to draw his attention away from the man who had carried that letter to him, at any rate.'

He fell silent. It was a long silence, both Basheer and Akram ruminating over all that had been told to them. It was Basheer who finally spoke. 'So,' he said. '*So*. My father was killed because he could have caused the downfall of Bijapur. Does his death actually avert that possibility, now?'

Muzaffar shrugged and put his now-empty goblet down on the white runner spread on the carpet. 'Who knows?' he replied. 'But, looking at the army the Diwan-i-kul was leading down south, and remembering the Shahzada Aurangzeb's forces: I doubt it. It would seem to me inevitable. I think Bijapur will fall, irrespective of whether your father were here to bribe its merchants to side with the Mughals, or not.'

Akram sat back against the bolster he had been leaning on. 'There is still one loose end, Muzaffar,' he said. 'Ibrahim. What about him?'

'Yes. Ibrahim.' Muzaffar pursed his lips. 'That is the other problem. And one that I am more wary of approaching than this one. I'll go and visit him tomorrow. Will you come with me?' He glanced at Akram.

'Of course I will. When do we start?'

'Not very early. Perhaps after the second namaaz of the day. I have an important task to complete in the morning.'

19

SHIREEN WAS THERE in the khanah bagh, waiting for him. It had been too much to expect, Muzaffar thought with a pang of annoyance, that she would come without a chaperone of some sort. It was not a female relative, or Zeenat Begum, or even a maid – at least he could be thankful for that. But the figure of the eunuch Khursheed hovered in the background, unobtrusive but still present.

Muzaffar murmured a quiet greeting to Shireen as she rose to her feet.

'I hope you are well rested now,' she said. 'All Agra is abuzz with your exploits. Everybody here is eager to know the details.'

'And you?'

She was startled; the way her head lifted with a sudden jerk, and the gasp that accompanied the action, were proof enough. Muzaffar himself was startled at what he had said. He swallowed, waiting for her to say something.

'I can wait for the details,' she replied. 'Though I suppose I have the advantage of knowing that your adventures involved an interesting – and possibly uncomfortable disguise.' There was that chuckle in her voice again, that sense of humour that he found so attractive. Like so much else about her. Her intelligence. Her calm, level-headed way of looking at things. The decidedly non-conformist streak that made her see the Baadshah and his heir apparent as something less than divine beings.

Muzaffar blinked. She had said something, and he had been too busy thinking of her to pay attention.

'I beg your pardon; you said –?'

'You had made me promise I would meet you when you returned,' she reminded him.

'Ah. Of course. Yes. I – Zeenat Aapa had spoken to me. A few days ago.' He could feel her gaze upon him, and it made it even more awkward for him to speak. 'She said that your aunt – um – had indicated...' His courage failed him. He did not know how to say it.

Shireen turned her head away, her shoulders sagging. 'It is all right, Jang Sahib,' she said in a barely audible voice, a mere wisp of sound. Muzaffar had to strain to hear her. 'I –I don't agree with what my aunt said. I mean, I do not think it right of her and of my uncle to try and push you into something. Please do not mind them, Jang Sahib; they think only of my welfare, you see. And they are not always as tactful as one would want them to be.' She had forgotten her initial humiliation, that agonizing despair he had seen in the drooping of her head. The words were pouring forth now. 'I was mortified when I came to know. I apologize, on my aunt's behalf. On my uncle's behalf. To you and to Zeenat Begum, for putting you through this. I hope you will forgive them. Forgive us. It was unpardonably gauche, I realize. But –'

Her distress made him ache, too. A tangible ache that began as a lump in the throat and then seemed to spread all over, clutching at his heart and at the same time causing it to swell. 'It is all right,' he said gently. 'I was not inconvenienced or annoyed by what was said. Do not trouble yourself.' He thought she was going to say something, but when she remained silent, head still bent, he said, 'May I take your leave now?'

She nodded hurriedly. 'Of course. And – Jang Sahib – please, do not feel that what my aunt said... that you must' – she gulped – 'offer. I will not be offended.'

'But would you be offended if I were to offer?' Muzaffar said. Shireen stilled and he heard her gasp. Then, with an incoherently mumbled word – was it goodbye? Was it no? yes? – she rushed away up the steps and down the corridor, towards the mahal sara.

Muzaffar watched as Khursheed followed, walking at a more sedate pace.

Muzaffar turned away too, and with a smile on his lips, headed back towards the men's quarters of the haveli, and beyond, to the stables.

Ibrahim was sitting on a cane stool in front of the little house he shared with Mahmood. The sunlight on his face lit up each wrinkle, each scar and purple blemish of age, throwing into stark relief the still-bright eyes that watched Muzaffar with wariness. He had noticed Muzaffar and Akram walking towards him long before they reached; Muzaffar had seen the brief glance in their direction, and the subsequent turning away. Ibrahim had remained studiously aloof until they arrived and Muzaffar greeted him. Even then, he acknowledged their presence with only a blink.

'If you're here to meet Mahmood, he's away at the rauza,' he said. His pet mongrel appeared in the open doorway, yawned, and shook its head vigorously, its ears flapping audibly against its skull. It stood stock-still for a moment or two, then came to its master, eagerly shoving its head under his hand, begging to be petted. Ibrahim obliged.

'I know,' Muzaffar said. He stood in front of Ibrahim, hands on hips, head swivelling around as if in search of something. His gaze alighted on a broken charpai, half of its ropes missing, which had been stood up, leaning against the side of the hut. It was the work of a few moments for him to pull down the charpai, drag it – with the help of Akram, who had realized a little late what Muzaffar was about – and sit down. Akram perched himself a little precariously on one of the corners of the charpai.

'We stopped by at the rauza on our way here,' Muzaffar said. 'They've made a lot of progress on the work, haven't they? No more malicious attacks by the jinn, I think.' He leaned forward, his eyes boring into

Ibrahim's. 'Not that you *really* believe in malignant jinn who prowl the earth looking to harm us poor humans, do you? You didn't believe in them all those years ago when you were working on the Empress's tomb, and you didn't believe in them that day, when you said the jinn were to blame for that accident at the rauza when the scaffolding collapsed.'

Ibrahim did not blink. 'Why do you say that?'

'Because there never were any jinn in the story, to start off with! Because all the jinn that crowd into this tale can be ascribed to you!' Muzaffar inhaled sharply, trying to calm himself. 'Mohammad Hussain, Mangal, all those others who were there during those days – all of them said there were moving shadows and dancing flames, in the night at the mosque of the Taj Mahal. That *you* said those were jinn. And that those shadows, those lights, appeared just a couple of days before your friend Fakhru crashed to his death. Just a day after your wife disappeared, never to be seen again – yes, we met Mahmood at the rauza just now, and he confirmed that he has never heard from his mother since the day she vanished.'

Ibrahim did not react. His hand continued to stroke the dog. Akram shifted uneasily, trying to find a more comfortable position on the charpai without plunging through the large hole in its centre.

'But that was just your imagination, wasn't it, Ibrahim? Or shall I say, it was your attempt to divert suspicion from yourself?' Muzaffar's voice lowered to just above a whisper. Off in the undergrowth on their left, a barbet began calling, its distinctive kot-roo, kot-roo syllables echoing in the silence. 'Because you knew exactly what happened to your wife. Fauzia did not run off, either by herself or with another man. And she wasn't kidnapped, or anything of the sort. She was killed – and by none other than her own husband.'

Somewhere further away, deep among the ber trees nearby, another barbet began calling, answering the first one. Akram, after a gasp of surprise, had lapsed into a silence brimming with curiosity. Muzaffar, glancing at his friend, could see the plea in his eyes, begging to be told all. He turned to look at Ibrahim. The old stone cutter still sat hunched on his stool. His face was impassive, but the hand that had been petting the dog had moved away now and was clutching the edge of the stool. It was clenched tight, the knuckles standing out bony and white.

'You married Fauzia years ago in Bijapur,' said Muzaffar, when he realized that Ibrahim was not going to speak. 'She had been fending for herself for some time – and in that time, she had worked as a maid in the household of a wealthy young Bijapuri merchant. She told all her past history to Fakhru's wife, you know; it was from her that I learned what had happened. The Bijapuri merchant must have been good to her, because when she married you and was leaving Bijapur to accompany you to Agra, she went to say farewell to him. He gave her a gift, too: a bidri bracelet, black and gold.

'She was already pregnant by the time you got back to Agra. You *were* happy, weren't you, when Mahmood was born? Both Fakhru's widow and Mangal told me you doted on him. He was a youth then, twenty-five years back, when the Empress's tomb was being built. The one thing that surprised Mangal was that, in the wake of your wife's disappearance, you seemed to have suddenly changed from a loving father to one who couldn't stand the sight of his son. And I can vouch for that. A father may be forgiven, if he is ill and in pain, for being short-tempered or abrupt; but a father who deliberately sets out to accuse his son of murder?'

Ibrahim shifted and scowled, but maintained a stony silence. The dog, perhaps sensing the man's discomfiture, whined.

'Mumtaz Hassan, incidentally, just a few weeks before he was killed, had given his current lady love a distinctive bracelet. It was a valuable item that was identified for me as being a piece of bidri jewellery: gold wire inlaid in black metal. I showed that bracelet to Fakhru's widow, and she was surprised to find it in my possession, even temporarily. Because she had last seen it on the wrist of your wife, Fauzia. And Fauzia had told her that it was a gift from that merchant in whose house she had worked in Bijapur for some time. Which, when one pieces together the facts, makes sense. Two Bijapuri merchants, both giving an identical bidri bracelet to two different women? Too much of a coincidence. It had to be one man. Mumtaz Hassan.'

There was a flicker of reaction now from Ibrahim. He frowned, looked up at Muzaffar for a moment, and looked as if he was about to speak. But the moment passed, and Muzaffar continued. 'Twenty-five years ago, while you were working at the Taj Mahal construction site, Mumtaz Hassan arrived in Agra from Bijapur. He had shifted to this city. You didn't know then, did you, the past he shared with Fauzia? And how did she come to know of his arrival? Did –'

He was interrupted, oddly enough, by Ibrahim himself. The man spoke in a low, hoarse voice, as if the words were being forced out of him. 'I,' he said. 'It was *I* who told her. I didn't know! I hadn't known then, I hadn't known all those years, how she had deceived me!' He was almost sobbing now, but these were sobs of rage, of a sense of ill usage that had festered for years on end. 'I was introduced to him by the overseer, Mohammad Hussain. Mohammad Hussain told me that this – this merchant – was from Bijapur, and would be supplying us with the gems we worked with. He was carrying some samples with him; he showed them to us. They were beautiful, far superior to any stones we had worked with before. When I went home that night, I told my wife.' He gulped and the sobs subsided, choked off in mid-flow. 'If only I had not!' he added, so vicious now that spittle flew. Akram cringed and leaned back. 'If only I had kept quiet, not said a word to her of my work!'

Muzaffar wondered if, considering the unsatisfactory state of their marriage, that would have helped matters much, but he held his tongue.

As abruptly as he had begun speaking, Ibrahim fell silent.

'So,' Muzaffar said. 'She learned of Mumtaz Hassan's arrival through you. And one day, while you were away at work, she went to meet him, dressed in her fine blue clothes and wearing the bracelet he had gifted her all those years earlier. Fakhru's widow saw her going, and remembered her as being excited and happy... Fauzia came back later, that same afternoon, and sometime between then and the time you returned and raised the alarm – she disappeared. And the bracelet disappeared with her. Fakhru's widow told me that when the search for Fauzia began, she accompanied you inside the house, and that you showed her Fauzia's blue peshwaaz lying bundled into the top of the chest. She said she did not see the bracelet.'

'But Hassan Sahib gave that bracelet to that – that other woman, just this year,' Akram blurted.

'Exactly. How did the bracelet vanish from Fauzia's wrist, and resurface in Mumtaz Hassan's possession, for him to give away, twenty-five years later?'

Akram's eyes widened. 'Ya Allah,' he whispered, horrified. 'You mean Hassan Sahib murdered Fauzia, somehow, and took away the bracelet –'

Muzaffar shook his head. 'No, I don't think so, not at all. Why should he? He had loved her very much, or at least been not just intimate' – he flushed, aware that he was referring to the long-dead wife of the man sitting opposite him – 'but also, perhaps, felt a good deal of affection for her. If he had been jealous, he might have stepped in way back then, in Bijapur, when she was getting ready to marry Ibrahim. But he didn't; he let her marry another man. He even gave her a wedding present, the bracelet. And if he was simply trying to make her keep quiet about his relationship with her – well, that seems a little uncharacteristic of Hassan Sahib, doesn't it? He's never made a secret of his fondness for the fairer sex. Yes, perhaps in his latest affair he has been discreet, but that may be because the lady in question is too well-born – and has relations who could have made things exceptionally uncomfortable for Mumtaz Hassan.

'And you remember, of course, that Fauzia returned alive and well from the rendezvous,' Muzaffar pointed out. 'Fakhru's wife saw her. If we even assume that Mumtaz Hassan came to visit her after she had returned, then how did he approach the house or get away from it? There were people around, in the neighbourhood – that boy herding goats – and everybody seemed to be unanimous in their belief that nobody out of the ordinary had been seen in the vicinity. Even if Mumtaz Hassan managed somehow to sneak in, what happened? Why should the bracelet – which he had gifted her willingly – be suddenly so important to him that he would kill her for it? Why not ask for it back? He could even have bought it back, if he was so desperate and she so unwilling to part with it. Why murder her? And if he *had* murdered her, what did he do with the body?' The questions came pouring out of him. Answers, really, all of them; not questions at all.

'But Fakhru's widow recalled seeing something strange in your house, Ibrahim,' he said, turning to the old man. 'A gash, fresh and large, as if someone had flung an axe at the wall. And someone had mopped the floor below that, she said. She was surprised, because a gash like that would only have made dried earth spill onto the floor – dried earth that any woman would simply have swept out the door. Why wipe it?

'But that might have been *necessary*,' he added, looking straight at Ibrahim. Muzaffar's usual charm and gentleness were nowhere to be seen; he now put Akram in mind of a watchdog, alert and on the prowl. His eyes were narrowed, his jaw tense. 'If blood had been spilled inside the house. I was told your chisel broke around the same time as your wife disappeared. How did *that* happen, Ibrahim?' He waited in token silence for Ibrahim to respond, but when the old man stayed silent, Muzaffar carried on. 'You attacked her with it, didn't you? Did you fling it at her, only to have it fly out of your hand and embed itself in the wall behind her? And when you pulled it out and went after her again, it left behind a gash in the wall – and perhaps the chisel broke too, in the process? But you finally succeeded. You killed her, leaving a pool of blood that you had to mop up before one of the neighbours arrived. And you had to dispose of the body.'

Ibrahim stared back at Muzaffar. He was glassy-eyed now.

'I don't understand,' Akram burst out. 'Why should Ibrahim kill his wife? I mean – yes, of course if I were in his place,' – he glanced towards the stone cutter – 'I would have been angry, too, to discover that my wife had had an affair with another man. But that had been years ago. It was over and done with.'

'Was it? Really?' Muzaffar did not look at his friend; he continued to gaze at Ibrahim, and when he spoke, his voice was grave.

'Wasn't it?'

'She went to meet that old lover of hers – dressed in her finest clothes – as soon as she found that he was in Agra. That does not sound like it was really over and done with.' Muzaffar sat up straight, gripping the worn wooden frame of the charpai to steady himself. 'But perhaps it was, too. Perhaps she went to see how he was, after all these years. Perhaps she went to return that gift he had given her all those years back – that, I suppose, was how it turned up again in Mumtaz Hassan's possession, for him to be able to bestow it on another woman, years later. *And perhaps she went to tell him how his son was.*'

Akram, who had begun to slump on the sagging charpai, snapped upright. He stared wildly at Muzaffar, then at Ibrahim – who was looking angry and miserable, all at once – and then back at Muzaffar.

'What was it,' Muzaffar said, still addressing Ibrahim, 'that made you realize Mahmood was not your son, but Mumtaz Hassan's? Did you notice a fleeting resemblance between the two? Something in the eyes, and in the smile? I did, you know. That day, when the accident occurred at the rauza and I came here with Taufeeq. I saw Mahmood then, smile briefly – and it seemed to me that I had seen that smile and those eyes somewhere before. But it was a ghost of a thought; I was not able to lay hold of it and remember whom it reminded me of.' He looked up, a frown creasing his forehead. 'It's such a minor resemblance, so small a similarity, one could easily overlook it – or put it down to coincidence. And sometimes, it can be difficult to compare a full-grown man, in his forties, with a youth who is not even twenty. But you guessed, did you? Or did you have a quarrel with your wife, and did she fling it in your face? That the son you were so devoted to was not yours at all?

He waited for Ibrahim to say something, to admit to what had happened on that momentous long-ago day. But the old man still stayed quiet.

'So you killed her, stuffed her body in the chest, spread the peshwaaz on top to prevent it being seen, and mopped up the blood that had spilled on the floor. Then you went out and raised the alarm, called the neighbours together and organized a search for Fauzia. Nothing came of it, of course. Sometime – was it that same day, or the next? – you spoke to your dearest friend, who was Fakhru. What did you tell him? That there had been an accident, that Fauzia had died and you didn't want it known because people, knowing your marriage was not especially happy, might accuse you of having done away with her? Or did you tell him the truth?

'Whatever it was, he agreed to help.' Muzaffar was now speaking to Akram, explaining what he had guessed. 'Do you remember what I told you of my visit to Mohammad Hussain, the man who had been the overseer? He had some odd recollections of those days – he remembered, very well, all that had happened: Ibrahim's wife's disappearance, Fakhru's death, Ibrahim's being struck down by disease – and a strange little fact: that someone had committed an inexplicable theft, stealing stone slabs from the storeroom, only to use them in the paving in front of the mosque anyway. Mohammad Hussain could not fathom why anybody would do that. Neither could I – until later, when everything fell into place, and I realized why Ibrahim had begun yammering about jinn around that time, and why Mangal himself had seen what he thought were jinn – and why Fakhru died the way he did.'

He turned back to Ibrahim. 'I can imagine a man, in a rage, killing his wife for being unfaithful. But to then dispose of her body in that cold-blooded fashion? And then silencing the one man who helped? That requires a lack of feeling few men have.'

From somewhere not too far came the sound of men talking: voices rising and falling in conversation, as if the speakers chatted as they walked along. The dog, which had dozed off, raised its head and looked fixedly in the direction of the sound. Whoever was coming was still a way off.

Muzaffar glanced around, then turned back to Ibrahim. When he began speaking, it was in hurried tones, as if he wanted to finish what he had to say before the newcomers arrived. 'You persuaded Fakhru to help you. In the night, the two of you took Fauzia's corpse with you – in a cart? – to the site of the Empress's tomb, and buried it in the one place where there was very little chance of it ever being discovered. In front of the mosque, where the paving was in progress. You simply extended the paving a little beyond what had been done *that* day. That was why you broke into the storeroom and stole those slabs that Mohammad Hussain couldn't account for later. And because you knew that a watchman – such as Mangal – may have noticed something, shadows, whispers, a candle flame – the next day you began putting it about that there were jinn at the site.'

The voices were closer now; one, Muzaffar had already recognized as Basheer. The other, he was not sure about, but thought might be Mahmood. 'You also, just to make certain he wouldn't get you into trouble – or later think of blackmailing you – shoved Fakhru off the scaffolding. People said you extended an arm out to try to stop him falling, but that wasn't true – it was just to add more force, to send him surely to his death.'

He eased himself off the charpai carefully, so that it would not tip over and deposit Akram on the ground. Behind him, Akram too rose to his feet. Muzaffar's gaze did not waver for a moment from Ibrahim, though his voice dropped significantly. 'And when you heard, some days ago, that Mumtaz Hassan had been killed, you decided it was a fine opportunity to wreak vengeance on the man you had once thought your son. Was it really vengeance, though, Ibrahim? *What was Mahmood's fault?* Has he been a bad son to you? Has he ever treated you as anything but a father? Even in those days when you inexplicably turned away from him, just after his mother had vanished?' He pulled up short, suddenly aware that contempt was making his voice rise.

He glanced away then, finally. Up at the warm, welcome sun, now flooding the plain below with its light. And then back again, at the bent old man who sat hunched on the stool. Ibrahim looked older, greyer, than he had less than an hour back, when Akram and Muzaffar had first made their way to his hut from Mumtaz Hassan's rauza.

'Mumtaz Hassan was killed, and *not* by his own son,' Muzaffar said quietly. 'You may have been wronged, Ibrahim, all those years back – by Fauzia and by the man she had loved. But today, it is you who has to answer for *her* death, and for the death of Fakhru. Basheer is coming; what shall I tell him?'

Ibrahim looked up at Muzaffar, his eyes dull and lifeless. The misshapen face twitched briefly, as if he was going to say something; but he did not. Behind him, on the ground beside the wall of the hut, lay his crutches. He bent down and lifted them up – Akram, starting up from the charpai, reached forward to help him – and hobbled away into the house. The dog followed, faithful as ever.

'I will tell Basheer the truth before long,' said Muzaffar as he rode back to the haveli with Akram. 'Not today; let him and the others think it was sheer old age, illness, whatever. Perhaps tomorrow, I shall go to Basheer and tell him all that happened.'

It had taken them some time to realize, after his departure, that Ibrahim did not intend to emerge from his home to greet Basheer, who had come by with Taufeeq to enquire after Ibrahim's health. By the time they had entered the house and gone to the still figure lying on the bed and shaken its shoulder and called its name – Ibrahim was dead. Not cold yet, but certainly beyond the reach of human help. Beyond the reach, too, of the Kotwal of Agra, thought Muzaffar. The old man must have known that justice would catch up with him sooner or later; he appeared to have swallowed some fast-acting poison which he had probably kept hidden in his house. All these years? wondered Muzaffar. Or just these past few days?

'And Mahmood?' Akram asked. 'Will you tell him?'

Muzaffar nodded. 'He, more than anyone else, needs to know. It will not be a kind discovery – to find that the man you had always thought of as father was actually not your father, and was the man who killed your mother... but Mahmood is a grown man, not a child to be shielded from all that is dreadful. Yes, I'll tell him. And perhaps he and Basheer will come to some sort of understanding, something better than one being the master and the other the employer. They *are* half-brothers, after all.'

They let their horses trot on, leaving Mumtaz Hassan's half-completed rauza looming above the surrounding landscape. Ibrahim's suicide had not affected the pace of work to any palpable extent; Mahmood had left his assistant Zulfiqar in charge. Muzaffar guessed that most of the workers at the site did not even know that Ibrahim had killed himself.

'I wonder what will happen now,' Akram murmured, more to himself than to his friend. 'It will come as a shock to both Basheer and Mahmood, I suppose – to suddenly discover the existence of a half-brother. That *must* be uncomfortable. What's more, a half-brother in such different circumstances from one's own.'

'People are resilient,' Muzaffar said, after a while. 'They'll recover. They will get used to the presence of each other in their lives.'

'An absence is less easy to get used to than a presence, I daresay,' Akram said quietly. 'Or, for Basheer's sake and for the sake of his half-brother, I hope so.'

'Come in, won't you?', Akram said when they neared Basheer's haveli a little later. 'Basheer should be back soon, too. Maybe once we've had a bite to eat and something to drink, I'll leave you to break the news to him.'

Muzaffar shook his head. 'I'll leave the two of you to your refreshments. I have a couple of tasks to fulfil, and fast.'

Akram looked quizzical. Muzaffar reached into his choga pocket and pulled out a silver coin which had been punched and strung on a length of thick grimy twine. 'This,' he said, 'belongs to a servant of Omar's, the man whom I had to pretend to rob in order to lure Omar out of Sajjad Khan's haveli. It's been weighing on my conscience these past several days; it's time I returned it to that man.'

'And? You said you had a couple of tasks. What more?'

Muzaffar slipped the coin and its string back into his pocket, heaved a deep sigh – as if mentally squaring his shoulders – and then grinned suddenly, his eyes lighting up with a joy so obvious that Akram blinked, taken aback.

'I have to go and begin negotiations for a marriage,' he said with a wink, and dug his heels into his mount's flanks, urging the horse forward.

The gardens in Qureshi Sahib's haveli would never rival Sajjad Khan's gardens near the Mehtab Bagh – they were not even meant to – but by the time spring came around a month later, they were as full of flowers as any well-tended garden could hope to be. Roses bloomed, vivid red and deep pink, in the parterres; there were lilies, the fragrance of jasmine, even some carefully-nurtured tulips. It was the jasmine that had surrounded Muzaffar as he sat, cross-legged and feeling terribly self-conscious in his crimson clothing. From the sehra tied around his forehead hung string upon string of jasmine, down almost to his waist, their fragrance overpoweringly sweet.

It had been a hectic month, beginning with the engagement. His gift to Shireen, a ring set in emeralds and diamonds, had been formally presented to the bride by Zeenat Begum. The equally formal acceptance, in the form of a paan leaf, had come to Muzaffar through her – passed on from Qureshi Sahib to his begum, and from her to Zeenat. That done, and a date fixed for the wedding, the would-be bridegroom and his sister had hurried back to Dilli to make arrangements. To buy gifts for the bride and suitable clothing for the groom; to spread the word among their friends and acquaintances and to invite them to a banquet following Shireen's eventual arrival in Dilli; to make preparations – as much as was possible, this far back – for that banquet. And most importantly, to convert the household of a bachelor, and a none too fastidious one at that, into a house a woman would fit into. Zeenat Begum had worn herself out, scurrying through the haveli and issuing instructions by the dozen to Muzaffar's equally harassed steward Javed. There had been much cleaning of utensils. New sheets had been stitched for the mattresses in the dalaan, the kitchens inspected and each chiraghdaan polished till an eagle-eyed Zeenat could see her face in it. 'It will have to do,' she had said finally, on the evening before they were to set out for Agra. 'Shireen is a forgiving girl; she will be gracious, I think.'

They had arrived in Agra a month after leaving it. This time they were accompanied by Muzaffar's brother-in-law and Zeenat's husband, Farid Khan, the kotwal of Dilli. Qureshi Sahib and his begum had insisted that Zeenat Begum and Khan Sahib stay at their haveli; it would, said Shireen's aunt unctuously, 'give them a chance to renew their friendship' – a remark that made Zeenat Begum direct a haunted look at Shireen, who had suppressed a giggle.

The incident had been recounted to Muzaffar – who was staying, at Basheer's insistence, at his haveli. Muzaffar was in the midst of his hennabandi, reluctantly getting his feet and hands daubed with henna. The henna, along with a set of clothing, gifts, more paan leaves and some sugar candy, had been brought from Qureshi Sahib's haveli. Akram had grinned mightily to see Muzaffar being forced to dress in finery he did not wish to flaunt. The hennabandi done, Muzaffar had finally stood up in his glittering garments, surrounded by well-wishers – he could even see Mahmood, Taufeeq and Haider amongst them. He had been sprinkled liberally with perfume, and Khan Sahib had fed him the sugar candy, a symbol of good luck. A feast had followed, with much singing and music and gourmandizing by Basheer, who seemed to be more interested in the food than in Muzaffar's wedding.

And now the day had finally arrived. They had come, a self-conscious Muzaffar leading a modest but lively procession that bore gifts of rich clothing, jewellery, nuts, and money for the bride and her family. There had been fireworks and much laughter and good-natured ribbing from those who were secure in the knowledge that *they* were not the ones being stared at. At Qureshi Sahib's haveli, there had been more gaiety, more fireworks, a warm welcome. Then, once Muzaffar had been seated, Qureshi Sahib, considering himself in loco parentis, had withdrawn; the bride's father, according to custom, did not attend his daughter's wedding ceremony. Shireen's brother Shaukat, who had managed to come from his military camp in Lahore just in time for his sister's wedding, had sat quietly by instead.

The maulvi had read the Sura Al-Fatiha, the first chapter of the Qur'an, and had asked Muzaffar for his consent to the match. He had done the same for Shireen. She was in another room, hidden, even now, from her husband's eyes.

Muzaffar had sat through it all, waiting. Congratulations had poured in, the men patting him on his shoulder or on his back, the more ribald – and closer friends, like Akram – offering advice or making jokes. Haider and Taufeeq, coming forward together, had been gentle and soft-spoken, wishing him much happiness in his life. Mahmood, though he looked still tense, and distinctly uncomfortable in the fine choga he was wearing, had been dignified.

The feast had been far grander than anything Muzaffar had had while staying at Qureshi Sahib's haveli. He had been too distracted – a little apprehensive, too – to pay much attention to what was placed before him, but fleeting impressions had stayed in his mind: of processions of servants bearing platters of fancy biryanis, of desserts finished with sheets of silver beaten thinner even than the finest paper, of Basheer praising the delicacy of a simple qabooli, spiced rice and lentils cooked with prunes, plums and apricots.

The feast had gone on long, and had been lengthened even more by the lively conversation of friends and relatives meeting after a long time. There had been dancing girls, twirling prettily on the carpet and using their long veils as a prop in their dances. There had been music, from men who played shehnais and kettle drums and tamburas, at times loud enough to drown out conversation. Muzaffar had ached for it all to be over.

And here, finally, it was. It was over. The friends and relatives had gone to their own homes, still chattering merrily. Those that were staying at Qureshi Sahib's haveli had gone to their own rooms. The ladies of the haveli – Qureshi Sahib's chief begum leading the pack – had welcomed Muzaffar into the zenana and taken him to Shireen's room.

The heavy curtains fell into place behind him, the murmur of the ladies' voices dying away as they moved off. Muzaffar prayed that they would go away, back to their own rooms, to sleep. He did not want a giggling gaggle of women – even if they were now related to him by marriage – to be lurking in the corridor outside, eavesdropping on his conversation with Shireen. At the other end of the room, he saw Shireen, sitting on the bed, clad in red and gold, her veiled head lowered decorously. He glanced at her once, then back at the doorway through which he had entered. From somewhere beyond – it sounded like a few yards away, perhaps more – came the sound of a woman laughing. He winced.

'Don't worry. They won't hang around here. I made it quite clear I didn't want any of that happening.'

His head snapped back, eyes wide. Shireen was still sitting in exactly the same position as she had been a moment ago. He grinned and strode across to her.

'And they'll listen to you?'

She nodded. 'Mmm-hmm.'

He bent, reaching out to lift her veil, and then stopped himself. Instead, he sat down beside her on the bed and then pulled back the dupatta, its delicate gold embroidery rustling as he did so. She was as he remembered her from that long-ago evening on the road to Ajmer: an oval face, large brown eyes – but she was far lovelier than his memory of her had been. She was beautiful. And she was smiling up at him, her eyes alight with what was certainly affection. A tiny dimple twinkled in her right cheek.

'I will not be able to look my fill at you in one night,' Muzaffar murmured, his thumb absently caressing that dimple. It deepened.

'You don't have to,' she replied. 'There are many years ahead of us.'

'Shireen,' he whispered after a moment, 'Allah has been infinitely kind to me, in giving you to me. I – am so grateful. Tell me what you want, and if it is in my power, I will give it to you.'

She continued to look up into his face, though, from the distant look in her eyes, he could tell that she was thinking. A brief while, and that look changed to one he could not quite recognize yet – he realized, with a start, that he had only now got to see well the face of the woman he would spend the rest of his life with; it would take time to understand her expressions. But the way her eyes shone, he was certain that she was at least not distressed in any way.

Shireen nibbled at her lip, and Muzaffar knew instinctively that she had something up her sleeve. She leaned forward, her cheek resting on his chest. 'Tell me, please,' she said – her voice brimmed with laughter – 'what your investigation was all about. I have only heard bits and pieces; the gossip and the speculation. I would love to know how you did it.'

Muzaffar burst out laughing. 'Ah, Shireen,' he said, putting his arm around her shoulder and pulling her closer to him. 'You prove Sa'adi, don't you? "He has obtained his heart's desire whose beloved is of the same mind as himself."'

Shireen looked up, her eyes sparkling with mischief. 'So you intended to spend this time telling me all about this adventure? Very well, Jang Sahib. Tell on.'

Author's Note

The history of Mir Jumla, described in the first chapter, is accurate. As Bamber Gascoigne writes in *The Great Moghuls* (Constable and Co. Ltd, 1998), '...*the interesting case of Mir Jumla, a Persian adventurer – son of an oil merchant of Isfahan – who like many of his countrymen had come to the Shia kingdoms of the Deccan to seek his fortune... As merchant turned conqueror Mir Jumla ensured, hardly surprisingly, that his personal wealth and power kept pace with his prestige...*' After the abortive siege of Golconda, Mir Jumla made his way to Delhi, loaded down with gifts – precious stones so dazzling that they played a part in tempting Shahjahan to invade Bijapur rather than his originally-intended Kandahar. Shahjahan appointed Mir Jumla the Diwan-i-kul, or chief minister, and following the death of Mohammad Adil Shah in Bijapur, sent Mir Jumla and Aurangzeb off to annex Bijapur.

Mir Jumla marched with his army from Delhi in the winter of 1656, headed for Aurangabad, where he joined Aurangzeb. The two armies set out for Bijapur on January 18, 1657. Mir Jumla had (as also mentioned in this book) already offered mouth-watering bribes to Bijapuri officers to defect to the Mughals. The expedition, however, came more or less to naught. As at Golconda, at Bijapur too, local links with Dara Shukoh led to Shahjahan agreeing to accept an indemnity in return for the lifting of the siege.

I have not been able to find any record of Mir Jumla having stopped at Agra en route to Aurangabad. But Agra, though no longer the Mughal capital, was still a major city and commercially very significant. Despite the shifting of the capital to Delhi, it remained a major entrepôt for goods from all across India and abroad. The Sarai Nur Jahan (described in Chapter 9) now long gone, once bore testimony to Agra's importance in trade.

The descriptions of the Taj Mahal and its construction – including how the exquisite parchinkari or inlay work was done – are accurate, as well. For these, I must thank Michael and Diana Preston's absorbing and informative *A Teardrop on the Cheek of Time* (Transworld Publishers, 2007).

Acknowledgements

Many thanks are due to my sister, Swapna, who came up with the 'puzzle of the paving stones' and suggested it as an idea for a story. To her, Gourab, Neeti, Deb, and Tarun, too, I am grateful for accompanying me to Agra for the research trip: all of you made it an interesting – and very fulfilling – experience, rather than just work.

Thank you, also, to Nandita Aggarwal and Rohan Chhetri, my editors at Hachette India, whose valuable feedback and advice helped polish this book and make it what it is.

Praise for *The Englishman's Cameo*

'The mystery is intriguing, but it is Liddle's historically accurate portrait of Shahjahanabad, complete with the moonlit Yamuna, the paandaans, the palanquins, the noblemen's parties and bustling market places, which make the novel come alive. The plot will intrigue you and the narrative will enthral you.'

– Damini Purkayastha, *Hindustan Times*

'*The Englishman's Cameo* is a genuinely promising debut. Its originality and freshness is its strongest point, and – after the dramatic resolution – one shuts the book hoping that Madhulika Liddle will continue with her literary project and act as a path-breaker for other history-mystery writers in order to build this fabulous genre's South Asian avatar.'

– Zac O'Yeah, *Deccan Herald*

'The writing style is vivid and descriptive. The Red Fort, bustling market places, moonlit Yamuna and the traditional palanquins; the symbolic imagery of yesteryear Mughal court erupt alive. With the young and hot-blooded Muzaffar Jang following the trail to help his friend from being executed we have an Agatha Christie-style plot in hand.'

– Shakti Swaminathan, *The Hindu*

Praise for *The Eighth Guest and Other Muzaffar Jang Mysteries*

'The writing is crisp and taut, just the way a good mystery tale should be told. At the same time, the essence of the book is not lost... *The Eighth Guest and Other Muzaffar Jang Mysteries* still stands as a testimony that Indian writers can write a good mystery. Madhulika Liddle is a writer to watch out for.'

– Vivek Tejuja, IBN Live

'It is vividly descriptive with attention to detail and it is simply delightful to read the way the words just flow with no attempt to flummox the reader. It's as if you were in Shahjahan's Dilli, roaming the *galis* and visiting the *sarais*, part of the audience that Jang is addressing, waiting for him to make sense of the muddle and provide the answer... Where others would be lost for being too commonplace, Liddle has been ingenious in creating a detective who is set in a time which places him far ahead in any competition.'

– *Asian Age*